To MISTY
HAPPY CH[...]
LOVE

Jane Sanderson is a former BBC radio producer, and has used some of her own family history as background for *Netherwood*, her first novel. She is married to author and journalist Brian Viner. They have three children and live in Herefordshire.

Netherwood

Jane Sanderson

SPHERE

First published in Great Britain as a paperback original in 2011 by Sphere
Reprinted 2011

A CIP catalogue record for this book
is available from the British Library.

ISBN 978-0-7515-4763-4

Typeset in Sabon by Palimpsest Book Production Ltd,
Falkirk, Stirlingshire
Printed and bound in Great Britain by
Clays Ltd, St Ives plc

Papers used by Sphere are from well-managed forests
and other responsible sources.

MIX
Paper from
responsible sources
FSC® C104740

Sphere
An imprint of
Little, Brown Book Group
100 Victoria Embankment
London EC4Y 0DY

An Hachette UK Company
www.hachette.co.uk

www.littlebrown.co.uk

To Brian,
for his love, faith and friendship.

And in loving memory of Nellie Sanderson
(1901–1999).

Acknowledgements

Where better to begin a list of thanks than with my parents, Anne and Bob Sanderson, whose encouragement, interest and fund of books and memories have helped *Netherwood* on its way, from the first sentence to the last.

To my agent, Andrew Gordon, I should like to say thank you for spotting the potential, for taking me on and for guiding me from conception to publication, with patient advice and great good sense. Thanks, too, to Joanne Dickinson at Little, Brown, who fell as completely as I did for Eve, Anna and Henrietta, and the rest of the *Netherwood* cast.

I've had expert help from Brian Elliot, a fount of information about Yorkshire and its mining heritage. Andrea Tanner willingly supplied details of Fortnum & Mason, plundering on my behalf the company archives for price lists and products. And Catherine Bailey's peerless research into the history of the Fitzwilliam family in *Black Diamonds* was an essential source of authentic detail and inspiration. Thank you.

To my beloved husband Brian, thank you for your wit and your wisdom and for sustaining me with frothy coffee, lunchtime platters and an unshakeable belief in my book and me. And to Eleanor, Joe and Jacob, our three wonderful children, thank you for keeping me so firmly rooted in the realities of life whenever fiction threatened to take over.

Finally, a heartfelt and posthumous thank you to Nellie Sanderson, my grandma, in whose kitchen the seeds of the book were unwittingly planted and whose cooking, like Eve's, fed the soul as well as the body.

PART ONE

Chapter 1

It was morning but the bedroom was still as black as pitch when Eve Williams opened her eyes. Wednesday, she thought. Nearly payday, and it couldn't come a moment too soon. The housekeeping tin on the kitchen shelf was already empty, except for a button that was still waiting to be sewn on to Eliza's pinafore. Miserable business, buttons in the housekeeping. They made the tin rattle and then sat there, worthless, when you opened it.

She lay still for a while, pressed flat by the weight of the blankets, staring into the blackness. There was the merest sound beside her, the soft and steady rise and fall of Arthur's breath, but that was all, and from the quality of the darkness and the depth of the quiet, she could tell it was early, probably too early to rise, though that had never stopped her before. She gave herself a few seconds longer in the warm hollow of the mattress, and listened for clues. Nothing. Even Clem Waterdine wasn't about yet, shuffling on bandy legs along the terraces, knocking up the day shift. He was generally the first soul out in Netherwood on these merciless winter mornings, but Eve was almost always awake to hear him and however reluctantly she might leave the warmth of her bed, there was

3

always a particular pleasure to be had by stealing a march on the day, pottering about in the kitchen, waiting for the kettle to boil and the tea to brew.

The cold hit her like a wall when she slid from under the layers of heavy wool, going carefully so as not to wake her sleeping husband. Her bare feet made contact with the linoleum floor and she winced, noiselessly, thinking for the umpteenth time that she needed a rug there. It was only ever first thing in the morning that it crossed her mind. Speed was of the essence now that she had left the protection of the bed, and she groped blindly on the floor for the thick stockings she kept there for just such emergencies as these. They were coarse and heavy, the sort of wool that pricked at the skin and that the children hated to wear, but they gave instant relief from the shocking cold. On they went. Next, a shawl, which she wrapped and tucked tightly around her upper half like swaddling. Then, sufficiently well clad to risk the journey, she moved carefully across the bedroom floor, sidestepping the loose boards and making her way through the inky darkness. In her head she held the coordinates for the bed, the dresser, the known creaks and the exact position of the doorknob, so her progress across the small room was efficiently managed even though her arms remained pinned to her side by the shawl. At the door, she released a hand to turn the knob and pull it open, but then she stood still for a moment, listening. Arthur's breathing continued regular and undisturbed, and she stepped out of the bedroom and on to the small landing where all her strenuous efforts to be silent were almost undone because right behind her a small voice whispered: 'Mam.'

It was Eliza, so close that she almost knocked her over. Eve, heart hammering, managed to hold in the scream but took a few moments to recover herself, then crouched down to the same height as the little girl. Still Eve couldn't see her, but Eliza's breath was on her face.

'You scared me 'alf to death,' Eve said, whispering too.

'I 'ad a bad dream. Is it morning?'

'Not for you. Back to bed. T'dream's gone now.'

''as it? 'ow do you know?'

'Because they do when you wake. Especially when you wake and tell your mam.'

'Mam?'

'What?'

'Seth's snoring.'

'Let's give 'im a shove on our way past then. Come on, back you go.'

Eve stood and, finding Eliza's shoulders with her hands, she steered her into the children's bedroom. Seth was indeed snoring, though very softly. He slept the way his father did, flat on his back, like someone had just knocked him out in the ring. She gave his shoulder a gentle shake and he protested sleepily, but shifted position and the snoring stopped. Eliza, back in bed, said:

'Mam?'

'Shhhh. Quieter. What?'

'Is there stewmeat gravy?'

Only Eliza would think of her next meal when the house was in darkness and dawn was still some hours away. She was thin as a lath, but was always first at the table and last to get down.

'Not if I don't get downstairs,' said Eve. 'Go to sleep now, else you'll be droppin' off in t'schoolroom.'

'See you in t'mornin' then,' said Eliza.

'You will.' She found the child's head, and kissed it, then navigated her way carefully out of the room. Nothing much could wake Seth when he was sleeping but the baby, Ellen, seemed always to be on red alert, determined not to miss anything. It was a wonder that Eliza hadn't already woken her, with her night-time wanderings. Again, just as she had in her own room, she paused at the open door, listening. Then she turned and went downstairs to the kitchen.

Eve and Arthur lived with their three children in Beaumont Lane, a short terrace of eight stone houses without front gardens, but backing on to a cobbled yard, which was shared by the residents of Watson Street and Allott's Way. The streets ran at right angles to each other, forming three sides of a square, the fourth side being completed by the privies, which were housed in a long, low-roofed building divided into separate stalls, one for each family. A narrow entry part way down Watson Street led into the yard, enabling residents and visitors to enter the houses via the back. Nobody used the front doors. They could have been bricked up and not be missed.

The houses had been built in 1850 by William Hoyland, the fifth Earl of Netherwood, father of the present earl, and a man whose great fortune was matched by a desire to do good. He had thrown himself with philanthropic zeal into the expansion and improvement of Netherwood town, and had conducted exacting interviews with a number of architects before settling on Abraham Carr, who demonstrated by word and deed his belief that the working classes were as entitled as anyone to finials, fan lights and front steps. Mr Carr drew up plans for several hundred new dwellings for the folk of Netherwood, and while all his terraces differed subtly from each other, they shared the same sturdy integrity and solidity that seemed to declare an intention to stand there for ever.

Eve loved her home from the day she moved in, even though there was a full five days' cleaning to be done before she felt she'd made it her own. She and Arthur had taken the tenancy when they married, she a lovely girl of seventeen, him an old man of thirty and a miner at New Mill Colliery. They were filling a dead man's shoes, taking up residence two days after the burial of old Digby Caldwell, who had clung on to life for some years longer than his neighbours expected him to, and for many years longer than they would have liked. He had stubbornly sat out his dotage with an unapologetic disregard for health or hygiene, leaving for Eve the charming housewarming gift of twenty-five makeshift chamber pots in varying shapes and sizes, each one brimful and reeking and dotted at random through the rooms. Arthur had been all for keeping some of the vessels as there were one or two decent saucepans and basins among them but Eve had given him short shrift. She would rather manage with what little they had than picture Digby Caldwell relieving himself every time she steamed a pudding.

And then there'd been the kitchen range, turned through disuse into a devil of a job, the iron rusted and the flue cracked. There was a dead crow up the pipe; Arthur had felt it as he groped up there checking for blockages and had pulled it out by one wing, stiff and sinister, its beak open in outrage. At the time it seemed to Eve a portent of sorrow, but she'd long ago forgotten it. The estate sent a welder to mend the flue but the rest was up to her, and she had scrubbed at it inside and out with wire wool and sandpaper until her fingers bled, then had black-leaded it back to a showroom shine. She'd made a good friend that day, though; she and the range were allies. It performed for nobody as well as it performed for Eve.

Arthur had watched in bewildered silence as his wife went through the house like a dose of salts. He couldn't step out of the back door without some small, womanly improvement springing up behind him. His young wife had some fancy ideas. Deep lace curtains around the base of the brass bed to conceal the pot underneath. Brodded rag rugs, made not from the usual dreary mud colours but in brighter shades, blues and greens and yellows, worked into clever designs from a collection of carefully hoarded scraps. Jolly little jugs and jars of wild flowers made a seasonal appearance in unexpected places, and at the windows were pretty curtains made from a bolt of cloth that Eve had been given by the draper in exchange for two of her meat-and-potato pies. Her ingenuity astounded Arthur, though he never told her so because he felt foolish for noticing, and anyway he lacked the language of compliments and endearments. But he admired her silently and treated her well, and he never sat down to a meal in his muck from the pit but sluiced it off in the tin tub first, no matter how famished he was. These small acts of kindness were his way of showing appreciation, and for Eve, who knew this, they were enough.

She had been downstairs for over an hour this morning before she heard the distant tattoo of Clem's pole. Turnpike Lane, she thought, head cocked, listening. No, Brook Lane. In this stillness before dawn she could track his movements and if the kettle wasn't on by the time he reached Watson Street, she knew she was running behind. She moved quietly around the small kitchen, going about her business, performing the rituals of early morning. This was her domain. She had mended the fire in the range, coaxing the barely smouldering coals back into life until she could safely pile a proper shovelful of new fuel into the hatch behind the bottom door. Now the water in the vast copper set pot was slowly heating, shuddering with new warmth, promising comfort. On a floured board, under clean linen cloths, three softly plump mounds of risen dough were waiting for her attention. Taking up a broad-bladed knife, she sliced a quick, deep cross in the top of each then opened the top door of the range and gingerly popped in a square of newspaper from a tin on the dresser top. The paper curled in the heat and began, in a leisurely way, to turn golden brown – not bucking and blackening as it did when the oven was too hot, but gradually colouring over the course of half a minute. Eve fetched the loaves and slid them into place in the oven. Then she set a pan of stewmeat to reheat at the back of the range, filled the kettle from the set pot and placed it to boil on the heat.

By now the sound of Clem's stick on his customers' windows was loud enough to raise the dead, let alone the sleeping. Hard of hearing, that was his problem. A whack sounded like a tap to Clem. Really, thought Eve, he'd be cracking the panes at this rate, spending the few coppers he earned on repairs. She wrapped the thick shawl tighter around her shoulders and pulled back the bolts on the door. Bracing herself for the cold she stuck her head out into the morning and waited for the old man to pass the entry. And there he was, bent against the chill, pole in his right hand, an oil lamp in his left.

'Clem,' she hissed. 'Clem!'

She startled him and he stopped dead, peering suspiciously towards the sound.

'It's me, Clem. Eve,' she whispered, as loudly as she could.

He came closer, and in the feeble light from his lamp was able to pick out the extraordinary sight of Eve Williams in a nightdress, shawl and woollen stockings, standing on her doorstep.

'Ey up, lass,' he said, astounded. 'Tha'll catch thi death!'

'Never mind me,' said Eve. 'It's you! Shoutin' an' 'ammerin'. Pipe down!'

Clem grinned at her, toothlessly. His walnut face was pinched and blue-tinged with cold, in spite of the heavy overcoat, thick scarf and old flat cap he'd been wearing for half a century, but his rheumy eyes were full of pleasure at seeing Eve. She looked pretty as a picture, he thought to himself, with her long brown hair loose and that stern look in her bonny eyes. Aye, even in a temper she was a fine-looking lass.

'Just doin' my job, flower,' he said. 'If I don't wake 'em, no bugger else will.'

9

He sniffed the air and nodded towards the kitchen behind her. 'That's a grand smell comin' from in there,' he said, his artful old face adopting a wistful look. And Eve, who was fonder of Clem than she chose to let on and who never could resist a plea for food, ushered him in.

Chapter 2

A stranger walking the streets of Netherwood, hoping from there to find Netherwood Hall, would almost certainly fail unless he resorted to asking directions from a local. Unlike many great country houses, the hall had been built not on high ground with commanding views of its own parkland and beyond, but in a wide, shallow valley whose gently sloping sides sheltered the house and its inhabitants from prying eyes.

A stone wall, mellowed over the years by lichen and more than ten miles in length, encircled the park and gardens of the house, although it by no means marked the limits of the Hoyland family's ownership, which extended for many square miles beyond. Within the walls lay the usual trappings of wealth and power – gently undulating pasture and parkland dotted with coppices and cattle and leading eventually to a majestic garden of many different elements, each one more charming than the last. A network of paths led the visitor on a tour of the varied delights; an oriental water garden with a miniature pagoda at its centre and a collection of ancient goldfish, whose lazy circuits of the pond gently broke the still-ness of the dark green water; a rose garden with numerous fragrant blooms of every possible hue, whose blowsy heads graced silver bowls in the entrance hall of the great house; a circular maze of dense yew, which successive generations of young Hoylands had mastered by sheer perseverance, but which always foxed the unsuspecting newcomer; a shady grove of rhododendrons and azaleas with flowers as big as Sunday hats and branches old enough and tall enough to climb; hothouses that cocked a snook at the northern climate with their abundant display of exotic blooms and tropical fruits; and lush acres of sweeping lawns, immaculately kept, bordered on all sides by wide paths of dusty pink gravel, swept daily into soothing stripes by one of the thirty-five gardeners employed at the hall.

The house itself could be reached from the outside world by any one of four tree-lined avenues, one north, one south, one east and one west of the property, and each one leading from massive ironwork gates bearing the Hoyland crest. The avenues were each a mile in length and each, at its end, converged on the same broad circular carriageway that surrounded the house. The four avenues had been planted with their own different species of tree, and were named after them; Oak Avenue was perhaps the most frequently used and therefore the most admired, leading as it did from the gate closest to the town of Netherwood on the south side of the estate, but Poplar, Lime and Cedar avenues, though less often seen by visitors, were stately and handsome, and maintained to the same lofty standards.

As befitted the splendour of its grounds, Netherwood Hall presented a magnificent face to the world from whichever direction you chose to view it, although naturally its front aspect was the most impressive. To the family who dwelt there, the Earl and Countess of Netherwood and their four children, this was simply home, but to anyone else it was a glorious, grandiose masterpiece. Built in 1710 for John Hoyland, the first Earl of Netherwood, whose forebears had ensured his fortune through judicious marriages and the canny acquisition of land, the hall was the largest private house in England. An earlier, humbler, timber-framed manor house built in Tudor times by an ancestor was pulled down to make way for this new and potent symbol of the family's wealth and status. At its furthest extremities, the east and west wings were identical, massively built square towers which jutted forwards like vigilant stone sentries. At the top of each tower was a cupola housing a great iron bell, and when both were rung together, on high days and holidays, their peals were said to be heard as far away as Derbyshire. Between the east and west towers, the main body of the house ran flat and simple, with two long rows of eighteen windows, each one identical to its neighbour. At the centre of the building stood a proud, eight-columned portico with curved stone staircases left and right leading up to a gallery from which one could view the gardens, and also to four towering French windows, each giving potential access to the fine reception rooms on the first floor. However, these doors were rarely used for any practical purpose, the portico being intended primarily to declare to the world the full pomp and circumstance of the noble family inside. Instead, the house was generally entered through a pair of great brass-studded wooden double doors in the shady recess beneath the portico. They opened on to a pillared entrance hall with a marble floor that rang out underfoot and a domed, painted ceiling depicting richly coloured images from the lives of the Roman emperors. Many a titled guest, visiting for the first time and being themselves the owners of a fine country estate, were nevertheless rendered temporarily speechless by the grandeur.

To enter the gates and progress through the park and grounds of Netherwood Hall was to leave behind all trace of the corner of northern England that it inhabited. There were stately homes up and down the country where visitors gasped at the splendour of the estate yet barely noticed a change in the landscape as they left the great park for the Surrey – or Sussex or Worcestershire or Norfolk – countryside beyond. But at Netherwood Hall, the contrast could not have been more marked between the worlds within and without the perimeter wall. In a thirty-mile radius there were just short of a hundred collieries, so that whichever direction you journeyed as you left, you were before long assailed by the scars inflicted by heavy industry on the hills, fields and valleys of this corner of the county. As their barouche or landau rattled its way north towards Barnsley or south towards Sheffield, the traveller's view through the carriage window would be of slag heaps, headstocks, smoke stacks and railway tracks. Only with the blinds of the carriage window pulled down was it possible to imagine the verdant meadows of the agricultural past.

But verdant meadows never made anyone's fortune; it was the stuff beneath them that counted here, and which was the continued source of the now-fabled fortune of Edward Hoyland, sixth Earl of Netherwood. Because in 1710, when the building of the great hall began, John Hoyland unwittingly laid the foundations of the family seat on a wellspring of seemingly limitless wealth. At the end of the eighteenth century, when the prosperous family already wanted for nothing, their Yorkshire estate was discovered to include, far beneath it, one of the richest seams of coal the country had to offer.

New Mill, Long Martley and Middlecar. These were the three collieries owned by the Earl of Netherwood and mined by his men. They were small pits by some standards – just over six hundred miners at each of them – but they were productive, yielding half a million tons a year of fine quality coal to help stoke the fires of industrial progress. The third earl, Wilfred Hoyland, had named the collieries back when they were sunk, and nobody knew where or what he was thinking of, except that by leaving Netherwood or Hoyland out of the matter he hoped to distance his family from any socially ruinous associations with industry. Of course, everyone knew anyway and rather despised him for it, and in any case his efforts went unappreciated by subsequent earls of Netherwood, who had the good sense to recognise the truth of that old Yorkshire maxim: where there's muck, there's brass.

Certainly Teddy Hoyland, the present earl, saw no conflict between his status in society and the fact that his vast fortune was increased daily by the efforts of the eighteen hundred men and boys employed at his collieries. And the mining of coal was truly a profitable pursuit. When his father died in 1878, Teddy had inherited a legacy of dazzling proportions; a private fortune of £2.5 million, a mansion in London's Belgravia, a small, sturdy castle in Scotland and twenty thousand acres of the West Riding of Yorkshire, with Netherwood Hall at its heart. His prestige and position were unassailable and he saw no reason on earth to curtail what his wife considered a vulgar compulsion to speak openly about business matters. In the countess's view, one's wealth was a given, and the source of it neither interesting nor relevant, but Teddy Hoyland was proud of his collieries and proud of his men and, broadly speaking, he was liked and respected by them for his fairness and decency. It has to be said that Lady Netherwood was less of a favourite, though this gave her not a moment's unease. A true daughter of the aristocracy, she was entirely defined by her impeccable pedigree and found there were quite enough people of her own class and position to provide diversion without having to bother much about those at the bottom of the heap. Even the county set, those neighbours and acquaintances whose situation was less grand than Lady Netherwood's but nevertheless whose lives ran along the same lines, didn't get much of a look in. Clarissa preferred the stimulation of

London society: the attack, feint and parry of cocktails in Cheyne Walk or dinner in Devonshire Place. Still, the countess was known to have a heart; it was she, after all, who forbade the Netherwood Hall kitchen staff to throw away leftover food after supper parties and banquets, and ordered instead that it should be distributed among the needy of the town. This was a mixed blessing, since devilled eggs, sole *bonne femme* and chocolate parfait, while all individually delicious, were not necessarily as palatable when slopped together in the same tin. Her motives were good, though. And her beauty and elegance, when she did deign to appear in public in the town, always caused a stir of excited interest, as if a rare and endangered bird had flown over Netherwood.

Chapter 3

In Eve's kitchen, Clem had taken off his cap but left his coat buttoned and his scarf tightly wrapped. He eased himself into a chair, exhaling audibly with mingled pain and relief as his arthritic knees adjusted to their new situation. Eve filled an enamel mug with stock from the pan of stewmeat on the stove and handed it to the old man, who inhaled the beefy vapour appreciatively.

'Champion,' he said.

'There's no bread yet,' she said. 'It's only just in.'

'Never mind, lass. This'll warm t'cockles.'

'Well sup up – you've folk to wake, I've things to be gettin' on with, and Arthur needs 'is brew,' said Eve. She opened the door of the range to check the loaves and the kitchen was suddenly full of the aroma of freshly baking bread.

''e's a lucky bugger is Arthur,' said Clem. He applied himself to his fortifying broth; it was scalding hot and he took it in tiny, delicate sips out of necessity, not good manners.

'By 'eck that's grand,' he said to himself. Then, to Eve: 'They've started wi' buntin' out there.' He tipped his head in the general direction of outside.

'Aye?' said Eve. She leaned her back against the stove and

17

folded her arms, settling in for a chat. The warmth seeped through her woollen layers.

'Aye,' Clem nodded. 'Fireworks an' all, they say, and ten bob for all of us.'

'Never!' said Eve.

This was everyone's subject of choice these days: the preparations for Tobias Hoyland's coming-of-age on Saturday week. The oldest son of the Earl and Countess of Netherwood, and heir to the great Hoyland estate, was a familiar figure to all of them, largely, it has to be said, on account of his fondness for pale ale. He wasn't the type of local figurehead who could be depended on to give his time opening a village fête or laying the foundation stones for a new library, but the landlords of the three Netherwood public houses wouldn't hear a word against him, and his excesses certainly provided the town with an infinite supply of mirth at his expense. Now though, there wasn't a soul who didn't wish him well since the news had got about that, to mark the greatness of the occasion, Lord Netherwood planned to include every last one of them in the celebrations. In the summer, six months hence, the park and gardens of Netherwood Hall would be thrown open to all tenants and employees, however lowly, for a jamboree of epic proportions, and now here was Clem, at Eve's kitchen table, telling her that bunting was being strung up, as if the fun was starting already. They'd had some for the king's coronation last year – red, white and blue flags hanging like lines of jaunty washing between the gas lamps – but it hadn't felt right then. It had been eighteen months after the queen's death, but there'd still been a subdued air, as if her famous disapproval of Bertie must be considered even when she was gone. But the coming-of-age of Toby Hoyland – Lord Fulton, to use the heir's historic title, though no one ever did – was another matter. A proper shindig, funded from the earl's deep and plentiful coffers. It was something to look forward to.

18

'Aye, ten bob for us all. Well, every 'ousehold, like.'

Clem drained his mug and wiped his mouth on his coat sleeve where, by the looks of the oily slick, he'd wiped it many times before. He sighed deeply then stood up to leave.

'Best get on,' he said. Then: 'Bad business at Grangely today, ey?' He was speaking to Eve's back because she had turned to fill the big brown teapot with boiling water, but she stopped what she was doing and looked at him over her shoulder, puzzled. The Grangely miners were on strike, but there was nothing new in that – they'd walked out weeks ago. She felt sure Arthur would have told her if something new was afoot.

'What bad business?' she said.

'Aye, a poor do. It's evictions day. They say there's nigh on four hundred bobbies drafted in to chuck 'em out.'

Eve stared at him, horrified.

She said, 'You must 'ave that wrong.'

Clem shook his head. He reached for his cap and pulled it low over his ears and brow so that he had to tilt his head back to see Eve from under the peaked brim.

'True as I'm standing 'ere,' he said. 'They say there's plenty o' folk goin' up to watch.'

'Are they sellin' tickets?' Her voice was suddenly harsh.

'Nay, lass . . .' said Clem. He hadn't meant to wipe the smile off her face.

'They should be turned away, if they're not there to 'elp them as needs 'elping,' she said. 'Those folk need kindness, not curiosity.'

She made no attempt to hide her bitterness – couldn't, even if she'd wanted to. She'd seen it all her life in the coalfields; strangers gathering at a scene of misery or misfortune, travelling miles, some of them, to watch the afflicted. Bad news always spread so effortlessly. When a fire-damp explosion had killed sixty miners up at Middlecar pit last month, there were so many onlookers and journalists that for a full hour after

19

the bodies came up, the wives of the deceased couldn't be found in the crush.

'Aye, it's a bad business,' said Clem again. 'Anyroad, best be off.' He was uneasy now, anxious to be on his way; all he'd intended was to pass on a bit of gossip. He walked to the door, then turned and tipped his cap at her. 'Good day, lass.'

'Quiet, mind,' called Eve as the door closed but she said it absently, without conviction, then, standing idle for a rare minute in her warm kitchen, she reluctantly allowed her thoughts to journey into the past.

Eve was a Grangely girl born and bred, and when Arthur found her twelve years ago at the chapel dance, people had warned him off her because everyone knew that nothing good came out of Grangely. Arthur knew it too and yet there she had been, proving otherwise.

In Eve's home town, miners and their families lived cheek-by-jowl in squalid housing, built in haste from cheap, yellow brick which fifty years on had taken on the colour and the smell of the coalface. The town was owned by a syndicate of Birmingham businessmen who paid other men to run the pit, and who probably couldn't have picked out Grangely on a map. It was a place riddled with misery and sickness, a bad beginning for a child, a bad end for an adult, but what saved Eve was an extraordinary resolve – formed in childhood, hardened in adolescence – to rise above it.   Her feckless drunkard of a father had hanged himself out of self-pity when the death of his wife left him with sole charge of five children, and Eve, at thirteen, took over. She sent twelve-year-old Silas to the pit in place of his father and tried to raise the little ones herself, then watched helplessly as they died of typhoid, one after the other, with such terrifying speed that for days afterwards Eve kept forgetting they'd gone and, remembering, would be stricken with new grief. She and Silas would sit together of an evening and plan a future away from the leaden, hopeless grind of Grangely, though neither of them knew quite how bad it had been until they had escaped. When she married Arthur – relief flooding her body as she repeated the vows and heard him do the same – Silas upped and left, heading on foot for Liverpool where he hoped to find work at the docks or on a merchant ship. He was sixteen by then, sharp as a tack and all but penniless. He promised her a bunch of bananas from the West Indies if he ever got there, but they never came; at least, they hadn't yet. She liked to imagine him somewhere hot and exotic and the fact that she heard nothing from him sustained the possibility that she still might.

These memories of another world were as indelible as etchings on glass, but they were fainter now than they once had been and were losing their power to cause Eve pain. She had learned to relish the small details of her life, and she did so now: the warmth of the range that she leaned against, the comforting smell of new bread and beef gravy. These everyday blessings were plentiful but none the less precious for that, and she offered up a prayer of thanks for her own good fortune. Then she poured a mug of hot, strong tea for Arthur and climbed the stairs to wake him.

Chapter 4

‿∾‿∾‿

It had surprised and pleased the earl that his wife had raised no insurmountable objections to his plans for the twenty-first birthday celebrations of their eldest son Tobias. Given her aversion to encouraging the masses, he had expected an attack of the vapours at the suggestion that a party should be held on a scale never before seen in Yorkshire. There would be thousands of guests, from the highest-born aristocrat to the lowliest tenant. Clarissa had only insisted that there must be strict segregation, and her husband had agreed; even Teddy Hoyland couldn't countenance the Duke of Devonshire stripping the willow with a Netherwood scullery maid. But nevertheless every family, however mighty or humble, would receive the same embossed invitation to the party, which would take place in June.

He was immensely pleased with the prospect, which was more than could be said for the birthday boy. Tobias Hoyland, made in his father's image, was nevertheless absolutely not cut from the same cloth. There was a long list of things in life that Toby enjoyed – girls, clothes, horses, beer, baccarat, dancing – and very few things he disliked. But one of them, and the thing he loathed above all else, was being obliged through birth to do what he didn't wish to. If only, thought Tobias, he could swap places with Dickie and be second son. All the privilege and none of the obligations. When Dickie's twenty-first dawned, there'd be a family breakfast and a glass of fizz and that would be that – lucky devil. Toby, on the other hand, would have to endure a veritable festival of a celebration populated by thousands of people he'd never seen before and would never see again. He knew how it would play out, too. He'd be stuck indoors at a banquet with the blue bloods, while under his nose but out of bounds would be the beer tents and the pretty girls. It was six months away and already it loomed like an endurance test, clouding the blue skies of his existence. When he allowed it to, as now, it put him quite out of sorts.

He was hemmed in by other people's expectations, he fumed inwardly; cornered by his damned *noblesse oblige*. Even now he wasn't able to do as he wished. He had assumed that his actual birthday, in ten days' time, might at least be spent in London where the multitude of diversions would take his mind off his wretchedness. But no. His father had insisted that he remain at Netherwood because there was an air of excitement among the people, and Toby would be obliged to wave at them from the back of a motor car before he was free to please himself. The countess – in truth just as keen as Toby for the delights of London and the comforts of Fulton House – had agreed that as soon as duty was done, they would flee south. This, at least, was a crumb of comfort.

He was in the library, the best place for Toby to be when he didn't want to be found, being the last place anyone would look for him. He sat crossways on a green leather wing chair, his long legs dangling over one arm, and he gazed morosely at nothing in particular. The past half hour had been spent aiming scrunched up balls of unused writing paper at a nearby waste-paper basket, and the evidence of this sport lay in and around the target, as if a frustrated writer had tried and failed again and again to frame the perfect letter. As a form of entertainment, Tobias had found it perfectly acceptable, and infinitely preferable to the alternative, which had been a site meeting with his father and the land agent at the newly dug Home Farm cess pit. At the thought of it now, Toby's face puckered in distaste. His father's enthusiasm for the disposal of human waste seemed to him to be deliberately controversial, as if he was displaying to his family that, though he was an earl, he was first and foremost a countryman with a countryman's tolerance for the stink of decomposing ordure. Well, if he expected Toby to fall in behind him on his endless tours of duty, he could whistle for it.

A squeal followed by a sharp bark of laughter outside stirred him from his mutinous lethargy. In a moment he was out of the armchair and crossing the library towards the window; if there was merriment to be had, Tobias was your man. At first, with his face pressed against the glass, he saw only the usual dull vista of neatly swept gravel and serene swathes of lawn. There it was again, though: a breathless squeal of laughter, evidence that there was the possibility of amusement on this dreary Wednesday morning. Tobias frowned, looking this way and that for the source of the fun. And then his face broke into a great grin because, all in a rush and none too steadily, his older sister Henrietta travelled past the window on a large black bicycle, her expression grim with concentration as she tried to keep her balance, momentum and dignity intact. The squealing, Tobias discovered, came from Isabella who, somehow released by her governess, ran behind her big sister, red-faced with the effort of keeping up and clutching at her skirts in a manner most unbecoming to a fine young lady of eleven years old.

Tobias hammered on the pane. 'Bravo Henry!' he shouted. She turned to look at him – big mistake – and started a wobble from which she had no hope of recovery. By the time Tobias

24

appeared on the path outside, she was on the ground with the bicycle on top of her. She made no attempt to get up, however, but lay rather contentedly on the gravel, making the most of the unscheduled break.

'Good God, what happened there?' Toby said, standing over her. He hauled the bicycle upright then held out a helping hand which, for the moment, she declined.

'You distracted me,' Henrietta said. 'It seems I can't steer, work the pedals and look over my shoulder at the same time.'

'So it's my turn now,' said Isabella. 'As you fell off.'

Henrietta shook her head.

'Skedaddle,' she said.

Isabella considered tears but opted for a scowl instead, Henry being in general immune to waterworks.

'Don't you have some French to translate or flowers to catalogue, Izzy?' said Tobias, in a conciliatory tone. 'If Perry catches you out here she'll have your guts for garters.'

Isabella knew he spoke the truth. Miss Peregrine had taught them all at various stages in their lives, and while she was kind enough when obeyed, she could show a heart of flint when her instructions were flouted. She'd left her reluctant charge alone in the schoolroom with a variety of irregular verbs and the ominous promise of a short test in half an hour. But, like Toby, Isabella had seen Henry through the window, and the bicycle had proved too great a distraction to keep her at her books. Anyway, Isabella had reasoned to herself, as she had no plans ever to visit France, indeed could only imagine herself in either Netherwood or London, the point of mastering the language was lost on her. Mastering the art of bicycling, on the other hand – now there was a useful pursuit. But now she was being thwarted; Henry and Toby were being beastly and Perry's wrath was a fearful thing. She glowered as she flounced away. Tobias returned her scowl with an amiable grin.

'*Au revoir, ma chérie. À bientôt,*' he said.

'Gosh, well done,' she said, without turning. 'Sum total of your command of French, all in one go.'

Henrietta laughed, if a little grudgingly. As a general rule she tried not to encourage Isabella, who in her view lacked the firm parental control that she herself had been subject to at the same age. The youngest of the Hoyland offspring was indulged and precocious, the undisputed darling of the earl, with the capacity – indeed the tendency – to be what the household staff, in the privacy of their own quarters, called 'a proper handful'. It piqued Henrietta, for example, that the child had been dining with the adults since she was ten, and often ended the meal on her father's lap as he popped petits fours into her open mouth. The rest of them – Henrietta, Tobias and Dickie – had all been confined to nursery suppers until well past their twelfth birthdays, and when they finally graduated to the dining room it was backs straight, elbows off the table, and woe betide you if you spoke out of turn. However, Henrietta found little support when she voiced this particular complaint to her brothers, both of whom claimed they would still rather be eating shepherd's pie with Nanny than enduring the tedious ritual of family dinners.

Henrietta stood now, unaided by Toby. She was as tall as her brother, though there the resemblance ended because she was the only one of the four Hoyland siblings who possessed none of the physical characteristics of either their father or mother. Isabella was the countess in miniature, a doll of a child with an adorable cupid's bow mouth which was always primed to pout. Toby and Dickie each shared the earl's sandy hair, high complexion and distinctive pale-blue eyes. Henry, on the other hand, was simply herself; thick blonde hair, which tended to unruliness despite the best efforts of her maid, eyes more green than blue, and a determined set to her mouth and chin that gave an outward indication of her personality. Some people thought her beautiful, others thought her plain, while

Henrietta herself thought the matter barely worth consideration. This blithe indifference was of grave concern to her mother, and four seasons after her society debut Henrietta was still resolutely single; she attracted suitors but then would somehow, infuriatingly, turn them into friends. The countess was at a loss: she herself had married at twenty and was considered one of the great beauties of her age. It was said that Clarissa once caused an orchestra to stop playing when she walked into a ballroom, such was her beauty. No one would ever stop what they were doing to stare as Henrietta passed, but no one ever forgot her after they had met.

The gravel had left imprints in her palms and there would probably be bruising from her impact with the ground, but she'd suffered worse many a time when riding. She dusted her skirts and smiled at her brother.

'Have a go?' she said, indicating the bicycle which he was still holding upright.

'Whose is it?'

'Parkinson's. Isn't that a scream?' The two of them enjoyed for a moment an imagined snapshot of the butler, revered in the household for his dignity and rectitude, wobbling along on two wheels. 'It's for his health, apparently,' said Henrietta. 'Modest exertion to quicken the pulse.'

'Good Lord, I can think of more interesting ways to quicken the pulse than this,' said Tobias.

'Doubtless. But you're you, and Parkinson's Parkinson. Any pulse-quickening on his part has to be morally defensible. Go on, have a go.' She stepped back to allow Tobias a clear run. 'Be bold and forthright as you begin with the pedals. He who hesitates falls off.'

Tobias swung his right leg over the saddle and settled himself into position. Then he pushed off strongly with his left foot and began to move, precariously at first but more securely as he gained momentum, away from the front of the house.

'Oh I say! Well done,' called Henrietta.

She stood, hands on hips, and watched him go, and Toby, with the confidence of one who knows he is watched and expects to be admired, raised an arm and waved it in triumph. Henry realised that her own experiment with the bicycle was clearly over, though she didn't begrudge Toby in the least; it was an unnatural contraption in her view, and in any case she had an appointment with Dickie in the stable yard in thirty minutes to canter out to the top coppice and back before luncheon. Much more fun. She turned and ran back into the house to change.

Meanwhile Tobias, pedalling furiously up the gentle incline of Oak Avenue, had had the sudden, marvellous thought that if he carried on all the way into Netherwood he might pay a social call on a certain warmly pliable barmaid, the latest in a succession of local girls to delude herself into believing that a willingness to please the young heir to the Netherwood fortune might result in a wonderful, glamorous twist of fate. Tobias smiled at the thought of her, even as he puffed at the effort of keeping the pace of his forward and upward trajectory. It was all that talk of pulse-quickening, he thought to himself. Henry's fault entirely.

Chapter 5

A rthur Williams had a miner's build. He wasn't tall, but he was strong, and his power was concentrated in his torso and arms, the parts of his body that needed strength for hewing coal from a seam. He could walk the mile-and-a-half to chapel with Seth on his shoulders and Eliza and Ellen in each arm, and never have to pause for breath. He always said he could carry Eve along with the children, but she never gave him the chance to try. She didn't doubt it though. He was barred from the bell-and-mallet game when the feast came to New Mill Common, because four years ago the prizes had run out as Arthur delighted the crowd and infuriated the owner by hitting the sweet spot with every easy blow.

It was his strength that had drawn Eve to him in the first place; his strength and his steadiness, certainly not his looks. He had the Williams ears, jutting out like jug handles, and rather forbidding dark eyebrows which gave him the appearance of being cross when he wasn't. But Eve, the most beautiful lass at the chapel dance, had looked at no one else after Arthur sauntered into her life. She knew instinctively, without any promises from him, that he would love her and provide for her and keep her out of harm's way. It was the feel of his hand on the small of her back as they moved together around the dance floor, and the directness of his gaze when he looked at her; she was reassured by him, without words, that after a childhood and adolescence racked by poverty and uncertainty, all would now be well.

For his part, Arthur had dreamed of Eve long before he met her. He told no one this, not even Eve herself because it sounded soft, but he had seen her, in precise detail, and it was the only dream he ever remembered having. His unconscious mind had summoned her and she had stood before him and lifted her hand up to his cheek and caressed him softly, and the image of her face – the shape of it, her features – had stayed with him as clearly as if he had her photograph in his waistcoat pocket. So when he saw her for the first time, he recognised her at once. Their engagement had followed so swiftly that folk had talked, but he had known that Eve was his intended. Their union was meant to be.

His faith in fate had been well rewarded, although the casual observer wouldn't necessarily have thought so had they chanced upon the scene in Eve's kitchen that morning, as Arthur brought his fist down on the kitchen table, making spoons and crockery bounce on the oilcloth surface and overturning the jug of milk, as if a small earthquake had struck in the bowels of Beaumont Lane.

He rarely lost his temper and more rarely still lost it with Eve, because when he did his anger swelled and heaved within him like a separate entity, more powerful than himself, and it alarmed him. But today she had maddened him, going on and on as he ate about the evictions at Grangely. Had he heard about them? Of course he had. So why hadn't he said owt? Because there's nowt to say. Nowt to say about thousands of men, women and bairns cast out into the street on a January

30

morning? Eve, fire in her eyes, had spat the words at her husband, challenging him to claim indifference.

'It's colliery business,' he'd said. 'They mun go back to work if they want to keep a roof over their 'eads.'

'Ha!' Eve, hands on hips, stalked the brief distance between table and range as if the small room could barely contain her. 'Go back to work? Twenty-five weeks of strikin' and near-starvation for no gain?'

Arthur pushed his bowl aside. 'Nob'dy said it's fair, Eve,' he said. 'I'm sorry for 'em, like you. But it's a plain fact – them 'ouses are for working miners. If you ask me, they're lucky not to have been turfed out before now.'

'If you ask me,' Eve spat back at him furiously, 'those miners are 'eroes, and if you can't see that then you're no better than the buggers who own that 'ell 'ole.'

She knew she'd gone too far, even before Arthur smashed his fist on to the table top, and if she'd been swift with an apology he might not have reacted so violently. The whole wretched row could have been defused and reduced to a difference of opinion. But Eve was never swift with a sorry; sometimes it didn't come out at all, no matter how badly she wanted to say it or how clearly a situation demanded it. She knew, of course she did, that between Arthur and the profiteers at Grangely Main lay a world of differences; she knew he was as loyal to his peers as he was to her, that he would lay down his life for a colleague as readily as he would for his children. But today, in her fury, she chose to take him for a craven wage slave. It was unjust but, for a fleeting moment, profoundly satisfying.

'Oh aye,' she said with a sneer. 'You can chuck your weight about at 'ome right enough. But there are two lots of strength, Arthur. Strength of body and strength of mind, an' it takes a real man to stand up for 'is rights an' the future of 'is bairns.'

How in God's name had this started, thought Arthur. Not twenty minutes ago she was rousing him from his bed with a cup of hot, sweet tea and now she stood before him like one of the three furies. He pushed back his chair and got to his feet, leaving the table in disarray. His snap tin was on the sideboard, already packed by Eve with bread and beef dripping and an apple. One of them had to stop this, and he reckoned by the look on her face that it had to be him. He picked up his snap and dropped it into the pocket of his jacket. She watched him, hiding her anxiety that he would leave for work without fighting back, but unable to be the first to break the silence. He turned to her and his face was dark with the struggle to stay calm.

'Everything I do,' he said quietly, 'everything, is for you an' t'bairns.'

'Aye, an' Lord Netherwood,' said Eve, prolonging the bitterness even as she told herself to stop.

'Aye, for 'im an' all,' said Arthur. 'For 'im as provides me with a good living and puts a decent roof over us, and cares for t'sick and t'needy in Netherwood. 'e deserves my loyalty, and I'm not ashamed to say it. But them up at Grangely, they 'ave bad bosses and they mun act according to their lot. The only thing they'll get from railing against their miserable lives is more misery.'

He pulled on his cap and tied a plaid scarf snug round his throat. He felt the pleasure of being in the right and it made him generous towards his feisty wife.

'There's nowt to be done about it, Eve,' he said. 'It's a bad do, but not our business.' He opened the back door to leave. 'I'll see thi at two.'

'You won't,' she said, far from ready to make her peace. 'I shall still be at Grangely. Them folk need as much 'elp as they can get.'

He turned back, goaded into delaying his departure for

work. Until she said it, Eve had no real notion of going anywhere, but now she'd uttered the words she wouldn't retract them. She cursed her quick tongue, silently. She'd have to take Ellen with her, and there was work enough here at home to keep a small army occupied. But there was no backing down now, not for Eve Williams. She'd committed herself to an eight-mile walk – four miles there and four back – in mid-winter with a child strapped to her hip, just to shock her husband out of his complacency. She expected him to protest now, to raise objections, to attempt to forbid the fool's errand but he just stood for a moment, letting the cold into the kitchen and regarding his wife with an expression she couldn't read.

Then he said, 'Why?' and Eve heard herself give him a pious earful about duty and compassion, yet still her husband wouldn't be drawn.

'If tha's got to go, then go,' he said, maddeningly. 'But take care o' thissen.' He pulled the door to and was gone. Eve listened bleakly to his receding footsteps, then she heard Lew Sylvester's greeting – 'Ey up' – as he fell in with Arthur, then they were too far away to be heard.

Arthur had had to strike once himself, ten years back, in 1893, when the earl's miners all walked out – many of them without conviction – in support of the Great Coal Strike. They were out for months, reliant on soup kitchens and handouts, but it wasn't memories of the deprivation or the hunger that had stayed with Arthur, it was the shame he felt when four platoons of mounted troops rode through Netherwood, called to defend the earl and his family from the insurgents. There was no need, of course; there was nothing personal in the strike action, at least so far as the Netherwood miners were concerned. So although the dragoons and lancers held their positions on the great lawn of Netherwood Hall for almost three months, they never saw action. At the end of the strike the earl had written an open letter to his employees, and Arthur had hung his head at the words: 'I am at a loss to understand why you would lay my pits idle,' he wrote. 'I had expected the loyalty of my men to match that of mine to them.' There were, of course, employees of Lord Netherwood who were unmoved by the admonishment, but not Arthur. The day the pits were re-opened and the miners returned to work – all of them forbidden by the earl to join a union or ever again withdraw their labour – was one of the happiest days of his life.

Arthur's shift began at five o'clock in the morning and his home in Beaumont Lane was ten minutes' walk from New Mill Colliery, but he always allowed twenty minutes for the journey in order that he could take his time. He hated to rush anywhere, and wherever his destination, Arthur would undertake the journey with his customary unhurried stroll. Plus, just as he hated to rush, he also hated to be late. He'd worked for Lord Netherwood since he was a lad and he had never yet failed to clock on, not once in over thirty years. Indeed his punctuality had become a matter of honour and – since the strike – a manifestation of Arthur's deep-rooted loyalty to his employer. There were younger men at New Mill who muttered among themselves about long hours and low pay, but they didn't have an ally in Arthur and would fall silent if they saw him coming. His deference to the master was increasingly out of step with the times, but there were few men at New Mill with the stomach to tell him. Arthur Williams commanded respect among his colleagues.

The truth was that Arthur was unusually content. Even as a ten-year-old lad, when he first started at New Mill, he had felt part of an endeavour that was almost noble and certainly supremely worthwhile. He arrived with honour already conferred upon him by his father, killed in an explosion six years previously and still spoken of with reverence at the colliery. Arthur had imagined he would be sent down the mine, but his first job had been on the surface, at the screens; he stood at steel conveyors in a dimly lit and dusty hut and sorted lumps of stone from the piles of coal, throwing them into wagons which then carried the unwanted muck to the stacks outside. The iron plates of the belt squealed demonically under the strain and the dust was sometimes so thick that he couldn't see the boy next to him, but Arthur was stoical. Every day, though, he asked the overman when he could go down, and every day received the same reply: 'Soon enough, lad, but tha'll rue the day.'

At twelve he got his wish and was given the job of trapper, waiting for coal wagons and opening and closing the wooden doors that controlled the flow of air underground. Other boys shivered in the dark passages, whimpering when their lamps were accidentally extinguished, longing for the time when their shift would end and they could be carried back up to the surface of the earth, but not Arthur. It was as if he had a bright ember of self-sufficiency burning at his core to sustain him. At the end of his first underground shift, he stepped into the cage next to a boy taller and older than himself but whose face was rigid with trauma.

''ow's tha got on?' said Arthur.

'Shockin',' the boy said. ''ow about thee?'

'Aye, shockin' an' all,' said Arthur, to be kind. But he hadn't meant it, not at all. The subterranean sounds and smells didn't startle him, just as conditions underground didn't faze him. All these years later, he still walked to the pit with purpose and walked home with satisfaction, and there wasn't a job at New Mill that Arthur couldn't turn his hand to. He was a miner now, of course, a hewer of coal, pitting himself against the earth, hacking at the seams until they yielded their treasure, unwillingly, lump by lump. And he enjoyed the effort of it, even when he was blinded by mingled sweat and coal dust and his arms ached to the marrow of their bones; he liked the camaraderie too, the dry Yorkshire humour of his workmates, their bluntness, their dependability. But all of this he barely acknowledged to himself, let alone shared with anyone else.

Chapter 6

Certainly Arthur wouldn't have let on to Lew Sylvester or Amos Sykes, the two men who generally worked alongside him. Just as, this morning, he wouldn't let on to them about his blazing row with Eve. It was a private matter, nobody's business but his own. Nevertheless he felt a throb of disquiet when the subject of the Grangely evictions came up on their way to work. Amos had joined Arthur and Lew, as he always did, on the corner of Brook Lane, and as they clomped their way through the sleeping streets of Netherwood, Lew said, 'What about them poor bastards at Grangely then?'

'Aye,' said Amos. 'Poor do.'

'It's all over now.' Lew's voice sounded foolishly gleeful. 'Waste o' bloody time that were.'

Amos shot him a withering glance. The local radical, he saw possibilities in the Grangely strike that reached far beyond regional concerns. Lew's ill-informed fatalism disgusted him.

'It's folk like thee that're a waste o' bloody time, lad,' he said now. 'Grangely men mun stand firm, stick to their guns. They mun say what needs to be said.'

His vehemence was met by silence; Lew wasn't equal to a response, Arthur wasn't in the mood. This was usually the case. Amos – clever, widely read, politically well-informed – could be impressive when his dander was up, but his intellectual energy rarely found a satisfactory outlet; he was a soapbox orator without a crowd. He knew Arthur's views well; they were commonly held in Netherwood, where the earl gave his workers little to kick against. But Amos had travelled the country. He had taken part in miners' rallies in Nottingham and Durham, had once heard Keir Hardie speak in Merthyr Tydfil, and, while he was forced to keep a low profile in his own region, he was on nodding terms with Ben Pickard, the great tub-thumper of the Yorkshire Miners' Association. These were good men, God-fearing men, and they spoke from their hearts about strength through unity and the rights of the working man. Like an apostle of the Lord, Amos longed to spread the truth of their message, but here he was, walking to work with Lew and Arthur, and one of them wasn't worth the argument while the other didn't want to hear it. Amos blazed silently and chewed the inside of his cheek.

Arthur, his mind still a ferment from Eve's outburst, violently disagreed with Amos, but had no appetite for another fight. For a while no one spoke and the silence that fell between them was soothing. Arthur hoped Lew would keep his mouth shut. He took comfort too from the familiar rhythm of other men's footsteps ringing out with their own in the darkness. Hordes of men were walking towards the colliery, but they were matched by the numbers walking away from it, the night-shift workers, their eyes livid white against their coal-blackened faces. Some of them nodded silent greetings as they passed, but none of them spoke, or were expected to. It was no time of day for pleasantries.

Arthur, Lew and Amos swung left off the main road and on to the track that led directly to the colliery. The winding-gear towered up ahead of them into the early morning sky. A man who wanted to be heard had to raise his voice now above the hiss and whoosh of the steam that powered its engine. Lew, unfortunately, had thought of something to say.

'I know what I'd do if I were a Grangely man,' he said.

'Oh aye?' said Amos. 'What's that then?' His face was clouded with contempt; Lew had a tendency to repeat whatever opinion he thought would reflect best on himself. Amos would take Arthur's wrong ideas any day in preference to Lew's borrowed ones.

Lew laughed grimly and said, 'I'd get back to bloody work.' He glanced at Arthur, sure the older man would agree, but Arthur strode alongside him, looking ahead, saying nothing.

'Tha knows nowt, Lew Sylvester,' growled Amos.

'I know this,' said Lew, recklessly defiant, still banking on Arthur's support. 'I'd rather 'ave a roof over my 'ead tonight than not.'

Amos hawked and spat. 'If they cave in at Grangely, it'll be bad for us all,' he said. 'Tha can never see t'bigger picture, Lew. Tha's 'ad too many blows to thi 'ead.'

It was all so predictable, thought Arthur. Lew was stung, again, into surly silence and there'd be no more out of him now on the subject. He was a fierce-looking, powerfully built young man, whose face had been knocked ugly by countless illicit bare-knuckle fights, organised and promoted by his older brother Warren, a shady character who made his living exploiting in various ways the weak and the feckless. Lew was a harmless soul but he was tall for a miner, and broadly built, and Warren had shoved him into the ring when he was still a boy. If he won, Warren paid him. If he lost, Warren only paid himself. So there was some truth in Amos's jibe because regular maulings seemed to have had the effect of gradually slowing Lew's responses. He wasn't exactly simple but neither was he quite all there, was the general consensus. Certainly he was no match for Amos, and too often he found himself retreating into wounded silence in the older man's company.

It didn't help that he was the younger of the three by fifteen years. With a gap between them of half a generation, casual disdain was all he could expect. Amos had set the tone on Lew's first day at the pit, greeting him with expansive bonhomie then sending him off to the stores for a long stand. Lew, waiting fruitlessly amid the comings and goings for upwards of an hour, had finally, tentatively, spoken up.

'Erm, I still need a long stand, mister,' he said.

'Tha's 'ad one,' said the stores manager. 'Nah bugger off,' and a red-faced Lew had run the gamut of jeering miners who had chanced upon his humiliating initiation. Of course it wasn't personal; similar indignities had been endured by every man at the colliery – even Amos, on his first day, had waited for almost an hour in the boiler room for a bucket of steam. But somehow the balance between Lew and Amos had never been adequately redressed, as if the younger man had lost his dignity on the first day and still hadn't entirely regained it.

It was Arthur, as usual, who finally took pity on Lew this morning as they joined the crowd of miners at the time office. The cloud created by his clash of words with Eve had evaporated on arrival at the pit. He knew what was expected of him here and this, being profoundly comforting, in turn enabled him to talk Lew out of his sulk. He steered clear of the subject of Grangely Main, though, sticking to the safer topics of the ten-shilling birthday bonus and a knur-and-spell match at the weekend, until Lew's pride was restored by the attention. Sidney Cutts, the colliery timekeeper, called out their numbers and handed out two brass checks per man: one square, one round. Arthur waited until Lew had pocketed his before heading off with him to the lamp room and, from there, up the wooden steps to the pit bank and the great two-deck cage at the top of the shaft. The banksman took their round checks – the square ones were for the return journey – and they stepped in. Amos was there already, and he acknowledged Arthur and Lew by making room for them beside him. There was a moment for everyone to settle and brace, then the cage dropped like a stone down the shaft and no one spoke then because no matter how many times a man went down a mine, the plunge of the descending cage seemed to leave his stomach at the pit top and made conversation all but impossible. But goodwill had been restored between the three men, which was how Arthur liked it at the start of a shift; there was discomfort enough at the coalface without ill-feeling squeezing in alongside them.

It was cold in the mine at the foot of the shaft's yawning mouth but the further into the labyrinth the miners went, the warmer the air became until their thick clothing, until recently entirely necessary, became almost unbearable. Just before they left the main roadway they all stripped down to vests and shorts, hanging their discarded jackets, shirts and trousers on a wooden girder to collect at the end of their shift; even so, as they progressed further into the mine, sweat sketched pale lines on their limbs and faces. They were heading for Harley End, the farthest-flung tributary of the great Netherwood seam, almost three miles from the entrance to the pit, and they each carried the same items: a lamp, a pick and a shovel, a snap tin and a two-pint dudley, full of water.

It took them three-quarters of an hour to reach the cramped chamber where they were to spend their shift. The three men knew the seam so well that they reached it in half the time than would have been possible for a newcomer. This was the furthest outpost of New Mill's coal production – anything beyond three miles meant a man might spend as long walking as he did mining, and there was no profit in that.

Lew peeled off his vest and took a deep drink from his dudley. He sweated more than his colleagues – was famous for it, along with his gormlessness – and sometimes worked naked but for his boots, rather than endure the clammy embrace of sopping-wet singlet and shorts. Amos and Arthur were already on their bellies at the foot of the seam by the time Lew was ready to work, but he joined them soon enough, contorting his big body into the L-shape required to hack at the coal from the bottom up.

They were hand-holing – cutting underneath and around the coal with the pick, supporting the seam with wooden sprags as they went. It was difficult work, not least because of the limited space, and it called for technique as much as strength. They laboured alongside each other, their heads and shoulders inching into the space they were creating under the seam. Amos grunted with each swing of his pick, a habit that used to annoy the others but which they had long since accepted. Arthur liked the noise now; it acted as a metronome by which he paced his own swing.

From time to time, as the shift passed, the men would knock out the sprags and let a section of coal drop, using their shovels to break it up and heave it into the waiting tubs. It was good stuff in the Netherwood seam: bright coal, they called it, because of the way it shone. It was clean-burning, too, and so was much in demand. More than that, it was famous; it had caused a sensation at the Great Exhibition in 1851, when the Hoyland family sent a three-hundredweight lump of it for display. It sat there like a monolithic black diamond, securing by its very presence the reputation of Netherwood coal in London and beyond. It was still the very devil to extract though; poor coal gave itself up much more easily than this superior product and, five hours into their shift, Arthur, Lew and Amos dragged themselves upright, having advanced only six yards along the coalface. Four tubs had gone, two more awaited collection, and they sat beside them, backs against the wall, facing the seam.

Amos pulled a pocket watch out of his shorts and consulted it.

'Just gone eleven,' he said, although no one had asked the time.

'Right,' said Lew, pushing himself into the standing crouch that the space demanded. 'My belly thinks my throat's bin cut.'

He reached along a rocky shelf and took down the three snap tins they'd lodged there at the beginning of the shift. His own contained the same meal his mother put up for him every working day: two slices of bread, thickly spread with white lard and scattered with a crust of salt. He took the slices between black fingers and wolfed them down in great, wet mouthfuls, then signalled the end of his meal with a prolonged belch. In a body of men not known for standing on ceremony, Lew was particularly uncouth.

'My bulldog's got better manners than thee,' said Amos. Arthur laughed.

Lew, whose prodigious appetite was never sated by the contents of his own snap tin, now eyed Arthur's speculatively. The smell of beef dripping – a superior version of his own meal – hung in the air, and it wouldn't be coming from Amos, Lew reckoned, because his missus had passed away and he fended for himself, poor bugger.

'Tha worse than t'bloody rodents, Lew,' said Arthur, but he held out the tin. Eve had managed to press six slices of bread into it, and he knew there was plenty more where that came from. Lew took a piece, Amos declined. Lew set about chewing with obvious relish.

'I swear it tastes better down 'ere than it does up there,' he said.

'Soft bugger,' said Amos. He was silent for a moment, then he took out his old watch again.

'Ten minutes to 'alf past,' he said.

'Twenty past, then,' said Arthur, who knew where this opening gambit was heading.

'Aye, well,' said Amos. 'Long walk back, see? We've to be setting off by twelve at t'latest. There's nowt to be done 'ere in 'alf an hour. We could call it a day, walk back slow, no 'arm done.'

He had a point, but not one that Arthur was willing to accept. Amos, with only a dog at home to feed and shelter, had a tendency to be cavalier at the tail end of a shift, but Arthur never was. Half an hour longer at the coalface meant more money in his pocket. He shut the snap tin and moved from his sitting position on to his knees. Lew watched silently, waiting to see how things panned out.

'One more crack at that seam then,' said Arthur, as if Amos hadn't spoken.

'Aye,' said Lew. Amos glared at him, a wasted gesture since Lew was now looking down the tunnel at the looming bulk of a stocky little pit pony. A new, much younger voice cut through the darkness.

'I'm to take these tubs but not leave new 'uns,' said Tommy Hart, a lad of fifteen, who sat like a drayman behind his pony. He'd been put in charge of Sparky today, everyone's favourite among the New Mill ponies, a lionhearted little Shetland who knew every yard of the underground workings. Once, when a rockfall had blocked the main route back to the shaft and Tommy's lamp had guttered and failed, Sparky had led the terrified boy to safety, walking for miles through long-abandoned districts until they reached the entrance to the mine. Tommy had held Sparky's tail all the way, and as they went they'd collected other lost souls until a stream of men and boys were trailing behind the pony, entirely dependent on him for escape. He achieved legendary status that day, and still reaped the rewards in the form of regular

44

treats from the miners. Now, as Tommy clambered down, his movements awkward in the confined space, Arthur fed Sparky the apple from his snap tin.

'Tha' to take these, but not leave new uns?' said Amos, in mock-bewilderment. 'Now, why's that?' His nostrils twitched like a hound after a fox. The scent of moral victory was in the air.

Tommy began to tug at the pony's halter, coaxing him round to face the other way. He was a placid little steed and he did as he was bid then stood quietly as Tommy busied himself, coupling the tubs of coal to the sling gears on either side of the pony.

'Mr Gilford says there's no time to collect another load this far out, an' you're to make your way back,' said Tommy. ''e says you'll be paid fair an' you'll lose nowt by finishin' now.'

'Mr Gilford says that, does 'e?' said Amos, prolonging his moment. 'Mr Gilford, our esteemed pit deputy?'

Tommy nodded innocently. With the two tubs attached, he took hold of Sparky's halter. 'Walk on,' he said, and the Shetland heaved the load into motion.

Amos grinned at Arthur. 'Better do as t'boss says,' he said. And Arthur, magnanimous in defeat, grinned back. The three men gathered up their lamps and tools and began the long walk back to daylight.

Chapter 7

The industrial town of Netherwood had once been a pretty village, back in the halcyon days of its rural past when no one knew the riches that lay underneath the fields and hedgerows. Then there had been simply a scattered handful of farms and cottages set in the lush and gently undulating pastureland of Lord Netherwood's estates. And still, here and there in the Netherwood of today, were vestiges of the village of centuries gone by. Steadman's Farm – the only working farm left in the area – dated back to the sixteenth century, and its long, low farmhouse with stone mullioned windows stood as a reminder that Netherwood had once existed for something other than coal. From the farm a lane led directly to Bluebell Wood, an ancient and beautiful beech wood which every May donned its glad rags, just as it had done for hundreds of years. But little else remained of Netherwood's verdant past; the march of industrial progress cared nothing for aesthetics.

Like other villages in the coalfields, Netherwood had grown with the speed of an American frontier town. From 1850, when the railway came to Barnsley, prospectors began buying up land and sinking shafts, frantic to maximise their share of the riches. There was an urgent, desperate quality to these early explorations, a fear that the coal boom wouldn't last – and indeed not all of the mineshafts struck gold. Abandoned pit workings became as much a feature of the local landscape as the working collieries. But enough of them succeeded to establish Barnsley and its environs as the coal capital of the county – and the ships, trains and factories of the British Empire were hungry for more.

So Netherwood village, five miles from Barnsley and sitting atop one of the longest and widest seams in the coal-rich county, had grown so spectacularly swiftly in size and significance that some of its older inhabitants still remembered a time when you could hang your washing outside to dry without it ever turning black, and when the view from Harley Hill was more green than grey. The Netherwood of their memory had just one main street; it was still there now, but it was longer, busier and had a new name – Victoria Street – and it had been joined by many others. There was also a railway station, a brickworks, an old flour mill – though this was disused now – and three public houses: the Hare and Hounds, the Hoyland Arms and the Cross Keys. There was a new branch of the Co-operative Society and two thriving places of worship: St Peter's for those with a taste for High Church and the Methodist chapel for those who saw popery in a brass candlestick. Soon these would be joined by a third; the Primitive Methodists, who until now had been without a proper meeting place, were awaiting completion of a fine new chapel on the corner of Tinker Lane. Its unblemished stone stood out among the blackened buildings around it.

Eve Williams, hurrying through the town on this Wednesday morning, paused by the new building, struck by its size and the progress that had been made in so short a time. She and Arthur, hereditary Methodists, dutifully marched their children to the chapel on the other side of town every Sunday morning without ever considering the whys and wherefores. Now here was this brand new barn of a building, big enough for three hundred worshippers and intended for those for whom John Wesley no longer cut the mustard. Eve wondered what she was missing. If God was up there listening, could he possibly care what building you stood in while you sent up your prayers? She thought she might have a look inside when it was finished, mind. See what they had by way of heating. Never mind theological differences, a warm chapel would fill the pews. She smiled and pressed on before the cold morning had a chance to take hold in her bones.

By the time Eve had set out for Grangely, a wintery, watery sun was making a half-hearted attempt to warm things up, but there was no real strength in it and its efforts were thwarted anyway by the habitual grey ceiling of chimney smoke created by the burning hearths of every dwelling in town. Eve had mourned the comfort of her kitchen the moment she left it, which she had done as soon as she had been able. Seth and Eliza had been hurried off with indecent haste, each of them bristling with indignation at the stern warnings dinned into them about behaving themselves after school until she was able to come home. In the event, Ellen had been left next door with Lilly Pickering, whose brood – seven of them now, with the new baby boy – was of the size where one more hardly mattered. Ellen was only just turned one but she was an independent little soul, as happy to wave her mother off as she would be to see her again. She had walked at ten months, being in too much of a hurry to wait any longer, and had bowled into Lilly's already over-crowded kitchen this morning with the purpose and authority of a natural leader. Lilly looked wan and exhausted – nothing new there, thought Eve, who had felt a stab of guilt at having asked the favour. She had handed over a batch of parkin along with her daughter, partly as an apology for the additional burden and partly to be sure that Ellen would be given something to eat. Lilly's children always looked famished – 'like little streaks o' whitewash,' said Arthur – and Lilly herself appeared almost concave, drooping inside her shabby clothes as if she barely had the strength to support their weight.

Eve had said a swift goodbye before her conscience got the better of her. Far from regretting her impulse to go to Grangely, she was now full of fire for the scheme and she set off at a brisk pace, efficiently sidestepping puddles as she hurried on to keep her clogs dry for the long walk. The streets of Netherwood were quiet this morning; most of the shopkeepers hadn't opened up yet and there was still a Sunday feel to the town.

She cut through Draper's Lane from West Street, then turned right into Victoria Street, but she was already leaving Netherwood and walking south along Sheffield Road before she saw another living soul. Then, like an answer to a prayer she hadn't thought of uttering, the massive, unmistakable bulk of Solomon Windross suddenly emerged from a junction several yards ahead of her, driving his pony and cart out of town. Eve broke into a run, hitching up her skirts in both hands.

'Solomon!' she shouted. 'Sol, stop!'

The old man was hard of hearing at the best of times but above the rattle of his cart and the steady clop of his horse's hooves on the road, he was as good as deaf. It was only when Eve drew level with him, red-faced and running perilously close to the wheels of the cart, that Solomon pulled on the reins with his big hands. Bessie, his black mare, stopped obligingly, as if trotting or standing were all the same to her. She gazed ahead passively and awaited further instruction. Solomon nodded at Eve, as if nothing were more normal on a Wednesday morning than for her to be running away from home at full tilt.

'Now then,' he said.

His stately bearing and his vast cloud of white whiskers gave Solomon the appearance of a civic dignitary – a mayor perhaps, or a magistrate – but rag and bone was his trade, although Eve noticed that today his cart was entirely empty of its usual motley cargo.

'Any chance of a ride?' she said breathlessly. She clutched her side to ease the stitch brought on by her sudden sprint. 'I need to get to Grangely.'

Solomon, who never did anything for nothing, considered Eve's request. She knew him well.

'Two steak-and-kidney puddin's,' she said.

Solomon considered further, then said, 'Two steak-and-kidney puddins an' an apple crumble.'

Eve laughed. 'Go on then, but no errands on the way, mind. I want a straight run for that price.'

Solomon heaved his bulk fractionally to the right and Eve clambered up beside him on to the wooden seat. He smelled of tobacco, which Eve found quite pleasant, and unwashed undergarments, which she didn't. He flicked Bessie's reins, and the old mare resumed her steady trot. Eve tried to put a little distance between herself and Solomon but his rump left so little space on the seat that it was impossible. Never mind, she thought. Rather Solomon's horse than Shanks's pony.

'So, where're you off to?' she asked. Solomon's rag-and-bone rounds were always Monday and Friday, regular as the church clock.

'Grangely,' he said.

Eve shot him a hard look. 'You mean, you were going to Grangely anyway?'

'Aye,' said Solomon.

'Well, you crafty old sod,' she said. 'You never said.'

Solomon was indignant. 'Tha never asked,' he said.

Eve harrumphed with annoyance and folded her arms. Two

50

steak puddings and an apple crumble for a journey he was making anyway. The cheek of it. He could bring her home again as well for that.

'Why are you goin', then?' she said suddenly. She had a horrible feeling she might know the answer.

Solomon, who in general cared very little what anyone thought of him, looked distinctly uncomfortable now. He made no reply.

'If I catch you pillagin',' said Eve grimly, wagging a finger at the old man's stony profile, 'the deal's off. No puddins, no crumble. And I want a ride home an' all, so I shall see what you're cartin' off.'

'Bit o' business is all I'm after,' said Solomon grumpily. 'Way I see it, if folk dunt 'ave a roof, they dunt need all them goods and chattels. I'll be doing 'em a favour.'

'Oh aye, Saint Solomon,' said Eve. 'Well, just you be sure to pay good money for owt you take. They've got precious little without you robbin' 'em as well.'

Solomon Windross scowled but held his peace. If it wasn't for those puddings, he thought to himself, he'd stop the cart and chuck her out.

No matter how inured a person was to the grim realities of the industrialised north, the squalor of Grangely was in a class of its own. Like a slap in the face or a blow to the stomach, it had the power to stop you in your tracks. Squatting at the bottom of a wind-whipped valley between Sheffield and Doncaster, in the shadows cast by its towering headstocks, it was a living monument to the legacy of greed over humanity. The mineshaft, one of the deepest in England, was the nucleus of the town and from every street the colliery dominated the view. Radiating outwards, just beyond all the workings and the pit yard, a thousand ill-built dwellings were packed tightly in dense rows, separated by the open middens which ran between them. When the wind blew, you could smell Grangely before you saw it. In dry weather, it was a dustbowl: in rain, a quagmire.

'It's a rough 'ole, in't it?'

Solomon, master of the pithy understatement, sucked his teeth thoughtfully as they looked down at the town. They had stopped on the crags, a chain of south-facing hills outside the town, and from here they could see lines of people in the streets below, small and eerily silent at this distance, and behind them a collection of empty carts and drays sent by well-wishers, waiting to be loaded with the contents of the houses. It was a sorrowful sight and Solomon, having brought Bessie to a halt, was uncertain how to proceed; he felt awkward now that he could see how things were. His intentions – which had never been entirely honourable – now began to seem downright wicked.

'There's none rougher,' said Eve, although in fact it struck her that Grangely looked strangely peaceful. With the pit workings inactive, the coal wagons empty and immobile on their tracks, and all the chimneys free of smoke, the blanket of pollution above the village had cleared and from their vantage point Eve could see all the way beyond Sheffield to the Derbyshire hills. In all the years she'd lived in Grangely, it was a view that she had never seen before. It made her want to weep, and she might have done were it not for the fact that suddenly behind them a column of policemen, some on foot and some on horseback, hoved into view.

'Good God,' said Eve quietly. She watched as the uniformed men drew closer. There were perhaps a hundred and fifty of them – nothing like the four hundred Clem had predicted, but still a forbidding sight, those on foot marching in two columns behind the mounted police. The men's faces were shuttered, unreadable. How must they feel, wondered Eve, charged as they were with the devil's work? They filed past the cart, paying no attention to Eve and Solomon, and began their descent into the village. The pale faces of the crowds below turned to face the approaching policemen and Eve knew, then, that she had been right to follow her instinct and come here this morning. But for the grace of God, it could be her down there, waiting for her possessions to be flung like rubbish into the street. She may have only sympathy to offer, but she had plenty of it.

'Don't go back without me,' she said to Solomon as she clambered out of the cart. 'I'm walkin' in from 'ere.'

'Please thissen,' said Solomon. He watched Eve as she set off, as determined and formidable as any of the men she was following, then he clicked at Bessie and joined the unlikely procession down the hill.

Chapter 8

Barrington Short was a prosperous Midlands businessman
with an impressive portfolio of interests, most of which
were connected in one way or another with stoking the fire
in the belly of the Empire. From his large, comfortable office
in a tree-lined avenue of a Birmingham suburb, he had invested
not inconsiderable sums in a number of railway companies, a
steelworks in Sheffield and the Gas Light and Coke Company
in London, all of which were producing satisfying returns for
his trouble. Grangely Main Colliery, on the other hand, of
which he was principal shareholder, was turning out to be a
veritable poisoned chalice. It had seemed, on paper, such a
golden opportunity; one of the most productive pits in the
Yorkshire coalfields, producing three-quarters of a million tons
of good, saleable coal every year. A man with his insight and
ambition had to be in coal, and Mr Short had seized the
opportunity when it had been offered ten years ago.

He had never actually visited the pit; he didn't need to, since
there were a number of reliable managers in place there,
appointed by the board. He understood that the miners were
decently housed in convenient dwellings close to the pit, and
that the Grangely Main Colliery Company, in the interests of

the community, had built two public houses for the inhabitants – a clever stroke, since any money the miners spent on ale went straight back into the company coffers. Everyone was happy. Or at least they should have been.

But it now appeared there was ruinous sedition at the heart of the colliery. What the company – and he himself, if he were entirely honest – had foolishly taken for sporadic, ill-organised and easily quashed grumblings had turned out to be something much bigger and far more costly. Six months ago, when the Grangely colliers had downed tools over withdrawal of payments for bag muck, the board of directors – Barrington Short among them – had held a brief meeting at which the consensus had been that the whole ridiculous business would be over before the end of the week. They had laughed – laughed! – at the audacity of the union men who were demanding to be paid for the hours they worked, not for the coal they produced. Damnable cheek! What profit-making concern would pay good wages for the removal of muck that couldn't be sold? The geology of the mine meant a thick seam of useless dirt had to be shifted before the coal could be got at, and as far as Mr Short could see this could only be accomplished by the miners. It was their bad luck, not his, that they worked in a mine where clearing the worthless muck took a couple of hours each shift. He had no doubt, no doubt at all, that if the company paid them for the removal of bag muck, it would suddenly take twice as long. No. Capitulation on this matter would be an open invitation to idleness and time wasting.

Barrington Short had said as much this morning in a tele-gram to Bill Bramley, manager at Grangely Main and the company's man on the spot, as it were. His reply had been infuriating: 'Much outrage at evictions stop . . . Inform soonest if board reconsiders stop'

Reconsider indeed! Mr Short would see the whole colliery swallowed back up into the earth and covered over for ever before he would let the miners win. So he sat at his mahogany desk in his thickly carpeted, oak-panelled Edgbaston office and waited for the welcome news that those workers who had chosen to withdraw their labour were now homeless. The sooner those houses could be filled with new men with a proper regard for authority, the better.

The silence of the crowds on the streets of Grangely held for longer than the policemen found comfortable. The rasp of their boots on the road rang out like artillery shots as they marched as a body into the row of houses farthest from the colliery, closest to the outskirts of the town. The mounted police now hung back; their instructions were to advance only in the event of the mob growing nasty.

Eve had been absorbed by the mass of humanity. She stood near the front of the crowd and looked about her. There wasn't a single soul she recognised here. Grangely had always been populated by incomers, who left as soon as they were able to for work in other, happier collieries. Most people didn't stay here long enough to put down roots, and those that did remained only out of poverty or inertia. No one understood better than Eve the desperation to flee Grangely; in many ways it was the undoing of the place. Without the succour and support of generations, a soul was too easily cut adrift. Eve looked at the children around her and pitied them with all her heart for the awful stigma of their birthplace. Their little faces appalled her: white with cold and fear, and filthy. Their clothes hung in rags about them and they rustled when they moved, hampered by the sheets of newspaper layered under their garments to help keep them warm. The men and women, too, were gaunt and hollow-eyed with hunger. The strike had lasted nearly twenty-eight weeks; desperation lined their skin and gave young men and women the appearance of great age. For months now they had had no coal for their fires and scant food for their bellies. There seemed no likelihood of a fight today, thought Eve; these people were already defeated.

By now the police had taken up their positions, two of them in front of each house. There were a few seconds of uncertainty as the policemen, self-conscious, waited for orders, then a shout went out from behind – perhaps from one of the mounted police, no one could be sure.

'Get a bloody move on!'

It was as if an electric current passed through the uniformed men; as one, they started forwards and into the homes, and still the assembled crowd stood motionless, their watchful silence a more powerful reproach than any words. But as the muddy road in front of the houses began to fill up with the trappings of domestic poverty, a hubbub began, low at first but rising, though not of complaint so much as resignation. It was remarkable how swiftly the work was being done. Until this point the miners and their wives had not been certain that the evictions would really take place, so the sight of their threadbare rugs, thin, stained mattresses, tin baths, tables and chairs, all stacked in careless heaps or upended in the dirt, was shocking to them. The police, in their haste and embarrassment, were dragging large pieces of furniture out of the houses and flinging smaller items out of opened windows, heedless of where they landed. From where she stood she saw a small box of children's playthings fly from an upstairs window and spill its contents on the ground: a ball, a shabby dolly, a spinning top. It was an outrage and an insult, thought Eve. She imagined her own possessions being handled in such a way, and bridled at the thought. She wanted someone to scream at the policemen, demand that they stop their callous work, but remarkably there seemed to be no anger brewing in the crowd around her.

'Why don't you rail against them?' she said, voicing her thoughts but addressing no one in particular.

'Nay, lass, it's not t'bobbies fault,' said an old man. His eyes were rheumy and red-rimmed with cold and Eve felt a powerful longing to feed him with hot soup. 'It's them bastards want stringin' up,' he said, tossing his head contemptuously in the direction of the pit offices, which were unoccupied today. 'An' there's not one of 'em man enough to face t'music.'

'Oi!' a woman on the other side of Eve shouted, as a well-trodden rag rug sailed from her bedroom window. 'Watch what you're doin' with that carpet – it's priceless!'

She cackled at her own black humour and there was a smattering of laughter from the crowd. Someone else had struck up an accordion, adding a bleakly festive air to the grim proceedings. Another man, standing on a footstool and ringing a small brass handbell, began an ironic auction of his own belongings, as if his furniture was piled around him by choice, not force.

People were moving quickly now, galvanised into action, hauling the contents of their houses on to waiting drays. Only the very old and the very young hung back, out of the way, watching the show with bewildered eyes. Eve took one end of a chest of drawers and its owner, a young woman with a sweet, sad face, accepted the help wordlessly. Together they lugged the piece of furniture to a small cart and heaved it into position. Back and forth they went until all the pitiful pieces of a domestic life were out of the dirt and on the cart. Eve moved on, to see how else she could help. Ahead, on a low wall, a man was standing berating God, the police force and the colliery owners in a stream of colourful invective. But he was drunk and no one paid him much attention except for a small group of children who had gathered round him and were listening, solemnly. A light rain, insubstantial but insidious, began to fall.

'Marvellous. Now we can all be wet as well as cold and miserable,' said a familiar voice. Eve turned towards it and smiled.

'Reverend Farrimond,' she said. 'You're a sight for sore eyes.'

'As are you, dear, as are you.' Samuel Farrimond, Grangely's Methodist minister, beamed at her and clasped her cold hands briefly in his own. He was a handsome man in his late fifties, urbane, well-read, mildly eccentric and entirely incongruous in the largely illiterate community in which he lived. But he'd come to Grangely twenty-five years ago and saw there a project so worthy of his energy and so needful of his Christian commitment that he had never been able to leave. Eve, whom he had known for almost all of her life, regarded him as the saving grace of her childhood, a fount of kindness and integrity in a cruel and uncertain world. For his part, Reverend Farrimond saw in Eve the living embodiment of what made his task here worthwhile. She stood before him, beautiful as she ever was, eyes lit with indignation and her skin glowing from the exertions of the brisk march down the hill into town. She looked unlikely here: well-nourished, properly wrapped against the cold, unburdened by defeat. Seeing her now reminded him how very much he missed her in his congregation. It was six years, at least, since he'd seen her.

'Excellent young woman, to come here today,' he said.

''ow are you bearin' up?' said Eve. Unused to compliments, she was not adept at receiving one and usually chose, as she did now, to ignore it.

'These are trying times,' he said. 'Man's inhumanity to man makes countless thousands mourn.'

Eve smiled. Reverend Farrimond had literary leanings and a rather theatrical delivery which sometimes gave the impression of ostentation, but Eve knew there wasn't a kinder heart in the county. He was a very dear man, she thought.

59

'Where will they all go?' she said, coming back to the point.

'Ah, Eve, pertinent and practical, as ever,' he said. 'Some of them have family elsewhere and therefore places to go, albeit temporary. Many, however, have nowhere to turn.'

'But they do 'ave you,' said Eve.

'Indeed they do,' he said. 'Indeed they do. As many as we can manage will be housed in the chapel and my own home, be it ever so humble. Also, as I speak, a canvas village is being erected for the rest.' He waved an arm in a vague southerly direction, indicating the fields beyond the town.

'Tents?' said Eve, incredulous.

'Army bell tents, fifteen of them, each one large enough for thirty people, perhaps more in extremis. A padre friend of mine took pity on our plight. Not a permanent solution, but, for now, nothing short of a godsend and what we lack in comfort we shall make up for in compassion. Spare blankets and hot food gratefully received. Do spread the word. Now, my dear, I must take my leave. Much to be done, much to be done. Bless you for coming.'

Reverend Farrimond swept off. He had spoken lightly to Eve, but she knew he would be feeling the burden of every sorrow, fear and pang of hunger suffered by his flock. Their cares were his own.

'Reverend Farrimond!' she called out on an impulse, but he had been swallowed up by the crowd. She stood for a moment lost in thought, then, aware that the rain was making the task in hand more urgent, she threw herself back into the common effort.

By nightfall Grangely's houses were evacuated. They stood blank-eyed and bereft of life in the dark, some of them with doors or windows still open to the elements. A few meagre possessions lay scattered in the mud, discarded by the inhabitants or dropped inadvertently from departing carts. Two hundred men, women and children were billeted in the chapel, twenty-four were in Samuel Farrimond's small house, and a further five hundred were sheltering in army tents, a stone's throw from their former homes.

Eve got her lift back to Netherwood with Solomon Windross, but had to wait for him up on the crags in the teeth of the wind for almost an hour. He'd been busy, he told her somewhat sheepishly, moving three families and the contents of their houses to Sheffield. They had family there, he said, but no means to make the journey.

'Solomon Windross, I do believe you have a 'eart after all,' Eve said.

'Aye. Well,' said Solomon. He clicked his tongue at Bessie. 'Get on,' he said, and stirred her into a steady plod home.

Chapter 9

The earl was alone in the dining room. That is to say, he was alone at the table, for in fact there was rather a crowd in the room. Strategically and discreetly placed around the perimeter were four footmen in green-and-gold livery, while Parkinson, soberly clad in his immaculate black tailcoat with silver buttons, stood motionless near the door. The table was set for six, but Saturday luncheon was always an informal, come-when-it-suits-you affair, so Lord Netherwood was in no way perturbed at the absence of his family members. On the contrary, he found his newspaper rather better company than his family, with the notable exception of Henrietta who could always be prevailed upon to talk rationally on the subjects closest to the earl's heart: the estate, the collieries and the damnable impertinence of the Yorkshire Miners' Association.

On the long sideboard was a cold collation, pickles, bread and a pat of butter, the Hoyland crest now incomplete on its surface since the earl had started tucking in.

'What's your take on the Grangely affair, Parkinson?' he said.

The earl was prone to this, a sudden unlikely question to whoever was closest, be they family, friend, servant or complete stranger. His valet was more accustomed to it than Parkinson, being more frequently with him in close quarters, but the butler, too, had to be always on his mettle.

'A regrettable business, m'lord,' he said now. A typical Parkinson response, nicely ambiguous, leaving him free to join his master on whichever side of the debate he favoured. He had a whole arsenal of non-committal replies for just these occasions.

'Quite, but entirely predictable, what?'

'Indeed, m'lord.'

Lord Netherwood folded the *Chronicle* and set it to one side. It was the local weekly, which he read every Saturday and which every Saturday got his dander up with its tendency to romanticise the struggles of the proletariat.

'If I owned this blasted newspaper I'd veto strike coverage,' he said. 'Why pay the troublesome blighters the compliment of publicity?'

'Quite,' Parkinson said.

'What mystifies me is that the whole damn business dragged on for so long.'

'Baffling, m'lord.'

'Mind you, the owners are scoundrels. No interest in mining, except what it can earn them, what!'

'Shameful, m'lord.'

'And the colliers are wastrels. Wastrels employed by scoundrels. If you ask me, they deserve each other.'

'Oh, Papa, do leave poor Parkinson alone.'

This was Henrietta, who breezed into the dining room with a rosy outdoor flush to her cheeks and a beech leaf caught in her hair. She was fresh out of the saddle, brimful of energy and good health. She grinned at the butler.

'You're off the hook now. He can harangue me instead.'

Divided now in his loyalties, Parkinson executed a graceful, all-purpose incline of the head and pulled out a chair for the new arrival.

'May I serve you with lunch, your ladyship? Or would you prefer to help yourself?'

'A slice of everything going, please,' she said, then turned to her father. 'Simply gorgeous out. Cold, though. By the way, Jem said to say he's repairing the fencing by the gallops if you want to find him.'

Lord Netherwood reached across to extract the rogue leaf and said: 'Any sign of Tobias? I want to take him to New Mill today. I thought, if he's actually there in the thick of it, as it were, it might help him take an interest.'

Henrietta said nothing, though her expression was easy enough for her father to interpret.

'I know, I know,' he said. 'Uphill struggle.'

'Losing battle, more like. Ooh, yum. Thank you, Parkinson.' A brief silence descended while the butler placed a loaded plate in front of her, then she said: 'Terrible business at Grangely. Have you been over there?'

'To Grangely Main? Don't be absurd. None of my business.'

'Well, no. But perhaps we could help. I'm sure they must be desperate for donations.'

The earl, irritated by her wrongheadedness, spoke sharply.

'Condone the strikers? Preposterous notion.'

'Mmmm,' she said mildly. 'I suppose it was more the children I was thinking of.' Her face clouded briefly, then immediately brightened.

'Tell you what, though, Daddy. I'd love a trip to New Mill with you.'

He looked down and sawed at his roast beef. 'Also preposterous.'

'Why? I'd love to. Nothing I'd like more, in fact.'

The earl looked at his daughter fondly.

'Do let's,' she said, sensing weakness.

'It's no place for a lady, Henry.'

'I'll go in disguise. Toby's trousers fit.'

He raised an eyebrow.

'I shudder to think how you discovered that.'

'Look,' she said. 'You won't get Toby there in a month of Sundays. So take me – in a dress, something dowdy though – and I'll tell him what he missed. We'll snare him that way. Make him feel he's missing all the fun.'

He smiled. There was perhaps method in her madness.

'Your mother mustn't ever know,' he said.

'Marvellous!'

'You'll need sturdy boots. And a hard hat when we get there.'

'Even better.' She beamed at him. 'When do we leave?'

'Meet me at one. I'll have Atkins keep the motor in the yard so we can slip out the back way.'

They shared a complicit smile, then gave their food the attention it deserved.

Saturday was, without any shadow of a doubt, Seth's favourite day of the week. Eve and Arthur's eldest was an earnest, thoughtful boy, who spent more time than your average ten-year-old contemplating life and all its facets. So when he settled on Saturday as the first of the seven contenders, it was after scrupulous consideration of the merits of the other six. Even so, his careful list of the attributes of every day put Saturday ahead by an indisputable margin. There was no school, of course – a significant point in the day's favour but not, in fact, the chief source of the boy's pleasure. Unlike most of his peers, Seth found schoolwork easy enough to be enjoyable and any dread he claimed to feel on a Monday morning was entirely feigned. His only school-related complaint was Miss Mason's insistence on openly praising Seth's 'thirst for knowledge' or 'inquiring mind', with which unwelcome compliments she singled him out from the pack. He wondered time and again at his teacher's failure to understand that the pack was where he wanted to be.

No, the absence of school wasn't part of it at all. What Seth loved about Saturdays was the mixed array of special qualities that each one held in varying measure. The smell of a ginger cake in the oven, perhaps, on this one day of the week that Eve baked what she called 'fancies'; the spring in her tread that meant his mother was neither cross nor tired; an idle quality in the air, a feeling of liberty and leisure that sometimes evaporated if he didn't make himself scarce quickly enough to escape a chore, but at least existed as a possibility when he first woke; the certain fact that the next day was Sunday and his father's cap and jacket, with their smells of outside and underground, would still be on the hook with everyone's things when Seth came downstairs in the morning. All these things, and more, had accumulated over the years in Seth's subconscious mind to make him treasure the prospect of a new Saturday. And today was more special still, since his father had promised Seth he could accompany him to the knur-and-spell match on Netherwood Common. Not to play, of course; the visitors this time were near-neighbours from Rockingham way and they were a sly lot, not above stamping a good, long ball into the ground so it couldn't be counted, so there was no room for a novice on the Netherwood team. He would be allowed to carry Arthur's pummel, though, and his prized stash of clay balls, and he was bound to be needed as a seeker – his young, keen eyes could follow the small, white knurs as they flew through the air, no matter how many yards they went, or how awkwardly they landed.

Arthur, sitting in the tin tub in front of the parlour fire, was in a cheerful frame of mind too. He'd got in just after half-past one after a satisfactory shift at New Mill and walked into the kitchen to be granted a warm smile from Eve, which boded well for his Saturday-night prospects in the marital bed. Added to this pleasing train of thought was the match later this afternoon, piping hot water in the tub and a mug of strong tea just within reach on the mantelpiece. What else could a working man ask for? More hot water, that's what.

'Seth,' he shouted and, as if he'd been waiting for the call, the boy stuck his head round the door.

'See if your mam can manage another bucketful, son,' said Arthur.

Seth staggered in moments later with a fresh pail of hot water which he'd dipped into the great set pot in the kitchen.

'Tip it over mi 'ead,' said Arthur. 'In a steady stream, like. We don't want a flood on yer mam's rug.'

To Seth, the water seemed to be still simmering in the zinc bucket, and it scalded his hands where it splashed, but he had never yet fetched water that was too hot for his dad. Arthur tilted his head back to receive it, and let it pour over his face, through his hair, down over his shoulders. He handed Seth the long-handled brush and the boy diligently scrubbed at the parts of his back that were still dirty. Arthur liked to be clean, scrubbing at his nails and jiggling fingers in his ears, winkling out the coal dust from every cranny and crevice. Seth's grandfather, Ephraim Williams, had never let anyone scrub his back. He left it black, the dust ingrained like oil on a wooden table top, to keep it strong. Seth never knew Ephraim, but Arthur had told him stories, especially about the black back, so that in Seth's mind he held a clear image of his grandfather: doughty, heroic, deeply superstitious. Ephraim believed coal dust had healing qualities; wash it away, he told Arthur, and you sap your strength. He died in a fire-damp explosion and was carried out of the pit with his eyes, nose and mouth packed with the stuff, so Arthur took against the theory and Eve was grateful for it. The wives of black backs had the filthiest linen in the country.

'It's good weather for t'game, Dad,' Seth said, more in hope than in confidence since outside the afternoon sky was looking uncooperative, and as grey as an elephant's hide. The steam from Arthur's bath had misted the windows and Seth had to rub a small, face-sized patch to see out. 'No wind to speak of.'

'Nowt wrong wi' wind, as long as you're not hittin' into it,' said Arthur.

Seth coloured. His father never allowed him an opinion. It was annoying, when all Seth wanted was a sage nod of agreement. 'No, but too much wind an' it's not a fair contest,' he said. 'Mr Medlicott said.'

Arthur heaved himself upright and stood naked and unselfconscious, one arm outstretched for the dry towel. 'Well if Percy Medlicott says so, it must be right,' he said.

Seth passed his father the towel. He felt pretty sure of his ground this time.

'Mr Medlicott said in a fair contest, every player should 'ave same advantage. If you 'it t'knur and t'wind carries it, it's not a true length.'

'Aye, well, if Percy Medlicott 'its t'knur, it's a blasted miracle,' said Arthur. ''E's t'only fella I know who calls 'imself an expert at a game 'e can't play.'

It was true, Seth conceded to himself, that Mr Medlicott was better at the game in theory than in practice, although he wasn't alone in this. The knur was so small, and the split-second timing so crucial, that many a man swiped at fresh air while the ball plopped to the ground at their feet. Percy Medlicott wasn't the only player to be made a fool of, although he was more likely than most to take all ten of his permitted strikes and never hit the ball once. But Seth liked him all the same; he was kind, and he was generous with his time, always happy to explain the ins and the outs of a match to him. Seth wanted an acknowledgement of this from Arthur.

'If it weren't for Mr Medlicott, there'd be no matches at all,' he said. This was a fact; all local contests were organised by him, and there was even a Medlicott trophy, played for every year on the Saturday before May Day and named after him because he bought it, not because he'd ever won it.

'I'll give thi that one,' said Arthur. 'But it doesn't make 'im a world authority. If tha wants to learn, watch them as can play instead o' talkin' to them as can't.'

Seth was silent. He felt both vindicated and chastised, which was unsatisfactory. But he felt he might sacrifice his small triumph – and possibly surrender his invitation to the match – if he continued to press his point. Arthur, oblivious to his son's internal struggle, whistled a tune of his own invention and pulled on the clean clothes Eve had laid out for him earlier.

'Nah then,' he said. 'A bit o' summat to eat and we'll be on our way.'

Chapter 10

Up on Netherwood Common a sizeable crowd had assembled by the time Arthur and Seth arrived. Warren Sylvester was running his usual book and hectic bets were being placed, names and odds dashed off on scraps of paper in exchange for hard cash, the slips then pinned under a rock for safe-keeping. Warren, a fixture at every local sporting event, would take any bet except for multiples – he was careful to protect himself against heavy losses – but he was mean with the odds and took constant verbal abuse from disgruntled punters. He was a punily built, pinch-faced man, with suspicious, darting eyes and a mind as sharp as a steel trap. Nobody liked him, including his own brother Lew, but he serviced the local appetite for gambling and made a useful profit in the process. His only expense, apart from honouring winning bets, was to slip the occasional few shillings to the Netherwood constabulary in order to continue his trade without harassment from the law.

Arthur despised Warren, and had never gambled in his life. Mug's game, he told Seth time and again, and he could never drop it on occasions like this so as they passed Warren now, Arthur said loudly, 'Good day's fleecin', Warren?' and Seth, his eyes lowered, wished he wouldn't. The boy scurried on ahead, but Warren was either too preoccupied, or too indifferent, to bother framing a reply. He just glanced up and snorted contemptuously – the low opinion was mutual.

At the playing pitch Arthur took from Seth the pummel and the bag of knurs and joined his team mates, who acknowledged his arrival with barely discernible dips of the head. Percy Medlicott – officiating today, not playing – was making final, minute adjustments to the spell, the spring mechanism that threw the knur up into the air to be struck. The four-man visiting team watched him closely, as if only their scrutiny would prevent foul play. In turn, as custom required, the four players from New Mill Colliery eyed their opponents just as suspiciously, the implication being that if there was any cheating to be done, it would be at the hands of the Rockingham lot.

Discharged of his duties as equipment carrier, Seth jogged away from the crowd towards the part of the common where the knurs were likely to fall. He was the first down there, and he chose his spot carefully, though he knew there was no saying exactly where and how far the knurs might fly. He adopted the attitude of an official and stood, arms folded, legs planted apart, looking back up towards the players with an inscrutable frown. He would have liked to be the only seeker, solely responsible for locating the knur, watched by everyone with bated breath as he sought out each shot then triumphantly signalled his success. But already there were men ambling across the common to join him: Solomon Windross, Stanley Eccles and a couple of fellows from Rockingham who Seth didn't know. He nodded fractionally at them in the way he'd seen his father do on countless occasions, and they paid him the compliment of returning the gesture.

A sharp wind was getting up. They were exposed on the common, where there were few trees to offer shelter, and Seth could tell, even from this distance, that the spectators wanted to see some action. They'd be getting angry with Mr Medlicott by now, chelping about the time he was taking at the spell. He could see his father talking to Jonas Buckle, who was whipping a new head on to his pummel with cobblers' thread. Percy Medlicott straightened up and stepped away from the spell, indicating with a raised index finger that play could commence. A coin was tossed between the two teams and Seth could see that Rockingham lost the call because they drew back, their expressions dour, preparing to be unimpressed. Jonas stepped up to the spell and Arthur, Wally Heseltine and Lew Sylvester took a few judicious paces in the other direction. Jonas was their big hitter – his record shot of 290 yards was still unbroken after ten years – and none of them wanted to risk feeling the power of his backswing.

Jonas carefully chalked the head of his pummel, then placed a knur on to the spring of the spell. He took two practice swings, then all of a sudden and in one fluid movement he tapped the spring to release it, swung the pummel smoothly backwards, then brought it forwards with one great stride just as the knur began its descent. Seth watched intently, his eyes never leaving the ball. Jonas missed. He picked up the knur and placed it gently back on to the spring. Two more practice shots, then the same swift sequence of movements. This time Seth heard the hollow pock of the wood striking its surface and saw the small, white knur sail up and out towards him.

'Look out, lad,' said Solomon Windross, but Seth could see the ball and it was close but it wasn't going to hit him. He was there almost as it landed, and he shouted joyfully and raised his arm to stop the search.

'Seth lad, tha faster than my Jack Russell,' said Stanley Eccles. 'Next time I go rattin', I'll take thee instead.'

Seth grinned. This was perfect, he thought. He stood importantly next to Jonas's knur and watched Mr Medlicott and a Rockingham umpire make their way down towards him with the long surveyors' chains they used to measure the length of the shots. Each chain was twenty-two yards long and they were carefully laid end to end, pulled taut to give an accurate reading all the way from the spell to the knur. Seth counted them as they were set down. He hadn't been born when Jonas made his record strike, but he knew it had needed thirteen chains plus a measuring tape for the last few yards, feet and inches. This one looked likely to need twelve, Seth reckoned. He wondered how his father would do and the thought made him seek him out again. This time Arthur saw him and gave him a salute, which Seth returned. Then Arthur turned and shrugged off his jacket, preparing to take his turn. He could never play in anything other than shirt sleeves, whatever the weather. Wool sleeves hampered the swing, he said. Seth wondered if he was feeling nervous. He knew he would be, if it was him up there with all eyes on him.

Percy arrived at the ball and Seth moved his foot away to allow the measuring of the last few inches.

'That's it, son, well done,' said Percy. 'Keep well clear now. Let t'dog see t'rabbit.'

His Rockingham counterpart sighed audibly as the tape measure was slowly and meticulously unrolled until it just touched the knur. Percy looked at Seth.

'Twelve chains, and eight-yards, one-foot-three on t'measure. That makes . . .?'

'Two 'undred and seventy two yards, one foot and three inches,' said Seth.

Percy nodded his approval. 'Correct,' he said, writing the figure on his slate. 'Now stay put, and watch thi dad. 'E looks to me like 'e means business.'

The Rockingham official, satisfied that there had been no funny business, set off back towards the players but Percy remained by Seth's side, his eyes on Arthur as he carefully rewound the measure into a tidy spool. He had a soft spot for the boy, who seemed to be able to listen as much as Percy liked to talk.

'What your father 'as, Seth lad, is a very good eye,' he said. 'What 'e lacks in length, 'e makes up for in consistency. All these years I've watched 'im play, and I could count on one 'and the number of times 'e's missed t'knur.' He paused. 'Well, two 'ands, maybe.'

'I wish I could 'ave a go, Mr Medlicott,' said Seth.

'Aye, well, tha 'as to be taller than t'pummel, lad,' said Percy. 'Tha's got some growin' to do first. Now look,' he pointed across the common to where Arthur stood at the spell. 'Your dad, 'e never takes 'is eye off that knur. See?'

Seth wanted to say he was already considerably taller than the pummel, but the moment was missed as they both watched Arthur clout the knur on its first rise and send it sailing through the air. Seth shot off after it and Percy, Stanley, Solomon and the two men from the opposition let him run.

'Twelve chains again, Mr Medlicott,' he shouted as he went, though he didn't look round because he was watching the knur, just like his father.

Wrapped up against the cold and watching from the relative comfort of the Daimler, Lord Netherwood and Lady Henrietta saw Arthur take his strike. They were driving home from the colliery, where Henry had proved herself a sensible and well-informed companion, though her evident grasp of technical matters was a mystery to the earl. She had quizzed the pit manager about productivity as if she was, well, there was no other way of phrasing it – a chap. It made the earl at once proud and regretful; her mind and her temperament were of the highest quality, he thought, and yet were no asset to her, given her gender. Some lucky fellow would take her from him and reap all the benefits of her natural intelligence while the Netherwood estate would fall to Tobias, who went at life like a child in a fairground. Perhaps, if Toby was lucky, Henry might settle close enough to still be of use to him, if her husband would allow it. These internal musings were interrupted by the sight of Arthur Williams, some distance away on the common but still quite visible from the lane, rolling up his shirt sleeves and preparing to address the knur. Lord Netherwood leaned forwards and ordered Atkins to stop.

'Watch this, Henry. This chap can really play,' he said, then, 'Oh I say, good shot!' as the knur soared high and long through the sky. He'd played himself as a youth, from time to time, and hadn't been half bad. But the years had passed, and decorum and responsibility meant his presence at these working men's gatherings would no longer be considered appropriate by them or by him. It was sad, but there it was. He sighed, remembering the supreme satisfaction of striking the rising knur. There was golf, of course, up in Scotland. But that stationary ball on its obliging tee just didn't cut the mustard.

'Wouldn't mind another crack at that myself,' he said.

'Well why don't you? We'll wait, won't we, Atkins?' said Henrietta.

But the driver wasn't required to answer, because the earl shook his head emphatically and said, 'Drive on.' Then he sat back in the seat, feeling rather disconsolate, and fell silent for the rest of the short journey home.

Chapter 11

E ve stood on her back doorstep and upended the last bucket of cold water on to the cobbles of the yard. She watched as Eliza and Ellen and two of Lilly's children from next door shrieked with laughter and jumped back and forth across the miniature torrent. On another occasion Eve might have snapped at them to stop, but today she felt almost high spirited, in spite of the fact that her back ached, her hands were chapped and her skirts were wet on account of the countless trips between the tin bath and the back door with pails of grey water.

She went back inside, through the kitchen and into the parlour. There was now just an inch or so of water in the bottom of the tub and Eve could easily lift it at one end and drag it over to the door. The girls skipped out of her way as she emerged backwards, pulling the bath by one of its two handles. Using the doorstep as a ramp, she lay the tub down then stepped around it to the other side.

The girls waited. Eve might make them stand out of the way for this last, most thrilling, part of the game and Eliza watched her mother closely to gauge her mood. Ellen, who took all her cues from her sister, watched Eliza. Eve, however, had already decided to indulge them.

'Ready?' she said. 'One . . . two . . .'

She paused, holding the tub almost vertical.

'Three!' shouted Eliza, and Eve swung the bath over on itself. Water flooded out and down the yard and the girls danced over it as it made its way into the rain gully and out into the street. Eve lifted the empty bath and hooked it, still dripping, on to a great iron peg in the wall, then she took a stiff broom from just inside the kitchen and chased the last of the water away with it. She rested, briefly, using the broom handle as a prop, listening to the girls' laughter out in the street. It sounded as though there were a few of them now. She'd leave them a while to play. No sense having them under her feet, and Eliza could be relied upon to keep an eye on Ellen.

'I 'ope they're not sodden.' Lilly Pickering's peevish voice made Eve jump and she turned, a little flushed, to look at her neighbour.

'Afternoon,' she said, cheerful in the face of Lilly's determinedly joyless expression. 'They're not sodden, but I am.' She brushed ineffectually at her skirts. 'Your Minnie and Bet 'ave more sense than to get their stockings wet.'

A thin wail rose from inside the Pickering house and both women listened for a second, wondering if it required attention. The wail continued, but seemed complaining rather than urgent. Eve smiled at Lilly.

'Your Victor up at t'match?' she said.

'Aye, 'e flamin' well is,' said Lilly. Her words were bitter, but her voice was flat, as if even she was bored by her incessant carping. 'Life o' bloody Riley.'

'Ah well, they deserve a bit of recreation,' said Eve. 'They're none of 'em idle.' She stepped inside her house and closed the door. On one of her bad days, and this looked like one of them, Lilly Pickering's expression could turn milk sour and Eve wasn't going to let it spoil her mood. She dried her hands on the linen cloth that hung by the range, and took a dab of salve from an earthenware pot, rubbing it into the backs of her hands where the skin was red and cracked. Then she took a basin from the cupboard and shook flour into it, a little sugar and a good pinch of salt. Nothing was weighed; instinct and practice had taught Eve just how much to use. She moved with a practised fluency and hummed softly as she added a handful of currants and a small scoop of bicarbonate of soda to the mix, then used the base of the scoop to make a small well in the centre, just big enough to hold the egg she now broke into it. She took a wooden spoon from its jar on the shelf and began to stir, while at the same time adding a steady stream of milk until she had a smooth, thick batter. Then she let it rest while she reached for the cast-iron skillet, blackened with use, rubbed its ridged surface with a piece of mutton fat, and set it to warm on top of the stove.

Eve was at her most content. She was alone in her house, which was clean and in good order, the fires in both rooms were burning bright, the children were out in the fresh air, there was money in the housekeeping tin – an extra ten shillings too, thanks to Lord Netherwood – and food in the pantry, and in a few moments there would be the incomparable smell of drop scones cooking on the griddle. Arthur and Seth would soon be home and they would all sit at the table and share a pot of tea and warm scones spread with a little of the strawberry jam Eve had made last August. On such small pleasures was Eve's happiness built.

There was a knock on the door. Sighing, Eve wiped her hands on the front of her apron. She didn't mind unexpected company as a rule, but hated to be interrupted on a baking day. She opened the door and found a small, scrawny child on the doorstep, hopping from foot to foot. He had no clogs on his little feet, which were blue with cold where they weren't black with filth. He was a stranger to the bath tub, was Willie

Waterdine, and by the looks of his encrusted nostrils wasn't over-familiar with a handkerchief either.

'Bissis Williabs, Grandad sent a bessage,' he said, still jumping about on the step like an outsized flea. Willie was cursed with chronically blocked nasal passages and as a result his bottom lip hung slack in order to draw breath. He needed half an hour over a basin of camphor and hot water, thought Eve, but the Waterdines were far too numerous for any of them to warrant individual attention.

'Did 'e now,' she said. 'Stand still, then, an' tell me.'

Willie settled, but only slightly.

''e said, ad allotbent's cub free a'd Bister Williabs is next on t'list,' said the boy. ''e said does Bister Williabs still want it?'

This was news indeed. The allotments were a relatively new addition to Netherwood, just two years old and still with a vulnerable, newly planted look about them. The countess, in a rare moment of community-spirited zeal, had decided that the landless poor of Netherwood should be allowed access to a few fertile acres of their own on which to produce food and flowers. Her vision, grandiose in scope and scale, occupied her mind for almost two days, after which she lost interest and handed the scheme over to Jem Arkwright, the earl's land steward. He had ideas of his own about the value of land and its potential uses, and had proceeded to allocate a meagre site out of town, butting up against the railway tracks and comprising just a dozen narrow plots. Arthur had been too slow to snap one up, much to Eve's vexation. Clem Waterdine, however, had been first in the queue and now, two years on, he seemed to have become the self-appointed – and increasingly autocratic – manager of allocation. A peppercorn rent had to be paid to the estate, but it was Clem who had the power of approval or refusal over all applicants and stood in judgement over any gardener who neglected his plot. Clem's domestic habits were famously unwholesome but he had turned out to be a fanatically tidy and rigorous gardener. Eve wondered briefly if the old despot had winkled someone out for falling short of his own high standards. Not that she cared, if it proved to be her route to home-grown veg.

'Tell your grandad yes,' she said to Willie. 'An' tell 'im to drop in whenever he likes for a bite o' breakfast.'

Willie nodded. 'Right,' he said. His eyes were huge in his grubby face, as if astonished, and he was still jigging on the spot on the top step.

'Bissis Williabs?'

'What now?' said Eve.

'Cad I use your privy?'

Eve returned to her mixing bowl, lifted it and began to drop the batter on to the surface of the hot pan where it spluttered and immediately set in small, irregular rounds. The smell, sweet and familiar, rose in the steam and filled the small kitchen. There was another knock at the door, this time truly unwelcome. Eve looked round with a scowl. It was probably Willie again. She certainly wasn't about to leave the scones for him; they would scorch in moments if unattended.

'What now?' she shouted, irritation evident in her voice. She turned back to the pan; the exposed, uncooked surface of the scones was beginning to bubble and she started to turn each one over with deft flicks.

The door opened and still Eve didn't turn. She was so fully expecting to hear Willie Waterdine that she started quite visibly when instead she heard the melodious, cultured tones of Samuel Farrimond.

'Ah, nothing evokes a feeling of wellbeing quite so strongly as the aroma of drop scones,' he said, and he inhaled flamboyantly as he closed the door and entered the kitchen.

This was an extraordinary occurrence indeed and Eve, though delighted to see him so soon after her trip to Grangely, flushed a deep shade of pink as she greeted him. She was mortified now at the way she'd spoken but, equally, nothing would induce her to allow her scones to burn.

'Reverend Farrimond!' she said. 'I . . . I'm sorry, I must just . . .' She indicated her pressing business at the skillet and he smiled.

'Please, please, don't let me stand between you and your scones,' he said. 'No one will suffer more than I if they're rendered inedible.'

Eve laughed. With her back turned to him she was able to regain her composure. She couldn't imagine what had brought him here, but he would be properly received as an honoured guest, just as soon as the scones were safely out of the pan. For his part, Reverend Farrimond used the moment to consider the pleasing details of the kitchen in which he stood; it was humble enough but it seemed to him, coming as he did from the squalor of Grangely, to shine from every surface. The floor, the table, the range, the great copper pan, all of them the ordinary trappings of a miner's kitchen, nevertheless seemed more than the sum of their parts. The room was aglow with pride and purpose.

One by one, Eve placed the batch of scones on a clean linen cloth. Reverend Farrimond, left to his own thoughts, took the opportunity to admire her. He wondered if anyone ever told her how lovely she was. He presumed Arthur thought her pretty, but he knew how sparing these men were with their compliments. He knew, too, that Eve's appearance, if she was aware of it, would be of no consequence to her; beauty didn't feed the children or wash the clothes or keep the cold at bay.

In another person's life, he mused, her physical attributes

would have been highly prized. Her chestnut hair was long, and though she rarely wore it loose, when she did it fell in gentle waves almost to the base of her spine. Her features were regular, delicate, and her brown eyes were wide and thickly lashed. But Reverend Farrimond was right to suppose that Eve, though she remembered caring about her appearance when she was young and unmarried and her future was still perilously uncertain, hadn't gazed at her own reflection in a looking glass for many years. Vanity and self-regard were privileges of the idle rich; the only time Eve saw her own reflection these days was in Matthew's butcher's shop in Netherwood, where a mirror hung on the wall behind the counter, bearing the outline of a bull, its body divided into sections to demonstrate the various edible parts of the beast. And if she caught sight of her own face on the rib or the flank or the brisket, she certainly didn't think to admire it.

She turned now, having wrapped the scones into their linen parcel to keep warm, and smiled at the minister.

''ello,' she said, with mock surprise in her voice, as though he had just walked through the door.

'Hello to you,' he said. 'And forgive me for bursting in on you unannounced.'

'Well, there's no other way of bursting in,' said Eve.

Reverend Farrimond laughed. 'No, indeed, very true.'

''ow are you?' said Eve.

'Quite dreadful, inasmuch as my wellbeing is tied up with the people of my parish,' said Reverend Farrimond. 'Indeed it's difficult to imagine how things could be worse. Abandon hope, all ye who enter there.'

Eve's face fell, and the minister smiled fondly at what he read as compassion. But what Eve was feeling was more akin to shame than sympathy; his words had no hidden meaning, but to Eve's ear they held reproach. In Grangely she had resolved to return with the offer of further help – food, perhaps, or extra clothing for the evicted families. She had called to Reverend Farrimond as he left her, but her words had been lost in the din. Had he turned, she might now have been back in there helping to ease the suffering of those whose fate could have been hers. But since coming home, their plight, desperate though it was, had been eclipsed by the simple rhythms of her own domestic life and she had barely spared a thought for those poor unfortunates. In a rush, she blurted all this out to Reverend Farrimond. He, however, would have none of it and held up a hand as if to stem the flow of words.

'Nonsense, Eve, nonsense,' he said. 'It's only Saturday! What could you possibly have achieved in that short time? No, it pains me to hear you berate yourself.'

'But what should I do?' said Eve. 'I do wish to be of some 'elp.'

Reverend Farrimond did have a proposal to make, but he felt it had better wait until Arthur was home.

'What you should do, young woman, is put the kettle on the stove,' he said.

Arthur and Seth bowled into the warm kitchen on the crest of their triumph over Rockingham to find Eve and the Grangely minister seated at the table. Arthur was surprised, Seth disappointed. He wasn't sure who this man was, but by the looks of the dog collar he wasn't likely to want to talk about knur and spell, or hear him describe his first bitter shandy at the Hare and Hounds, a victory drink with the team, awarded to him with elaborate ceremony by Mr Medlicott for dedication above and beyond the call of duty. Seth had had to sit on an old bench outside the pub with only Jonas Buckle's dog Barney for company, which took the gloss off it a bit, but he still felt proud as punch. Now he was going to have to hold it all in until the man left.

Eve saw the struggle in his features and understood instantly what Seth was feeling. She saw him now through the minister's eyes; a comically miniature version of his father, ears stuck out like chapel hat pegs and a flat cap perched on his head. He'd been born with an old man's face, and he still looked older than his years. She smiled at him.

'This is Reverend Farrimond, Seth, say 'ow d'you do,' she said.

''ow d'you do,' said Seth, obediently but coolly. Arthur pulled off Seth's cap, then his own, and shook the minister's outstretched hand.

'Reverend Farrimond buried Mam's mam.'

Eliza's voice came from under the kitchen table where she'd been sitting with Ellen for the past half hour. It was her favourite spot when grown-ups were talking. Some years ago she'd realised that if she sat still and stayed silent, adults assumed she couldn't hear what they were saying. Eliza had learned all sorts of things using this reliable method.

'And christened your mother and married her to your father,' said the minister, lifting the cloth and stooping down to see the child. 'I don't only deal with the dead, miss.'

She stared at him, unsmiling; she was shocked to be directly addressed, and wished she hadn't spoken. Eliza's sixth sense for gossip told her that the main purpose of his visit hadn't yet been discussed, and now she was likely to be sent out of the room.

'Out you come, young 'un,' said Arthur. 'Call on Minnie next door, see if she's laikin'.'

'Minnie's gone in for 'er tea,' said Eliza, but it was useless, she knew. Eve bent down low enough to give her a hard look. Eliza immediately crawled out from under the table, followed, predictably enough, by Ellen. The two girls left the kitchen,

84

Eliza stomping her feet, Ellen trailing amiably behind, but on the threshold of the back door Eliza turned and said, 'Why's 'e staying?' and pointed an accusing finger at Seth.

''e's 'ad no tea and 'e's 'alf starved wi' cold,' said Arthur. 'Not that it's any o' your business. Now sling yer 'ook.'

The door slammed shut, and Eve stood to pour tea for her husband and son. Arthur sat in the chair she'd vacated and got straight to the point.

'Now then, Reverend, what's your business?'

Chapter 12

Arthur Williams had lost his wool scarf. It usually hung with his hat and his coat on the pegs at the foot of the stairs, but this morning it wasn't there and the search for the scarf was now in its seventh minute. It really didn't matter that much, thought Eve. A man wouldn't perish without a scarf, just the once. At this rate he would be late for work, and that was unthinkable.

'Go without it,' Eve said. She had stopped looking anyway. It seemed to her that if an object didn't present itself within the first few moments of a search, it should be left to turn up when it was ready. There was enough to be done in the day without finding extra work.

'One o' them bairns must 'ave 'ad it,' Arthur said.

'Aye, well, that's as may be,' Eve said, by which she meant that it wouldn't serve her purposes to have them woken before it was necessary.

There was still a great deal unsaid between Arthur and Eve since Reverend Farrimond had taken his leave on Saturday evening; somehow, in the hours between then and now, the opportunity to properly discuss what had been proposed and agreed to had eluded them. And now Monday morning had come round again in its inexorable fashion and Arthur, scarfless, was about to leave the house.

On the threshold of the back door, he turned to his wife.

'It'll just be temp'ry,' he said.

'I know it will,' said Eve.

'Right,' he said. 'Ta-ra then,' but he still looked unsettled and stood, on the brink of departure, unable to leave. Eve saw Seth in his hesitancy and she took pity.

'Wait,' she said, and she walked across the kitchen, took his familiar, beloved face between her hands and planted a warm kiss on his mouth.

'You're a good man, Arthur Williams,' she said.

He smiled at her, a little bashful now, and opened his mouth to say something, but outside in Beaumont Lane Lew gave a shrill whistle, so Arthur turned and left the kitchen, closing the door softly behind him.

Reverend Farrimond's request had not been for food, or clothing, or any of the charitable schemes Eve had had in mind. What the minister had asked was for Arthur and Eve to take in a family from Grangely. A particular family, and a very small one, but one in the direst need. The husband, a hard-working, God-fearing man, had died on the day after they were evicted. He had been desperately ill for weeks, said the minister, and the upheaval of being carried out of his bed and into the cold had proved fatal. He had died on a makeshift mattress of straw in the crowded tent that, for the foreseeable future, was to be his home. His young wife and baby were now utterly helpless. Even if the strike ended – which everyone suspected it would – and the miners and their families were allowed back into their former homes, the widow and child were no longer the responsibility of the Grangely Main Colliery

Company. She was twenty-two, said the minister. The baby, a girl, was six months old. Could Arthur and Eve have them, just for a few weeks? It was a great deal to ask, he knew, but other people had taken in the needy and Eve had seemed to want to offer help.

Arthur, seated next to Reverend Farrimond and opposite his wife, had thrown her a look that the minister couldn't see. It was a challenge, a gauntlet, flung on the table. It seemed to say, 'Now we'll see how far your conscience takes you.'

Seth was still in the kitchen too, and he looked at the minister with wide, horrified eyes. There was no room for anyone else in this house, he thought. Why was he even asking?

Eve said, ''ow long would they have to stay?' betraying her unwillingness by her choice of words, even though she kept her voice level.

'Just a matter of weeks, really,' Reverend Farrimond had said, mistakenly encouraged by her response. 'The young widow wishes to travel back to her homeland, and there's every chance that the church distress fund might be able to help her do this. She's willing to work in the meantime. She could be a great help to you, Eve. Eve?'

Eve forced herself to look up. She had stopped listening after the minister said 'homeland' and she gazed at him blankly. Arthur spoke up.

'Where's she from then?' he said.

'Russia,' said the minister, quite cheerfully, as though there was nothing at all unusual being discussed and he was simply responding to Arthur's polite interest.

'Leo and Anna Rabinovich,' he went on. 'Just Anna now, of course. Not sure what the baby's called. Fascinating, really, how they ended up in our little corner of Yorkshire. We have two other foreign families in Grangely, you know. Polish, though.' He chuckled. 'Oh yes, we're quite international.'

He looked at Eve then back to Arthur. Seth, forgotten by

everyone, said, 'Then they should go to them. They should go to the foreign people, not come 'ere. We're not foreign.' He spoke quickly, out of panic, and his voice cracked. He felt maddening tears pool in his eyes.

The three adults looked at him and the boy waited to be sent out of the room, but the stranger said, 'We are to them, Seth,' then they all simply looked away again, and their behaviour made him feel more afraid. He wanted his mother to banish him in the normal way instead of staring at the table. More than that, he wanted this man to get up and leave. He had walked in on their perfect Saturday and ruined it completely. The boy glared at the minister with hatred, but nobody was watching him any more.

'You wouldn't ask this of us if you weren't desperate?'

It was Arthur who spoke, not Eve. She looked at him, aghast. He seemed to be speaking her line, asking the question she should ask, but her compassion for the needy of Grangely and her desire to help them had been a poor, stunted impulse in the end, she thought.

'That's right, Arthur,' said Reverend Farrimond. 'I truly wouldn't.'

'Then they can come,' Arthur said.

'No!' said Seth. 'They can't!'

Now his mother did turn on him.

'Seth Williams, get up them stairs now and stay there till you're told otherwise.'

He hesitated a fraction too long and she gave him the look she reserved for such moments, the look that conveyed the seriousness of her intent, the firmness of her resolve. He fled through the doorway at the foot of the stairs, pulling it shut behind him so that his mother couldn't see he was still there, his face pressed into his father's coat. It still smelled of beer fumes and tobacco from the Hare and Hounds, and Seth breathed it in, wishing they were still there.

The door swung open, and there was Eve, alerted to his attempt at defiance by the absence of footsteps up the stairs. 'Up,' she said. 'Now.'

So he went, but he surreptitiously slid his father's woollen scarf from the peg and took it with him. It was bitterly cold in the little bedroom and he was glad; shivering on the bed helped him feel as wretched as he believed the situation demanded. He wondered how long he'd be made to stay here. He rolled the scarf into a pillow and, curling up on the bed, shoved it under his cheek and lay listening to the voices in the kitchen below. They were muffled, but he could still tell it was his mother speaking, and Seth wondered what she was saying. She didn't want those people to come any more than he did, thought Seth, and that's why she was angry at him. He was only a boy, but he understood that well enough.

Chapter 13

Lew Sylvester's brother Warren had picked up a copy of the Sheffield *Telegraph* on Saturday, and had seen an advertisement in it for miners to fill the vacated positions at Grangely Main. There were similar adverts, too, he'd heard, in newspapers in Birmingham, Newcastle and Liverpool. Only a matter of days now before the striking miners slunk back to work, Warren had said. He had no sympathy for them, not an ounce. The miners should put up and shut up or get on and do something else for a living. That was his view. Warren had no time for self-pitying whingers.

Lew was full of this news as he walked along the dark streets with Arthur and Amos, but disappointingly Arthur would only nod, as if it was only to be expected, and Amos walked ahead so he didn't have to listen. And then, when they got to the colliery, it turned out not to be news at all – the talk in the time office and the lamp room was of nothing else.

'Waste o' bloody time,' said Alf Shipley, who had no faith in the power of the working man to improve his lot. 'All them weeks, kiddies starvin', folk dyin', an' all for nowt.'

'They should stick it out,' said Amos. 'If blacklegs take those jobs, there'll be riots on t'streets.'

'Oh aye, an' what good'll that do anybody?' said Sidney Cutts.

'Keeps it in t'newspapers,' Amos said. 'Makes' folk realise we can't be subdued by capitalist tyrants.'

'Keep thi revolutionary claptrap to thissen,' said Alf. 'Tha'll 'ave us all out o' work wi' that kind o' talk.'

'Death or victory,' said Amos loudly, punching the air. He grinned broadly.

'Bloody 'ell, Amos, I didn't know tha could smile,' said Sidney. He handed Amos his brass checks.

'Puts Yorkshire miners centre stage,' said Amos, ignoring Sidney and continuing with his theme. 'Right under Balfour's nose.'

Lew said, 'Aye, an' right up it an' all,' and was pleased to earn a brief laugh from Arthur, who stood by him in the line.

'Fact is,' said Arthur, 'Balfour's never 'eard o' Grangely an' never will. Nowt to do wi' 'im.'

Amos shook his head. 'Balfour best sit up an' listen then,' he said. 'The workin' man will 'ave 'is day.'

Arthur, displeased with this casually seditious talk, walked to the bank ahead of Amos and Lew, exchanged a friendly nod with the banksman who took his check, and stepped on to the cage. He was the last man on, and it plunged downwards almost immediately. At the bottom of the shaft he set off alone to the Parkgate seam where he was to spend his shift. It was only a mile from the shaft bottom but it was a devil of a place to work, hot and dry and dirty. The water carriers – young lads hauling tanks of water on wheels – went back time and again to fill the dudleys of any miner working there.

There was no need to stoop in the main roadway through the mine, the roof being several inches higher than a man's head and wide enough for tubs and ponies to pass each other with room to spare. Arthur strode along, content to be alone. Amos and Lew would join him soon enough. He thought about Eve; he knew that what Samuel Farrimond had asked of them was harder for her than for him. Arthur was underground as often as he was at home anyway. The house in Beaumont Lane was Eve's domain, and almost sacred to her. Arthur understood this, and it was because he understood that he had spoken as he had; Eve would not have been able to utter the words, yet Arthur knew that, at the same time, she would never forgive herself for failing to make the offer. So he had spoken for her and offered their home as a refuge for strangers, and foreign ones at that. He hoped her kiss earlier that morning had meant she forgave him.

He turned into another tunnel, hotter now, and lower. Arthur had to move more cautiously and he stripped off his jacket and shirt. He passed two men, Fred Greaves and Frank Ogden, youngsters not long graduated from the screens and sent by the deputy with replacements for two of the wooden props that supported the roof; they had twisted under the weight of the tons of rock and shale they held at bay. It was a common enough sight, these bowed and buckling posts, and it was a full-time job to keep up with the maintenance. Arthur knew the two lads – there was no one at New Mill he couldn't name – and they exchanged brief nods as he passed.

'On thi own?' said Frank, watching him go.

Arthur said, 'Sykes and Sylvester an' all,' but he spoke tersely and didn't stop walking or look back, because nobody ever worked alone and Frank Ogden should know that.

Arthur was stripped to his shorts by the time Lew and Amos arrived at the coalface; the temperature in this section of the pit was pushing ninety degrees. Lew, crouching in the confined space, took a deep drink from his dudley then began to strip too. Arthur was already lying on his side finding if not exactly a comfortable position then one which was at least tolerable while the work was done. Amos made no move to join him. He waited, stock still, with his head slightly cocked.

Arthur looked at him. 'When you're ready,' he said drily.

'Summat's amiss,' said Amos.

Immediately, Arthur pushed himself away from the floor and up on to his knees; he'd noticed nothing awry himself, but Amos was almost as experienced in this pit as he was, and many a man had been saved before now by gut instinct. Lew sniffed the air; it was hot and full of dust, but it didn't carry the foul stink of gas. Arthur checked his lamp for any change to the flame; it burned bright and was yellow, not blue, and he looked at Amos questioningly.

'What's up?' he said.

'Summat's shiftin',' said Amos, and he began to shuffle back down the tunnel, away from the coalface. Arthur and Lew exchanged a look and, without saying a word, agreed to follow him. Lew left just ahead of Arthur, who stayed a fraction longer, listening, before picking up his lamp. The merest scrap of shale, no bigger than a flake of snow, fell from the ceiling on to his bare shoulder. More followed, soft and sinister. Bent almost double, moving as quickly as he could in the confined space, Arthur set off out. Lew was just in front, Amos had moved out of sight. He'd be heading all the way back to the main roadway; if something was happening, that's where they needed to be. It was a nuisance, creeping away from the face in this way when it was likely they'd be back before long, but there was not a shred of doubt in Arthur's mind that it had to be done. The wooden props lining the tunnel creaked from the strain of supporting the earth. They did this every day, Arthur told himself. It meant nothing. Nevertheless he tried to step up his pace, but he'd caught up with Lew now, and the taller man moved more slowly underground, always had.

They shuffled on and were making good progress, were so

nearly out. Just a few yards more and they'd be in the roadway, where Amos waited. And then, with heart-wrenching certainty, Arthur knew that it was all over. In a few, short, terrible seconds, the creaking became a splintering and the splintering became a demonic creak and grind, more final than anything he had ever heard before, and the noise was ahead of them, not behind. Amos, still unseen, shouted, 'It's comin' dahn!' and Lew turned in panic to see where Arthur was, wasting precious moments to twist himself round in the confined space. There was Arthur, almost on top of him, and their eyes locked for the briefest moment before Arthur gave Lew a powerful shove with his shoulder, propelling the younger man further down the tunnel as one of the props, then another, snapped like matchsticks under the impossible weight, and the roof of the tunnel pressed down with all the might of the earth above it. The rockfall was loud and swift and brutal; it filled the tunnel with dust and noise so that nothing was visible and even the sound of Lew screaming was lost in the din. Then, with obscene suddenness, it was finished. Lew was pulled away, dragged backwards by unseen hands as the last rocks settled into place and a silence descended, more terrifying by far than the noise.

Lew, half-crazed by the trauma, struck up a low, animal moan like an injured bull. Amos left Lew with the men who'd run to his aid and shuffled forwards, as hesitant and vulnerable in the thick dust as a blind man. Groping with his hands, he found the edge of the fall and, stooping, felt along its fringes for any sign of Arthur. He could see, at this close range, the extent of it, floor to roof, and nothing to show that Arthur was there, though still a chance, thought Amos, that his friend could be safe on the other side of it. Standing again, leaning in to the wall of rock, he began to pull at the rocks nearest the tunnel roof, loosening them, letting them slide. Behind him, Lew's wailing had finally ceased – or, at least, ceased to be audible – as he was helped further along the roadway to the pit bottom. Fred Greaves, plucky for a youngster, had stumbled towards Amos, coughing and choking on the dust, to join him in his task. Together, wordlessly, they clawed at the rock; if a space could be made at the top of the fall, perhaps Arthur's voice might be heard. Perhaps if they worked hard enough, there might be space for a man to crawl to safety.

They laboured at the task for almost an hour, Fred driven by youthful inexperience, Amos driven by grief. He knew, now, that it was hopeless. Enough of the fall had been shifted out of place to see just how far back it extended. Unless Arthur had turned and run in the opposite direction – and Amos knew he hadn't, knew he would've been right there with Lew – then his body had to be underneath these rocks.

He slid away from the top section of the wall, back down to the tunnel floor. The dust had finally begun to clear, and visibility was improving. Amos heard Reg Gilford, the seasoned old deputy, calling him back. There were reinforcements, said Reg, men with unsapped strength and energy. Fred, too young to pay no heed to the deputy, clambered gingerly down the irregular slope of the wall and retreated but Amos stayed put, heaving rocks from the base layer, showing no sign of flagging.

Then he saw it, revealed by the removal of a large, flat section of stone: Arthur's hand, emerging outstretched from the debris as if straining to touch him. The palm was down, the fingers splayed, the nails rimed with black. Tears began to course silently down Amos's cheeks at the sight.

He sat back on his heels and hung his head. Behind him, Reg Gilford had arrived to coax him away, and he saw, immediately, why Amos had ceased his efforts. Any further attempts at rescue would be fruitless. Now it was simply a matter of retrieving the body.

It could wait a minute or two though, thought Reg, hanging back respectfully from Amos, who appeared to be praying.

But Amos had nothing to say to God, whose presence could never be felt at the bottom of a mine. Instead his head was full of grief, curses and impotent fury.

It took no time for the pit to rob a man of his life, thought Amos. No time at all.

Chapter 14

Monday was wash day, the one day of the week when Seth and Eliza were happy to get out of the house and off to school. Breakfast on Mondays was always rushed because by the time they got themselves up and downstairs, Eve was already busy fetching in extra water, bringing it to the boil and piling soiled linens into a great basket in the kitchen. Years ago she had got Arthur to install a barrel outside the back door to collect rainwater from the spouts; it was softer than water from the spigot in the street, and better – Eve believed – for the clothes. She guarded her rainwater jealously; it was forbidden to use it for the bath tub, and she made Seth and Eliza go back and forth to the tap with buckets when water was needed for any purpose other than the weekly wash.

In silence, the children ate bread and dripping and drank a glass of milk at the table. They watched as Eve bustled about, lifting the mats from the kitchen floor and shifting the fire irons and fender away from the rising steam. She pushed the empty dolly tub nearer to the stove and then dragged the mangle across the floor too, positioning it by the tub. Eliza, a helpful little soul, collected the empty plates and carried them to the sink where she briefly rinsed them and stacked them to dry on the ridged draining board. Ellen, far too young for school but old enough to understand that she should keep out of her mother's way, slipped down from her chair and into the parlour, away from the commotion. Then Seth and Eliza, wrapped up warm and ready to go, came to Eve for a brief, distracted peck on the head before leaving the house to join their friends on the short walk to school.

Alone in the kitchen, Eve filled the dolly tub with boiling water and dropped in the first batch of whites: sheets, pillow-slips and a few bits of the children's underwear which looked in dire need of a hot wash. She left them there to soak and went out into the backyard to stretch out her drying line, unhooking the coil of thin rope from its place by the kitchen window and unravelling it until she reached the privy wall, where there was another hook at the same height as the first. She looped the rope around it twice then walked back at a slight angle, making another line which was finally secured on to a third hook on the other side of the window to the first. She tied the loose end tight, yanking on it hard, to be sure it wouldn't give way. It wasn't a bad drying day, she thought. Even if the weather turned and the washing all had to come back into the house, they would still have the smell of outdoors about them. Hilly appeared; her line was already up, and she had a basketful of wet clothes resting on her hip. The two women exchanged a smile but didn't linger to chat. No one had time for that on wash day.

Back inside, Eve took the wooden dolly in two hands and plunged it into the mass of wet and steaming linen in the tub. Up and down she worked the stick, her face set in an expression of grim determination. There was nothing half-hearted about Eve's approach to washing; she was all vigour and concentration. When she was satisfied that the clothes had taken enough of a pummelling she took up a pair of wooden tongs and began to hook out the items one by one and pass them through the mangle. It was heavy work; sheets that had dropped in so easily when dry were now made leaden with water. Eve puffed slightly as she fed them into the jaws of the mangle and turned the great iron handle. The water, slightly greyer now but still hot, ran on to a sloping wooden tray then down through a hole and back into the dolly tub. Soon she could make a start on the next batch. All being well, by the time the children came home at dinner time, the bulk of it would be done.

Eve was pegging out sheets in the backyard when she heard the sound that had the power to render her catatonic with fear. Somewhere in the town a housewife had begun to strike a poker against the grate of her fire and the sound, carrying easily through the walls of the terraced houses, had been heard and replicated by her neighbour, and hers, and again hers, until it seemed that hundreds of pokers were striking hundreds of iron grates, to relay the news more effectively than any telegraph that there had been an accident at the pit. Eve listened to the hollow, chilling sound of metal on metal and prayed with all her heart that it wasn't at New Mill, and if it had to be New Mill, then it wasn't Arthur. Let it be anyone else's husband, she prayed, but let it not be my Arthur.

Eve had walked up to the pit with a growing crowd of women, but she felt alone among them and drew no comfort from their presence. On the contrary, she regarded them as rivals in their joint desire to be spared the grief and uncertainty of widowhood. There was no comfort, either, in the fact that on previous occasions Arthur had survived unscathed. New Mill was a safe pit compared to many, but Eve had made this journey twice before, her mouth as dry with fear as it was today, and had stood as close as she was able to the pit head while bodies were carried out and the dead named. That Arthur was not among them then made it more of a certainty, to Eve, that he would be this time.

She knew, the instant she arrived. There were many women there before her and their expressions of profound relief, for which at that moment Eve hated them, changed swiftly to looks of deep compassion when they saw her. So she knew from their faces that it was Arthur, though she didn't know – at least not immediately – that it was him alone. That news was delivered to her later, as she sat motionless in the deputy's office not drinking her hot sweet tea, waiting for Arthur's poor, crushed remains to be brought up the shaft. She remembered, as if it were a glimpse of another person's life, that she must have left Ellen alone in the house. The realisation didn't alarm her; it simply crossed her mind, then was gone. The Earl of Netherwood came to speak to her; he always tried to attend an accident at one of his collieries, had even, on one occasion, joined the rescue effort underground. He sat by Eve for a while and spoke to her gently of his sorrow, but she didn't meet his eyes and barely heard his words; this encounter, to her, was no honour, but merely part of the ongoing nightmare. Lord Netherwood, giving up the effort but sitting in silence with her for a while, wondered what her future held. He didn't know Mrs Williams, had no idea what she was made of. He hoped she would find the resources – both inner and material – to stay in Netherwood. The earl was a fair man and his estate didn't evict women for being widowed, but rent must be paid all the same.

'Can we assist you home?' he said now, in the hope that practical help might be more welcome than words of sympathy. 'My driver's outside. You're more than welcome . . .'

101

She turned on him a gaze of such emptiness that he trailed off into silence again. Ah well, he thought. No point sitting here. So he took his leave and joined the pit managers for a debriefing; the priority now was to find unquestionable proof that the accident was unavoidable.

Eve sat on. Then Lew came to find her, one leg bandaged from the shin to the knee and blue and yellow bruising to one side of his face. He was weeping openly, like a child, though Eve was not. Arthur had saved him, he told her through great, messy sobs. Arthur had pushed him clear of the prop before it fell. He died a hero, said Lew, she could be proud of him.

Eve stared at him for a moment, then said coldly, 'I've always been proud of Arthur. He had nothin' to prove to me.'

Lew left her alone then, and she sat in silent desolation. Boast not thyself of tomorrow, she thought, for thou knowest not what a day may bring forth.

Seth and Eliza hurried home from school together, earlier than usual. The headmistress, informed in the vaguest terms of an accident at New Mill, kept all the children in ignorance for a while but then had decided they should perhaps return home. None of them knew what had happened, though, and they left the schoolhouse just before midday, more in excitement than in fear. The streets they ran along were festooned with flags of green and gold for Lord Fulton's coming-of-age; it was hard to believe in disaster while bunting flapped between the gas lights.

But when Seth and Eliza left their friends and turned the corner into Beaumont Lane, they saw immediately that the curtains at number five were drawn, as if the house had closed its eyes on the day. Curtains drawn in daylight meant death had come calling. Eliza began to scream and Lilly hurried out to scoop her up and carry her in to her mother. Seth followed them in, stony faced, his mind empty but for the thought that Arthur's scarf was still rolled into a ball under his bed, and how very glad he was for it.

Chapter 15

≈≈≈

The funeral was held on the seventeenth of January, the Saturday after Arthur died and the day of Tobias Hoyland's twenty-first birthday. It was a strange confluence of celebration and sorrow; the young Lord Fulton was driven around Netherwood to receive his birthday ovation, then not quite an hour later the carriage bearing Arthur's coffin followed a similar route to the chapel. People who had waved their flags and yelled cheerful birthday greetings to Tobias stood silent on the kerb stones and bowed their heads as Jeremiah Hague's funeral horse, adorned with black ribbons, pulled Arthur on his final journey. The earl had paid for the hearse; he always did when men died in his service. Other men, who lived without his protection, died without it too, and had to be carried by relatives to the graveside. None of it made any difference to Eve. She walked behind the hearse, supported by Samuel Farrimond, although she seemed to need no assistance and, though ashen-faced, was dry-eyed and upright. Seth, who had refused to stay at Lilly's with his sisters, walked on the other side of his mother, his likeness to Arthur adding extra poignancy to the occasion. Like Eve, Seth shed no tears, although unlike her he had cried a great deal in the days since his father's death.

As they processed the mile or so from Beaumont Lane to the chapel the cortège grew, joined along the route by people from the roadside, so that by the time Jeremiah drew to a halt in Middlecar Road, there were almost two hundred mourners. The coffin was carried by Lew Sylvester, Amos Sykes, Jonas Buckle and Wally Heseltine; the rest filed into the chapel and, seated or standing, they hung their heads and prayed for the soul of Arthur Williams.

Eve, at the front, prayed for her own. She felt cold and empty and, in spite of the great number of folk behind her, entirely alone. Seth, sitting beside her, trying so valiantly to be a man, was no comfort to her. At this moment, and indeed since she had first learned of Arthur's passing, she had felt nothing for the children: no compassion, no concern, nothing that she recognised as love. She harboured a dark fear that death, when it took Arthur, had robbed her of the capacity to feel. There was at least some small comfort in the thought that she would therefore be spared any future pain.

Wilfred Oxspring, the Netherwood minister, addressed the congregation. He was a local man, a former miner, and his face and voice conveyed the compassion he was truly feeling for Eve; he wished she would look at him.

"'I am the resurrection and the life,' saith the Lord. "He that believeth in Me, though he were dead, yet shall he live. And whosoever liveth and believeth in Me shall never die.'"

Eve had heard these words before, spoken at the funerals of others, but they had never then struck her as utterly meaningless. She barely listened now, her mind wandering to the previous Sunday when she had stood in ignorance in this chapel alongside Arthur and their three children. The girls had fidgeted and complained about the cold and Seth had fumed in his stiff Sunday collar. She and Arthur had been cross with them and a little cross, too, with each other. How they had wasted his last hours on this earth.

Reverend Oxspring raised his voice, as if to penetrate Eve's reverie with his prayer for the bereaved.

'O Holy Spirit, Divine Comforter, we know that Thy presence is among us in fulfilment of the promise of our Lord Jesus Christ; we ask that Thou wilt pour Thy comfort and strength into the minds and hearts of these Thy children. Grant that courage may rise within them to meet this test.'

Eve thought, Arthur is dead and gone and there is no comfort here. She hadn't realised until now that her faith had been in her husband, not in God. She sat motionless through the rest of the service, concentrating hard on not uttering out loud any of the words in her head. Then she felt herself being led to the graveside, and she watched as Arthur's body in its plain wooden casket was lowered into the hard earth. Seth, standing at her side, began to wail, but Eve, locked in private misery, could offer the boy nothing. Lew and Amos stepped forwards to cast a handful of dirt on to the coffin.

Back underground, thought Eve. At least he won't be afraid down there.

Teddy Hoyland, diary permitting, always tried to attend the funerals of men who died in his collieries and today he had insisted that Tobias accompany him, notwithstanding the fact that it was his birthday. A good and loyal man had died in their service and his memory should be honoured by them. Henrietta was with them too, though in her case through choice, and it gave the earl pleasure to have her on his left at the graveside and his handsome heir on his right. None of the mourners would ever know, of course, of the truculent resistance to this show of unity displayed by said heir the previous evening. For a young man of twenty-one, Tobias still had a great deal of the spoilt child in him, thought Teddy. The boy had proved peculiarly resistant to all notions of duty and responsibility over the years, but it was never more evident than now, when the time had come to help shoulder the burdens of his lands and title. Well, his hand must be forced, thought the earl. Waiting for Tobias to do the right thing, he had realised, bore no fruit at all.

So the earl and his son stood shoulder to shoulder at Arthur's graveside, two tall men with the same noble bearing, though Tobias's mutinous expression rather gave the game away. He'd had other plans for his birthday morning; Buffy Mountford, an old school chum with a country pile in Derbyshire, had proposed a day's snipe shooting followed by a steak and claret supper. But good old Pater, always to be relied upon to scotch a half-decent plan, had insisted he stay at home and – worse still – had requested in that tone of voice which brooked no objections that Tobias accompany him to pay his respects to a dead miner.

Mind you, thought Tobias, the widow was a bit of a stunner. He was on the opposite side of the grave to Eve, so was well placed to discreetly observe. Lovely hair, lovely eyes. The black looked well on her too. Altogether rather ravishing, he thought. He wondered, idly, how old she was, and whether he might take an interest in her. She would be in need of succour, he thought. He forgot where he was and smiled.

Tobias's stomach rumbled loudly, and he wondered what was for lunch. He'd felt too queasy to fully partake at breakfast, hadn't managed more than a scrap of dry toast. A corker of a night out in the Cross Keys, though. He smiled again at the memory of it, then looked across the cemetery and eyed the Daimler longingly. Soon be home. Forty winks, a slap-up lunch, then a ride out with Dickie and Henrietta, perhaps; a cobweb-blowing gallop through the park. He'd speak to the stable lad when they got home.

The mourners began to move away from the churchyard

now and there was a palpable, if slight, relaxation of tension among them. Tobias nodded and smiled at one or two familiar faces then realised that his father and Henry had moved around the grave in order to speak to the widow and he followed them in a spirit of curiosity. The woman was gazing steadfastly at the coffin in a rather unnerving manner and Tobias wasn't sure that he'd bother, if he was in their shoes. Leave her to it for the time being. But no, his sister and the earl seemed unfazed. Henry reached out and placed a gloved hand on the widow's arm, murmuring words of sympathy, and his father cleared his throat to speak.

'Mrs Williams,' he said. 'We spoke at New Mill on Monday but may I say, once again, how very sorry I am and how very much your husband will be missed.'

Eve dragged her gaze upwards, like a sleepwalker trying to get her bearings. There were no tears, but her face was rigid with trauma. Tobias felt awkward, exposed to her suffering in this way.

'Thank you, sir,' she said. Her voice came in a whisper.

'Please, don't hesitate to seek assistance if you need it,' Lord Netherwood went on. 'My land steward, Mr Arkwright, and my bailiff, Mr Blandford, act on my behalf, and their office is always open. Don't suffer in silence. We cannot offer charity to every needy case, my dear, and you doubtless wouldn't seek it, but we will always help if we can.'

Eve nodded again but found she was unable to speak. Reverend Farrimond, who had left the graveside to attend to Seth, now came back for Eve. He nodded a greeting to Tobias and Henrietta, then turned to their father.

'Lord Netherwood,' he said briskly, 'Reverend Samuel Farrimond.' He extended a confident hand, and the earl shook it.

'We haven't met, your Lordship, but it is a very great honour and I must thank you on Mrs Williams's behalf for acceding to my recent request.'

108

This fellow has aplomb, thought Tobias. Wonder what the dickens he's talking about?

'Not at all, not at all,' said the earl, who understood no more of the situation than Tobias but was rather more practised at appearances.

Reverend Farrimond went on: 'Mr Blandford and I agreed that the young woman and her child will remain with Mrs Williams until such a time as she is able to make the journey home. She arrives tomorrow.'

Eve, through her fog of silent grief, felt the unpleasant sensation that her life was no longer her own concern. Between Reverend Farrimond and Lord Netherwood, her fate was being busily arranged. Surely an agreement made when Arthur was alive was null and void now Arthur was dead? She made as if to speak and the men kindly waited, but weariness engulfed her and she looked away, defeated.

'Yes. Well. So,' said the earl. If Absalom Blandford had the details, he thought, he need not trouble himself with them. Time to be off; this churchyard was no place to linger. He raised an arm, signalling to Atkins that the Daimler should be readied for the short trip home.

'My good wishes to you, Reverend Farrimond,' he said. 'And to you too, Mrs Williams. Tobias, Henrietta?'

The earl and his son strode briskly off to their motor car, though Henrietta hung back, moved more than she could say by the young widow. She wished she had something meaningful to say, something other than platitudes.

'I am so very sorry, Mrs Williams,' she said. 'Please let us help if we're able.'

Eve directed her blank stare in Henrietta's direction but made no reply, and Reverend Farrimond, with a kind smile for the aristocratic young woman, took Eve by the arm and walked her away from Arthur's remains. He would bring her back, he thought, when the hole was filled with fresh earth and the reality of the grave, its depth and its darkness, was no longer so brutally evident. Ahead of them he could see Seth walking alongside Amos Sykes, holding his hand. The minister was glad of it; the boy needed compassion, and he'd had none yet from his mother.

Chapter 16

Anna Rabinovich, at the age of twenty-two, felt there was very little left for the world to show her that she hadn't already seen. She was mistaken in this, of course, but still, in her short life so far, she had known comfortable prosperity and extreme hardship, the heights of joy and the depths of sorrow; she had been treasured by her family then cast asunder from them; she had loved with all her heart then had lost the object of her love. Now Anna, always by nature cheerful and resilient, was adrift in a country that was not her own, among people who seemed to be perpetually bowed down under the weight of their own woe. When Anna tried to imagine her future, she struggled to see beyond a lonely battle for survival.

She and her young husband Leo had arrived in England three years earlier with the intention of travelling to Lanarkshire, where his brother was already making a living as a miner. Leo was Anna's romantic hero, and her financial downfall; she had defied her family of wealthy Ukrainian merchants to marry the penniless only son of their bookkeeper, although it was not that he was poor that inspired their wrath, but that he was Jewish. The depth of her family's anti-Semitism took even them by surprise. They had always employed Jews and

111

had believed themselves to be almost liberal, but their anger at their daughter's choice was immediate and immutable, and it grew in direct proportion to Anna's determination, the one feeding off the other until too much had been said and done on each side to ever reach a reconciliation. Anna's brother, Alexei, fought hard to win their parents round; he felt her banishment from the family home more keenly than she did herself. But the door remained closed on the wayward daughter, in the belief that only in this way might she return to them, contrite and begging forgiveness. Fate, however, had other plans. A wave of pogroms in their country and the threat of violence against them forced Anna and Leo to flee Kiev, where they had lived all their lives. With a few scant belongings they had travelled with other Jews, crowded like cattle on to a train, as far as Bremen, from where they were able to buy a passage on a packet steamer bound for Southampton. It was only on disembarkation that they realised how very far indeed they still were from Scotland.

Undaunted, they had used most of their money on two train tickets to Sheffield, where they planned to find work in order to raise the money needed to travel further north. Leo had been taken on at Grangely Main, and thus began their downward spiral from romantic adventure to relentless adversity. By the time their baby girl, whom they named Maya, was born, Leo was already showing early symptoms of tuberculosis; then the Grangely miners went on strike, and Anna discovered that what she had believed to be hardship had not been hardship at all but merely a rehearsal for the penury into which they were now plunged.

When Leo died, Anna envied him the release, though only for the briefest of moments. She was young; she was resourceful and clever too, quick to pick up not only the English language but also the Yorkshire dialect, so that she spoke in a lively hybrid of hard Russian W's and Yorkshire dropped aitches.

She spoke and sang to Maya in a mixture of her native tongue and her newly learned English. Her plan, she explained to Reverend Farrimond, was to strive to live as well as she could until such a time as she could buy a passage back to Russia. She would not, she said, write to request her family's financial assistance; she felt they did not deserve such a compliment.

Anna was tremendously relieved when Reverend Farrimond presented her with his proposal; leaving Grangely, she felt, was essential to their survival. She and Maya were ready, their few poor possessions gathered about them, when he arrived to accompany them to Netherwood. It was two days after Arthur's funeral, but they were almost halfway there before the minister explained how recently Eve had been widowed. Anna was all for turning round and returning to Grangely; she threatened to jump down from the carriage and walk back if the minister refused to take her. But Samuel Farrimond was a wise man and his quarter of a century in the ministry had taught him a thing or two about human nature. He believed Eve and Anna needed each other; Arthur's death, while utterly unexpected and unutterably sad, made perfect sense to him in the context of this arrangement. He had thought, when he heard the news, not that Anna must remain in Grangely, but rather that she should go to Netherwood as soon as possible.

They arrived at Beaumont Lane at shortly after ten o'clock on Tuesday morning. Seth and Eliza had gone to school, Eve and Ellen were in the house, the child pottering aimlessly about the kitchen while her mother, as was her new custom, sat silently at the table. At the back door, Anna stood beside Reverend Farrimond with Maya in her arms and a tight knot of anxiety in her belly; when he knocked, she longed to flee. Inside, Ellen looked eagerly at her mother, who pushed herself wearily to her feet, walked to the door and opened it.

The two women, face to face, held each other's gaze. There was a split-second jolt of recognition then Anna handed her baby to the baffled minister, stepped into Eve's house and wrapped her in an embrace that was so entirely natural and necessary that Eve was finally able to let go of the burden of unshed tears. She lay her head on Anna's shoulder and wept.

Anna and Eve had met before, on the day of the evictions, when Anna and Leo's belongings had been flung out of their house and into the dirt of the street. Leo, close to death, had been unable to help his wife, and she had struggled alone with their furniture until Eve had appeared, kind and capable, to silently share the load. Then she had seemed to vanish into the bedlam and Anna had wondered afterwards if her own imagination, fevered with fatigue and distress, had conjured up the lovely stranger. But here she was again, now pitiful and helpless, her own face white with trauma and exhaustion. Anna's protective gesture had been an act of instinctive compassion, one human being responding to the need of another; but, more than that, it was an unspoken acknowledgement of a kindred spirit.

Eve cried in Anna's arms for a long time; long enough for Reverend Farrimond to move beyond satisfaction at this promising beginning and into the realms of embarrassment. He was beginning to feel foolish, and more than a little voyeuristic, as the private moment between the women extended into minutes. The baby in his arms was becoming heavy and slightly damp at the rear end. It blew bubbles at him and pulled on his whiskers, so he was extremely relieved when Ellen, with all the insensitivity allowed to a one-year-old and bored now with the spectacle of her mother's noisy tears, pushed herself between Eve and Anna and shouted: 'Mam!'

The little girl's imperative tone of voice seemed to stem the torrent and Eve looked down at where her daughter stood, squeezed into the space she'd created between the women's skirts. Ellen smiled at her artlessly and raised her arms for a cuddle. Eve picked her up and kissed her.

'Now, that's better,' said Reverend Farrimond.

'It's a start,' said Eve.

Reverend Farrimond stayed for quite some time; long enough to fully observe the extraordinary and instant ease with which the two women accepted each other. He sat by Eve at her kitchen table with a mug of tea, his comfort levels returned to normal. Ellen and the baby were sitting under the table scrutinising each other amiably. Anna was busy at the sink. Earlier, she had put the kettle on and brewed the tea, and Eve had watched her with detached interest; she couldn't remember the last time anyone had performed this simple task for her. Her great bout of weeping had had a cathartic effect, leaving her drained but also peaceful. She felt she could sleep at last, and would in fact have dearly liked to lie down and close her eyes, but the minister demanded her attention, asking her questions for which she had no answers.

'Eve,' he said. 'Eve?'

She looked at him. 'Mmm?' she said.

'I said, you must give some consideration to your future.' His voice was kind but firm. 'What will you do to earn a living?'

She shrugged but didn't reply, preferring to stare hard into her mug of tea as though it might provide a vision of the future. Anna began to wash the dishes that were piled in the sink.

'You must apply yourself to this matter, dear,' said Reverend Farrimond. 'The Sheffield workhouse is full of women who found themselves in your position' – Eve looked up at him now, shocked out of apathy – 'and too often they were propelled into penury not so much by circumstance as by their own lack of will.'

'This is Netherwood, not Grangely,' said Eve. She sounded defiant, and the minister was glad to hear it. If Eve was to thrive without Arthur, she needed spirit.

'Indeed,' he said. 'But the fabled generosity of your benevolent earl is likely to be sorely tested if you can't pay the rent.'

Eve was silenced by the irrefutable truth of his argument.

Anna said, 'What do you do well?' She said *vot* and *vell*, and it sounded strange and exotic in Eve's little kitchen.

Eve looked at her. 'Nothing,' she said. 'I was t'wife of a miner, mother of his children.'

Anna left the sink and walked to the table. She made a dismissive gesture with her hand, sweeping away Eve's remark. 'But just think for a moment. What do you do well?'

'I was a good wife,' said Eve, bridling a little. 'I'm a good mother. But no one will pay me for that.'

'So. A good wife and mother has many jobs – which of these do you do best?' said Anna. Her tone was that of a patient teacher, coaxing an answer from a reluctant pupil. It seemed curious to Eve, in this most curious of situations, that this woman, this displaced foreigner, had such command. The vague notion flitted across her mind that she'd need to keep an eye on that.

Reverend Farrimond beamed. 'Ha!' he said. 'Of course!'

Both women looked at him.

'She cooks!' he said to Anna, then to Eve: 'You cook!'

'Everybody cooks,' said Eve. She was utterly perplexed.

'Everybody cooks, but nobody cooks like you,' he said.

Anna sat down opposite Eve at the table and smiled at her.

'Then you should sell you food,' she said.

'*Your* food,' said Eve.

'Maybe mine, but also yours,' said Anna.

Eve and the minister laughed, and Anna laughed too, though she had entirely missed the joke.

Eve said, 'Oh aye, I expect there's a fortune to be made in raised pork pies and drop scones.'

'If not a fortune, maybe a living,' said Anna. Eve looked doubtful. She'd exchanged food often enough for other goods and services, but to ask people to hand over their hard-earned money for food they could just as well make at home – it made no sense to her.

Reverend Farrimond said: 'Anna's right, Eve. All you need to do is open your front door at the same time every day and sell your marvellous pies and pastries. There'd be a queue from here to Turnpike Lane by the end of the second day.'

Eve shook her head. 'It's barmy,' she said. 'I'd be a laughing stock.'

'First, we must try,' said Anna. Eve, noting the 'we', felt a wave of comfort.

'And if it doesn't work, we try something else,' Anna went on. Under the table Ellen said '*sam-zing*', quietly to herself.

'So, it's settled,' said Reverend Farrimond, which Eve thought was hardly the case, but she let it pass because she had no better suggestion to make and, anyway, she was already thinking that she'd better pop out to the Co-op for more flour and lard.

Chapter 17

Down by the railway lines there was a long, straight cinder path which ran parallel to the tracks, so close to them that one small step sideways put you right on the ironwork. Seth and Eliza were forbidden from coming here; once, years before, a boy of eleven had been killed when he caught his foot underneath one of the rails. The train had sliced the foot clean off at the ankle like a knife through butter and the boy had blacked out then bled to death. That's how the story went, at any rate. Seth was sceptical; he spent hours down at the railway line – in spite of the ban – and he couldn't see how it was possible to trap a foot so thoroughly that you weren't able to pull it free. In any case, there was nowhere for a foot to fit – there just wasn't a gap big enough. Seth thought it was a tale invented to scare children, and it had certainly worked on Eliza, who had added it to the list of places she feared to tread, along with the cemetery and the kiln yard at the brick-works – all of them, in her view, arenas of certain death.

But Seth loved it, especially if he was alone, like today. There were two sets of lines on this side of town and if you walked away from Netherwood, towards Long Martley Colliery, there was a place where they converged, criss-crossing each other as if they'd had a change of mind about their destination. Seth would sit right on the sleepers, tracing with his fingers the geometric shapes made by the tracks at the intersection. If a train came, there was plenty of warning; even before the engine appeared, the tracks would vibrate under his hands and the birds would always fly up in alarm from the trees. It was another reason for his scepticism about the dangers lurking at the railway lines; the trains advertised their impending arrival in so many ways that even if you were deaf and blind you could still step out of danger. Seth thought you could only die here if you wanted to. That, he could understand. Time it right and bang, you'd feel nothing.

He wandered aimlessly back towards Netherwood, dragging a stick in his left hand so that it bounced rhythmically off the wooden sleepers. It was a fine stick, straight and long, and someone had whittled the end of it into a point, like a caveman might have done to hunt wild boar. He raised it above his shoulder like a spear and looked for something to aim at, but nothing seemed to present itself and he lowered it, letting it scrape on the track again. If it was early summer the path would be bordered on the right hand side by hundreds of foxgloves and Seth would have whipped the flowerheads to see the bees rise in alarm from the purple thimbles. But now, with no such sport to distract him, his thoughts strayed back to the unwelcome realm of home; it was so hectic this morning that his mother hadn't even noticed him leave, let alone ask where he was going. The house smelled constantly of baking and there were pies and puddings piled up on the table but he wasn't allowed to eat any of them because they were going to be for sale on Monday morning. Eliza and Ellen were playing a stupid game with that woman's baby, and that woman herself was bustling about the kitchen as though it were her own. She and her baby had moved into his bed, in the room he had always shared with his sisters, and now he had a makeshift mattress on his mother's bedroom floor and Ellen was in the big bed with her. Eliza had begged to sleep with the baby, so she slept where she always had. Seth hated the new arrangement and was three days into a silent protest, but no one had noticed yet. He longed for his father.

The big church clock struck three. At exactly this time, two weeks ago, he was on the common with his dad. To chase this thought from his head, Seth took the stick in two hands, raised it above his head and smashed it down on the iron track. It splintered but didn't break, so he brought it up again, and again thrashed at the track with it, and this time it split into two pieces, which he tossed on to the sleepers. Since Arthur's death, grief kept arriving unannounced in great, engulfing waves. It happened again now and he let himself be swept along, abandoning himself to the pain, wailing and shouting like a boy overboard. Then, like a miracle, he heard his father's voice: 'Seth!'

It wasn't close, but it wasn't too distant either. Certainly it sounded real, not ghostly. Seth looked wildly about him. He thought the voice wasn't behind him, and he stepped off the path and on to the railway line. Then he heard it again.

'Seth! Over 'ere, son.'

From where he stood Seth felt the rattle and boom of an oncoming train. He was on the sleepers now, between the tracks. Perhaps if the train hit him, he would see his dad. Perhaps that's what he had to do.

'Seth, lad, move!'

A man suddenly loomed into Seth's vision, smaller and stockier than his father. He was heading towards him, running frantically down the other side of the track, pumping his arms like pistons and hurtling forwards but looking backwards at the oncoming train. Then, just as it bore down on Seth, the man turned his head.

'Move, Seth, move!' he screamed, but his voice was drowned

out by the fearsome rush and roar of the train, and Amos Sykes had to wait until fourteen empty coal wagons had rattled by before he saw Seth standing safe on the other side of the tracks, staring at him with hostile eyes.

Amos had been at the allotments with Clem when he'd heard, from the direction of the tracks, an animal sound, a violent keening, like the scream of a vixen calling for a mate. Clem, cloth-eared, hadn't heard a thing and was mid-sentence when Amos, having turned to identify the cry, suddenly sprang over the back wall and ran down the embankment on to the railway. The old man was still scratching his head in puzzlement when Amos reappeared, now accompanied by young Seth Williams. Amos, puffing with effort – the embankment was steep behind the allotments – had to catch his breath before he could speak, leaning with his hands on his knees and his face dripping beads of sweat. The lad, though, just looked cold. He shook, and his face was grey, like putty.

Clem had a fire going in an old metal dustbin and he led Seth over to it, dragging an upturned crate to the edge of the heat so that the boy could sit. Amos, who was upright now and breathing more comfortably, said, 'Tha shouldn't be laikin' on t'railway.' His relief had turned bad, and his voice trembled with anger.

'I weren't laikin',' said Seth flatly. 'I were thinkin'.' He glared at Amos as he spoke, but his voice was hopeless, not defiant. By 'eck, thought Clem, this lad's in a bad way.

'Well, think somewhere else in future,' said Amos, glaring back. He'd recovered from the exertion of the run and the climb, but he was still feeling the effects of the shock. He had thought, for a few awful seconds, that he'd be visiting Eve today with news of a second tragedy.

Seth looked away and for a moment sat silently, watching the red glow through the holes that Clem had made around the bottom of the bin. Then he said, 'I thought you were my dad. You said, "Over 'ere, son," and it sounded like my dad.'

Amos softened at once. He went to Seth and placed a hand on his shoulder. It all made sense of course – Seth had been stricken with grief, but until Amos had shouted, the boy had been safe on the path. It was only after he called that Seth had put himself in harm's way.

'Ah. Right,' Amos said. 'Sorry, lad.' He felt awkward, because he hadn't had a lot of practice at giving comfort; his old dog Mac was his only companion at home, and even he was a self-reliant kind of animal who rarely sought physical contact. But a deep and barely acknowledged part of Amos felt he owed it to Arthur to watch over his boy.

'S'all right,' said Seth. He was sorry too. He didn't want to hate Amos; he liked him. He smelled a bit like his dad, and his hands, like Arthur's, were calloused and coal-marked, the black ingrained in the cracks and whorls of his skin like gradient lines on a map. Seth looked around at the hard brown soil of the vegetable beds, divided by rough paths of muddy brick. A low fence of woven twigs and branches divided this plot on either side from the next, and there was a small shed at one end with a selection of wooden-handled tools leaning up against it: a hoe, a spade, a shovel and a pick. Nothing grew, and the beds looked impenetrable as rock.

'What's tha think?' said Clem.

'It's a bit bare,' said Seth. 'Whose is it?'

'Well . . .' said Clem, looking at Amos for guidance.

Amos said, 'It was your dad's, not that 'e ever knew 'e 'ad it. It came free just before t'accident. That's what me an' Clem are doin' 'ere, like. It needs sortin' out.'

Seth digested the information for a moment, then said, 'Can I 'ave it?'

Amos's craggy face broke into a rare smile. 'There you go!' he said to Clem. 'It's just as I told thee.'

The issue of the allotment secured so recently for Arthur Williams had lain heavy on Clem Waterdine's mind for a day or two after the funeral. He was loath to bother Eve, yet felt it was a matter of some urgency. There were, after all, too many living men on the waiting list to let the plot remain in the name of one who was dead. On the other hand Clem knew that it was Eve, not Arthur, who had wanted the allotment in the first place, and it might seem unfeeling to hand it on to the next bloke in line without so much as consulting her. For her part, and to Clem's astonishment, Eve seemed to have forgotten about it entirely. He had seen her two or three times since Arthur died and she'd said very little indeed, and nothing at all relating to the allotment. Clem wondered if she had quite understood the honour conferred by ownership.

It was a vexed question, but nevertheless he had made up his mind to bite the bullet earlier in the week and had been walking down Allott's Way towards Beaumont Lane when he saw Amos Sykes coming towards him in his pit filth, on his way home at the end of the day's shift. Amos nodded at him and would have walked on, but something about Clem's manner made him stop.

'Ey up, Clem,' he said.

Clem, never in a hurry to get anywhere, looked uncharacteristically keen to move on.

'What's up?' said Amos.

The old man pursed his lips and pondered a reply, but thought better of it.

'Top secret is it?'

Clem cleared his throat. 'Allotment business,' he replied,

and his voice was loaded with such preening self-importance that Amos felt it was his civic duty to poke fun. He staggered backwards in feigned alarm and pressed his palms against his ears. 'Spare me!' he said. 'T'less I know, t'safer I'll be.'

Clem knew he was being mocked but decided nevertheless to unburden himself. Amos listened, and when the old man had related his tale he said, 'You're a daft old sod, Clem Waterdine.'

Clem bridled.

'Arthur's barely cold in 'is grave. Eve Williams 'as more to think about than a veg patch,' Amos said.

'Aye, well,' said Clem. 'She mun give it up then.' He felt belittled and, as a result, less certain about his mission. Even so, he made as if to move off. He had no desire to engage in verbal sparring with Amos, who could be merciless with his sharp tongue.

'Tell thi what,' said Amos, entirely oblivious to Clem's wounded pride and the complicated politics of the allotment system. 'I'll meet thi there on Sat'day, 'ave a look at it missen.'

Clem snorted derisively. If Amos Sykes thought he had any say in the matter, he had another think coming. He could get to the back of the queue, like it or lump it.

And yet there they were, come Saturday, agreeing that young Seth Williams, under Amos's guidance – and, for the sake of the paperwork, under Amos's name – would take the allotment intended for his father. More than that, the old autocrat Clem Waterdine had about him the rosy glow of the benefactor; if he felt outwitted by Amos, it was more than compensated for by the smile on Seth's face and the gratitude later that day from Eve that there would be fresh vegetables in abundance come next autumn, God and the weather permitting.

Chapter 18

A mean February wind blew the smile off everyone's face and thin, persistent rain fell from the pewter sky, as if to put the dampers on any enthusiasm for the new venture. Eve felt like a fool; a grown woman, playing shop. Earlier that Monday morning she had taken a large slate and placed it, doubtfully, outside her front door, leaning it against the wall. She hoped her writing would withstand the weather, because the slate bore the chalked-up products she was hoping to sell and their prices. Against her better judgement, but encouraged by Anna and Eliza, she had given her business a name, and this was carefully spelled out in fancy capital letters at the head of the list.

EVE'S PUDDINGS & PIES
open 9am – 2pm Monday to Friday

it said, and below it:

Meat and potato pie – 2d a slice; 6d whole
Raised pork pie – 2d a slice; 4d whole
Faggots – 1d each

Drop scones – 4 for 1d
Tea cakes – 4 for 2d
Eve's Pudding – 6d
All freshly made on the premises.
Thank you for your custom.

She'd used much of Tobias Hoyland's ten-shilling birthday present to buy the ingredients – a great sack of flour and a smaller one of dried fruit, a bag of waxy green Bramleys, a hessian sack of dusty potatoes, six blocks of lard, some stewing steak, pork shoulder and middle bacon, new pots of mace and allspice and a tiny bottle of anchovy essence. At Wilton's hardware stall on Barnsley market she'd bought a crisp stack of brown bags and waxed paper and made a down payment on twelve new pie dishes, promising Eli Wilton, more in hope than conviction, that he'd have the rest of the money by the end of the week. Her pies and puddings, if bought whole, were to be sold in the dishes they'd been baked in, and her customers – if there were any, and she was by no means sure there would be – were to be asked to wash and return them. Lilly next door thought Eve should be charging tuppence, refundable on return of the dish, just to be sure they kept it safe and brought it back, but it seemed to Eve that she should at least begin in a spirit of trust, even if experience might teach her the error of her ways. Anyway, she told Lilly, she wasn't selling to strangers; she could walk to their houses and fetch the dishes back if it came to it.

Lilly, who was a poor cook – 'Pigswill Lil' Arthur used to call her, though never, thank the Lord, within her hearing – had watched with studied bemusement as preparations next door reached fever pitch. She kept referring to 't'grand opening' in a sardonic voice that Eve only tolerated because she needed her help with the children. Lilly regarded Anna with deep suspicion; her accent, her Slavic looks, her oddly named baby, all these things inspired mistrust, and she simply couldn't comprehend why Eve would give them house room. But neighbours in Netherwood helped each other out – always had, always would, even when they were barely speaking to each other – so Lilly's house was the crèche and baby Maya was round there now, sitting rather glumly in the bottom of a crate so she didn't crawl into trouble in the kitchen. Anna, meanwhile, had pushed up her sleeves and begun scrubbing pots at Eve's sink, a task she had done, unasked and on a regular basis, since she'd arrived. A basket of dirty linen squatted in the centre of the kitchen and when the dishes were done she would make a start on the washing. Eve, a woman of high standards and set methods, worried a little that the blouses and bloomers, socks and singlets might, after washing, show the absence of her expert hands, but she was a pragmatic perfectionist and even she acknowledged she couldn't see to wash day at the same time as running a shop.

In any case, Anna had shown herself to be competent in every way, and cheerful too; she sang now as she worked, a Russian folk song about a dark-eyed lover, which reminded her of home, though she wasn't melancholy. Rather, she felt more full of hope now than she had since leaving Kiev, a fact which made her feel at the same time guilty, for it implied she had always harboured a lack of faith in her future with Leo. Her thoughts wandered to him often, but the memories caused little pain; by the time he died, the process of separation was well under way. His protracted illness reduced him by degrees, taking him day by day a little further away from her. For weeks, it seemed, he was defined only by his terrible illness; what little energy he had went into simply drawing breath. Anna would never confess it, for it seemed to her a shameful emotion, but she felt unfettered now, as if Leo's passing had not mired her in misery but released her from it.

Eve came into the kitchen from the parlour and interrupted her reverie. She gave Anna a crooked, uncertain smile.

'Nearly time,' she said. The clock said ten minutes to nine.

'T'grand opening?' Anna said, imitating Lilly, and Eve laughed.

'Hardly,' she said. 'Still, we won't go hungry.'

She nodded her head back towards their makeshift counter in the other room, which they'd fashioned out of a long board – courtesy of Amos – balanced on the backs of two sturdy chairs. It was effective, in as much as the height was perfect, but more than a little precarious; one wrong move on either side might send the display crashing to the floor. But what a display; in the past five days they had, it seemed to Anna, made enough food to feed a Roman legion. Eve, while always supposing no one would come, had nevertheless thrown herself full tilt into the task in hand. Pride played a part; she would be judged on the merit of her produce, and no one must find it wanting. She wanted to demonstrate abundance as much as quality, so a pyramid of pork pies, glossy and nut-brown, rose up at the centre of the counter and around them were arranged eight meat-and-potato pies in their dishes and an oven tray, scrubbed bright by Anna, bearing a pungent pile of knobbly round faggots. The drop scones and tea cakes were piled in baskets lined with linen cloths and, in a tidy line at the back, four Eve's Puddings – she hadn't been able to resist – completed the collection.

Anna dried her hands on the teacloth and together they walked into the parlour. 'In Ukraine, at Easter, we would make feast like this, with table bearing good food. But different food, like blinis and kulich. And not pig pies. These I don't know.'

'Pork,' said Eve. 'Say pork, not pig.'

'Yes, pork,' said Anna. 'Excuse me.'

'Never mind,' said Eve. 'My Russian lets me down sometimes. Right, shall we get it over with?'

She edged around the counter and stood at the front door, taking a moment to smooth her apron and pat her hair. And though it was more out of nerves than vanity, she tutted inwardly at herself, fussing and preening as if she was about to walk on to a stage. Just open the ruddy door, woman, she said to herself, there'll be no one there anyroad.

So she did, and she was wrong.

Samuel Farrimond had done Eve one last favour before returning to Grangely. After leaving Anna and Maya with her in Beaumont Lane, he had driven the pony and trap the short distance to the home of his friend and Wesleyan colleague Wilfred Oxspring, where he was to spend the night. The two men had much to discuss, and they chatted companionably over a supper of bread, cheese and Mrs Oxspring's famous piccalilli. But after the Oxsprings had retired, Reverend Farrimond stayed up and at a neat little roll-top desk he wrote, on paper he had begged from Wilfred, just short of four hundred announcements that home-made produce would be available for sale at number five Beaumont Lane from nine in the morning on Monday. It was a laborious task, scratching away with pen and ink by the light of an oil lamp in a room which grew chillier by the minute, and by the time he felt he could write no more, he owed his friend two new nibs and three pots of black ink. He went to bed for a brief interlude, before rising early and delivering his homespun leaflets. Then, his task completed, he headed through Netherwood to Sheffield Road, the hooves of his pony clipping and the wheels of his trap clattering along the quiet streets, and he wished only that he had written twice as many notices. Three times as many. No, four. He sent up a prayer to the Lord, to somehow help him spread the word and to make Eve's business a success.

So either God spoke to the people or the leaflets served their purpose, because when Eve opened her front door as the town clock struck nine, she found a queue of customers, wrapped up against the rain and snaking almost as far down the street as the corner with Allott's Way. She gaped at them for a brief, unfortunate moment, so that Meg Pickles, at the head of the line, said, 'Shut thi mouth, Eve Williams, or tha'll catch a fly,' which was embarrassing but at least had the effect of bringing her to her senses. She snapped her mouth shut and gave a bright smile.

'Morning!' she said. 'What can I get for you?'

By a quarter to ten the queue had been dealt with and a lull descended.

'Well,' said Eve. She looked at Anna, who was in from the kitchen again because it was dull in there at the dolly tub, and exciting in the parlour. Anna grinned gleefully and danced a spontaneous little jig. In that moment she looked more child than woman, and she reminded Eve of Eliza, who could never express joy in words alone, but always had to skip or spin as she delivered good news. Behind them the counter was much depleted; six whole pork pies had gone, and all of the meat-and-potato pies. The faggot mountain was diminished, but not so much as to seem unappealing, and Eve set to improving their appearance further by making strategic, swift adjustments to their position on the tray, picking up the rear guard and pushing them forwards to make them as tempting as possible.

Clem Waterdine appeared at the open door.

'Now then, young Eve,' he said. ''ow's it goin'?'

'Nicely, thank you,' Eve said. 'Can I 'elp you?'

'Time was when your cookin' came free,' said the old man. 'I've never paid thee for owt before.'

'First time for everythin', Clem,' said Eve. 'This is my livin' now.' Because Arthur's dead, she added, but to herself.

'Aye, well,' said Clem, who was thinking the same, and feeling ashamed. After all, he had the same ten-shilling bonus as everyone else and all he'd bought so far was a packet of Woodbine; he could take a few drop scones and a slice of pork pie, and still have plenty left. He placed his order, and watched as Eve cut him a generous piece of pie and wrapped it in waxed paper.

'Tell Amos 'e mun get crackin' in that veg plot,' he said.

'I shall do no such thing,' said Eve. 'Amos and Seth know what's what, an' Amos only gets there after a full shift down t'pit. I shan't be meddlin'.'

Clem sniffed. Eve popped four drop scones into a bag and handed it over.

'Thruppence,' she said. 'You can 'ave t'bag for nowt.'

He handed over the coins, still warm from his pocket, and she dropped them into her cash tin. Lilly walked into the parlour, coming in through the back. Her pinny was splattered with grease and her stockings formed fat wrinkles around her bony shins. She had Ellen by the hand and Maya on her hip. The baby, almost asleep, lolled her head as if it was impossibly heavy then, as if someone unseen had poked her, she jerked it back and the shock of it made her cry.

Clem regarded her, and sniffed. 'Babbies all speak t'same language then,' he said. Like everyone else in Netherwood, he knew that Arthur Williams's widow had a foreign woman and her bairn living in. Gossip spread effortlessly here, running like water from the source to the sea, because everyone had an opinion, even those – and they were many – who had yet to lay eyes on Anna.

She came in now, wiping her hands on the rough wool of her skirt, and they looked red raw from the hot water. Still, she was smiling as she took Maya from Lilly, and thanked her. Lilly managed an ungracious nod. Clem stared rudely.

131

'I put her to bed,' she said, and then, to Ellen: 'You want come help?'

The little girl nodded yes, and trotted off upstairs with Anna. Lilly watched them go then turned back to Eve. 'You be careful. She's got 'er feet right under your table,' she said tartly.

'Aye, she 'as,' said Eve. 'An' long may they stay there.'

Chapter 19

The days were consistently warm and there were bluebells underfoot in the woods by the time Eve paused for breath. At least, it felt that way to her, swept as she was on a tide of industriousness, buying supplies, baking half the night, selling her wares by day. There was barely time for grieving, though she did that too, in the privacy of the early hours when she should have been sleeping but often, instead, gave way to tears for Arthur. Eve wasn't inclined to self-pity, and it wasn't for herself that she cried; it was for her husband, who could no longer carry his children on his broad shoulders, or take quiet pride in their achievements, or marvel at how they grew. If Arthur came back now, she thought, if he walked back into the kitchen at the end of his shift, he would see that Seth was already an inch taller than he had been when he last bid him goodnight. She missed Arthur for herself, too, but that seemed the lesser grief to her than all he would now never see.

She wondered what he would make of this new life of hers. More than anything, she wanted to tell him about it: about the triumph of that first day, when the children had come home from school to find the shop sold out and Eve and Anna toasting their success with a mug of strong, brown tea; about the pride she'd felt as they had counted their takings and, as each day passed, had added to the sum total, so that when the bailiff's man came for the rent it was there, in the old tobacco tin, just as it always had been. She wanted to tell him about the stir she'd caused in Netherwood just by selling his favourite food, and how Everard Holt at the Co-op, recording her purchases in the society ledger, had joked she'd be retiring on her divi by the end of the year. All of these things she longed to share with Arthur, knowing full well that if he was here to tell, none of it would be happening.

She could tell Reverend Farrimond, of course. He called in when his duties in Grangely allowed, and he took a quiet, avuncular pride in what Eve was doing. And Amos took a friendly interest, asking Eve questions about the business with his serious brown eyes fixed on her face, as if her answers were of the utmost importance. He was a regular at her door, buying himself a slice of something on the way home from the pit. He had never passed much through Eve's mind before, except as a character sketched for her by Arthur: tough as old boot leather, quick-witted and sharp-tongued, and as reliable in his time keeping as the town hall clock. His only complaint about Amos had related to his politics which were too defiantly left wing for Arthur's tastes; he often said that Amos worked at the wrong colliery – no use getting angry with a boss that played fair, was Arthur's view. But socialism wasn't a mortal sin, and Eve had some sympathy with Amos's views. The day he told her that the Grangely miners were back at work on exactly the same terms they'd walked out for, she gazed at him, appalled.

'It were all for nowt, then,' she said.

'Aye, for them,' said Amos. 'But there's a bigger picture, an' if we keep chippin' away we'll get there. Things are changin', Eve.'

'Well I 'ope you're right, but if Arthur were 'ere, you'd've just found yourself an argument,' said Eve.

'Aye, well.'

'Arthur didn't see it like you do. Nobody ever 'eld a boss in more esteem. And,' she added, speaking for Arthur, knowing what he would have said, 't'earl's always treated 'is men well, you among 'em.'

'Aye, but it's all in Teddy 'oyland's gift, isn't it?' said Amos. ''E still gets to choose what 'e gives and when. An' we're meant to be doffin' our caps and bein' grateful for anythin' chucked our way.'

His face, thought Eve, was suited to anger, hard and unyielding. When it was coal-black like today, it could have been chipped from the seam he'd just been working. He prodded at the air between them as he spoke, as if it were a rally of miners before him, not his friend's widow.

'There should be rights for every miner, wherever he works, to be paid a decent wage for t'hours 'e works an' get sick pay when 'e can't work. An' I'll tell yer summat for nowt – the day of reckoning will come. I just 'ope to God I'm still 'ere to see it when it does.'

Just listening to him was exhausting. Out of respect for Arthur, Eve changed the subject. And, out of respect for Arthur, Amos let her.

Lew was a regular visitor at the front door too, though Eve made him stand well back from the produce if he hadn't been home for a bath. There was too much of him, and he loomed over the table like a hungry gorilla. The injuries caused by the accident were long healed but his face was always recovering from its latest bout in the ring. Eve hoped Warren was splitting the winnings fairly, at least. You wouldn't want to look like Lew and have nothing in your pocket to show for it. She felt sorry for him; he had a kind heart, but not much sense. Most folk were sharper than Lew

135

and he was, she imagined, easily codded. It'd taken him weeks before he was able to stand before her in anything other than abject apology for being alive, and she'd finally dealt with his discomfort herself, catching up with him in the street one day and telling him outright that she bore him no ill will.

'I've never wished it was you an' not Arthur,' she had said, speaking without preamble. 'The pit took 'im, not you.'

Lew, speechless, had simply nodded and watched Eve go on her way, but the next day he'd appeared at the shop, clutching the necessary coins in his fist like a boy with pocket money, and had bought a bag of drop scones which he devoured there and then, one after the other. Feeding time at the zoo, thought Eve, watching him. He shook the crumbs from the bag directly into his mouth, fully absorbed in the task in hand. Then he balled up the paper and shoved it into his jacket pocket.

'Grand,' he said.

'It's up to you, like,' said Eve. 'But most folk take their cakes 'ome.'

Lew tapped the side of his nose, conspiratorially. 'Destroyin' t'evidence,' he said. 'Mi mam'll bray me for buying your scones when she 'as 'er own at 'ome.'

Eve laughed. She considered alerting Lew to the crumbs lodged securely in the stubble round his mouth, but thought better of it. Let him feel the sharp side of Edna Sylvester's tongue. Big daft lump. She watched him amble off towards home. It wasn't true, of course, what she'd told him; she had hated Lew when it first happened, fervently, pointlessly, wishing Arthur had been in front of him when the roof gave way. She wondered still whether her husband had delayed his own escape in pushing Lew to safety; some instinct told her that was probably the case, knowing Arthur and knowing Lew. But she wouldn't release that thought, wouldn't speak it out loud, because to do so could bring no relief, so she held it in and offered, instead, a comforting lie. Since Lew was still alive, it seemed kind to bring him ease of mind.

Anyway, she thought, Lew knew the truth. If his conscience was burdened with responsibility, then that was punishment enough for any man.

Eve was thinking of diversifying. She was bored, she told Anna, of making the same things week in, week out. It was late evening; the girls were playing out on the street, and baby Maya was asleep upstairs. Seth was at the allotment, as usual. He only came home after school for as long as it took him to wolf down his tea, then he was off. His talk was all of pricking out and potting on, which was all a bit foreign to Eve though she enjoyed his enthusiasm. She had yet to see much evidence of his labours, though much was promised, but she was happy and grateful that her serious little son had a project. It stopped him brooding, kept him busy. And, if she was honest, it kept him away from Anna, to whom he could still be less than civil. Time, Eve was sure, would cure this, as it cured most things. And Anna was very clever at ignoring his rudeness; she planned to win him round by being consistently, though not excessively, pleasant. It was the best way with Seth, thought Eve; let him think it's his idea to like Anna, not hers.

The two women were busy in the kitchen raising pie crusts for a new batch of pig pies, as Eve now liked to call them. The lard and water, having come up to the boil, was added to as much flour as it took to make a good, pliable pastry. Eve never used scales, preferring to judge by hand and eye, and Anna – whose experience of cooking was less but who was quick to learn – watched her closely.

''ere,' Eve said. She passed the mound of smooth pastry across the floured surface of the table, and handed Anna a rolling pin. 'Now, beat the living daylights out of it for a minute,' she said.

Anna did as she was bid with great gusto, flattening the pile into a rough round then scooping it back together again and repeating the operation, just as she had seen Eve do on many an occasion. Then she wrapped the whole into a linen cloth and placed it by the range.

Eve, chopping pork into small dice, said: 'I mean, pig pies are all very well, but there's other things would sell just as well.'

'Such as?' said Anna. She took another knife and joined Eve at the table. There was ten pounds of pork still sitting in a vast stockpot. She fished out a glistening heap and began to slice it.

'Keep t'fat and t'lean separate,' said Eve, glancing up at Anna briefly before looking down again at the task in hand. 'Such as . . .' She paused, thinking. 'Pickles and chutneys, maybe. All that produce that Seth and Amos keep promising from Arthur's allotment is going to need preserving. Pickled cabbage. Green-bean chutney. And other things like, say, Scotch eggs. They'd sell nicely.' Anna looked lost. Sometimes Eve spoke too quickly for her to follow and sometimes there were new words to grapple with, such as Scotch, placed before egg. 'Never mind,' said Eve. 'All I'm sayin' is, we need to keep folk interested.'

'Deruny, maybe,' said Anna. She paused, for the briefest moment, to enjoy Eve's puzzled expression, before elaborating. 'Potato pancakes. Mmmmmm. Potato, onion, eggs, flour and good helping of sour cream.'

Eve wrinkled her nose in distaste. 'Sour won't sell,' she said.

Anna ignored her. 'Blinis. Stroganoff, though we need more dishes for this. Salted herring.' Her expression had taken on a dreamy quality. 'With iced vodka,' she said.

Eve snorted. 'Let's think on it,' she said, 'while we raise these pie crusts.'

She took the warmed parcel of pastry and unwrapped it, revealing just enough to break off two lumps of dough before re-wrapping the remainder. Then the two women set about shaping and smoothing the pastry into high-sided pie cases.

'Like top 'ats,' said Eve. 'But no brim.'

'At home,' Anna said, 'when I was little, my favourite thing to eat was golubtzi.'

Eve looked at her askance.

'Stuffed leaves of cabbage. Slowly cooked in tomato sauce.' Eve looked interested, so Anna continued. 'You make cabbage leaves soft in boiling water, then use them to wrap minced meat, or perhaps rice if you prefer. Or both. Then you pack them tight in dish and bake them in tomatoes and herbs.'

'What did you call them?' Eve said.

'Golubtzi.'

'Sounds like an ailment. Could we call 'em summat else? They're a suspicious lot in Netherwood.' Eve was smiling as she spoke, because Anna had her hands on her hips and was feigning indignation.

'Such as?'

'Pig parcels?' said Eve, laughing now. Anna took a swipe at her with a floury hand, but she was laughing too. 'Pig pies and pig parcels,' Eve said. 'Has a nice ring to it.'

They made eight raised pies from that evening's mixture, packing the pork closely into the prepared cases, two-thirds lean to one-third fat. Eve fitted the lids, pinching them at the edges to seal them, while Anna cut out leaf shapes from the left-over pastry, and fashioned roses for the centre which could be removed after baking to allow the stock to be poured in. She was deft with the knife, and her leaves were fancier than

Eve's, five-pointed with delicate veins. She gave them a slender pastry stem too, and trailed them like ivy around the top of the pie. It was a charming effect, and Eve was always happy when someone bought a pie whole instead of asking for a slice because it seemed a shame to cut into Anna's little works of art. They weren't appreciated by everyone, though. The first time they went on sale, Maud Platt from two doors down had refused to believe they were plain old pork; fancy decoration meant foreign filling, she suspected, and could she have one that Eve had baked? No, Eve had said, they'd made them together and they were perfect. But she'd had to cut Maud a free slice to try before she'd buy more.

Now they were all brushed with eggwash and placed in the bottom of the range. Eve yawned widely, pushing her hands into the small of her back to ease the ache. The pies would be baking for at least three hours, and there was bread dough still to make. The stewmeat was ready for the meat-and-potato pies, but the pastry lids would have to wait until tomorrow morning. Another four o'clock start then.

'Tea?' said Anna, who had the passion of a native Yorkshire woman for a strong brew.

Eve nodded. 'Lovely,' she said. Her face was flushed from the heat of the range, and tendrils of hair were plastered to her cheeks and down the back of her neck. She blew a little updraught from one corner of her mouth and smiled wryly at Anna, whose face, like hers, was pink and damp.

'You look like I feel,' Eve said, but Anna made a little piff noise and waved her hand, as if heat and hard work were nothing to her.

'Best get t'girls in,' said Eve.

'Leave them five minutes more,' said Anna. 'Sit down, drink tea, then get girls in.'

'Sit down, drink tea,' said Eve, imitating. She smiled. 'Go on then, you've talked me into it.'

And she sat, with a sigh, at the kitchen table, feeling immediate ease as the chair took her weight. Hard graft and small pleasures, she thought, that's what life was made of. Hard graft and small pleasures. And it could be a lot worse.

Chapter 20

The Hoyland Arms stood smack in the centre of Victoria Street, big and square, a dependable landmark that everyone knew but no one really noticed. It had been built at the time of Netherwood's expansion so was well-positioned to pick up maximum passing trade from homeward-bound miners as well as tradesmen, stall holders and shoppers on market day.

Being more recently built than the Hare and Hounds or the Cross Keys, both of which hailed back to Netherwood's rural past, the Hoyland Arms bore all the hallmarks of Victorian grandeur. But the high ceilings, fancy stained-glass partitions and handsome mahogany bar spoke of an ambition and vision which had perhaps been somewhat misplaced, since it had never in its history had a landlord who cared much for its upkeep or customers who cared much for its appearance.

The present incumbent was a newcomer called Harry Tideaway, a barrel of a man who had moved in with his plain and silent daughter Agnes a year ago. He wasn't popular, though to be fair, no one knew much about him – twelve months in Netherwood wasn't long enough for anyone to take an interest. There was no Mrs Tideaway, but his girl helped in the bar, drifting like a wraith around the tables, collecting empty glasses while trying to remain invisible. The pub was owned by the Hoyland estate, but was leased to individuals who were free to make as much money as they were able once their own rent had been paid. Thus far, Harry was making a better go of things than his predecessor, who had never fully grasped that by helping himself to free beer and brandy, he was stealing from his own till.

Harry had ideas. He was thinking of opening up on Sundays, if the estate allowed it, when the other pubs were closed. He thought he might fetch down the old piano from the living quarters above the bar, and find a fellow who could play it. Bit of a sing-song might pull in the punters. And he was at Eve's door early every Friday morning, to collect the pies he'd ordered for the bar. It was a custom he'd begun soon after Eve started her business, to supply free pork pie on market days, cutting it small and presenting it round the bar on wooden platters. There were those who said Harry should clean his windows and sweep his floors before bothering with titbits for the customers, and it was true that the floor of the Hoyland Arms hadn't seen a mop and bucket since he took over the post twelve months ago. But his free pork pie worked on customers much like cheese in a mousetrap, luring in drinkers who might otherwise have taken themselves off to the Cross Keys, a little further from the market place.

Like the pub he presided over, Harry aimed for imposing but achieved something much less. He dressed every day as if it were Sunday, but his bowler hat was dusty, his collars were frayed, there were buttons off his waistcoat and his fob watch had read twenty past eight for as long as he'd been here. Eve didn't much like him, not because of his dusty bowler or his useless watch, but because he was a compulsive gossip, leaning in towards her over the table of goods to pass on whatever nugget he'd picked up the night before while eavesdropping at his bar. He had a leering air about him too, greedy eyes that took in more than was decent. She preferred it when he sent droopy Agnes for the pies, but he usually came in person. Eve tried to discourage him by expressing no interest whatsoever in what he said, but Harry's money was as good as anyone's and four pies every Friday morning was one shilling and four pennies, guaranteed. It was one of the facts of her new life that she had to tolerate the company of those she might once have crossed the street to avoid.

This morning she wrapped the pies in waxed paper and slid them into bags while Harry told her that Edna Matthews had told Bradley Mason that Clem Waterdine had booted Ambrose Foster off his allotment for no good reason except to make way for Arthur, and now Amos Sykes had it and Ambrose Foster was taking his complaint to the earl's land agent. 'Our Seth 'as it, as well as Amos,' Eve said, lured against her better judgement into responding. 'And Ambrose Foster never planted so much as a pea shoot in that allotment.' She regretted it instantly, knowing her remark was being filed in Harry's head under 'matters pending'.

'I'm just sayin' what Bradley Mason told me,' said Harry disingenuously, sidestepping responsibility with the skill of the seasoned pedlar of tittle-tattle.

'One shillin' an' fourpence, Mr Tideaway,' said Eve, hoping to show him he'd taken a turning into a conversational dead end.

He handed over the money and Eve dropped it into the tin, but Harry stayed where he was. He had more to impart than Edna's version of Ambrose Foster's grievance. He stood there, clutching his pies and eyeing her up and down, while Eve made pointless adjustments to her table of goods, hoping he'd be gone when she next looked. No such luck.

'You might want to change into your Sunday best,' said Harry, inexplicably.

'You what?' said Eve. She looked at him now, unsmiling, but Harry wasn't in need of encouragement.

'I said, you might want to change into your Sunday best. You might be 'avin a visit from t'earl today.' Harry's expression was all triumphant glee, like a fisherman reeling in a catch.

'What you on about?' said Eve.

'Well, last Friday, Teddy 'oyland came in for a pint, like 'e does now an' again.'

This much was probably true, Eve thought. The earl's visits to the Hoyland Arms were infrequent, but not unheard of. He liked to mingle with his men periodically, and he kept a tankard behind the bars at all three of Netherwood's pubs.

'Anyroad, it bein' a Friday, 'is lordship 'elps 'imself to a piece o' your pie,' said Harry.

'I see,' said Eve. This story could go either way, she thought.

'Well, 'e eats one piece, then reaches for another, then straight off gets another again,' said Harry. 'Now, any other bugger, and I'd 'ave told 'em where to get off. But this bein' t'earl, I just says, "Glad to see you're enjoyin' t'pie, your lordship," and 'e says . . .' Harry, practised in the art of storytelling, paused for dramatic effect.

Eve waited, fascinated in spite of herself.

'. . . An' 'e says, "My good man, this his the finest pork pie hi 'ave ever tasted," just like that.' Harry, using his toff's voice, was getting aitches in all the wrong places. 'Then 'e says, "Where did you buy hit?" an' I told 'im it were from you, an' 'e says 'e's of a mind to buy some for 'imself.'

Eve, delighted, nevertheless felt compelled to underreact.

'Well, that's as maybe,' she said. 'But since when 'as Lord Netherwood done his own shopping? If they buy a pie for t'big 'ouse, it'll not be t'earl carrying it back.'

'Aye well, that's where tha wrong,' said Harry, with the air of a man who had saved his best for last. 'Lord Netherwood

145

'as an interest in thee, Eve Williams. Lord Netherwood said to me' – he cleared his throat again, ready for his flawed rendition of the earl's received pronunciation – ''e said, "Hi shall visit next Friday, see 'ow Missis Williams his getting on, and purchase one of these excellent pies."'

''e said that to you?' said Eve.

'Well, as good as,' said Harry. ''e said it to Jem Arkwright, but I was stood there an' all.'

Eve remembered what Arthur used to say about Harry Tideaway: 'Tell 'im nowt, an' 'e'll 'ave it in t'*Chronicle* by Friday.' She could almost hear him saying it now, quietly, from somewhere unseen. And then round the corner came Betty and Doris Ramsbottom, spinster sisters from Tinker Lane, here to buy their Friday treat of Eve's pudding, so Harry took his leave and Eve forgot all about their conversation until later that day when Lord Netherwood did indeed appear at her front door, asking for a pork pie and leaving her speechless with the surprise and honour of it.

By the close of business on that felicitious Friday, Eve had agreed to bake forty raised pork pies for Netherwood Hall on the occasion of Tobias Hoyland's long-postponed twenty-first birthday party the following month. She would be paid in advance, enabling her to order and buy the great quantity of flour, lard and pork needed for such an undertaking, and she was to report to the kitchens of the great house the evening before, and work through the night there to fulfil the order. The earl had bought a pie from her and asked after her family, and had behaved so entirely like an ordinary person that Eve began to wonder if the tales concerning his extraordinary fortune might be exaggerated.

'What did you imagine?' said Anna, later. 'That rich people

don't eat pies?' The daughter of an affluent man, she felt no awe in the company of wealth. They were sitting on the back doorstep, enjoying the late afternoon's warmth, mulling things over. A noisy mob of swifts ducked and weaved in the sky above the yard.

'No. Well. Yes,' said Eve. 'I suppose I wouldn't expect Teddy 'oyland to eat t'same as Clem Waterdine.'

'Well the difference is, Clem has no choice. Your earl can eat caviar one day, pie next.'

''e rolled up in that big car,' said Eve. 'It drew up outside in Beaumont Lane and everybody stopped to watch. And there I was, in yesterday's pinny and my hair all any'ow. I should've 'eeded 'arry Tideaway and put my good frock on.'

'And if you had, he would have ordered eighty pies, perhaps?' said Anna.

'Fair point,' said Eve. 'But still, even if 'e's not interested in what I'm wearin', I might 'ave felt a little bit less foolish if I'd smartened up.'

'Well foolish or not foolish, you're now most famous pig-pie maker in Netherwood, so – *na zdorov'ya*!' She raised her cup of tea, and leaned in to clink it against Eve's.

'Cheers,' said Eve. She smiled, then looked suddenly grave. 'I couldn't do any of this without you.'

'This I know,' said Anna. She smiled. 'But you don't have to, do you?'

PART TWO

Chapter 21

Tobias leaned against the casement of his bedroom window and took a deep, therapeutic drag on his first cigarette of the day. He was still fully clothed from the night before, eccentrically so, sporting his old punting get-up, cream flannels and a jaunty blazer. This college garb was his current outfit of choice for a night on the ale, and, along with a small selection of other garments – cricket whites, his (stolen) college gown – was all he had to show for his time at Cambridge. He had been sent down from Trinity in his second year, just before the end of Michaelmas term, for a persistent refusal to engage with the academic demands of undergraduate life. He had felt no sense of failure or remorse at this turn of events; Toby was a stranger to regret, and in any case had only gone up in the first place to oblige his father. He had enjoyed the japes though: the balls, the dinners, punting along the Backs, and his friends there had missed him after his dismissal.

Below him, wheeling a barrow-load of ivy leaves along the broad gravel path, Hislop, the elderly Netherwood head gardener, happened to glance upwards and did a startled double take. This happened often among the older members of staff, for Toby was the very image of his father's younger self. At the same age, Teddy Hoyland had been considered quite the beau and it was said that his handsome face and figure had been almost as responsible as his fortune for capturing the heart of Lady Clarissa Benbury. Now, of course, his penchant for rich food and tawny port had altered Teddy's appearance, and not for the better. But everyone saw the young sixth earl in his oldest son's features and they were not the sort of good looks that had gone out of fashion. Add to that his glittering prospects, and Tobias was considered just as much of a catch as his father had been, if he would only allow himself to be caught. But his tastes, thus far, had been for the unsuitable: earthy local girls with high spirits and low morals, offering accessibility without any tedious demands for commitment.

Toby's suite of rooms were among those which overlooked the main lawns at the front of the house. He had a large bedroom, amply furnished with fine mahogany pieces and a high four-poster bed. Adjoining this room was a small study with a walnut bureau cabinet, its concealed drawers well stocked with paper vellum, pens and ink, none of which Toby ever used. He wasn't much of a writer. Through a further door was his private sitting room, with two burgundy leather wing chairs placed at angles by the fireplace and a low green leather ottoman between them. There was a bookcase, too, stocked with all the volumes one might expect to find: Shakespeare, Milton, a little Wordsworth and Coleridge, some Thackeray, some Dickens and a rather beautiful first edition of *Gulliver's Travels*. Additionally, on the bottom shelf, was a row of pink, yellow and buff-coloured paper spines – Tobias's much-prized collection of Wisden's cricketing almanacks. Beside them, stacked in a pile and serving as a very effective bookend, were numerous copies of *Horse & Hound*. These, and the Wisdens, were well-thumbed.

He took one last, long, rather desperate drag of his cigarette and stubbed it out carelessly on the window sill, scooping the remains into the palm of his hand and, from there, blowing it on to the rug. He stayed at the window though, watching dispassionately as members of the household staff secured the guy ropes of one of five vast marquees that were being pressed into service for the celebrations.

He had no appetite for the day ahead, really he didn't. He rubbed his temples to ease the pain there, the last vestige of a very good night indeed, spent with a crowd of Netherwood lads in the locked tap room of the Hare and Hounds. Tobias, every inch a spoiled young aristocrat, would nevertheless down a pint with any man. This trait, a kind of innocent social democracy, had been roundly approved of by the earl when Toby was small. It boded well, Teddy had thought, that the future custodian of the Netherwood estate was on friendly terms with the under-privileged, and it had warmed his heart to see his son up a tree on the common or sledging down Harley Hill with a gang of local children. Now, however, the earl felt a certain distance between his son and his old friends was necessary – a distance that he had wrongly assumed would occur naturally as they grew up. What was commendable in boyhood lacked dignity in adulthood, particularly when beer became part of the equation. Last night had been a classic, thought Toby now. He'd only staggered home half an hour before and what he needed now was a long sleep, a hot bath and a plate of Mrs Adams's egg and chips, in that order. Instead, what he faced was all the pomp and ceremony of a Hoyland family celebration with brass knobs on. The very thought of it made him want to weep with weariness: his father's florid face puffed out with paternal pride and he himself made to smile modestly as he listened to all the damned embarrassing eulogies about his coming-of-age and his responsibilities – what a bloody torment.

Behind him, the door opened softly and a young under-footman crept into the room, staggering slightly under the weight of a brass coal scuttle. He stopped in his tracks when he saw Tobias, then retreated, closed the door and tapped on it, tentatively.

'Come!' said Toby sharply. He didn't look round.

The under-footman stepped into the bedroom once more, head dipped, eyes cast down. He swallowed anxiously. It was early days in his career in service at Netherwood Hall and he had been expressly instructed by the formidable head footman to remain invisible as he went about his morning duties. He was meant to creep into the room to prepare and light the fire before the young master rose, yet there he was, already dressed, gazing out of the window on to the garden. The bed, he observed, appeared to have been already made. Or possibly it hadn't been slept in. It was all most irregular, and the boy felt entirely unequal to the situation. However, something had to be done, so he steeled himself and coughed politely.

'What?' barked Toby. He turned and his head, which really did ache terrifically, throbbed at the sudden movement. He had a raging thirst too, which had not been helped by the cigarette.

'M'lord, sorry, m'lord. Should I see to your fire, m'lord?' The boy was white as alabaster with anxiety, thought Toby. He softened fractionally and nodded.

'Go ahead, might as well. Bloody June but it's freezing in here, as per usual,' he said.

The boy tiptoed over to the grate and began to shake out last night's spent coals. It had been chilly for the time of year, and all the family had felt the need for fires in their suites, morning and night. Toby watched the boy for a moment then lost interest and turned back to view the worker bees assembling the trappings for his party. Good God, there was a bloody pennant flying from the tents now, long, with a forked end, like something Henry V might have flown at Agincourt. He had a brief, rather disturbing flashback to Eton.

'"He which hath no stomach to this fight, let him depart,"' Toby murmured, because he hadn't forgotten everything he'd learned in the schoolroom. Then he barked; 'Depart! Ha! Fat bloody chance.'

The lad at the fireplace jumped in alarm and to his shame emitted an involuntary squawk. Toby laughed, but not unkindly.

'What's your name?' he said. 'I haven't seen you before, have I?'

The boy, encouraged by the young master's tone of voice but appalled nevertheless at the attention, squeaked his reply.

'Freddie, m'lord. Thomas.'

'Well? Which is it? Freddie or Thomas?'

'Both m'lord. Freddie Thomas, m'lord.'

Toby laughed again. 'So, Freddie Thomas, I trust you'll be coming to the party? Roast ox, free ale and pretty girls. You're not too young for pretty girls, are you?'

Freddie was all confusion, frantic with anxiety that a yes would seem too forward, but a no would appear insolent. However, he needn't have worried, since Toby wasn't interested in the answer.

'Light that then and get yourself off,' he said. 'I expect you've other tasks to perform before you can join the shindig.'

'Yes, m'lord. Thank you, m'lord,' said Freddie. He put a match to the newspaper in the grate and watched briefly to be sure it was going to take. The new flames wreathed themselves around the kindling and, satisfied, Freddie stood to leave, sneaking a look behind him. Tobias, Lord Fulton, the future seventh Earl of Netherwood, was facing the window again, smoking a new cigarette, his body and bearing the personification of gloom. But what troubles, thought Freddie, could a man like that possibly have? As he made for the great oak door of the bedroom, the boy was seized by a sudden bold impulse.

'M'lord?' he ventured.

Toby sighed and turned around.

'What now?' he said.

'Enjoy your day, m'lord,' said Freddie.

'Oh bugger off,' said Toby, and turned back to the window.

At Netherwood Hall the coming-of-age of an offspring, from the heir to the youngest honourable, had always been celebrated with a lavish family breakfast, before any other festivities began. Today was not Tobias's birthday, of course, but back in January there'd been a recent death at New Mill Colliery, a funeral to attend that morning and a general air of sobriety in the household. Therefore, on Lady Netherwood's instructions, Tobias's birthday breakfast was being staged today, six months after the event. There were to be gifts, too; Clarissa felt that, without them, the celebration would fall flat.

Birthday meals at Netherwood Hall were always an event, but for the oldest son and heir at his coming-of-age, new standards of excellence had to be set. This morning's fare was tremendously lavish: domed silver platters bore generous quantities of bacon, lamb cutlets, kidneys, grilled tomatoes, curried eggs, sauteed mushrooms, steamed smoked haddock and baked kippers. Baskets of toast and warm muffins had been placed on the table, one within reach of all the diners, as well as silver pots of marmalade and fruit preserves, silver coffee pots, jugs of cream and bowls of sugar. And, because it was a special day, a three-tiered platter of frosted glass had stood proud and splendid in the centre of the table bearing a dewy cascade of grapes, melon, orange and pineapple.

A pity, then, that the mood around the table at just before nine-fifteen was tense. For while every member of the immediate family understood that they were expected in the dining room by nine o'clock prompt, the earl and countess, facing each other at opposite ends of the long table, had thus far been joined by only three of their four children. Henrietta, Dickie and Isabella were all present and correct. Tobias, for whom an inviting heap of beautifully wrapped boxes had been arranged by his place setting, was not. Isabella fixed her gaze on the parcels; she yearned to open them.

While they sat in their uncomfortable silence, breakfast had been carried through and placed on the long sideboard by Parkinson, assisted by an under-butler and four footmen. Their immediate task complete, they now stood, silently impassive, at their various posts around the room, waiting for the family to begin their meal. The ormolu mantel clock chimed briefly, indicating a quarter past the hour. Lord Netherwood drummed a brief tattoo with his fingers on the table. He pulled out a gold pocket watch from his waistcoat and placed it on the table, then looked pointedly at Parkinson, who in turn looked pointedly at a footman. The footman, having no inferior to whom he could pass the look, stared at the floor. Tobias's late arrival was no one's fault but his own, but still there was a general shared sense among the household staff that they were somehow failing their master.

'Dashed bad manners,' said the earl.

He spoke mildly, conversationally, as if he was commenting on the weather. Everyone in the room knew better, however. Teddy Hoyland rarely raised his voice, so his family and staff were accustomed to looking for other signs of his displeasure. This morning, the mottled red skin of his neck above his stiff, white collar indicated that all was not well beneath the genial surface. They sat on in continued silence.

'Well,' he said, still pleasantly, all of a sudden pushing back his chair and getting to his feet, much to the consternation of Parkinson, who had been caught out by the unexpected change in circumstances and was too late to assist his master.

'I don't see why we should allow this fine food to go cold. Let us eat.'

He made for the sideboard, where Parkinson, back on his mettle, was poised to raise whichever lid the earl showed an interest in.

Lady Netherwood, her expression bland and pleasant, raised an objection. 'Ought we to begin Toby's birthday breakfast before he joins us?' she said.

'He really wouldn't care if we did,' said Henrietta evenly. 'In fact, he would probably regard it as a bonus to be spared the ordeal.'

'Henrietta!' said Lady Netherwood, with an annoyance born more out of habit than conviction.

'Well it's true,' said Henrietta. 'He's permanently worse for wear these days. I expect he's fully clothed up there, and out for the count.'

'Enough, Henry,' said Lord Netherwood, who had ignored his wife's objection and was returning to the table with a plate generously loaded with kippers and tomatoes. Isabella eyed it hungrily. She knew it was folly to displease Mama, but if Papa was eating, she wondered if she might too. Her father began to saw and stab at the food as if he had Toby's head on his plate. She watched him warily and wondered if she should risk asking permission to eat, but was prevented from speaking by Dickie, who volunteered, affably, to go in search of the errant birthday boy.

'Certainly not,' said Lord Netherwood, at the precise moment that his wife said, 'Thank you darling,' so Dickie unwisely laughed and Henrietta smirked. Lord Netherwood told her to wipe the insolent expression off her face. Dickie, with his characteristic inability to gauge an awkward atmosphere, sat back comfortably in his chair and began to whistle and Lady Netherwood, by now a ferment of anxiety and irritation, insisted that he stop at once because her head was beginning to ache. Henrietta said if everyone was going to continue to be so disagreeable, could she please leave the table, and Isabella burst into tears. At which point the dining-room door opened and in strolled Tobias. He bestowed a rakish – if rather jaded – smile on the assembled company.

'Darling boy,' said his mother, much relieved, instantly forgiving. She smiled warmly at him; her indulgence of her eldest son's excesses had been often tested but had yet to reach its limit.

'Morning, Mama,' said Toby. 'Gosh, what a spread. And presents! Here, Izzy, open this for me would you?'

To his youngest sister's huge delight he tossed a package across the table to her. She began to pick eagerly at the blue satin bow.

'You look perfectly ghastly,' said Henrietta, resolutely uncharmed.

'So do you,' said Toby. 'But I haven't slept. What's your excuse?'

She laughed. '*Touché*,' she said.

Toby, still standing, gripped the back of his chair for support and willed himself not to gag at the sight and smell of his father's kippers. Beads of sweat had erupted on his brow and a throb at his temple heralded the onset of another beast of a headache. He'd made the mistake of lying down on his bed for forty winks, and had fallen into a deep sleep from which he'd only been woken by the clattering arrival of a new posse of marquee builders outside his bedroom window. Now his body yearned for unconsciousness. Just endure the next half an hour, he said to himself, then retreat to quarters and sleep for a while. But the old man was clearly rattled. He hadn't yet spoken, his neck was as red as a turkey's wattle and he was using his fork like a bayonet. The proceedings were likely to be bloody enough without the pater giving him the evil eye all day long. Better make amends, and sharpish.

'Sorry, Papa,' he said. He sounded humble and sincere and, up to a point, he was. 'Awfully poor show to be late for my own party. Can't tell you how shabby I feel about it.'

He looked the picture of contrition. It was a look he had turned on Teddy many a time over the years but it was no less effective for that, on this occasion. His father was perfectly capable of giving Toby a roasting, but this morning – well, there was a big day ahead, a great deal to be done, a celebration to be had. And good Lord, thought Teddy, hadn't he drunk himself into much the same state himself many a time? The decision was made, a swift pardon issued.

'Indeed. Well. Let no more be said on the matter,' said Lord Netherwood. 'Fill your plate, young man, and let's get on with the day.'

Toby, reprieved, sneaked a look of triumph across the table at Henrietta, who smiled sweetly.

'Kippers?' she said. 'Or kidneys?'

Chapter 22

The cold weather was immensely vexing, but there it was;
one simply couldn't rely on the English summer. Lady
Netherwood, insulated from the chill inside her furs, leaned
on the balustrade of the first-floor terrace of Netherwood Hall
and surveyed the gardens. It was her domain, this outside
world, much more so than the house which, though lavishly
decorated and furnished, had always interested her less. It
seemed to Lady Netherwood that there was something intrinsically dull about interior design, however opulent the effect.
Nothing evolved within a faultless interior, and one could
hardly order the removal of the Gainsboroughs and Stubbs
simply to alter one's outlook.

The garden, however, was in a state of constant, seasonal
flux, and even now remained full of possibility. Under her
reign as the Countess of Netherwood the grounds had been
redesigned and replanted with a near-obsessive zeal and a tire-
less quest for perfection. The Oriental Garden had been her
idea entirely; she had researched the scheme rigorously, determined to achieve eastern authenticity in every detail. Plants
were sourced and imported from Japan and rocks, too, were
shipped at great expense from the Orient, Yorkshire stone

being deemed lacking in the necessary spiritual significance. They now formed stepping stones across the goldfish pond and were green with algae, but no one had yet dared suggest to Lady Netherwood that they had been, perhaps, an authentic detail too far. The rose garden, with its famously beautiful pergolas, the enchanting thirty-foot long wisteria tunnel, and the magnificent domed Palm House had also all been her innovations. There had been four glasshouses already at Netherwood Hall, but they were functional rather than decorative and Lady Netherwood wanted something with a little more dash. She had tried to commission Decimus Burton for the design but he had stubbornly refused to come out of retirement, even for the king's ransom the countess was prepared to pay. Instead, and rather defiantly, she had simply commissioned a replica – though slightly smaller in scale – of Mr Burton's famous building in Kew Gardens. If he objected to her audacity, his concerns were never made public.

Now, from her vantage point above the garden, Lady Netherwood allowed her eyes to settle briefly on the hubbub of activity immediately below her; four great marquees were now erected, parquet floors laid and tables and chairs installed. There would be a formal luncheon inside the house for fifty-four of the upper-tier guests, none of whom could possibly be entertained under canvas, while the lower tiers would be amply provided for in the marquees. Even among the lower tiers, of course, there were considerations to be made as to who would rub shoulders with whom. The squirearchy and gentleman farmers, for example, must not be expected to dine and drink with the professional classes, who in turn must be separate from the upper echelons of the estate workers who themselves might take offence at being seated among the miners – it was an exercise in finely tuned social etiquette, but one that the countess had no doubt would be beautifully managed. She had no objections to the town being invited, but she had every intention of observing society's rules during the celebration. Equally there was to be no lapse in standards and she had not stinted on her instructions for decorating the marquees; tables were covered with cream linen cloths – an unwise choice, in the event – and the gardeners and household staff alike were now trimming the interiors with trailing festoons of evergreen foliage, interspersed with hundreds of white and yellow orchids, cultivated under glass specifically for this day and freshly cut this morning.

Satisfied with what she saw, Lady Netherwood directed her serene gaze to the gardens beyond this industrious scene, and a look of supreme satisfaction settled on her face. How glad she was that she had vetoed Teddy's first plan, to hold Toby's birthday celebration back in January on the day itself. The borders, however impeccably pruned and weeded, simply lacked glory in the winter. The hellebores were always a triumph, of course; they grew abundantly in the damp and shaded fern garden where their petals of palest green, chalky pink and soft cream looked well against the lively foliage of the hart's tongue. There were delicate aconites in January too, pushing through the russet leaves in the woodland garden, and of course the snowdrop cascade, a vast grassy bank of nodding white heads, was ever-reliable at that time of year. But, charming though these features were, they were too modest to ever be a satisfactory backdrop to an important occasion. Whereas now, mid-June, the herbaceous borders were in full flight, the lilac bowers were still dripping with blooms, the rose garden was crowded with heavily scented flowers and the wisteria tunnel was simply glorious – it was all perfect, and a perfect garden was one of Lady Netherwood's greatest joys. The countess's happiness was almost complete, she thought to herself now. She had just the tiniest twinge of disappointment that the sun was refusing to shine. And a similarly tiny twinge at the fact that the London season, by now in full swing, had produced three delightful engagements for the coming weekend which had had to be declined. However, she refused to let herself dwell; the sun was outside her influence, and London would still be there next week. In any case, it rather amused her to hold her own delightful engagement up here in the frozen north.

And anyway, not a single person had returned their apologies for the house party and most were here already. They were drifting around the house and grounds now, at their various chosen pursuits, as comfortable – or more so – at Netherwood Hall as at their own homes. Their staff, the ladies' maids, valets and coachmen, were installed in the servants' quarters, in rooms correctly allocated according to hierarchy by the inestimable Mrs Powell-Hughes, Netherwood Hall's housekeeper. She could be so utterly relied upon to get it right, thought Lady Netherwood. Such an asset. She had been here almost for ever, and in living memory there hadn't been a single ghastly blunder of the type that was common in other, less well-run establishments. Mrs P-H had an extraordinary memory for rank and title, like Debrett made flesh. Of course there were sometimes disadvantages to following social convention to the letter; correct form meant that too often Lady Netherwood had to endure the close proximity round the dining table of various grand but tedious relatives. She often felt her natural place was with the spirited and amusing young men – in her heart, Lady Netherwood was still twenty – lower down the table, and this led her to wonder why, of the many charming people of her acquaintance, none of them were relatives. So unjust, she thought now with a conscious smile, since she was so very charming herself.

Today's seating plan for luncheon was a case in point. At least her own fate – diagonally adjacent on one side to the idiotic Bowlby and on the other to a painfully desiccated old duke who could only hear if one yelled into his ear trumpet

– meant she could stand up to Tobias when he complained, as he undoubtedly would, at being seated by his grandmama, Clarissa's mother, the Countess of Bromyard. Clarissa hoped the darling boy wouldn't too frightfully resent the arrangement. Lady Bromyard had been emphatic in the demand, and it had always been impossible to refuse her.

The bell in the cupola chimed briefly to indicate a quarter past the hour. The countess started – if it was eleven-fifteen, and she feared it must be, she had left Flytton very little time to undress and dress her in time to acknowledge the first outdoor guests at half-past noon. She stepped away from the balustrade and the instant she moved, the footmen, hovering behind her, opened the great French windows to allow her through. She swept graciously past, carrying on her furs and in her hair the fresh scent of outdoors. The drawing-room fire, lit against the unseasonal chill, crackled and spat within its wide marble surround, warming the room enough to make the countess instantly irritable inside her many layers. But there was Flytton, waiting for her. She disrobed her mistress with swift efficiency, then the two of them glided from the room, Flytton two paces behind and loaded with furs, to begin the elaborate process of preparing the countess for the party.

'What an absolutely marvellous wheeze!'

Henrietta, transported back to childhood from the lofty heights of her twenty-two years, screamed with laughter and yelled at Tobias above the noise of the engine and the rush of the wind. Her blonde hair, which had been respectably pinned up when she'd got into the car half an hour earlier, was now a disreputable tangle which repeatedly whipped her face and neck.

Tobias grinned at her, though he couldn't hear a word she

was saying on account of the tan leather driving helmet which, along with matching gauntlets, had come with the car. The jaunty little Wolseley two-seater rattled down the hill, perilously close to the hawthorn hedge, brooking no obstructions it might encounter. He really had thought he was too far out of favour with the old man to hope for anything as divine as a motor car of his own. Certainly there'd been no mention of it on his birthday, when the haul had been excessively dull. A gold fob watch was hardly likely to set one's pulse racing. But this morning, after breakfast, his father had led him downstairs, through the marble hall and out of the front doors on to the gravel, where stood this miraculous little motor car. The mere sight of it had done wonders for his crashing headache. Now, having barrelled rather recklessly out of the park and down the lane, he felt euphoric, invincible. Toby had always had the capacity to enjoy the moment, and the day's onerous filial duties were currently entirely eclipsed.

He steered adroitly, turning left along Wharncliffe Bank and beginning to climb Harley Hill. It was an ambitious project as the rutted track was more suitable for walkers than for vehicles, but the little car battled its way to the summit, and he and Henrietta sat for a while to recover from the bone-shaking motion.

'One day, my boy, all this will be yours,' Henrietta said, indicating the swathe of Yorkshire countryside. 'Warts and all.'

'Plenty of life in the old boy yet,' said Toby. He was in no hurry to inherit his father's title, along with all the dreary responsibility that went with it.

'When I was twenty-one,' Henrietta said, 'I was given diamonds and there wasn't any fuss made at all.'

They were parked in the shadow of a towering bonfire that would be lit at dusk in Toby's honour. It would blaze like a beacon, visible to all. There were to be fireworks too – again.

They'd had a lavish half-hour display of pyrotechnics on his birthday six months ago. This evening they were to be set to music. Henrietta thought it was all rather overblown.

'I do think it's a bit rum,' she said. 'Especially as I'd make a much better earl than you.'

Toby laughed, though she was only half joking.

'Well, you're welcome to it,' he said. 'I say, Henry, let's drive to London and skip the whole ghastly shindig.'

She gave him a look, part pity, part irritation. Henrietta loved her brother, but he was such an infant.

'Start the car, Tobes,' she said. 'I need to get back. I must look a fright.'

'Oh, you do,' he said. 'You're all smuts and rats' tails.'

He executed a tortuous five-point turn in a space not quite wide enough for the manoeuvre. Then, partly to irritate his sister and partly to entertain himself, he took a circuitous route home in order to make an impromptu, showy tour of Netherwood town, where the streets were once again festooned with bunting and the townsfolk were feeling particularly well-disposed towards Tobias since his party meant early closure of the pits and a free knees-up for all. The car attracted a most gratifying amount of whooping, clapping and hollering as it made its stately progress, moving slowly enough to encourage a jolly procession of children who danced along through the streets behind it. Toby, on familiar terms with many among the crowd – one or two of whom had picked him up and carried him home last night – waved wildly at everyone, while Henrietta's dignified profile went some small way towards making up for his boundless, boyish disregard for propriety.

By the time they reached the gates of the hall and chugged down the length of Oak Avenue, preparations for the day's events were complete and Tobias and Henrietta had been very much missed, their absence having shifted from the realm of high jinks into that of ill manners. The New Mill Colliery Band were tuning up and the smell of roasting ox hung deliciously in the air. Two under-footmen attended the siblings as they disembarked, smut-covered and dishevelled. Henrietta, rather mortified, hurried into the house to be dressed but Toby took his time, slapping the motor car's right wheel arch as if it were the rump of a fine filly and checking the sides for hawthorn-related damage. Lord Netherwood, regarding him from the drawing room upstairs, pondered his son's lack of urgency.

'He really has not a care in the world,' he said, speaking to himself but attracting the attention of the countess. She joined him at the window.

'Well, isn't that just as it should be?' she murmured.

The earl considered a reply but decided against it, not because he had nothing to say on the subject, but because he had rather too much.

Chapter 23

Henrietta stood before a cheval mirror clothed only in a simple cotton chemise and silk stockings which pooled in loose ripples around her shins. Her long hair had been returned to respectability, brushed, smoothed and twisted expertly into an elegant chignon, pinned with diamond clasps at the back of her head, but she still had to be dressed and Maudie, working swiftly, was fitting a long pink coutil corset, heavily boned and not built for comfort. She yanked at the lacing, pulling it tight at the waist; Henrietta yelped.

'Snakes alive, Maudie, you'll snap me in two,' she said.

Maudie tutted. She heard the same complaint, give or take the odd expletive, every time the hated corset was manipulated into position. There was nothing to say in response, because one way or another, it had to be done. The countess was a stickler for a silhouette, especially where Henrietta was concerned. She knew beyond doubt that without her example – and her vigilance – her older daughter would probably jettison the bones and laces and let nature reclaim her posture.

Maudie pulled up the stockings, smoothing them over Henrietta's knees and thighs, then clipped them securely to the suspenders. There was an air of urgency to her business;

outside, the New Mill Colliery Band were welcoming arrivals to the party with their first turn, a carefully selected medley of popular music and rousing hymns, intended perhaps as a reminder that, while the revels were beginning, a modicum of respectful behaviour might be expected throughout.

The maid held open a pair of long drawers and Henrietta stepped into them then stood passively, allowing them to be pulled up and arranged, their laces tied at the waist. Then came a series of petticoats, followed by pretty shoes of mint-green grosgrain, Maudie holding her mistress steady while she slid her feet into them. Next the dress, an elegant gown of pale yellow silk chiffon, newly purchased from the countess's London dressmaker, was laid in an open circle on the floor for Henrietta to step into. Maudie drew it up, pausing to allow her mistress to slip her arms into the sleeves, then fastened the tiny silk-covered buttons, moving deftly from bottom to top, before finishing the task by securing the hook and eye. They chatted comfortably as Maudie worked; Henrietta was as familiar with her maid as she was with her siblings – more so, in some ways, since she and Maudie shared real intimacy in their relationship. Every day, twice a day, sometimes more, Maudie's deft, cool fingers, brisk but gentle, drew stockings over her thighs, arranged her flesh inside her corset, placed jewels around her throat or coaxed the tangles from her thick blonde hair. It was natural that these acts of tender service should lead to shared confidences, and their friendship, while always and necessarily somewhat unequal, was important to each of them. They had been together for almost ten years now, since a grateful Maudie was promoted from housemaid to attend the young Lady Henrietta, and they were as easy together as their respective stations in life allowed. Awful, thought Henrietta, often, to have a lady's maid one couldn't stand. Awful, for example, to have the flint-faced Flytton, though Mama seemed quite content.

Now Maudie, her mission accomplished, stepped away from her charge and sighed with satisfaction.

Henrietta, gazing at her reflection in the cheval, said, 'Hate the colour. I look like an end-of-season daffodil. Get the pink, Maudie.'

Maudie, having none of it, shook her head. 'Nonsense m'lady,' she said. 'You're already late for lunch and t'countess won't thank you for 'olding things up further. And anyway . . .' – she looked Henrietta up and down appreciatively – '. . . you look just grand. Or you would, if your expression weren't dismal as a dishclart.'

Henrietta smiled at her. 'You really do take the most enormous liberties,' she said. 'I should dismiss you on the spot.'

'Aye, and a right pickle you'd soon be in if you did,' said Maudie. She smiled back at her mistress who – whatever she said to the contrary – looked striking in the new gown. If there was something unsatisfactory about her appearance it was just, thought Maudie, that Lady Henrietta's looks were out of step with her time; she never managed the appearance of fashionable delicacy, because nothing about her – neither face, figure nor manners – was fashionably delicate. Not that Henrietta lost any sleep over this immutable state of affairs. In her view her mother and sister more than compensated for her own shortcomings in the delicacy department. She pulled a face at herself in the mirror then turned away – nothing more boring than one's own reflection – while Maudie began to gather up from the floor and surfaces the jumble of discarded clothes and accessories. Outside, a rousing, brassy conclusion indicated that time was of the essence. Henrietta glanced out of her bedroom window and blanched at the size of the crowd already milling around the lawns at the front of the great house. Her clear instructions had been to join her family in the drawing room at a quarter past noon, in order to present a regal and united front on the terrace at half past. Henrietta

171

had no idea of the time, but if the band had finished their piece then she must be perilously late. She turned from the window and fled the room, then in seconds was back, her head peering round the open door.

'You'll make sure to have some fun yourself, won't you, Maudie?' she said.

The maid smiled at her mistress. It was so kind of her, and so characteristic, to spare her a thought. Maudie was, of course, invited to the party along with the rest of the household staff although she, like the others, had no idea how they were meant to find time for carousing when not only the family but also fifty-four house guests were in residence for the occasion. Far from being relieved of their duties, they had all been further burdened.

'I mean, will you find the time?' Henrietta said, pressing her point.

'You'll be in for it, m'lady, if you dawdle there any longer,' said Maudie, deliberately evasive. In truth, she had no idea when she might slip away to join the party; she had much to accomplish before she could even leave Lady Henrietta's rooms.

'I shall check later to make sure you're in the thick of it. Don't miss it on my account. I shan't care a jot if all these clothes are still on the floor when I come back to change this evening.'

Perhaps not, thought Maudie, but she'd be for the chop good and proper if Flytton should find the rooms in disarray. To oblige her mistress and hasten her departure Maudie said, yes, of course, she'd be at the party in no time. Then, with Henrietta gone, she went back to the business of restoring perfect order to the rooms and laying out the black and silver gown required by Lady Henrietta this evening. She might get away, she thought, if she worked swiftly, and didn't get landed with extra duties as she attempted her escape. She might even

172

get out there in time for a slice of that roast ox on a warm bap, which was more than could be said for the kitchen staff, the butler and the thirty liveried footmen currently required to attend to the needs of the luncheon guests in the great hall.

By three o'clock in the afternoon, there were twice the number of guests in the grounds as had been invited, and the household staff posted at the four gates earlier in the day had long since abandoned any attempt to check the influx of gatecrashers. Some eight thousand invitations had been sent – an extraordinary number by anyone's standards – but still the uninvited and the curious from outlying towns and villages had come in droves and it had proved impossible, in the crush of arrivals, to maintain any order or discipline at the gates. Only members of the house party – whose carriages and horses were already in the coach house and stables – and those guests whose transport was being returned whence it came, were allowed into the park to be deposited at the hall. Everyone else was expected to walk down to the house, so the surrounding lanes were crowded with abandoned carts and drays, their horses tethered to every available post or branch. The gates were all unmanned now, the temporary sentries having sloped off to the marquees for their fill of ale and food.

And who could blame them? The like had never been seen in the county, and quite possibly in the whole of England. As well as the spit-roast ox, a magnificent centrepiece and itself quite big enough to feed three villages, there were hogs, lambs, hams and chickens, all roasted and ready to carve. There were trestle tables which bowed in the middle under their burden of pies and pastries, both sweet and savoury, and vast oval platters bearing crusty bread and hunks of cheddar in great doorstop wedges. Earthenware pots piled with pickles

– onions, beetroot, cucumber and cauliflower – were placed at convenient intervals down the tables, and, at the back of it all, awaiting its moment of glory, was a towering four-tiered iced fruitcake, baked many months ago and basted with brandy every week since. There were barrels of bitter and bottles of stout, replenished from a mysterious limitless source whenever stocks appeared to be growing low, and for the children – and abstemious adults, of whom there were very few – there were punch bowls of lemonade and ginger beer; ladles were provided, but were quickly jettisoned in favour of the more efficient method of plunging one's cup into the bowl for a refill.

There was very little decorum and sobriety, though the party was yet young. Each marquee, even the one reserved for the upper tier of the lower-tier guests, and in spite of Lady Netherwood's cream linens and yellow orchids, was taking on the unwholesome character and appearance of a London tavern. Drinkers and diners sprawled at, on and under the tables, and gales of bawdy laughter and occasional, unharmonious attempts at song made ordinary conversation impossible. Outside seemed scarcely less crowded, though the fresh air had, at least, a bracing effect that was lacking in the increasingly fetid atmosphere of the tents. All attempts at social segregation had been abandoned by popular consent, the free-flowing ale having proved a great leveller. A small number of guests had left – including all the members of the local Temperance Society, who possibly should have declined the invitation in the first place, and the Methodist minister Wilfred Oxspring, who, while not actually disapproving of the merrymaking, felt he shouldn't wholeheartedly condone it either. But hordes of people remained and as afternoon turned to evening they stood, sat or strolled on the grass and the gravel, their faces flushed with the ale and the cold. Folk who would ordinarily doff their caps and bow their heads in submissive deference to the earl and countess were making themselves at home, turned loud and confident by the free-flowing beverages.

Into this surreal and dissolute scene walked Eve Williams. It was four o'clock and, though she had arrived at Netherwood Hall the previous evening, this was the first time she had stepped out of the servants' quarters below the house. Even now, back in the kitchens, there was still work to be done – the cleaning of those vast rooms was like one of the twelve labours of Hercules, and it was all hands on deck down there. But Eve had more than fulfilled her contract. Her mission now was to find her children in the mêlée.

This was easier said than done. Even before she could identify anyone by name, she could tell by their weaving, loose-limbed gait that most of them were pie-eyed; on the periphery of the main event, there even appeared to be bodies slumped on the grass and the gravel, sleeping off their first excess in preparation for the second. One of them resembled Amos who, if all had gone to plan, should by now be in charge of Seth, Eliza and Ellen, having taken over from Anna. Eve, anxiety rising in her breast, hurried over to the prone figure for a closer look but found she was mistaken; it was the earl's gamekeeper Walker Spruce, scourge of the poachers and relentless guardian of the Netherwood estate. His wiry body was stretched out full length at the foot of a flight of stone steps, arms folded behind his head as if he were sunning himself on the chapel outing to Blackpool. Eve watched his beatific expression for a moment, marvelling at the power of drink to make a feather bed out of a gravel path.

'I wish I were a poacher,' she said to his sleeping form. 'I'd miss t'party and bag enough game tonight to see me through to midwinter.' Walker stirred at the sound of her voice, smiled stupidly but slept on, so she risked a scornful little poke in the ribs with the toe of her clog, on account of all the game pie she might have made if it wasn't for him.

Eve moved on, pushing her way into the mass of people and scanning the crowd for Amos. She hoped to God that he was still standing and cursed him inwardly in case he wasn't. It was a near-impossible task in the crush all around her, and the more people she asked, the more she despaired. There was no menace in the air, but still Eve felt waves of panic beginning to break over her; a crowd of this size in the pursuit of earthly pleasures was an unfeeling thing. Few of the folk she asked spoke sense, and those that did hadn't seen Amos Sykes. Anna and Maya were nowhere to be seen, either. Eve cursed herself for a fool, for having stayed so long in the Netherwood Hall kitchens, for having failed to arrange a meeting place, for entrusting her children to a man when there was free ale on tap.

Then she saw Ellen, still some way distant but head above the crowds, up on Amos's shoulders in a state of dishevelled bliss, clutching his hair with one hand and waving a thick slice of roast ox with the other. Eve pushed on, her heart light with relief, and as she drew nearer she could see Seth and Eliza too, both held safe by the hand and both laughing, their faces tilted up to Amos. He seemed to be telling them a tale, holding their attention in spite of the noise and the novelty of everything around them. Eve felt a surge of emotion that threatened to overcome her; she checked her progress and stood still, watching the cameo unobserved for a few seconds. She felt a mixture of emotions: relief at seeing her children, remorse at having thought so badly of Amos and profound and painful sorrow that he stood there, in Arthur's place. Then Ellen saw her and squealed her approval, and Eve waved and began to move forward towards them.

Suddenly, she found her way barred by Harry Tideaway, glassy-eyed and swaying. He loomed large in front of her, peering at her as if through fog, then he steadied himself by placing his hands on her shoulders. She shrank away from the contact but he tightened his hold.

'Now where you off to?' he said, his face too close to hers, the aroma of roast meat and ale on his breath. 'I've a mind to take a kiss from you, by way of payment, like.'

Eve, appalled and repulsed, forced his hands away from her and tried to step away, but he detained her again, clutching the fabric of her jacket in his fist. He'd seen plenty of others kissing and canoodling this afternoon, and he didn't see why he should miss out.

'You're drunk,' she said.

'Never mind that. I think you're forgettin' what you owe me.'

'What you talkin' about?' she said. 'I owe you nowt.'

'Correct me if I'm wrong, but 'ow did you end up 'ere baking pies for this party? On account o' me, and my . . .' he paused to belch, then returned to his theme '. . . recommendation. You've me to thank. So come 'ere.'

He seized her round the waist with both hands and pulled her close so that she was trapped against his body.

'C'mon,' he said, all but licking his lips. 'There's plenty o' folk 'avin' a fumble this afternoon, an' no 'arm done.'

She kicked him sharply on the ankle, then brought her knee up into his crotch with all the force she could muster, and he immediately released her, doubling over in helpless response to the pain. And then Amos was there, standing between Eve and Harry, and he was baring his teeth like a dog and shaking with fury.

'Touch 'er again, an' you'll be sorry,' he growled. He gave the landlord a vicious shove, and he staggered backwards, still too absorbed by the pain in his testicles to fully comprehend the situation. 'You 'ear me? You'll wish you were dead, you miserable bastard.'

Then he turned to Eve.

'Did 'e 'urt you? Are you all right?'

'Aye, I'm fine,' she said. 'But thanks for askin'.'

And she bestowed on him a smile of such warmth and humour and loveliness that he knew for sure what he'd feared for a while now: that he loved her.

Inside the great house, the celebration lunch, which began at just after one, was at half-past five only just approaching its lavish conclusion. Toby had spent the entire meal seated between his grandmother – the forbidding Countess of Bromyard – and his simpering maternal aunt, Lady Thomasina Boxwood, a seating arrangement that he surmised, correctly, had been devised to ensure his good behaviour. His grandmother had watched him with gimlet eyes, like an old buzzard hanging in the air above its prey. She noted every sip of wine he took, and seemed, unnervingly, to shake her head at every unspoken rebellious notion he entertained, as if his thoughts were just as clear to her as his words. Meanwhile Lady Thomasina had prattled on, providing an unasked-for commentary on each stage of the meal and detailing precisely how it was superior to the New Year banquet she'd enjoyed at Chatsworth House six months before. Toby felt the boredom like a physical pain, his limbs afflicted by a creeping ache, as if influenza was taking hold. From the moment the gong sounded in the marble hall, the monstrous boom of it bouncing off the cold, hard floor and frescoed ceiling so that there was barely a room in the house not penetrated by the noise, Toby had felt like a condemned man. He yearned to be outside, drinking with the lads and squeezing the luscious backside of Betty Cross, a Netherwood dairy maid and his latest favourite among the local girls. Earlier, as the titled house guests had gathered in the drawing room, he had glimpsed her in a crowd down on the lawn, pink-cheeked and bright-eyed, directing her come-hither laugh at Will Tucker instead of at him. When the family assembled en masse on the terrace before lunch, smiling and waving indulgently, the local royalty acknowledging their subjects, Toby had found himself assessing the drop from the balustrade to the ground, as if there was even the slightest possibility that he might spring free. Self-preservation, not obligation, had kept him in his place.

The meal, even by the standards already set on previous occasions at Netherwood Hall, had been astonishingly complex and accomplished. No detail had been overlooked as the twelve exquisite, tiny courses were served with balletic grace by liveried footmen bearing heavy gold tableware, every item of which was stamped with the Hoyland crest. The table was decorated along its considerable length with an intricate, plaited garland of variegated ivy, interspersed with white and yellow roses, which snaked artfully up and around each of the twenty gold candelabra it met along its path, and at its centre arched dramatically upwards on either side, all the way to the great chandelier. Crystal glassware cast diamonds of light on to the burnished rosewood table and motes of reflected light bounced from the solid gold cutlery, which was arranged outwards from each place setting with mathematical precision in meticulous order of size and function.

The menu, handwritten for each guest in copperplate, was entirely in French, an affectation that irritated the earl; it seemed to him an unnecessary complication when English served perfectly well in all other aspects of life. Such matters were outside his remit, however, and the countess hadn't even thought of seeking his opinion. It very much pleased her to hear the guests' admiring murmurs as they perused the menus placed before them. *Caviar Frais, Consommé Froid Madrilène, Saumon en Croûte, Filet de Boeuf Charolais avec Sauce Béarnaise, Timbale de Homard Royale* – on it went, proof, if proof were needed, that the Hoylands could be relied upon to entertain elegantly, and in style.

The Duke of Bowlby, an extremely grand but limited first cousin of Lady Netherwood, who had been invited not so much for his own sake but for the suitability of his eldest son Charles for Henrietta, leaned across the table towards her.

'My dear Clarissa,' he said, in his unfortunate and much-imitated nasal drawl. 'This is simply magnificent. But what on earth will you do for Bertie?'

She eyed him coldly, much resenting his impertinence. King Edward, in spite of his long-established reputation for lively sociability, had still to bestow his favour at Netherwood Hall. As Prince of Wales he'd been three times and had an exceptionally jolly time, but since his accession to the throne their little corner of the kingdom seemed to have been temporarily forgotten. It hadn't yet gained the status of a full-blown snub, but soon that conclusion would be unavoidable. All this was an immensely entertaining state of affairs for the Hoylands' friends and acquaintances, though as a topic of conversation at the Netherwood Hall table it was entirely taboo. The duke, who in fact was innocent of anything worse than a clumsy assumption that the royal visit was only a matter of time, had nevertheless shown a lamentable lack of form and discretion. Lady Netherwood, prevented by good manners from cutting him entirely, instead answered his question with another on an entirely unrelated topic.

'Must you and Madeleine leave tomorrow?' she said, with practised sincerity. 'I do think the evening after a party is often more fun than the party itself.'

'Ha! Indeed,' said the duke, quite distracted from the king. 'Who said what to whom! I'll speak to the duchess. So kind of you to press.'

Hardly pressing, you old fool, thought Clarissa, but she smiled, her mission accomplished, and turned her attention politely away. She wondered if, after all, the Bowlby boy was perhaps not quite the thing for her daughter. She gazed down the table to seek out Henrietta and found her laughing – a little too loudly than was entirely becoming, as usual – with Jonty Ogleby-James. Only a second son, thought Clarissa, but frightfully dashing. And there, a little further along, was poor Tobias having no fun at all. Poor darling. The Countess of Bromyard, catching her daughter's tender expression, shot back a reproving, steely glance, which for all its familiarity to Clarissa had lost none of its power to chill. The old lady wore a dress of pale blue chiffon and a fine tiara in her soft, grey curls, but battledress – chainmail, perhaps, and a Norman helmet – might have been more apt.

On and on the miniature courses came, held aloft under golden domes until all the footmen were in place behind their pair of assigned diners, then placed and uncovered with unfailing symmetry of movement on to the table. A French pastry chef, with a team of unsmiling assistants, had been employed for the occasion for his continental flair and the cachet of his Parisian pedigree. Even the redoubtable head cook Mrs Adams, sceptical about the merits of foreigners in general and foreign chefs in particular, felt compelled to join in the spontaneous applause in the kitchens at the completion of Monsieur Reynard's confection; sixty edible baskets, crafted from closely woven spun sugar to resemble wickerwork. Concealed beneath their delicate lids was a clutch of wild strawberries dipped in chocolate, resting on a pillow of strawberry mousse.

Lady Thomasina, on Toby's left, bounced in her seat and squealed her delight when dessert was brought to the table; his aunt was long past the age when such girlish behaviour might have been excusable, but her essential silliness had proved to be a trait that hadn't diminished with advancing years. Dickie, diagonally opposite and seated, maddeningly, between the famously beautiful Adamson twins, pulled a fleeting, cross-eyed face at Toby, a device the brothers had used since childhood to lift each other's spirits in adversity. Toby appreciated the gesture, but he was too firmly in the clutches of gloom to smile. Though the meal was almost over – just savouries, fruit and coffee to endure – speeches would doubtless follow, and judging by the discreet activity at the end of the room, a string quartet was threatening to further prolong the agony.

Toby gazed wretchedly into the dregs of his wine glass. Another drink might ease the pain, but the sommelier appeared to be in cahoots with his grandmother and his glass hadn't been refilled for half an hour. Meanwhile his aunt was leaning in to him with what she thought was a winning smile.

'And how has the birthday boy enjoyed his luncheon?' she lisped.

'Very little, Aunt,' said Toby, smiling pleasantly. 'You?'

Lady Thomasina, confused by the contrast between content and delivery, was unsure how to respond, so merely giggled anxiously. The sommelier passed by once again without making eye contact. And at the head of the table, Lord Netherwood was rising to his feet and calling for quiet in order that the speeches might begin.

Truly, thought Toby, had anyone ever suffered as he did?

Chapter 24

Mary Adams had a reputation for being always formidable and occasionally fearsome, but in fact she was only ever either of these things when a situation demanded it. Her reputation may have had its origins in her size: she was an enormously fat woman – after all, no household should employ a skinny cook – with a belly that wobbled like a soft-set blancmange and a huge jutting shelf of a bosom. Added to this generous girth were fleshy jowls, hair the colour and texture of steel wool and large, mannish hands which were as scarred and calloused as a blacksmith's, all of which amounted to an appearance that was somewhat alarming. But Eve Williams, presenting herself for duty on the eve of the party and expecting to be coldly received by a cook with her nose out of joint, had instead been met with not exactly a warm welcome, but a welcome of sorts, at any rate.

'You must be Eve,' Mrs Adams had said, before introducing herself. She had held out one of her huge, floury hands and Eve shook it. She wondered, in passing, why she was Eve and not Mrs Williams.

'I shan't bother with any more introductions, because there'll be no time for talking,' the cook went on. 'You and your pies'll be over there' – she nodded her head in the direction of a large pine work surface – 'and your flour an' all that is over there' – this time she nodded at an open door leading to a series of larders – 'so if I were you I'd get crackin'. Forty-one pies teks some baking.'

'Forty, isn't it?' said Eve.

'Forty for t' marquees, aye. An' one for tastin',' said Mrs Adams. 'We 'ave nothin' but Lord Netherwood's say as to your pies, and that's all well and good but nothin' leaves my kitchen that 'asn't been tasted by me.'

I can see that, thought Eve. She smiled obligingly.

'I wish we could give you more room, but as you can see' – the cook waved a meaty arm in a general arc – 'we're 'ard pressed as it is.'

'No, no, this'll be champion,' Eve had said, thinking as she gazed around that Mrs Adams should spend a day in the kitchen at Beaumont Lane to understand the meaning of hard pressed. The room – there was more than one, in fact, since the kitchens extended further than Eve was able to see – was vast. It was busy as well; there were enough people to pack the platform at Netherwood railway station: a whole descending hierarchy of cooks below Mrs Adams, too many kitchen maids and lads to keep count and a couple of little barefoot village boys in ragged shorts who kept the fires stoked and staggered out with pails of peelings, and waited, silent and cowed, for a clout round the head, or further instructions, whichever came first. In a cooler room, ventilated by open windows, the visiting French pastry chef and his slavish entourage seemed to be spinning sugar into gold, the Rumpelstiltskins of the culinary world.

Oddly, perhaps, Eve found she wasn't nervous in this environment. More oddly still, given the humble dwelling she'd left this evening, she felt almost at home. She could see that, beneath the obvious grandeur, this was simply a kitchen where everything was kept in its proper place and was applied to its proper use. On the walls, the multitudinous pans, bowls and ladles had the burnished gleam of correctly tended copper; the four great ranges, though in near-constant use, shone a deep glossy black, like new; the work surfaces, where not in use, were scrubbed clean and wiped down; there were racks over-head with every kitchen utensil known to woman, and knife blocks well-stocked with sharpened blades for every function; decorative jelly moulds, round, oblong and square, had a long shelf all to themselves; a stockpot, large enough to have bathed Ellen in, simmered on a hob and on another, a wide and shallow bain-marie held ten lidded copper pans of delicate sauce to accompany this evening's supper above stairs. It was like landing in a well-run hive of bees with Mrs Adams as queen. Eve thought, this is my kind of place.

Where she stood, in front of her and just for her use, was a long worktop, about the length and width of her front door. It was equipped with scales and weights, mixing bowls, and an earthenware jug of wooden spoons and spatulas. A slab of cool marble, long and wide, had been placed on the right hand side, intended for working the pastry. The pork, fifty pounds of it, ordered at the beginning of the week from Ernest Simpson in the town – ''ow much?' he'd said – was in barrels, waiting to be chopped, and the bricks of lard and sacks of flour had been stacked on stone shelves in a cold larder, awaiting atten-tion. Eve hadn't really expected any help, but since there was such a great number of girls on hand for everyone else, she wondered if one might be offered. She continued on alone, however. Perhaps, after all, Mrs Adams harboured a little resentment and had decided to leave Eve to scale the pork pie mountain unassisted.

In any case, Eve didn't give a fig. She had never suffered unduly from self-doubt and if there was one thing she under-stood better than most, it was raised pies. She had made so many already in her life, she reasoned, that forty-one more could hardly present a problem, especially in this kitchen. She set about her work cheerfully, and had the first six in the bottom of the nearest range and another batch of pastry resting by the time a brass bell rang to signal supper in the servants' dining hall. There was cheese, gammon slices and bowls of fruit from the glasshouses, all set out on a long pine table, and tea in oversized brown pots or ginger beer poured from jugs. It was like a cross between a church picnic and a harvest festival, thought Eve, but she found she had no appetite, and instead helped herself to a mug of tea then slipped outside with it, to breathe air that wasn't suffused with the smell of pork or pastry. If she'd been at home she'd have sat on the back doorstep, but here she made do with a stone ledge, close to the kitchen door, and sat down with a grateful sigh. The horses, behind their stable doors across the courtyard, gazed at her with interest.

'Mrs Williams?'

Eve jumped, then turned to find Lady Henrietta Hoyland, emerging from the same kitchen door that she had just used. She began to get up, but the young woman protested.

'No, no, please don't get up. Sorry to disturb you. It's just, I recognised you, you see, from the, erm . . .'

'Funeral,' said Eve, helping her out. It was the last time they'd met, though it was months ago now.

'Yes, sorry. Didn't mean to make things awkward.' She smiled, a smile of great charm, and held out a hand to be shaken. 'Henrietta,' she said.

'Eve.'

'How lovely to see you. Daddy said he'd asked you to come and lend a hand.'

Delicately put, thought Eve. As if she was here as a favour, and not for the irresistible lure of eighteen shillings.

'Are you well?' said Henrietta.

'Thank you, yes I am,' Eve said. There was an easiness in Lady Henrietta's manner, and Eve felt no embarrassment at the attention.

'Hard work, I expect. All hands on deck for Toby's party.'

There was the slightest edge to her voice, the merest hint of disapproval, but neither of them acknowledged it. There was a beat of silence, then Henrietta said: 'I'm here to see Beetle. Stole a carrot for him from the kitchen. Plus the kitchen's a short cut, you see, much quicker than walking all round the house.' She leaned in, conspiratorially. 'Beetle's my horse, by the way. Not a groom.'

They both laughed. Gorgeous face, thought Henrietta.

'So,' she said. 'Better dash. Dinner seven-thirty sharp and I'm behind as always.'

'Well, dinner looks lovely, from what I've seen of it,' said Eve.

Henrietta rolled her eyes. 'I expect it is. But what I wouldn't give to skip it. Do you find you're always pleasing others, and never yourself?'

Eve nodded, smiling. Their lives, she thought, were hardly comparable, but perhaps they had that in common.

'Well. Cheerio. Good luck in there, and enjoy the party tomorrow.'

Henrietta smiled again, then left, and Eve watched her cross the courtyard. Polite small-talk with the aristocracy, she thought. Whatever next. She stood and went back inside, where Mrs Adams, on the far side of the room, caught her eye and smiled, showing a kind side. She had seen the first lot of pies, and approved of their shape and size. Proof would be in the tasting, but this young woman seemed to know what she was about and Mrs Adams, though she hadn't said and probably wouldn't, was grateful for the help.

It seemed there was no keeping the Hoylands out of the kitchen. Eve had always assumed, if she thought about it at all, that below stairs was a foreign country to them, but soon after her encounter with Henrietta, Isabella had danced in and demanded – none too politely – toast and jam. Then Tobias showed his face at just after eight o'clock on that busiest of busy evenings, dressed as if for boating, in a striped blazer with patch pockets and brass buttons. He had ducked out of dinner but was looking for a bite to eat before his night out in Netherwood, and Eve watched him turn his soulful, beseeching eyes on the cook, whose resistance melted like butter on the hotplate. You'd think these hungry Hoylands would simply ring a silver bell and wait for service, thought Eve. Instead they were in and out and under the feet like Seth, Eliza and Ellen in her own kitchen. And here was Toby now, tearing a corner from a freshly baked loaf and being greeted by Mrs Adams as if he were a favourite nephew. She called him Master Toby, and he called her Mrs A, and her face took on a delighted flush as he placed an arm round her shoulders, soft-soaping her into letting him have a pie or a pasty.

'Surely you have a morsel to spare,' he said. 'Got to line the old stomach, Mrs A. You don't want me the worse for wear now, do you?'

'It'll not be for lack of food if you are,' she said, trying to be stern. 'It'll be for excess of ale.' But she was laughing, and a little gaggle of kitchen maids were laughing too, edging closer in the hope that they might catch the young lord's eye. Eve stayed put, rolling out pastry and listening to the exchange but with no desire to be part of it, but then Mrs Adams put paid to her desire for anonymity.

'I'll tell you what I can spare,' said the cook. 'A slice of this young woman's pork pie.' She pointed over at Eve. 'It needs tastin' anyway.'

Toby looked across the kitchen to where Eve stood. Ah, the

188

beautiful widow, he thought, right here, just two floors below my bedroom. He widened his green eyes at her and she dipped a little curtsy out of respect for his title, but all the while thinking him an over-indulged dandy.

'Mrs Williams, isn't it?' he said, excessively pleased with himself for pulling her name out of the hat.

'It is, m'lord, yes,' Eve said.

'Oh heavens, don't m'lord me. Makes me sound ancient. So what brings you here?'

'Your father,' she said, obliging him and dropping the title. 'He liked my pork pies.'

'I'll bet he did,' said Tobias, with an inference that Eve found impertinent. 'Well, you're most welcome, Mrs Williams.' He boldly assessed her as he spoke, sizing her up and down with a seasoned eye. 'What a thoroughly decorative addition to the staff.'

Eve, with a whole volley of responses on the tip of her tongue, remained silent. How different he was from his father, she thought.

'She's temp'ry,' said Mrs Adams rather brusquely. She bustled across to where Eve's first batch of pies were now almost cool. They were fine-looking examples, each one perfectly formed and a deep golden-brown. Mrs Adams took a long knife from the nearest block and cut a triangle of pie, sliding it away from the whole with a surgeon's precision. She tipped it on its side, examining the component parts: crisp pastry, soft savoury jelly, tightly packed meat with its nice balance of lean to fat. Tobias, having joined her on Eve's side of the room, reached out to take it and received a slap on the hand from Mrs Adams.

'Manners,' she said. He grinned at her sheepishly and waited to be served.

She cut the slice in two, offered one to Tobias, and took the other for herself. Tobias, cradling the slice in one elegant

189

white hand, bit rather delicately at the sharp end of the triangle. Mrs Adams did the same with hers, though with less finesse, sticking out her tongue to catch the crumbs as the pie approached her mouth. Eve watched her as she chewed and pondered.

'That,' said Tobias, 'is the finest pork pie I have ever had the pleasure of tasting.' He turned to Mrs Adams. 'No offence, Mrs A.'

Eve ignored him. It wasn't his opinion she was interested in. Mrs Adams was still chewing thoughtfully.

'What proportion of fat to flour?' she said through her mouthful.

'For this batch, one stone of flour, four pounds of lard,' said Eve. 'Four pints of water an' a handful of salt.'

Mrs Adams bit again, and chewed.

'And t'jelly? Did you add anything?'

'Well, no. But t'stock comes from boilin' t'gristle I couldn't use in t'pie. It sets better.'

'What's in t'filling. Apart from pork, I mean, and salt and pepper?'

'Essence of anchovy,' said Eve. 'It's not somethin' I can always afford, but Lord Netherwood was generous and—'

'Yes, yes,' said Mrs Adams. 'Well, I can tell you this much for nowt: these pies are beautiful.'

'Thank you,' Eve said. She knew they were, but it was nice to hear it anyway.

'You have special 'ands,' said Mrs Adams. 'Pastry-maker's 'ands. Cool and sure.'

Eve looked at them; they were chapped at the knuckles and lightly dusted with flour. They looked entirely ordinary.

'Special everything, I'd say.' This was Tobias, temporarily forgotten by both of them, licking his fingers and gazing at Eve. He turned to Mrs Adams. 'Can we keep her?' he said.

This was too much.

'I'm kept by no one, as a matter of fact,' said Eve. 'And I'll thank you to remember that. Now I must get on.' She turned her back on him, shaking slightly, indignant. Mrs Adams, anxious that Eve's pastry-making hands should remain cool and composed, ushered Tobias away with a second piece of pie, a consolation prize he was happy to settle for. Entirely unabashed, he sauntered back out of the kitchens, whistling and pinching the occasional backside as he went, leaving behind him a general air of hysteria, as if a fox had just ambled through a chicken coop.

Eve turned and looked at Mrs Adams, unsure of herself, but unrepentant nevertheless.

''e's a good lad at heart,' said the cook. Her expression was part abject, part defensive, like the doting mother of a delinquent son.

Eve was unmoved. ''e thinks t'world's 'is for t'taking,' she said.

'Well, it very often is. 'e means no 'arm, it's just habit as much as owt.'

'If you ask me, 'e needs to resist. Easy enough to get into bad 'abits, devil of a job to get out of 'em.'

'Aye,' said Mrs Adams. 'Same as a big feather bed.'

Curious analogy under the circumstances, Eve thought. But she smiled, keen to draw a line and get on with her pie making. The cook smiled back at her. She had forgotten any trace of hostility she might initially have felt at Eve being hired without her say-so; had forgotten, in fact, that her recruitment was anyone's idea but her own. Because in Eve Williams she saw not a beautiful woman, or even a sensible one, but a woman with a God-given talent for sublime baking. This was indeed something to admire. And Mary Adams knew that unlike beauty or good sense, this gift didn't come ten to the penny.

Chapter 25

'I thought I might take Seth an' Eliza to see Buffalo Bill,' said Amos. 'If it's all right wi' you, that is.' He was walking with Eve and her three children through the park of Netherwood Hall, back towards town. Behind them the revelry continued, though now that the fireworks had been set off, most of those guests with children were making for home. Eve, dog-tired after her labours in the kitchen, and conscious of the picture they presented to the world, had urged Amos to stay. There were plenty of miners there still, and no one had yet thought to limit the supply of beer. But Amos had had enough, he said, and he'd see Eve home safe before turning in himself.

'T'Wild West show?' Eve said. 'I've seen posters in town.' It was a non-committal answer.

'Aye, a proper spectacle. It's summat they'll never forget.'

'When is it?' Eve said.

'October. Barnsley. Custer's Last Stand in t'Queen's Ground. It'll be my treat.'

'Oh no, if you tek 'em, I'm payin',' said Eve.

'But I've nob'dy to spend money on. It could be a birthday present for 'em both, from me, like.'

192

Seth would be eleven at the end of September, and Eliza's ninth birthday was two weeks after her brother's. Eve was both touched and vaguely alarmed that Amos was thinking this way, planning treats for five months hence. And he was carrying Ellen on his shoulders still. Eve had tried to take her before they set off, but Ellen had made a fuss and Amos hadn't helped, tickling Ellen back into a good humour and insisting she stay where she was. Eve wished Anna was with them; her presence would have made all the difference. But she'd left earlier to put Maya to bed and start the bread off for tomorrow. And now they looked like a family, with Amos in Arthur's place.

Still, thought Eve, the local gossips would find ammunition even if she didn't present it to them on a plate, so what was the point fretting? She knew, and Amos knew, that theirs was an innocent friendship, and that was all that really mattered.

'Arthur would've enjoyed today,' she said. Invoking his name was a comfort.

'Aye, 'e would that,' said Amos.

'It were a grand do,' said Eve. 'T'earl's a generous man.'

Amos didn't respond; there'd been two more fatalities in Netherwood since Arthur's death, one at Middlecar and another at New Mill. The wooden posts that held the tunnel roofs in place needed replacing in all three of the earl's collieries, and it was beyond Amos's understanding how Lord Netherwood could apparently jib at the expense, while roasting oxen and lighting rockets for his son's birthday. He regarded the celebration as a monstrous display of lavish personal wealth rather than an act of generosity towards the workers, but he thought that in present company he should keep that opinion to himself. They walked for a few seconds in silence, but it was comfortable enough.

Then Amos said, 'You did a grand job.' Complimenting Eve was safe territory. 'Your pies were flyin' off them tables.'

Eve smiled. 'So I 'eard.'

193

'I expect you'll pick up a bit o' business after this,' Amos said. 'Everybody knew they were yours.'

They walked along in silence again. Up on her perch, Ellen had fallen asleep, one soft cheek pressed against the top of Amos's cap, her head jogging gently with every step he took. Eve had Eliza by the hand, and Seth was well ahead of them, leapfrogging the lichen-covered posts that lined the path they had taken. Eve yawned widely.

'I could do with some of what 'e's got,' she said, pointing at her son.

Amos laughed. 'You've not done so bad,' he said. 'Pork pie queen o' Netherwood. 'ow many did you make?'

'Forty-one,' Eve said. 'Then Mrs Adams got me on game pies for a few hours, and loaves while t'game pies were coolin'.'

She'd stayed on, in fact, long after the terms of her contract had been fulfilled. Mrs Adams hadn't wanted her to leave. They'd had to send a messenger in the early hours of the morning from the big house to Beaumont Lane with a note explaining the situation. Eve had written it, her hand shaking slightly, on Netherwood Hall writing paper. She'd asked Anna to bring the children to the afternoon's entertainments, then to entrust them to Amos's care whenever she needed to leave. The kindness of friends, thought Eve now, was something on which she entirely depended. True, Anna had board and lodging for her part of the deal, but all Amos got was extra work after his shift at the pit. If he wasn't planting veg on her behalf, he was minding her children.

She looked sideways at him now, striding along beside her. Arthur used to say he'd come to resemble his bulldog, Mac, and while this was overstating the case, it was true that they shared a similar pugnacious set to the features. He was small – shorter than Eve and she was only five foot three – but he was wiry and strong. For a widower, he was a fastidious man, his nails always scrubbed clean of pit muck and his hair tidy. Eve thought about his late wife. She knew very little about her, only that her name was Julia and that she'd died in child-birth, then was followed to the grave by their first child a day later. They'd only been married for a twelvemonth. There was a headstone in the same churchyard where Arthur now lay; In Loving Memory of Julia Sykes and Frances Mary Sykes, it said, then came the dates which told the story, followed by the words May You Rest in Peace Together. There was a vale of sorrows contained in that simple inscription, thought Eve, and she felt a wash of shame that she'd never spoken to Amos on the subject.

'What was Julia like?' she said now, on an impulse.

He started slightly and Ellen stirred, up on his shoulders, then settled again.

'Sorry,' said Eve.

'No, no, yer all right,' Amos said. 'It's just, that's t'first time in years anybody's said 'er name out loud.'

'Oh, Amos, that's so sad.'

'Well, who is there to mention 'er? She's been dead more 'n twenty years.'

'So what was she like?' Eve said, again.

Amos thought about it. It wasn't easy for him to answer, not because it was painful, but because he'd lived so long without her. He remembered her not as a whole, but in small, disconnected details like the scar on her calf from a childhood dog bite, or the strange fleck of blue in one of her brown eyes. But he had to say something.

'She were nobbut a child when we wed. Just sixteen,' he said. 'Tiny, like a little bird. Not a beauty, but she 'ad summat.'

'Like Arthur. Not a beauty, but 'e 'ad summat.'

They both laughed fondly at Arthur's unquestionable lack of beauty. And they walked on to Beaumont Lane, where Amos

195

handed over Ellen, somehow heavier asleep than when awake, then said goodnight and carried on alone.

Inside, in spite of the long day and the lateness of the hour, Anna's face was alight with excitement.

'What?' said Eve, with the smallest of warnings in her voice. She was in no mood for revelations, wanting only to sink into a chair and let the healing properties of strong tea revive her for the work still to be done before bed.

'I have idea,' said Anna.

'*An* idea.' Eve corrected her automatically. Anna took it for encouragement.

'*Da*, an idea,' she said. 'You want hear?'

'Not really,' said Eve.

'Imagine scene. *A* scene,' said Anna, correcting herself this time. 'Small tables with pretty cloths, maybe jugs of flowers.'

'Sounds nice,' said Eve.

'Set for lunch.'

'Dinner,' said Eve.

'Or dinner.'

'Tea,' said Eve.

Anna conceded, with a nod of her head, that she should perhaps, by now, be using the local terms for meal times, though for her, dinner would always be a meal taken in the evening, while tea was always and for ever a hot drink.

'So. Daily menu, with simple hot meals, served to paying customers who sit at tables,' said Anna.

'Sounds like t'Central Café in Barnsley,' said Eve. 'Oxtail soup, sausage an' mash, poached egg on toast. Oooh, do we 'ave any eggs? I'd kill for a couple.'

'So,' said Anna, ignoring her. 'As well, we sell usual things

196

at door – pies, puddings – but also feed customers here, at our tables.'

'I beg your pardon?' said Eve, suddenly cottoning on.

'Eve's Café!' Anna, like a child on Christmas morning, was wide-eyed and pink-cheeked. She looks like Eliza's china doll, thought Eve. What a shame it was to disappoint her.

'No,' she said.

'But—'

'Absolutely not.'

'If you just—'

'Absolutely, definitely not.'

'Why?' said Anna.

'Because we haven't t'space. Because we haven't any tables and chairs. Because folk wouldn't come. Because we only have one pair of hands each.'

Anna, her voice beseeching, said, 'We do have space, if we move things a little. We buy tables and chairs. People will come. They love your food.'

Eve sat forwards in her chair. 'Anna,' she said. 'We're managing to run a good little business, but perhaps you 'aven't noticed that we're flat out doin' it. 'ave you heard t'expression "t'straw that broke t'camel's back"?'

Anna, a touch sulkily, said, 'No.'

'But you know what I'm getting at?' said Eve. 'Because between us we just manage all t'shoppin' and choppin' and stewin' and bakin', not to mention t'cleanin', washin' and feedin' of four children. T'very last thing we want to be doin' is inviting folk in to that parlour for their dinner or their tea. Especially miners in their mucky britches.'

Anna said nothing. She knew it was a good idea, just as she knew Eve would say no. Now, it was simply a matter of waiting.

Chapter 26

On Sunday, after church but before luncheon, the countess and Lady Henrietta left Netherwood for Fulton House in Belgravia, the family's London mansion. Lady Netherwood had felt in need of diversion since the house guests had dispersed, and London society would provide the perfect antidote to the ennui that had stolen over her since waking on Friday morning. Lady Netherwood craved variety. She liked a diary full of engagements, witty company, pretty garments that were Absolutely the Latest Thing. So she had proposed what she called a 'girls' jaunt' which generally involved the twin pleasures of shopping and tea-taking. Sometimes she went alone to London, in which case she also indulged her taste for elegant gentlemen, whose ardent attentions made her feel younger and more vital, and quite restored her *joie de vivre*. Pleasures of the flesh, in actual fact, held little real interest for her, though occasionally she would allow one of her admirers an intimate liaison, just to keep them panting. But her excursions to the capital weren't simply for social gratification, because in London, too, lay all the novelty of recent modernisation; the earl had just spent a fortune on bathrooms and lavatories throughout, and electric lights now performed daily miracles where once only gas lamps and smoky sconces had lit the scene. For all these reasons, Fulton House was absolutely her favourite place to be – that is, until she tired of it, and yearned again for her Netherwood garden.

The jaunt excluded young Lady Isabella, who was still by and large kept prisoner by her nurse and her governess. She knew her mother and sister would return in a few days' time with a tantalising collection of tied paper parcels and striped hat boxes, most of which would not be for her and it was a tragedy of circumstance that young Isabella, so much more generously endowed with materialism than Henrietta, was made to stay at home. She had watched them leave, gazing glumly from the rain-streaked nursery window as they processed down Lime Avenue away from the house. Henrietta and the luggage were squashed into the Daimler and they followed behind Lady Netherwood, who refused – at least in this regard – to move with the times and give up the landau. They were heading for the family railway station, a private facility known locally as Hoyland Halt, quite separate to the busy station built by the Midland Railway Company and used by the rest of Netherwood's population. The fifth earl, Lady Netherwood's father-in-law, had commissioned the building of the station and the laying of the tracks for the family's private use and it had remained entirely at their disposal ever since. The intervening years had seen an enormous increase in the comings and goings of passengers, goods and coal trains to the town, but the little station was never used for industrial purposes, and the handsome dark green locomotive bearing the Hoyland crest was ever available for the earl and countess. So much better, even the countess conceded, than rattling and bouncing one's way south in a coach-and-four. Mrs Adams had packed wicker hampers with a light luncheon for the ladies, and these were loaded on to the locomotive, along with padded baskets bearing produce from the kitchen garden and destined for the Fulton House kitchen.

199

The earl, like Isabella, had also watched the ladies leave. His expression was anxious as the Daimler bearing his older daughter juddered into life and set off down the driveway. His anxiety stemmed not from their imminent absence from the family home, however, but from the fact that the last time Atkins had driven the car, its motor had inexplicably failed to start for the return journey, and he'd had to be ignominiously towed home by a couple of plough shires borrowed from the farm. So Lord Netherwood breathed an audible sigh of relief as, now, the vehicle accelerated smoothly then receded, diminished still further, and finally disappeared altogether from view.

The earl was dressed in his shooting tweeds with Min and Jess, his two black Labrador retrievers at his side, though all he actually intended to do was take an instructive stroll through the estate with Jem Arkwright, his land steward. There was flooding at the Home Farm again and Jem had some new ideas about improving the drainage. Teddy's ruddy face bore the expression of a man profoundly satisfied with his lot; there was little he enjoyed more than a long discussion with Jem about the condition of his land, his buildings, his stock or his boundary fencing. All of this and more would be covered in their walk today, which would conclude with a pint of ale at the Hoyland Arms in the full and certain knowledge that, on his return, he would not be required to dress for dinner. He watched a thin plume of smoke rise from the lower lawns and trail into the cloudless sky; Hislop had a bonfire of wet leaves on the go. You could keep your colognes and your potpourris, thought the earl. Bottle that smell and you'd be a wealthy man.

Teddy stooped to slap his dogs heartily on their glossy, muscular haunches. 'Always a red-letter day when the old girl takes off, ey?' he said to them. He was fond of the countess, but fonder still, on balance, of his Labradors. Fortunately he had never been forced to choose between them, and found

200

that the way Clarissa organised her life meant that he managed to spend more time in canine company than in hers. They had both realised, soon after their marriage, that a prolonged period together was good for neither of them, since the more time they spent in each other's pockets, the less they seemed to have in common. Once upon a time, many years ago, they had at least shared a physical attraction for each other, and Teddy's bedtime visits to her rooms had been frequent and mutually fulfilling, not to mention extremely productive, having provided an heir, a spare and a brace of lovely daughters. But that was then. These days, the earl was stout and occasionally gouty, and he neither sought nor received encouragement from his wife. When he needed it he found sexual relief with a discreet widow in Bloomsbury, whose clients were only of the very best kind, and in Netherwood he managed perfectly well without. There was enough on the estate to occupy him, frankly. And in any case, if he was honest, the quest for sexual ecstasy was proving increasingly exhausting. All that thrashing and straining seemed barely worth the goal.

None of this, of course, was passing through the earl's mind as he fussed his dogs and inhaled the restorative garden air. Jem Arkwright was usually to be found at his desk even on a Sunday, so the dogs sprang down the steps followed a little stiffly by the earl who crunched round the gravel sweep to the courtyard at the back of the house, a cobbled quad made up of stables and coach houses on two sides, and by estate offices on the other. Dickie had announced his intention to ride after church and his stallion, Marley, was saddled and ready in the yard, and, judging by the strenuous efforts of the little groom who held him, in a state of eager anticipation. The earl nodded to the boy, who stood to attention like a private on parade, while still hanging on to Marley's bridle.

'Walk him round the yard before he makes a bolt for it,' said Teddy. The boy nodded respectfully.

'Yes m'lud,' he said, although he didn't move from where he stood. There was a whisper among the stable hands that the master's head had been turned by motor cars and his judgement skewed when it came to the horses. It was nonsense, of course, a theory born out of resentment that the coach and horses often lay idle while the Daimler was pressed yet again into action, but nevertheless Marley, just short of seventeen hands high, was a headstrong, restless beast and the young groom knew that once he was saddled he really needed the weight of a rider to keep him in check. If he set off with him round the yard, the horse would be halfway to Lancashire by the time Master Dickie had pulled his riding boots on. Groom and steed watched the earl warily but, having issued his instruction, the earl didn't linger to see it carried out because Jem was emerging from his office, shrugging his broad shoulders into a mud-spattered waxed jacket, and greeting the earl heartily. The two men swung in unison out of the yard, followed by the dogs.

Teddy had hoped that Tobias might join them. By his age the earl had known the features of his land better than he knew his own reflection in the looking glass; he'd been walking the estate since boyhood, and there was no aspect of its maintenance, improvement or upkeep that didn't fascinate him. Toby, on the other hand, showed a lamentable indifference; he just wasn't interested. He knew nothing about the collieries either, nothing about coal production, nothing about the workforce. Not once in his twenty-one years had he asked a sensible question about anything relating to estate matters. Henrietta, now, was a different story. Damned shame she was a girl, because she would have made a splendid heir. But there was no altering the order of things. The title would be Toby's, and he would have to be made to face his responsibilities. He was a slippery customer though, thought the earl, as he and Jem strode out towards the Home Farm. This morning he had declined his father's invitation with such charming and courteous regret that Teddy had quite forgotten he meant to insist.

'We shall 'ave to dig new gravel pits, run the water off the grazing land,' said Jem. His words brought Teddy back, most willingly, from the vexing issue of his first-born son, and he gave his full attention to the poor drainage in the lower fields and Jem's fascinating theory that if the trenches were this time dug in a herringbone pattern, the matter might be resolved once and for all.

It was always cold in the dairy, necessarily so, considering the purpose of the place, and always, lingering in the air, was the smell of cheese. Sour, but not unpleasantly so. Even at the height of the summer the sun never fell directly on to this building, thanks to its clever positioning, and all along the walls, one inch from the floor, little openings let in air to further cool the cream and the milk and the cheese. The floor was made of stone flags, the walls were roughly plastered and whitewashed and the single small window had slatted shutters, which today were closed, though not for shade but for privacy.

Tobias lay spent and spreadeagled on the floor. His britches were round his ankles, and the flagstones were cold against his bare buttocks, though the rest of him was warm enough. Betty Cross knelt astride him, fully clothed except for her drawers, which had been pulled off and tossed aside half an hour earlier. She smiled at him lazily and squirmed, fractionally, from side to side. Tobias moaned, half in ecstasy, half in pain, as his newly flaccid penis registered the movement. He watched her through hooded, sleepy eyes; her fingers slowly unlaced the ties of her coarse cotton chemise to reveal more of her breasts, then she leaned forwards, supporting herself on her arms and hanging over him, dropping low until his mouth was so close to her flesh that, had he wished, he could have taken a bite.

'Well, well, Lord Fulton,' she said in a mocking tone. Her breath smelled of Parma violet, and her teeth were sharp and white, like a cat's. Her eyes were feline too, and they gazed directly at him, bold and challenging. 'What business do you 'ave on t'dairy floor?'

He smiled back, then with a practised manoeuvre he heaved to the side, tipping Betty over and round and supporting her with one arm until she was underneath him, grinning up at him now rather than down.

'The same business as you, Betty Cross,' he said. He felt her legs widen and her pelvis tilt, inviting him in. She was bold and greedy, and Toby marvelled at her brazen desire. This was his kind of girl. Her face was flushed, but her throat and breasts were the colour of cream. He'd noticed this about girls who worked in the dairy and wondered vaguely if there was a connection but the question for now remained unanswered, as the blood rushed away from his head and robbed him of rational thought.

Chapter 27

Harry Tideaway had pushed on with his plan to open the Hoyland Arms on Sundays, but it hadn't yet become the money-spinner he was hoping for. Sometimes he would stand behind the bar on the Sabbath, drumming his fingers and watching the hands creep round the clock face, while old peg-leg Bill Whitlow made a half of best last until the bell rang for time at half-past two. Still, he told himself, it was early days, and there was a regular handful of reliable Sunday drinkers who just about justified the trouble of sliding back the bolts on the big front door at midday. The fact that one of them, more often than not, was the earl meant he had moral authority on his side too – Lord Netherwood's endorsement being as good as a legal document in these parts.

It was almost closing time this Sunday when the earl entered the public bar, followed by his dogs and Jem Arkwright, and their appearance caused a small ripple of respectful interest. Harry Tideaway stood a little straighter behind the bar and rolled down his shirt sleeves, fastening them quickly at the cuffs with the studs he kept handy in a dish. Agnes smoothed her apron and looked down at her clogs. The assembled customers, few as they were, tipped their caps and murmured a collective greeting and in response Teddy boomed a general hello around the room, addressing no one and everyone. In any case, it was difficult to make out individual faces in the gloomy interior: dark-brown paint on the upper walls, dark-brown panelling on the lower portion, a warm fug of tobacco smoke suspended permanently in the air.

'Good day to you, Mr Tideaway, Miss Tideaway,' said the earl, full of fresh air and bonhomie. 'Two pints of best, if you please.'

Harry was already filling the pewter tankard reserved for Lord Netherwood's exclusive use.

'Your very good health, gentlemen,' he said.

They drank, silently, intently, then sighed in unison as their initial thirst was slaked. Jem wiped the foam from his whiskers.

'By God,' he said. 'That 'it t'spot.'

Harry, still standing before them on his side of the bar, said: 'Grand do last week, yer lordship.' Apart, he thought, from the injury to my bollocks – an insult that still seethed, unredressed, in his private musings.

Jem scowled. He had earned his own familiarity with the earl through fifteen years of loyal service and shared interests, but Harry Tideaway was a Johnny-come-lately and had no business being so forward. Teddy, however, rarely pulled rank. Also, he was rather proud at the way Tobias's party had passed off.

'Good show, good show,' he said, which was rather meaningless, but inspired further confidence in Harry, whose broad face now beamed at the earl with a significant smile.

'I gather that lad o' yours 'ad t'time of 'is life,' he said.

Jem bridled. The earl looked at Harry, askance.

'I beg your pardon?' he said.

Dismissive as he generally was about the complexities of the social pecking order, there was something in the cut of this fellow's jib that Teddy found impertinent. Jem stared hard at Harry; he considered speaking out, then decided to let the landlord go hang himself, which he duly did.

'T'young lord,' he said. 'I gather 'e was scooped up and carried off in t'cart with t'drunks by accident.'

He gave a hearty bellow which rang out in the room, loud and inappropriate.

Teddy said, 'Is that so?' in a perfectly pleasant tone of voice, but the ticking of the big wall clock was suddenly the loudest sound in the pub.

Agnes looked up from her clogs, and gazed at her father, mute but appalled. Harry, uncomfortably aware now that he had misread the situation, tried to regain lost ground. It was only idle gossip, he said, and it was almost certain to be unfounded. Foolish of him, really, to repeat it, and could he refill that tankard?

But the damage done was beyond repair. Harry Tideaway had unwittingly broached the one subject on which Teddy Hoyland had no sense of humour. He left his unfinished beer on the bar, snapped his fingers irritably at Min and Jess, and stalked out of the pub. The door swung shut behind them, and all eyes were on Harry.

Jem drained his glass of beer then said, 'Tha'd do well, 'arry Tideaway, to take a leaf out o' thi daughter's book and keep thi gob shut.'

Then he walked out too, though he judged, rightly, that his company was no longer required, and he set off back on an alternative route to the one taken by the earl. Harry, perspiring slightly, watched him leave then turned to Agnes.

'What you bloody staring at?' he said nastily, and she shrank from him like a whipped cur.

Harry Tideaway, of course, was only saying what all the town knew – that Tobias had been piled unceremoniously into the horse-drawn cart that was sent through the grounds after the party to clear away the drunken sots. They were thrown on top of each other, like carcasses on their way to the meat market, and driven outside the gates where they were dumped in the wet grass and left to sober up. Before this point Tobias, feeling noble and heroic, had endured the protracted family celebration until late evening; he had listened to the string quartet, he had flirted with all the titled young ladies towards whom he was steered by his mother, he had even played a couple of rubbers with his ridiculous Aunt Thomasina, whose bridge-playing skills and strategies were as limited as a kitten's. Only when his hawk-eyed grandmother announced her intention to retire did Toby make his bid for freedom, slipping from the proceedings and making a circuitous journey down the servants' staircases and out into the night through the kitchen wing at basement level.

Like a condemned man given an eleventh-hour reprieve, Toby sought, and found, the raucous company he had been craving all night. The last thing he could recall, when he woke up on the scrap heap of bodies the following morning, was lying gaping-mouthed underneath the open tap of a barrel of ale, gulping at the free-flowing liquid in a race towards oblivion, egged on in his endeavour by a braying crowd.

Lord Netherwood had known nothing of this. In fact, he had been under the illusion that Tobias's behaviour, once the celebrations had begun, had been exemplary, and had even entertained the notion that perhaps his oldest son was at last beginning to behave with some dignity. He stomped along Victoria Street and on to Stead Lane, heading out of town past the silent headstocks of Middlecar colliery, past the brick-works and on towards home. The roads turned to lanes and the shops and houses gave way to hedgerows, but he noticed none of this because he'd been made to feel a fool, and he was fuming. A robust, imagined dialogue between himself and his errant son was occupying his mind: he was an apology for a son, an embarrassment to his title and the family name was being dragged into disrepute as a result of his antics. The earl would make Toby see, once and for all, that aristocratic privilege could not be enjoyed without a proper regard for one's responsibilities.

On he strode, towards and through the magnificent gates of Oak Avenue, and on down the gentle slope of the driveway where the towering trees stretched out their great leaf-laden boughs against a blue, early summer sky. The house hoved into view, imposing and implausibly grand even from this great distance, its windows flashing in the sunlight, as if to welcome the earl back from his travels. But he remained unmoved by the sight, lost in his thoughts, and continued on until he was close enough to Netherwood Hall to see the figures moving within; maids would be setting out tea things, lighting the flames beneath the great silver pot, pulling the wing chair just so in front of the fire, ready for his return. Now, finally, the earl registered pleasure at the unaltering glory of home and the limitless comforts within, and he felt the merest lifting of his dark mood. Earl Grey, crumpets and perhaps, given Clarissa's absence, a cigar. He would summon Tobias to the drawing room and over tea, in a civilised and gentlemanly fashion, he would set out his expectations for his son's future conduct.

The footmen at the great front door stood to attention at the sound of the earl's boots on the gravel, but he swung past the main entrance to the rear of the house and into the stable block where the Daimler, long returned from its jaunt to the railway station, was being buffed back to its newly minted shine by Atkins, the driver. The sight of the handsome vehicle warmed Teddy's heart still further, and he congratulated Atkins on his scrupulous guardianship. The earl's black mood had

209

dissipated now, leaving him with a purposeful but peaceful resolve. He left the Labradors with a stable lad to be cleaned off and kennelled, and stood for a moment to admire the sun which at this time of day hung low enough in the sky to be framed by the arch of the clocktower. As he stood, he heard a tap-tapping on glass, and he turned and looked up to see Isabella, his darling baby, waving at him from an upstairs window. He waved back and made as if to move, but she shook her head, ringlets bouncing, and began to push open the sash window.

'Papa,' she said through the gap. 'Wait there!'

Teddy did as he was bid, smiling indulgently up at the window. Isabella had dashed off, but almost instantly she was back, with something quite flat and white in her hand.

'Bet you can't catch this,' she called, and with a deft flick of her wrist she launched a paper dart through the gap in the window. He laughed indulgently, watching it loop-the-loop on its downward trajectory. It weaved crazily, impossible to catch, and ended its journey with a final, desperate lurch before landing nose down, several yards from where Teddy stood.

Isabella, in a manner she knew to be enchanting, blew a kiss to her father. She had none of the reserve that her siblings showed towards him. She said, 'Fetch the dart, Papa, I'm coming down,' in a peremptory tone which would have earned a reprimand for any of the other three at the same age, and she flitted from the window, a blur of blue cotton and brown curls. Teddy gazed for a moment at the space she'd left, then, still smiling, he ambled over to the paper dart, which had flown surprisingly far, insubstantial as it was.

The earl crossed the courtyard and stooped to retrieve the dart. Its nose was bent and slightly damp, and he tried to straighten it before Isabella appeared, pulling at the tip with his fingers and sharpening the crease along its spine. As he stood there an incongruous yet familiar noise began to penetrate his consciousness, muffled but none too distant. Intrigued, he followed the sound, which took him just out of the courtyard to a long, low run of outbuildings.

It was unmistakably the sound of rutting, thought the earl, and it seemed to be coming from the dairy. Intent on discovery, he quite forgot that Isabella was approaching and he flung open the wooden door just as his young daughter arrived by his side, to reveal the unedifying and shameful sight of Tobias and Betty Cross *in flagrante delicto* on the flagstone floor.

In the fuss that followed, the chief crime became the terrible shock to Isabella's sensibilities, the fatal blow to her childish innocence, though in actual fact it wasn't the first time she'd caught Tobias similarly engaged. She knew his favourite haunts and she was a careful, crafty little spy. But, while she was very attached to her oldest brother, she was also too fond of the limelight to forgo the opportunity of causing a scene. Afterwards, with the benefit of hindsight and considering the almighty row that ensued, she felt she might have screamed a little less and certainly wouldn't have pretended to faint. But she did scream tremendously and collapsed magnificently to the floor, and her doting father – who had taken his fair share of servant girls in his day, many of them rather less willing than Betty – nevertheless found he could not forgive or forget.

Chapter 28

~~~~~~~~~

Amos sat underground eating his snap and listening to the idle chat of the men around him. Since Arthur's fatal accident, he and Lew worked apart; he was in a team of four these days with Jonas Buckle, Barry Stevens and Sam Bamford. Long ago, when death was an even more regular occurrence than now, it had been considered bad luck to simply fill the place of a dead collier with someone new in an established team. Now, though, it was avoided less out of superstition than as a mark of respect for a dead colleague. It suited Amos, who couldn't tolerate Lew without the moderating presence of his old friend. And it suited Lew, for similar reasons. They didn't even accompany each other to work any more – Lew had been given a day's paid compassionate leave by the earl after the accident, then when he returned to work he felt awkward about passing the Williams's house on Beaumont Lane where Arthur had always joined him. Instead he'd taken himself off on an alternative route; it took him slightly longer, but it meant he often hooked up with young Frank Ogden, whose junior status at the pit gave Lew a new and pleasant feeling of wisdom and superiority. He and Amos were still on nodding terms at work, but their paths didn't cross so much as they once had.

Barry Stevens, foul-mouthed and lewdly funny, was describing, with actions, exactly what dowdy young Agnes Tideaway needed to put a smile on her face. Jonas was sniggering and Sam was laughing so hard that tears left ludicrous tracks down his dirty cheeks. Amos, serious-minded and with no appetite for the pantomime, sat watching with an expression that rattled Barry.

''s'up wi' thee?' he said, sitting back down. He wasn't best pleased at working with Amos Sykes. There was something unsettling in his steady gaze. Barry liked to entertain, but Amos was a poor audience.

'Nowt's up wi' me,' Amos said evenly.

'Miserable bastard,' said Barry.

'Mucky sod,' said Amos.

There was no real animosity in the exchange and they continued to sit together, backs against the rocky tunnel wall, chewing their way through the predictable contents of their snap tins. Amos let his thoughts wander to Eve, as they often did at times like this when his mind and body were unoccupied by hard labour. He carried his feelings for her like a heavy load and he had no idea how to unburden himself. He wished he had more words at his disposal. Not poetry, just something other than the vocabulary that served well enough for a humdrum life, but let him down in the event of this extraordinary occurrence: the blooming of love in his miner's heart.

'Grudge match this Sat'day,' said Jonas. He was referring to the knur-and-spell fixture against Middlecar at the weekend, but Jonas always spoke in shorthand, preferring not to waste time with verbs.

'Aye,' said Amos. He'd been asked to step in for Arthur, and had done so not for himself but for Seth. He'd thought the lad might have been upset at the prospect, but in fact he'd begged Amos to take his father's place on the team and had tagged along to every home fixture so far, carrying Amos's equipment, cleaning the knur, even whipping new heads on to the pummel when the conditions called for it. He'd be a grand player himself in due course.

'Am surprised tha'r available,' said Barry, still feeling hostile towards Amos. 'Thought tha'd be with thi comrades this weekend.' He lingered over comrades, investing it with contempt.

Amos ignored him. There was a fair pay march through Barnsley on Saturday, and though he risked his job every time he showed his face on such occasions he damn well would be there, just briefly, before coming back for the match. Barry didn't need to know though; that was information he could use against Amos if the fancy took him so why supply him with the ammunition? Amos felt only disdain for the likes of Barry Stevens, who would be happy enough to reap the benefits of the struggle but was constantly sniping from the sidelines all the same. The march on Saturday was a peaceful protest – if the police allowed it to be – with modest ambitions, but Barry and his ilk liked to pretend the Yorkshire Miners' Association was after world domination, and as for the earl, with his bans and his edicts, well, Amos wondered what it was he feared.

Sam Bamford said, 'It's time tha started marchin' thissen, Barry. Tha'll be t'first in t'queue on pay day when we win a minimum wage.'

Barry laughed, a short, cynical bark.

'Sam's right,' Amos said. 'Fair day's pay for a fair day's work – tha don't 'ave to be a revolutionary to want that.'

'No, but tha'd 'ave to be an idiot to think it could 'appen,' Barry said. 'Anyroad, I've no complaints about my wages.' He patted his rump, as if the money was there now, waiting to be spent on the way home.

Amos rolled his eyes, partly bored, partly exasperated. He was sick to death of this argument. He'd thought the cold-blooded defeat of the Grangely miners might fan the political flames at New Mill. In fact, the reverse was true; he seemed to be surrounded by men with an I'm-all-right-Jack mentality. Who needed union membership when the earl drove round town in his big car, dishing out ten-bob notes? Folk were too easily bought, he reckoned.

Jonas, with no strong opinion either way, brought the conversation back to Saturday's match. A knur-and-spell victory against Middlecar was very much uppermost in his mind, and he was worried now that Amos wouldn't be there after all. Bugger the fight for better pay and conditions, he was thinking; more to the point, could New Mill field a full team?

He voiced his concerns and earned a withering look from Amos. Yes, he said, he'd be there. But he wondered at the intellectual calibre of his colleagues, when the greater good of the working man came a very poor second to a couple of hours' entertainment on Netherwood Common.

It turned out that Anna was a fine needlewoman – the legacy of her idle, affluent youth, when a tapestry cushion cover was the only task requiring her attention on long winter's evenings. Now, on those rare occasions when there was nothing more pressing for her to do, she took up a needle and thread, and sitting in the circle of light cast by the old paraffin lamp she mended holes and tears in the children's clothes and even ran up new garments from odds and sods she picked up for next to nothing from Solomon Windross. In fact there was enough money these days to buy bolts of cloth from the draper, but Anna seemed to take real pleasure in reinvention. A blue serge door curtain had become two extremely serviceable pairs of gardening overalls for Seth, who kept putting out the knees of his trousers, kneeling to plant pea plants and broad beans. The new trousers, like Anna, had a foreign look about them, but Eve couldn't put her finger on what it was. The cut of the leg and the depth of the waistband somehow had a flavour of the mysterious world she'd come from, just as her knotted headscarf or her centre parting and thick plaits twisted into a crown around her head gave Anna the same indefinably un-English quality. Eliza and Ellen now asked for their hair to be done the same way, and when they wore the red pinafores made by Anna, with two bands of ribbon trim around the hem of the full skirts, she called them her little matryoshkas.

'See,' Anna said. 'We take off your head, Eliza, and pop Ellen inside!'

There were no Russian dolls in Netherwood so the girls had looked at her blankly. Anna had to draw a set for them, showing five little gaily clad, apple-cheeked women in descending order of height. Eliza thought they looked more desirable than anything she'd ever seen.

There was no talk of Anna going home. Her presence was as completely necessary to Eve as Eve's was to Anna. Like two cogs in a machine, their lives were mutually dependent and though no conversation had been held, no conscious decision taken, it was agreed that Anna was home already. It was a shame Samuel Farrimond didn't realise this, thought Eve, when he came over one evening, waving a copy of the London *Times* and reading aloud in his sonorous, pulpit voice about continued violent unrest in Russia: Jews murdered in their beds, houses and businesses looted and destroyed. Anna muttered to herself in her native tongue and Eve could see conflict in her face, a mix of shame, sorrow and regret for her homeland.

'"The mob was led by priests,"' read Reverend Farrimond. '"And the general cry 'kill the Jews' was taken up all over the city." Can this be so, Anna?'

She shrugged her foreign shrug, all arms and shoulders.

'Perhaps. I don't know. There is much fear and ignorance in Russia.'

He drove home his message, which Eve had come to realise was the purpose of all his visits to them; 'Well, I know you're not a Jewess, my dear, but you must stay here until it's safe to leave. Who would return to such a country, where these atrocities are carried out and the authorities merely look on, unmoved.'

'Sounds like Grangely,' Eve said, to get him off the subject. He folded the paper and set it down on the kitchen table.

'Well, we haven't seen murder on the streets or religious persecution yet, but I do take your point,' he said. Grangely was as sad a town as ever, the fire in the bellies of the militant miners entirely quenched, the dismal little tied houses occupied once more. It was as well for Grangely, thought Eve, that their Methodist minister had such a strong calling and that he wasn't inclined to pack his trunk and take up a picturesque post in the Lake District or the Derbyshire Dales. There wasn't much to celebrate in Grangely but Reverend Farrimond's genteel, intelligent presence was, literally, a godsend.

'So,' he said now. 'What tidings? How's business?'

'Brisk,' said Eve, which was an understatement. Her front-door shop continued to sell out daily, and on top of that she had – as Amos had predicted – picked up new customers from Lord Fulton's party. Orders from some of the more well-heeled guests had started to arrive the day after the function. Eve had answered a knock on her back door and found a smart young delivery boy from Wilkinson's Comestibles. He wore a short navy jacket and a peaked hat with the company name stitched in red across the front; Wilkinson's was a shop for the monied middle classes and they dressed their staff accordingly. If he hadn't been about the same age as Seth, Eve might have felt a little overawed by his military bearing. As it was he made her laugh, clicking his heels and introducing himself very formally as Albert Osgathorpe, before handing her a letter on thick vellum requesting a regular consignment of twenty raised pies every Thursday morning. A representative of Wilkinson's, it said, would collect the produce from her at eight o'clock prompt each week. She was to entrust her reply to young Master Osgathorpe, who would cycle all the way back to the shop's distinguished premises in Market Street, Barnsley.

Eve – lacking her own headed notepaper – had told Albert to pedal back with the answer yes, and she gave him a slice of new bread spread with beef dripping before sending him on his way.

She'd no sooner closed the door on him when Mavis Moxon, housekeeper at the rambling old vicarage by St Peter's, stopped by to ask Eve for ten pies for the church fête two weeks on Saturday. And while she and Mrs Moxon were still speaking, a lad turned up from Squires' butchers with an order for raised pies to sell in the cooked meats counters in all three of their branches.

In the weeks since then, there'd been still more requests for regular deliveries, while the line outside her front door when she opened up in the mornings was never less than the length of the street. News was exchanged, gossip was spread and friendships were formed and broken in the queue for Eve's Puddings & Pies. She'd branched out a little, selling dishes of Anna's stuffed cabbage leaves and a clear brown chicken soup made from simmering the bones of the bird for hours in the bottom of the range. Anna said it was Leo's recipe; he had called it Jewish medicine, the cure for all coughs, colds and even sadness of the spirit, and they sold it in jars with rubber seals and metal clasps. The initial general suspicion towards Anna and her foreign food had been eclipsed by the enthusiasm for how good it was – enthusiasm, that is, expressed in the traditional Yorkshire way, which is to say that although no one complimented it, every day it sold out. There was a penny charge these days for the dishes, repayable on return. In the early days Eve had sent Eliza to fetch them back, but she proved an unreliable courier; always at least one would be dropped and smashed on the trip home.

So when Eve said 'Brisk' in answer to Samuel Farrimond's kindly interest, she was hiding the fact that the business, though undoubtedly thriving, was threatening to run her into the ground. She fell into bed every night dog-tired at gone midnight, but would be awake again before dawn with the weight of her new responsibilities closing in on her. She had anxiety-induced dreams where angry customers bore down on her shop with blazing torches, or where all her stock was eaten by a pack of crazed fox hounds. Being asleep, she said to Anna one morning, was more exhausting than being awake. Anna told her she should embrace her success, not resist it.

'Expand,' she said, illustrating her point with widespread arms. She was such a physical speaker, thought Eve; she used her body as much as her voice. 'You are businesswoman, Eve. You must act like one.'

Eve didn't much like her tone, and huffed a little about how expansion was hardly on the cards given they were barely managing the current workload. But Anna knew all about speculating to accumulate; she understood that overheads were sometimes higher than income. Daughter of a wealthy merchant, daughter-in-law of a bookkeeper, she saw income and expenditure as simply a list of numbers in an accounts book.

'When my father wanted to make bigger his business,' she said carefully, as if speaking to an infant, 'he found wealthy men who could lend him money to grow. Then, when he grew, he paid them back, with extra on top for having faith in him.'

'Are you suggestin' I go to a moneylender?' said Eve, scandalised. 'Because I most definitely will not. If I spend money on my business, it'll be my money and nob'dy else's.'

Anna laughed. 'Not moneylender, no. Another businessman, perhaps. An investor, not a crook.'

'It amounts to t'same thing,' Eve said. 'Why spend money I don't 'ave?'

'Because your little business is telling you it wants to be bigger. You could take new place, with more ovens; you could have people work for you; you could make ten times this, twenty times.' She waved a hand at Eve's cash box, dismissing its contents with a disparaging gesture. 'You think too small,' she said. 'You need think big.'

Then Maya, waking from her nap, began to cry in her cot upstairs and Anna went to attend to her, leaving Eve all in a turmoil as she started on yet another batch of pie pastry. And as she worked, the familiar ritual soothed her so that she was able to apply rational thought to what Anna had said. It was quite true that the business was bursting at the seams. She simply couldn't make any more pies or puddings than she currently did. The very next new order would have to be turned down, and that seemed plain wrong. Amos and Seth were already harvesting the vegetables and soft fruit they'd been nurturing for months, and that had opened up new possibilities for dishes she could sell. Eve, up to the elbows in a sticky mass of damp flour, wondered if Anna perhaps had a point. Maybe all this was just the beginning, she thought. She tipped the pastry out of its bowl and pounded and pulled at it for a few seconds, absorbed in the task. And then suddenly, with a flash of clarity which lit up her face, she thought of Lord Netherwood.

Chapter 29

⚜

A bsalom Blandford, the Netherwood bailiff, was a man with two faces, one for the earl and another for the rest of the world. So while Teddy Hoyland knew him to be an excellent chap, amenable, dependable and trustworthy, everyone else he dealt with thought him an out-and-out swine. It was a testament to his own ingenuity and consistency that these two entirely diverse impressions had been successfully maintained for so many years.

Of course, being an out-and-out swine was a useful quality in a bailiff, whose typical daily workload didn't generally call for empathy or good humour. Absalom worked alongside, though independently of, Jem Arkwright; while Jem was responsible for the estate's outdoor concerns, Absalom had complete control over all the dwellings, businesses, farm buildings and any other brick-and-mortar structure upon which he could place a rent. His efficiency and commitment was such that he also doubled as the earl's accountant, there being nothing more fascinating to him than a row of numbers. He took nothing – nothing at all – on trust. There wasn't a single tenant on the Netherwood estate who was above his suspicion. When he'd been appointed, twenty-five years earlier, he cast aside his predecessor's books and ledgers and conducted his own general survey of every building entrusted to his care, making an inventory that then formed the basis of his scrupulous execution of duty. Over the years, regular memoranda and amendments were entered on the pages; notes relating to deficiencies, improvements, insurances, dates of leases, rates, changes of use, changes in tenancy, lapses in rents. The history of Netherwood could be told from the pages of his estate books and most of it – perhaps all, though he'd never been tested – was committed to his prodigious memory. If a person were to ask Absalom Blandford what date Arthur and Eve Williams moved into the house vacated by Digby Caldwell's corpse, he would say 19 April 1891, without pausing for thought, let alone having to check his facts in the ledger.

But his encyclopedic knowledge of key moments in the lives of others was accompanied by a chilly lack of interest in humanity. His fascination lay not in the people, but in the buildings they inhabited. Tenants were just that; names in his books, significant only if they either failed to pay up on time, moved away or died. He wasn't a bad-looking man, and if he'd learned how to laugh or to love he would have been downright attractive: slim, tidy, always dressed immaculately and with not inconsiderable style. His distinguishing physical feature was a fine head of glossy black hair which was as abundantly luxurious as his spirit was mean. He was unmarried – matrimony held no appeal – and entirely friendless, but in his own, emotionally barren way, he was content. And on the fine Monday morning in early July when Eve Williams presented herself, without appointment, at the estate offices, Absalom Blandford was in what passed for him as a good mood.

Not that Mr Blandford was the person Eve was hoping to see. She cursed inwardly when she realised that she would have to put her request to him instead of the somewhat surly but infinitely more approachable Jem Arkwright. He, however, was out with Walker Spruce and his terriers, mending fencing and – if truth were told – enjoying the sunshine. So it was the basilisk gaze of Absalom Blandford that greeted her when she knocked on the office door and was bid to enter.

As it was, Eve's heart was pounding with fear – had been since she left Netherwood and entered the gates of the park to walk the mile down Oak Avenue. She looked the part, but she didn't feel it. Anna had made her a little red flannel jacket, the first such garment Eve had ever owned; it was beautifully dapper, with a cinched-in waist and narrow lapels, and it looked very well over her good white blouse and grey skirt. She had real boots, too, in tan leather, newly purchased from a shoe shop on Cheapside in Barnsley, and although she still preferred the feel on her feet of her old clogs, she hoped the boots lent her a professional air because she needed all the help she could get.

It was all Anna's fault, she said to herself as she walked along under the towering trees. The liquid feeling in her gut and the dryness of her mouth were Anna's doing. She had chivvied Eve out of the house this morning and was now safe at home, darting between the dolly tub and the front-door shop – Monday was Monday, after all, and Anna was juggling the demands of wash day with those of a busy trade in pies and puddings. Well, thought Eve, she'd swap places with her now. Aye, she would that; let Anna come to the big house with a hare-brained scheme to borrow money. No, to raise capital. She had to remember that, because apparently it was the correct term. Reverend Farrimond had told her, when he heard of the plan, that looking and sounding professional was the key to success in these matters. People in business raised capital, he said, they didn't borrow money – although he and Eve both knew it amounted to the same thing. Amos, never backward in coming forward these days, had weighed in with his own advice, which was not to go cap in hand to the earl under any circumstances. But Eve judged, quite correctly, that Amos's interest wasn't entirely objective, so here she was, smartly dressed, coached in what to say, hair brushed to a shine and pinned into a fetching twist – a vision, had she but known it, of loveliness – but still feeling like a small child on her first day at school.

What made it worse was that the gardens were swarming with staff, all of whom seemed fascinated by the novelty of her presence. Eve wondered, as she passed them, what on earth there was to do in a garden, however grand, to keep so many men and boys busy. Old Bartholomew Parkin, the Oak Lodge gatekeeper, had been the first person she encountered and he'd lifted his cap deferentially as she walked past before realising it was just Eve Williams and he needn't have bothered. That, at least, had made Eve smile. But she soon began to feel foolish again, as she ran the gamut of gardeners who stood and watched her lonely progress towards the magnificent cupolas and columns of Netherwood Hall. She kept in her head the words of Lord Netherwood at Arthur's funeral: 'We cannot offer charity to every needy case, my dear, and you doubtless wouldn't seek it, but we will always help if we can.'

What she sought this morning was an audience with the earl. And if Jem Arkwright had been sitting behind the desk instead of Absalom Blandford, her objective might have been far more easily achieved.

'Good mornin', sir,' she said.

'Yes it is. At least, it was,' he said. An unpromising start, but not disastrous. At least he hadn't demanded she leave at once.

'I'm Eve Williams,' she said.

Number five, Beaumont Lane, widow, three children, émigrée lodger, thought the bailiff automatically. He looked at her steadily with his lizard's eyes.

'I wondered if I could see you for five minutes?' Eve said.

'And can you? See me?' said Mr Blandford, coldly facetious. 'Or have I become invisible since arriving at work this morning?'

Eve blushed deep red and her train of thought crashed spectacularly into a brick wall of pure panic. She had expected discouragement but not mocking, naked hostility.

'Yes, sir. I mean, no. That is, yes, I can,' she said.

'Oh for the love of God, what on earth are you doing here?' he said. His nostrils twitched with displeasure; he was entirely unmoved by her confusion.

'I wanted to see t'earl,' she said, blurting it out helplessly. 'To borrow some money.' Oh bugger, she thought.

Absalom Blandford snorted derisively.

'Quite extraordinary,' he said, as if to himself. He indicated the door with one outstretched arm. 'Do close it behind you on your way out,' he said, then he balanced a pair of spectacles on his neat little nose and opened the ledger in front of him, not because there was anything there demanding his attention, but because it was the most effective way possible to ignore this preposterous young woman.

She stood for a moment looking at the crown of his head, until he looked up at her with an expression of such practised coldness that she turned and walked to the door. She had almost left the office when she was suddenly seized by the reckless urge to plead her case.

'I expressed myself badly just then,' she said. He didn't look up. 'I 'ave a small business, sir, a little shop – I'm sure you know that – and I need to raise some capital in order to expand.'

She sounded now as if she knew what she was about. He knew it, and so did she. But Absalom Blandford didn't like to back down or retract and he was one hundred per cent certain that the earl would have no interest in investing in a back-street pie shop.

'The usual channels for such matters are financial institutions,' he said. She seemed entirely uncomprehending, so he added: 'Banks,' spitting the word out contemptuously. 'Now, off you go. You were quite mistaken to come.'

Now Eve did leave, closing the door behind her with a defiant little bang and allowing herself an internal stream of colourful curses of which, to look at her, you wouldn't have thought her capable. Amos was right, she thought. She should never have come. The silent invective sustained her as she crunched along the gravelled carriageway and set off back up Oak Avenue just as Lord Netherwood emerged from the entrance of Netherwood Hall. Serendipity, Samuel Farrimond said later, though Eve called it a simple stroke of good luck. The earl, surmising that Mrs Williams must have emerged from the estate offices, briefly postponed his own departure by car in order to enquire after her business there. Absalom Blandford, secure in the knowledge that he had protected the earl from an inconvenience, told him with the sycophantic bonhomie he always used in Teddy Hoyland's company that the impertinent tenant had been sent packing after asking to see his lordship.

'To borrow money, apparently,' he added, and let slip a bitter little cough of amusement.

There was no reciprocation, however. The earl looked thoughtful, then said, 'Get her back, Absalom. Atkins can fetch her in the Daimler. I'll see her in the morning room. Bring her to me, would you?'

Stunned into silent submission, Absalom Blandford watched his master return to the house before following his orders to the letter. Atkins swung the car out of the courtyard and set off in pursuit of Eve Williams, and Absalom positioned himself at the steps of the house in order to receive her when she emerged from the Daimler. He was, after all, a faithful and obedient servant as well as an out-and-out swine.

Chapter 30

Mitchell's Stone Ground Flour Mill, just off – aptly enough – Mill Street, had ceased production five years before, finally driven out of business by the Barnsley British Co-operative Society, which was producing better flour and selling it for less. Those workers who were willing to travel were given jobs at the Co-op's mill in Summer Lane, Barnsley, and the rest were out of work. But even those who grumbled at their lot knew that Mitchell's flour was of a poor grade; take a fistful from the sack and it crumbled to dry dust, whereas Co-op flour was strong and pure. It held the shape of your clenched hand and showed the indentations of your fingers. Eve would use nothing else.

She liked the old Mitchell's building, though, and the part of Netherwood it stood in. It was the highest part of town, where the air was fresher and the sky clearer. Mill Street itself was wide and well-paved with an almost affluent feel, partly because it was home to two of Netherwood's most appealing shops: Walker's Confectioners, its long bow window chock-full of glass jars of boiled sweets and boxes of toffee, fudge and coconut ice, and Allott's High Class Bakers, with a fancy delivery dray and horse parked permanently outside the shop.

The horse was a local landmark, but its teeth were rotten from two decades of being fed mint humbugs by Mrs Walker. Mitchell's Mill sat off this main thoroughfare at the end of its own walled lane, officially unnamed but referred to by locals as Mitchell's Snicket, and from the front it had the look of a fine old house, except for the gabled wooden gantry jutting out at the centre of the third storey and the peeling fascia declaring its original use. It was a sandstone building, heavily grimed but still attractive, with generously proportioned sash windows and an arched entrance in the middle, wide enough to allow a coach and horses to pass through to the rear courtyard. In a flat, smooth stone above the arch were inscribed the initials WEH after the present earl's father, who had commissioned the building and equipped it for business. It would have saddened him greatly to see it now, unused and down-at-heel. Absalom Blandford was all for demolishing it, but something – sentimentality, optimism, perhaps a little of both – had made Teddy resist.

And now, as he sat opposite Eve Williams in the sun-filled morning room, his instinct to preserve the old mill suddenly made sense to him. Her proposition was extremely interesting: that he invest in her fledgling business to allow it to flourish. She was such a plucky individual, he thought, as he watched her struggle to articulate her unformed ideas. She could teach his feckless son a thing or two about strength in adversity; sent for the summer to the family's Scottish residence, Tobias had reacted with lamentable pique, all but stamping his feet like Isabella in a temper when he learned his fate. It was no hardship, really, to oversee the renovations to the exterior of the castle – Teddy himself at the same age would have considered it something of a treat – and they'd all be joining him up there in early August anyway for the shooting. But still Tobias had railed against his father's decision: he called it exile, banishment. Poor show, thought Teddy, very poor show indeed.

It hadn't helped in the least that Clarissa made such an almighty fuss too. She was as bad as the boy, almost hysterical at the prospect of him missing the rest of the season in London, as if all that mattered in the world was his attendance at one silly gathering after another. Well, it was done now and Tobias was gone. He hoped a couple of months in his own company might teach the boy something about self-reliance and responsibility.

Eve had stopped speaking and was looking directly at the earl. He hasn't heard a word I've said, she was thinking. And she didn't blame him for letting his mind wander. Why, Ellen would've made a better job of it than she had this morning, rambling on about pies and orders and ovens as if an earl would have the remotest interest in any of it. He'd brought her into this lovely room, flooded with light, smelling of lilac, and had sat her opposite him at a rosewood table you could have used as a mirror, such was its gleam. He'd ordered coffee – the first Eve had ever tasted – and it was served from a silver pot by a girl Eve knew from town but who gave not a flicker of recognition as she poured. The girl was still within earshot when the earl had said, 'So Mrs Williams, how can I be of assistance?' so she was probably out there still, ear pressed flat against the door, so that she could take a full story and not a fragment of one back to the kitchens with her. Eve wished she'd written out her piece and brought it with her; she might have looked foolish, reading it aloud, but at least her words would have come out in the right order.

But then the earl said, 'Do you have half an hour to come with me and look at something?'

Eve hadn't expected anything other than a kind but firm dismissal. She stared at him, uncomprehending.

'I have an idea, you see.' He stood and, walking around the table, took hold of the back of Eve's chair for her to stand, just as if she were a guest at one of his famous dinner parties. 'A solution that might serve us both equally.'

They walked to the door. Eve hoped they might catch the housemaid in the act, but she was gone, although she glimpsed Maudie Staniforth crossing an upstairs landing with an armful of dresses; she would have waved, but it seemed that different rules applied here. No eye contact, let alone anything so bold as a greeting. Apart from that brief encounter, she saw no one else as they made their way through the great house, and Eve was observed only by the grave and disapproving subjects of countless ancestral portraits as she walked with Lord Nether-wood – at his shoulder, not a few steps behind – out of the morning room, down the plushly carpeted corridors, through the cavernous marble hall – she was glad then that her clogs were at home and not showing her up with the racket they'd make on this unforgiving floor – and back into the outside world. Two footmen attended them as they descended the steps and settled back into the handsome leather seats of the waiting Daimler. Oh, Arthur. If you could see me now, thought Eve.

The motion of the car, the smell of petrol and the bitter, unfamiliar taste of coffee all combined to make Eve feel sick on the journey through Netherwood. She preferred Sol Windross's cart as a means of transport; even taking into account the swaying and the old man's stink, it was still preferable to this unnatural, hemmed-in feeling and the violent lurch every time they had to stop. Lord Netherwood had taken the wheel and Atkins was in the front passenger seat, which seemed an odd business; perhaps the driver's function, she thought, would be to wait with the car when they reached their destination, keep the urchins off the bonnet.

The earl had a lot to say, shouting at her over his shoulder but fairly comprehensively thwarted by the noise of the engine. Eve strained to listen. She only picked up about one word in four, but what she heard made her worried that he had the wrong idea entirely; they were heading for Mitchell's Flour Mill, he said. She knew it was a grand old building but it was far too big for her purposes. What Eve had had in mind, if anything, was one of the pit workshops down near New Mill Colliery. One of those, kitted out with a couple of stoves, would do the job. She held her peace, though, partly out of sheer nerves at the situation she found herself in, but mostly because she feared that if she opened her mouth she'd vomit all over the Daimler's immaculate interior.

In King Street she perked up, adjusting to the novelty and enjoying the attention the motor car attracted. Lilly Pickering was drifting down the street with a line of little children following her like unkempt ducklings. She looked stick-thin and almost weightless, as if the only thing tethering her to the pavement were the bags of shopping she carried in each hand. Eve gave her a cheery wave and had the very great pleasure of seeing her neighbour drop both bags in disbelief as Eve Williams sailed on by in a fancy car driven by the Earl of Netherwood.

'You see,' she thought she heard the earl shout, 'it's a damnable shame to have it go to rack and ruin.'

Eve nodded, hoping she was picking up the gist. They turned left into Mill Street, startling the baker's old horse with an unexpected explosion from the rear end of the vehicle. Atkins and the earl didn't bat an eyelid, so Eve presumed it was perfectly normal, but she and the horse exchanged looks of sympathy as they passed. At the corner with Mitchell's Snicket the earl slowed to a crawl to negotiate the turn, then approached the flour mill at the same snail's pace. They gazed at the building, and it gazed back at them, with sad sash windows that were either smashed or spotted with bird muck – the pigeons had moved in when the humans had moved out.

They drove right under the arched entrance at its centre and into a cobbled yard at the back, where the earl made some adjustment and the motor car spluttered and wheezed to a halt, though the engine continued to tick over.

'Splendid!' he said, clapping his gloved hands together. He jumped out of the car and sprinted round to Eve's side to hand her out. I could get used to this, she thought, a hand every time I step up or down.

'Very good, Atkins, take her back,' he said.

For an awkward moment, Eve thought he meant her to leave, but it turned out he meant the car because the driver simply slid over into the seat vacated by the earl and drove it – her – out of the courtyard.

'Hope you don't mind,' the earl said, turning to Eve. 'I like to walk home, work up an appetite for luncheon, what!'

'No, sir, not at all,' she said. 'It's nobbut five minutes for me.' She flushed a little, remembering she was speaking to an earl, not to a nobody like herself. 'I mean, it's no distance,' she said. It still seemed all wrong, speaking to Lord Nether-wood in this familiar way, but by his expression, his tone of voice and everything he did, he positively encouraged it.

'Quite, quite. Now. Look,' he said, turning to face the rear of the building. Eve turned too, seeing it from this angle for the first time.

'Oh,' she said.

Even accounting for the effects of neglect, it was an extraordinary sight, so different to the front of the building that Eve felt disorientated, as though she was suddenly somewhere other than Netherwood. Its principal charm, and what had temporarily taken Eve's breath away, was a pretty colonnade which ran the length of the ground floor. Above it was a double row of arched windows, each decorated by ornate pediments, and the whole was topped off by an elaborate cornice. Wisteria, still in bloom thanks to the late summer, dripped languidly from the columns of the colonnade, and had begun to climb above it on to the mellow stone wall.

Eve sighed. She wondered why she'd never seen it before. This lovely place, sitting here in Netherwood, churning out flour.

'It's grand is that,' she said.

The earl laughed. 'Couldn't agree more. My old father knew what he was at when it came to buildings. This place is, what, seventy years old? But it could be much earlier, don't you think? Italian influence you see – all the rage at the time. Harking back to the Renaissance.'

He might have been speaking Swahili for all Eve understood, but she recognised a lovely building when she saw one.

'I thought it was nice from t'front,' she said. 'But this is – well it's beautiful. It doesn't look English.'

'Exactly!' said Lord Netherwood. 'My father wanted to create the same Italianate feel that Nash had been producing, you see. Couldn't do it at the front, with the gantry and what-not. But the back of the building' – he swept his arm in an arc – 'was another matter.'

'But it was just a flour mill,' she said.

'Yes, well, he was a whimsical fellow. Shall we look inside?'

The brief lecture on architecture over, the earl strode purposefully forwards, looking back at her with a boyish grin to bid her follow. She saw Tobias in him at that moment, and briefly but earnestly thanked God she was at this abandoned building with the father not the son, before trotting along after him.

Together they toured the three floors, sending indignant birds flapping out into the sky and leaving footprints in the carpet of dust. There were very few rooms considering the size of the building, but they were lofty and wide and full of light. The workings were still in place of course: the massive gristmill, great discs of stone laid one on top of the other, pulleys and hoists to lift the grain, hoppers and chutes to send the ground flour to the sack floor – it was all still there, redolent of another more productive era in the building's recent past. The earl talked as they walked and his plan, still very much in its formative stages, was that the building should be completely stripped of the trappings of its milling days and be fully refurbished at his expense. Then, when restoration was complete, it would be equipped with ranges, work surfaces and sinks with running cold water. These latter items would also be paid for by the estate, on the understanding that fifty per cent of Eve's business would then be owned by the earl. She would pay a weekly rental for the premises, the amount yet to be settled by Mr Blandford – who of course was ignorant of any of this, but would be apprised of the situation as soon as he – the earl – got home. He rattled all this off nineteen to the dozen and she followed him, listening, although his ambitious scheme combined with the dusty half-light of the interior enhanced her increasing conviction that she must be asleep, and none of this was really happening. Except she was hot in her red jacket and the new boots were chafing at each heel – she'd rubbed blisters there, she was sure – and these uncomfortable, human details were not the stuff of dreams.

'What do you think?' he was saying now, looking almost anxious, as if everything hinged on her good opinion.

'It's big,' she said stupidly.

'Yes, yes,' he waved her words away like so much chaff. 'Bigger than you had in mind, doubtless. But let's say you only use the ground floor for now? The upper floors might be let to other businesses, perhaps. Or they could be converted to dwellings, you know, apartments – very continental, what!'

His 'what!' came out like a little bark, and she wished he wouldn't do it. It reminded her of the little Jack Russell that Stanley Eccles went about with. Plus, she didn't know the correct response to it, though it seemed to be an exclamation rather than a question, because he was off again.

'I see this as an opportunity, not a favour, you see. This lovely old place, restored to glory.'

'Well,' she said. 'I can't promise glory. Only pies.'

He grinned his Tobias grin. 'Forgive me, Mrs Williams, but glorious is the only adjective for your raised pies – no, no,' he held up a hand to stop her modest protestations, 'credit where it's due. You have reinvented the product, my dear. And imagine what else you might do, with the space and the facilities to achieve it, what!'

There it was again, but she was ready for it this time and took it in her stride.

'Lord Netherwood, you're a very, very generous man, and I would be honoured to move my business 'ere' – his face was alight with pleasure, and even with the gulf of class and wealth between them, she felt excessively fond of him – 'and thank you.' Her words seemed inadequate; a hug and a kiss would be going too far, but it was what she felt like doing.

'Marvellous, marvellous,' he said. 'Do you know, I feel rather invigorated myself at the prospect.' He held out a hand which she took, and they shook. 'I shall return to the estate office now, have a chat with Absalom' – I wish I could witness that, she thought – 'and then we'll draw something up in writing. It'll be a few weeks, of course, before the building is habitable, but time flies, you'll be in before you know it. I'll leave you here, let you have a wander on your own. Watch these floorboards,' he stamped one foot by way of illustration. 'Some of them feel a trifle shaky.'

And he marched off and out, all purpose and energy. She waited until she could no longer hear his footsteps outside,

235

and then she hugged herself tight and spun wildly so her skirts flew out around her, whipping up the dust from the floor and sending it dancing in the shafts of light and she laughed for the sheer joy of it all. Then steadying herself and taking deep, calming breaths, she did as he'd suggested and walked solemnly around the ground floor, trying – and failing – to see herself there. She stood at one of the front windows, looking out over Mitchell's Snicket. There were shoppers to-ing and fro-ing in Mill Street, going about their workaday business. Eve wanted to climb the stairs to the gantry and stop them in their tracks, shouting out her good fortune. Instead she chose the more sober option of walking back outside into the courtyard to sit on a step, where she unlaced and removed her boots and massaged her damaged heels for two minutes before walking home to Beaumont Lane in her stockinged feet.

Chapter 31

It was after midday by the time Eve got back, and Lilly had long beaten her to it, so Anna already knew that the earl had taken her for a drive in the Daimler, but that was all she knew because Lilly hadn't been fast enough to follow them. Eve walked up the entry into the backyard to find Anna pegging out the last batch of washing.

'Lovely dryin' weather,' Eve said.

'Pish!' Anna said. 'Never mind weather! What happened?'

Lilly's head popped out of her open doorway.

'Well?' she said. 'What's going off?'

It made Eve laugh to see her disembodied head, its brow knitted in cross perplexity: there were few things happened in Netherwood without Lilly Pickering knowing the details from the thread to the needle.

'Who's looking after t'shop?' Eve said.

Anna looked a little defensive. 'I close for lunch,' she said. 'I cannot be two places at same time.'

'Can't you?' Eve said. 'Shame on you.'

Anna laughed, a little reluctantly because she felt aggrieved. If it wasn't for her, Eve wouldn't have gone to see the earl this morning, and now here she was, keeping secrets.

Eve said, 'Come on then, come inside and I'll spill t'beans.'
She looked at Lilly. 'You an' all,' she said.

Lilly, who really preferred bad news to good, feared from
her neighbour's expression that congratulations might be in
order. But good news was better than no news at all, so she
gathered up her two littlest babies and followed Eve and Anna
into the house.

Down at the allotment, Amos and Seth were harvesting peas,
runner beans and spinach, picking the pods and the leaves
and laying them carefully in wooden crates that Amos had
lined with newspaper. They worked in silence, both of them
fully absorbed in their task. The allotment was a different
place from the one they'd taken over back in January. Now
it was a model of its kind, the vegetables growing in orderly
fashion in raised beds that Amos had made using old railway
sleepers from a stack down by the lines. They were seeping
tar in the hot sun, but apart from that they were ideal for
the job and there were other gardeners down the row of
plots who were eyeing them covetously. They had three
wigwams built out of silver birch for the runners to climb,
and the tender leaves – lettuces and sorrel – grew under a
cloak of netting impenetrable to slugs and snails. Raised
furrows bore the bushy crowns of Red Duke of Yorks, and
there were the highly promising beginnings of a prize-winning
marrow bed; Amos had put the wind up Seth by saying he
should start sleeping by it in case of theft or sabotage. Dotted
all around were marigolds to further ward off the pests, and
cosmos and larkspur to attract the bees. The still air was
heavy with the scent of sweetpeas, which grew abundantly
up both sides of a flat trellis of woven willow. The more
Seth cut them the more they came; the house was full of

them in jam jars, and Eliza had a little stall in the street after school, selling posies.

Amos was learning on the hoof. He'd never had his own patch of land to tend, but he was catching on fast, watching what the other gardeners were up to and, on occasion, swallowing his pride and asking Clem's advice. Seth, on the other hand, was going at it with his usual forensic intensity; the school library was inadequately stocked with gardening books but Miss Mason had brought him some of her own and he currently had *The Gardener's Assistant* by his bed, and was marking pages of interest as he progressed. He was nagging Amos to build a melon pit, but was getting short shrift.

Their immediate neighbour in the run of allotments was Percy Medlicott, which meant Seth was truly among friends. Percy didn't mind who he talked to, as long as they'd listen, and even though Seth was not quite eleven, he paid solemn attention to Percy's pearls of wisdom so was a worthwhile, as well as willing, audience. Percy knew with wistful certainty that the day would come when Seth would know considerably more than he did. But he was enjoying his advantage while it lasted, and he gave the boy hours of his time. For a little lad who'd lost his dad, thought Amos, Seth was doing all right. Eve told Amos – swearing him to secrecy on pain of death – that he was wetting his bed and was mortified by it, because it was something even Ellen didn't do any more. But Eve had refused to let Seth fret. This too would pass, she told him. He seemed to Eve to be not entirely happy, but happy enough. Certainly he loved being with Amos in the allotment.

'Right,' Amos said now, breaking the diligent silence and stretching his back against the ache. 'Let's get this lot dahn to yer mam.'

Carrying a crate each they took their leave, unwillingly on Seth's part, but with some relief on Amos's. He'd drop the boxes off at Beaumont Lane, then treat himself to a pint at the Hare and Hounds. Percy Medlicott, who never seemed to leave his allotment – at any rate never left before them – gave them a farewell salute. He was basking like a cat in the evening sun, sitting on his old stool, chewing on the stem of a pipe. His tobacco tin was empty but the memory of his last smoke was strong enough, in taste and smell, to give him pleasure.

'How come 'e's stayin' and we're goin'?' said Seth truculently.

'Because 'e's got Madge Medlicott at home,' said Amos. 'Think on, young Seth. When you take a wife, be sure you'd sooner be at 'ome with 'er than on thi own wi' yer pipe.'

Seth did think on. Then he said, 'Would you sooner be at 'ome wi' my mam than alone wi' yer pipe?'

Amos clipped him round the back of the head. 'I don't smoke,' he said. 'Cheeky beggar.'

They staggered into the kitchen ten minutes later, hamming it up as if the weight of the vegetables had them nearly on their knees. The dry washing was in and Anna was pressing the linens with the smoothing iron, hot work on any day, but barely tolerable on a day like this. Her face was damp with sweat, though she looked cheerful enough. Seth, still cool towards her, though even he didn't know why, pushed through to the parlour where Eve was whisking crumbs off the shop table and into her hand. She turned and smiled at him.

'Good gardenin'?' she said.

'Champion,' said Seth. 'Amos's 'ere.'

Amos is always here, she thought. And she knew why he was here now – he'd be wanting to find out how she got on up at the Hall. Hoping it'd all come to naught, no doubt. She tossed the crumbs out through the open door and, wiping her hands briskly down the sides of her skirt, followed Seth back into the hot kitchen.

'You should do that in t'yard,' she said to Anna. 'You'll be a puddle on t'floor before you've done.'

Amos said: 'Now then.'

She smiled at him. 'Thanks for all that,' she said, indicating the two laden vegetable boxes on the table. 'Will you take some of it with you?'

'Not till you've turned it into summat I can eat,' he said, grinning at her. He smiled more these days; people were almost getting used to it. It had a lot to do with Eve, and the time he spent with Seth, but it was also partly to do with the gardening. He reckoned it was making him more peaceful, this connection with the soil and what he could coax from it. He sometimes thought if Lord Netherwood provided a few hundred allotments, his pits would be safe from socialism. All that fresh air and fruitful labour could take the fight right out of a man. Not that he was giving up the struggle, but he could see how others might.

Eve wasn't volunteering any information so Amos said, '"ow did you get on then, this morning?'

She told him, and as she talked his face lost its smile.

'If I were you,' he said carefully, when she'd finished, 'I'd think very 'ard before signin' up for life wi' Teddy 'oyland.'

'Well, you're not me. And who's signin' up for life?' she said.

'You'll never be free,' Amos said. 'You've been bought by 'im, an when—'

She stopped him, mid-flow: 'Don't you dare, Amos Sykes. Don't you dare preach to me. I've been bought by nob'dy. Lord Netherwood is an investor in my business, and I for one am pleased with t'connection. If you can't be pleased an' all, it's your problem, not mine. The earl's a good man, an' your blindness to that just makes you sound foolish.'

Amos's expression was thunderous. It was rare for anyone to take him on, and rarer still for it to be anyone whose high opinion he cared about. But this, instead of making him conciliatory, consumed him all at once with a hot anger, and though there was nothing, in truth, in his relationship with Eve to merit it, he felt betrayed.

'You're t'fool, Eve Williams, if you think any good can come from this.' His voice was raised and Seth stood watching the scene with an expression of abject dismay. Anna tried to steer him gently out of the kitchen but he shook her hand from his arm, wouldn't even look at her. She shrugged, and left the room.

Eve was shaking with a powerful emotion she couldn't name. Amos was wrong, she thought, and not only that, he had presumed too much in speaking to her in this way. She took a deep breath and said, 'You'd best leave.'

It was shocking, the coldness in her voice, but there it was, and they all heard it. Amos didn't linger; he stalked across the kitchen and out of it with such haste that his cloth cap lay forgotten on top of the spinach leaves, like a reproach for treating him so ill when he'd worked so hard. Seth snatched up the cap and clutched it to his breast, swept along on the melodrama of the moment.

'I 'ate you,' he said to his mother, in the same controlled and chilly tones she'd used herself, then he followed Amos out of the door.

Chapter 32

Custer's Last Stand turned out to be a triumph, though not for General Custer who ended up, as he always did, dead at the hands of Chief Sitting Bull and his terrifying braves. The Queen's Ground in Barnsley was the Wild West, dense with spectators who had never witnessed a spectacle like it. Amos arrived early with Seth and Eliza and they placed themselves near enough the front not to miss anything, but not so near as to be able to see the whites of the Red Indians' eyes, which Amos said would put the willies up them.

The crowd was warmed up with a show by the Rough Riders of the World; Turks, Gauchos, Cossacks and Arabs in outlandish national dress, careering about the arena on wild-eyed stallions, drenched in sweat. As they exited stage left, the Red Indians entered stage right, whooping their battle cry, bare-chested and fearsome in war paint and feathers. There was a thrilling attack on the Deadwood stagecoach, gunshots ringing out in the October afternoon, arrows flying, horses rearing.

Then Annie Oakley sauntered on, twirling her pistols and shouting, 'howdy pardners!' to the crowd. She had two hundred glass marbles fired one after another into the sky and shot every one of them to tiny shards; she invited spectators to toss pennies into the air – 'First time ah've seen Yorkshiremen chucking their money away,' said Amos – then handed them back punched through with a perfect hole; she shot the ash from a cigarette dangling from a man's mouth; and with the thin edge of a series of playing cards facing her, and at a range of ninety yards she shot the cards from their moorings and peppered them with holes as they fell to the ground. Eliza's eyes were wide as she imagined a whole new future for herself. She wondered how, and when, she might have a pistol.

And then finally, on a crescendo of applause and to raucous cheering, Buffalo Bill himself cantered on playing General Custer astride a heroic grey stallion, and the Battle of the Little Bighorn was played out in all its gory detail. The horses, skilled actors every one, fell with their wounded cavalrymen or Red Indians until the arena was strewn with the lifeless bodies of men and their steeds. Seth watched with a rapt and fervent concentration, as if the afternoon's entertainment might be followed by a test on the sequence of events; Eliza had lost her voice and could only croak her excitement; and Amos, along with every other grown man in the grounds, hollered and hooted, roared and whistled, stamped his feet and waved his cap in the air as the Last Stand drew to its inevitable conclusion and Chief Sitting Bull polished off Custer with a deadly arrow to the heart.

'Is 'e a goodie or a baddie?' Eliza said, pointing at the Red Indian chief who was executing an immodest triumphal circuit of the battleground. He had paint daubed on his face, which was old but curiously unlined. The feathers of his headdress were impossible primary colours, not at all birdlike in Eliza's opinion, and he had long dark hair which he wore in two plaits, as Anna sometimes did. His fringed shirt and trousers looked to be made out of shammy leather, like her mother's window cloth. His horse danced past Eliza and the chief seemed to pick her out in the crowd, his stern brown eyes settling on her for the briefest moment; she shivered in the grip of a strange ecstasy.

'Depends on yer point o' view,' Amos said. 'Depends if yer an Indian or a paleface.'

Seth was reading the programme. 'I wish I 'ad a Red Indian name. Sitting Bull, Crazy 'orse, summat like that,' he said.

Eliza said: 'We could call you Smelly Pig if you want,' and Amos laughed. Then Eliza immediately lost her adantage by saying, 'So is that man t'real General Custer, Amos?' and Seth gave her a look of shrivelling disdain.

'No, 'e's dead, you clown,' said Amos. ' That there is William Cody, Buffalo Bill, see?'

He was on his feet again, the dead general, and hopping back on his horse to join Sitting Bull. Behind them the rest of the fallen were also rising, men and horses alike, preparing to take their share of the riotous applause, but there was a smell in the air of onions and sausages frying and potatoes baking, and it was drawing the fickle crowd away.

'Can we 'ave summat to eat?' Eliza asked.

'Mam should 'ave come, sold 'er pies an' that,' said Seth. He was always doing this, invoking Eve at every opportunity then watching Amos's face for clues.

'Yer mam 'as bigger fish to fry,' Amos said, an unsatisfactory result for Seth; he wanted a straightforward agreement.

'Bigger pies to bake, you mean,' said Eliza, who was still at a very literal age.

'That an' all,' said Amos. He pulled his cap lower on his head and stared out gloomily from under the peak. The Wild West was melting away, Indians and cavalry on the same side now as the props were dismantled and the horses led away.

'Amos?' said Eliza.

He looked down at her upturned face and she smiled gappily. Her front milk teeth were long gone but there was still no sign of their replacements. It gave her a soft lisp, so that Amos was Amoth.

'Right then, toothless Aggie,' he said. 'Thpud or thauthage?'

245

The earl had thrown himself into the Mitchell's Mill project with the zeal of a man who had money, energy and ample time on his hands. Three months after the contracts between himself and Eve Williams had been drawn up – by a stunned but obedient Absalom Blandford – the renovations were all but complete. Stonemasons, carpenters, builders and painters had swarmed over the building every day for weeks. Alfred Hague, the earl's electrical engineer, was brought out of the pits to do the wiring, enigmatically threading and twisting his strange brown cables under floorboards and up channels in the plaster of the walls; a small crowd assembled and applauded when, for the first time, the wall lights were switched on.

The great gristmill had been fetched down from the upper floor – in itself a full day's work for fifteen labourers – and placed as a centrepiece in the rear courtyard. Lord Netherwood was wondering if it might not be turned into a water feature. He rather hoped Clarissa might show an interest, if he could only winkle her out of the drawing room, but the weather had turned poor and she seemed to be temporarily hibernating. The fine arched windows, front and back, had been reglazed, and the frames rubbed down and repainted. The wooden gantry – on consultation with Eve, much to her bewilderment – was to remain; there would be little or no use for it, but it was attractive enough, and was, after all, part of the town's history. The wisteria-clad colonnade had been pretty much left alone. Once it had been swept of dead leaves and mopped free of bird droppings, the original floor tiles were properly revealed, black-and-white chequered like a giant chess board. Its inherent glory needed no improvement and when the tradesmen left for the day and Eve was alone there, she sometimes gave in to the urge to perform a short, celebratory tap dance on it.

New timbers had been laid on the upper floors and waxed to bring out the grain, and there were York stone flags in the kitchen. The ranges – four of them, brand new with a showroom shine – were of the old, coal-fired type, which was what Eve was used to and what she very much preferred. Mr Hague had talked about electric ovens, but Eve had had the final say. Electricity might well be cleaner, she told him, but nothing could turn a pie crust brown like a coal fire.

There was a long work surface running down the centre of the main kitchen, with a cool marble top for pastry-making and three butler sinks set into wooden stands with blue-and-white tiled backs and storage cupboards beneath for soap, dishcloths and pot brushes. Everything, every single thing, was brand new. Eve, given carte blanche to furnish the kitchen with what she needed, had been directed by the estate to Micklethwaite's Household Emporium in Sheffield, proud purveyor of high-class kitchen goods; the bill was to go directly to Mr Blandford.

'Them 'oylands 'ave more money than sense,' Eve had said to Anna as they wandered together through the hallowed halls of Micklethwaite's. It was a fine old establishment, two-storeyed and with none of the clutter and chaos that generally characterised such enterprises. The goods were displayed in tasteful fashion on fine tables and dressers, so that even the most workaday items achieved the status of an exhibit. There was a country-house smell of beeswax and Eve, noting the yards and yards of polished wood panelling on the walls, wondered which poor soul was given that job once a week. Not the uppity Miss who seemed to be keeping them under surveillance at the moment, she'd wager. The place was quite unlike any Eve had ever been into; a showpiece of a shop, all gloss and gleam and outrageous prices handwritten on linen tags.

'Look at this,' she said to Anna. 'I mean, a wooden spoon's a wooden spoon. Why pay a ha'penny more 'n you 'ave to?'

She plucked the spoon, a perfectly ordinary example of its kind, from its Cornishware jar and stroked its curves. They were waiting for the attentions of the assistant manager, a Mr Francis Micklethwaite, who was expecting their visit but had been detained, as he told them in a fruity basso profundo dripping with regret, by 'an erroneous delivery at the rear of the premises'. The two women were happy enough to stroll through the shop while the crisis was dealt with, but Eve was discovering that a lifetime of thriftiness was a hard habit to break, even when she was spending someone else's money.

She waved the spoon at Anna. 'You can get four o' these at this price from Eli at t'market,' she said.

Anna took it from her and adopted the affected air of a connoisseur. 'But look at grain, so beautiful, and handle, so slender. Probably it stirs all by itself.'

Their mirth was coolly regarded by the supercilious young woman watching their progress. Hilary Kilney, great-niece of the original founding Micklethwaite, was steeped in her own sense of superiority. On this occasion, however, she was at a distinct disadvantage; she had no idea why Eve and Anna were there, and was quite certain that they had no good reason to be.

She coughed, and the two women looked at her properly for the first time. Miss Kilney had presence, a brass name badge and a fine silk blouse. Eve felt a little awed. Not so Anna. Three hard years on the breadline in Grangely had been merely a passing phase in her life, not a defining one; it hadn't made so much as a dent in her self-esteem. Shop assistants were her social inferior, of that she had no doubt.

Miss Kilney said, 'Can I help you?' politely enough, but her expression belied the courteous question. She wore an unpleasant smirk and held her head rather too high, as if sniffing out fresher air.

'Perhaps. Perhaps not,' said Anna, in her heavy accent. Perheps. Perheps not. She leaned in to read the name on the badge, then added: 'Hilary,' and managed to make it sound like an insult: hil-lair-ree, just one syllable short of hilarious.

Eve gawped at her, as did Miss Kilney, though she recovered more swiftly.

'Let me put it another way,' she said. 'Do you intend to buy that implement?'

She indicated the wooden spoon, which Anna still clutched.

'Because if you don't, you should replace it.' She smiled, not warmly.

Anna shrugged her Russian shrug. 'When we make up our mind, we let you know,' she said. She made a swift little sweeping motion with the fingers of one hand, as if to brush something out of her way. 'Eve,' she said. 'Come.'

And she swept off, like a young and offended Queen Victoria. Eve threw an appeasing look at Miss Kilney before following her.

'What you playin' at?' she hissed.

'Playing? Not at all,' Anna said. 'Like you, I shop.' She looked genuinely baffled.

'But t'way you just spoke to 'er,' Eve said, still whispering. 'Like she was muck you'd stood in.'

Another shrug. 'She was rude,' she said indignantly. 'She forgets her position is to serve. And don't whisper. It makes you look like thief.'

Eve, grudgingly impressed but nevertheless affronted, decided it was time to retrieve the upper hand from her haughty friend. These flashes of imperiousness were all very well, but Eve wasn't going to stand there and be told how to behave.

'Put that back,' she said briskly to Anna, pointing at the spoon. Then she turned to Hilary Kilney, who had retreated slightly from this discomfiting pair, but was still within earshot.

'If t'Earl of Netherwood 'appens to ask why we bought nothing from you,' she said, 'I shall tell 'im your prices are too 'igh and we took our business elsewhere. Give our apologies to Mr Micklethwaite.'

She turned back to Anna and, in a deliberate and skilful parody, said, 'Come,' and stalked out of the shop. Only when they were outside in the throng of the street where needles of rain were falling steadily from a leaden sky did she remember that their transport – a pretty brougham picked out in Hoyland colours – wasn't to meet them until a full hour from now. Still though, it had to be done; Hilary Kilney and her top-end wooden spoons were not to be countenanced.

'Let's find a pot of tea,' Eve said, cheerful now and feeling like herself again. 'We'll order some scones and mark 'em out of ten.'

They set off down the street in search of a tea room, arm in arm, heads together, laughing at nothing very much. And in the shop, Miss Kilney spent an uncomfortable five minutes explaining herself to Mr Micklethwaite who, in addition to anticipating a profitable morning's business, had rather looked forward to assisting the delectable young woman with clogs and shawl and access to the bottomless Netherwood Hall account.

Four days later and for the first time in living memory, the estate offices of Netherwood Hall received a slightly grubby bill from Eli Wilton's Hardware & Housewares stall on Barnsley Market. It was for just short of twenty-four pounds and the order had almost cleaned Eli out of stock, but the shelves and cupboards at the old flour mill were now primed and ready for business, and Eli took his wife Melody off for a week in Bridlington to celebrate the unexpectedly happy turn in their fortunes. Meanwhile Absalom Blandford made a mental note to speak to Mrs Powell-Hughes and Mrs Adams about the Netherwood Hall housekeeping receipts and wondered whether either of them might be prevailed upon to visit the market in Barnsley next time they needed supplies.

Chapter 33

Opening day was to be the twenty-sixth of October – just a fortnight away – and Eve wanted as little ceremony as possible. No red ribbons cut or colliery bands playing, though she had a sinking feeling that Lord Netherwood, with his taste for the big gesture, had something along those lines in mind. Her principal concern at the moment, though, was the training of her staff – the three women hired by her to help in the new venture. She hadn't advertised the posts, because she had known who she wanted: Alice Buckle, Nellie Kay and Ginger Timpson, competent women who kept a clean home and whose children were all at school or grown. There were other women who Eve knew better – Lilly Pickering and Maud Platt, right there outside her own back door – but she'd need more than a fortnight to coax anything edible out of Lilly, and Maud, though she had a good heart, was sloppy when it came to domestic hygiene. Mucky Maud, Eliza once called her, and ever since Eve had been unable to think of her as anything else.

So Alice, Nellie and Ginger were offered new jobs at a starting rate of five shillings a week, when all they'd done was pop out to buy pies from Eve's front-door shop. Alice,

Jonas Buckle's shy, plump, likeable little wife, was first to be asked, and though her blue eyes widened with pleasure, she had to ask Jonas first before she could accept. Alice had been Jonas's child bride – they married on her sixteenth birthday – and the ten-year difference in their ages had skewed the balance of power in the relationship. She was twenty-eight now, and the mother of five boys and one girl, but even so she had retained something tenderly youthful about her appearance and her manner, and she deferred to her husband in every matter. When Eve spoke to her about the job, Alice bustled off home to seek permission, then bustled back within the hour, full to bursting with the gift of Jonas's blessing. Ginger, on the other hand, had no such compunction. She couldn't remember the last time she'd asked Mervyn's permission for anything.

'Why not?' she had said to Eve, there and then. 'It'll be grand to get out more.'

Her name was actually Edna, but it seemed too lumpish and plain for the vivacious creature she was and now that her parents were dead, no one ever used it. Her hair had softened over the years to the burnished brown of a prize-winning conker, but she'd been Ginger since childhood and always would be. She had a touch of glamour, a rare commodity in Netherwood town; even on wash day you'd never catch her without red-tinted lips or perfectly drawn eyebrows. She liked to sing while she worked, though she was more generously endowed with enthusiasm than with natural talent: Eve hadn't known this when she hired her, but discovered it soon enough.

Meanwhile Nellie, prim and particular and taking the job offer as entirely her due, deferred agreement until she knew exactly what her hours and duties would be. She had to be certain, she said, that there'd be plenty of time in the day to keep her own house in order. She was a woman of high standards – her kitchen floor was as fit to eat from as her crockery. Clogs and boots had to be left by the door, and her husband Alf had to bathe at his old mother's after his shift at Long Martley, to get the worst of the black off before he went home, where there'd be a second bath ready for him. He suffered a good deal of stick from his colleagues over this, but he knew he'd suffer more from Nellie if he didn't oblige.

Eve, who heaven knows was houseproud enough herself, thought Nellie a perfect tyrant in her own home, but just what she needed in the new venture. And the combination of Alice's willingness to please, Ginger's confidence and Nellie's obsessive cleanliness seemed like a promising package of assets. So this past week all three of them had been presenting themselves at the old mill at half-past eight every day so that Eve could show them the ropes. It was an odd situation. Eve didn't feel at all like an employer, and certainly didn't feel remotely qualified to teach these seasoned housewives anything. To her own ear she sounded hollow and foolish as she told them, increasingly hesitantly, what she expected of them. She wished she could keep the apology out of her voice. They all listened obligingly enough, but she feared they were simply hiding the contempt they were actually feeling for her feeble instructions. It struck her that Anna would have made a far better job of it, with that high-handed bossiness she could adopt at the drop of a hat. But Anna was at home with Ellen and Maya and the little shop, which for the time being was still a going concern, though now she was alone in the house, Anna had instigated strict and limited opening hours from which she refused to bend.

'Four hours open, from ten until midday, and from one until three,' she said bluntly to Eve. 'If folk can't get here, then they go without.' She sounded almost like a Yorkshire-woman.

"ark at you!' said Eve. 'You make it sound like you're doing them a favour.'

'And so I am,' Anna said.

Eve, thinking of Hilary Kilney, said, 'You forget, your position is to serve,' then ducked before the wet dishcloth made contact with her head.

In fact, there were no seeds of resentment germinating behind the pleasantly attentive faces of Alice, Nellie and Ginger, but that's not to say they were not growing elsewhere. Personal success and entrepreneurship were rare as hens' teeth among the mining community in Netherwood. There were, down the years, occasional exceptions: Herbert Roscoe, a miner turned professional boxer, was doing nicely but he wasn't what you'd call an out-and-out success, with those cauliflower ears and busted nose. And Warren Sylvester, of course, self-employed in his own weaselly fashion, was doing all right. But they were men, by and large masters of their own destinies. Eve Williams, though, was a woman, who prior to Arthur's death had relied entirely on her husband for support. Never in living memory, no matter who you asked and how long they ruminated, had a miner's widow turned her fortunes about in the way Eve Williams had. In the Middle Ages, she'd have been drowned for a witch, but as it was, her detractors had to satisfy themselves with peddling idle rumours and peevish gossip.

Much of it was harmless, generated by women such as Lilly and Maud, who knew no better or couldn't help themselves. Eve Williams was getting fat on her own pies. Clem Waterdine had eaten one of her faggots and spent all day Saturday on the privy. Seth, Eliza and Ellen were calling Anna Rabinovich 'Mam'. Madge Medlicott had threatened to leave Percy if he spent so much as a farthing more on Eve Williams's food. None of it was true, and none of it – when it worked its inevitable way back to Eve – was particularly hurtful. But there was other, more vicious tale-telling that had its roots in genuine bad feeling, and the chief exponent among the ill-wishers was Harry Tideaway.

The publican's own star had fallen since his loose tongue had put him out of favour with the earl. Not that Lord Netherwood had spoken of his feelings after the encounter with Harry on that Sunday afternoon back in June – it was, after all, very much in the earl's interests to say as little as possible on the subject, since it principally concerned his feckless son. But Jem Arkwright, land agent and avenging angel, made sure that Harry was made to pay for his indiscretion. A quiet word here and there and most of the regulars were easily persuaded to drink at the Hare and Hounds or the Cross Keys. It was a very simple equation: Jem was highly regarded in the town, while Harry was hardly regarded at all.

With his trade and profits whirlpooling down the drain, Harry had ample time to nurture his resentment against Eve and it combined with his naturally savage streak, which for the past twelve months had been confined to occasional acts of violence towards Agnes behind locked doors. He began to pass on to anyone who would give him the time of day that Eve Williams was servicing the earl in the bedroom, for which sexual favours he had paid generously by setting her up in the old flour mill. The day she stopped lifting her skirt for Lord Netherwood would be the day she went out of business. It was God's honest truth, he said.

Nobody really believed him, but plenty of people passed it on, though most of them had the good sense to keep it from Amos Sykes. Except, that is, for Barry Stevens, who at the end of a shift at New Mill, when Amos had angered him with his prudish refusal to find him funny, decided to get a rise out of him with the details of Eve Williams's dodgy business arrangement. They had just stepped into the cage for the ride up to the top, so Amos didn't hear first time and said, 'What's tha' say?'

Barry put his mouth closer to Amos's ear.

'Ah said, Teddy 'oyland's stickin' 'is dick into Eve Williams.' He paused to snigger. 'What d'yer think's put that smile on 'er face? It's not thi bloody veg plot, that's for certain.'

The cage burst through into daylight and lurched to a standstill. The banksman hauled open the doors and collected the brass checks as the men stepped out. Barry's face wore a familiar smile, sly and triumphant; he'd floored Sykes, the smug bastard. Head down, he walked off at a lick, but Amos was right there, by his side.

'An' who told you that shite?' he said.

'That's fo' me to know,' said Barry, and suddenly found himself backed up against the brick wall of the lamp room, his throat in the vice of Amos's clenched fist.

'Who told you that shite?' said Amos again. By God, it's like goading a bull, thought Barry.

'It were a joke,' said Barry, with difficulty. 'I were 'avin you on.'

'Who told you that fuckin' shite,' Amos said. He knew Barry Stevens well enough to know when he was lying.

'If ah tell yer tha'll let me go, right?' Barry was all mouth, but he was no fighter.

'Aye, yer miserable bastard,' Amos said. 'I'll let thi go.'

'It were 'arry Tideaway,' Barry said, his voice strangulated, his eyes bulging.

Amos relaxed his grip and Barry thought he'd got away with it, but he was wrong because although Amos did let him go, it was only to free up his right fist for a powerful uppercut which split the skin on contact and opened up a gash through which the white of the jawbone was just visible. He left, without so much as a backwards glance, tossing his helmet in through the open door of the lamp room, and stalking out of the pit yard at a pace fired by fury. At the Hoyland Arms he stopped, took a few deep breaths, rearranged his face, and walked in.

The pub was empty except for Harry, who had his till open and was counting his pitiful takings. He looked at Amos with surprise. 'I've called time,' he said.

'Shame,' said Amos. 'Ah well, ni' mind.'

They regarded each other across the bar, Harry wary and Amos working hard to keep his expression unreadable.

'Just 'eard summat interestin' from Barry Stevens,' he said, as if he was merely passing time.

'Oh aye?' said Harry, perking up. If he'd lived longer in Netherwood – and hadn't been so much of a scoundrel – he might have sensed treacherous waters.

'Aye. Eve Williams and Lord Netherwood. Y' know.' Amos nodded suggestively. He couldn't bring himself to frame the words. 'Probably not true, mind,' he said.

'Every word, true as I'm stood 'ere,' Harry said, sealing his fate. 'Mind you, who wouldn't shaft 'er, given t'chance?'

He laughed a deep, fat man's laugh that shook his jowls and his belly, a dirty, lascivious laugh that provoked in Amos such a fierce rush of pure hatred that, small though he was, he found the strength to reach over and haul Harry up and across the top of the bar, the buttons of his waistcoat scratching the mahogany as he travelled. Then, when Amos had him where he wanted him, he punched Harry twice, square in the face, and shoved him backwards against the panelling where he slid down the wall and slumped like a sack of coal on the floor.

Amos snarled, more beast than man. 'One more word about Eve Williams from your wicked mouth, an' tha dead,' he said.

Harry couldn't speak, even if he'd had anything to say. His

flesh was swelling above the left eye, and blood ran in a steady stream from his nose into his open mouth. He was immobile. He watched Amos Sykes leave the pub then sat there in his wretched stupor, waiting for Agnes to come back from the butcher's. She'd feel the back of his hand if she was late.

In a roundabout way, Barry Stevens did Amos a favour. He and Eve had patched up their friendship since their argument – it was months ago now – but still, it wasn't the comfortable, easy thing it had been. Amos had told Seth he mustn't side against his mother, but at the same time he himself had privately nursed a grievance against Eve, keeping his disappointment and sense of betrayal alive, quietly hating the earl for his ability to give Eve what she seemed to want. But suddenly, today, the picture looked different. Eve was vulnerable to harm from folk who didn't wish her well. She needed Amos, whether she knew it or not. He walked home that day with a spring in his step and a lightness in the general area of his heart that made him almost take a detour to Beaumont Lane. Instead, he counselled himself to be cautious. A man couldn't declare himself to the woman he loved with blood on his knuckles and coal dust on his face. Amos didn't know a lot about romance, but he knew that much.

Chapter 34

The day of the opening dawned fair and bright, one of those crisp, late gifts of a day that England has made its speciality, a last, joyful hurrah before we're all forced to remember the arduous trudge of winter ahead. At Netherwood Hall, the countess was up early; Flytton, arriving to assist with her lengthy morning toilet, was alarmed to find her out of bed and gazing out of the window. This was most irregular.

'Well, thank goodness,' Clarissa said, without turning. 'I thought you'd never come.' It was habit, not irritation, which compelled her to speak so brusquely.

Flytton bridled. She looked at her fob. It was seven-thirty; to her certain knowledge, Lady Netherwood hadn't asked her to be any earlier today.

'I'm here at the same time as always,' she said tartly. The countess gave her a reproving look, which Flytton staunchly returned.

Their partnership was ten years old, and, like a marriage of the same length, the relationship had settled into entirely predictable patterns of behaviour. Flytton was a formidably efficient lady's maid who had once had an offer from the Duchess of Devonshire, and although she had chosen to remain in post at Netherwood, the interest from Chatsworth had raised her further still in both her own esteem and the household hierarchy, with the effect that any deference she might have once displayed was quite evaporated. For her part, Lady Netherwood met Flytton's occasional insubordination with often unreasonable behaviour and appalling rudeness. She saw no conflict between this and the great value she placed on her maid's judgement and opinions. It was a finely tuned act, perfectly understood by each, and a cause of concern to neither.

Flytton crossed the room, barely disturbing the immaculate line of her skirt as she moved. She gave the impression, Tobias once said, of having casters for feet.

'Good morning, ma'am,' she added pointedly, as if to remind Lady Netherwood of her manners.

'Don't be petulant, Flytton,' said Lady Netherwood. 'The dove-grey chiffon, I thought?'

'Certainly, ma'am. If you think so,' said Flytton, with the inflection she used when she disagreed.

Lady Netherwood sighed. 'Why not?'

'Wigmore Hall, ma'am?'

The countess blanched and brought her hand to her lovely mouth at the unwelcome reminder. She'd forgotten, though she didn't quite know how, that it was indeed the dove-grey, with its modish train, that had been responsible for a most humiliating public come-down. In the very same gown, just this season past, Clarissa had swept into an afternoon recital carrying a banana skin and the stubs of two cigarettes in the folds of her trailing skirts. More unfortunately still, the famously spiteful Lady Aldney had been first witness to this.

'Clarissa, dear,' she had boomed in her carrying voice, her bosom already heaving with mirth. 'How very public-spirited of you to clean the streets of detritus as you promenade.'

She had flicked the offending items out of the chiffon and on to the floor of Wigmore Hall as she spoke, so that they skittered across the marble foyer and had to be collected by a menial. The assembled company laughed gaily at Lady Aldney's great wit, and Lady Netherwood had been obliged to join in.

It was an unwelcome memory but Clarissa, recovering her composure and still keen on the dove-grey, said, 'Yes, but does anyone eat bananas in Netherwood?'

'It's not banana skins you need to worry about here,' Flytton said, expertly lifting out of the wardrobe a selection of alternatives to the dove-grey. 'It's the blessed coal dust.'

'Well I hope you're not suggesting the black silk. That wouldn't do at all. It's super fun, this little pie-shop venture. I'm rather pleased with Teddy for getting involved.'

She rifled through the dresses, which now lay on the bed. Her tiny nose, a Benbury family trait and a great asset to the girls who inherited it, though not so fetching on the men, wrinkled charmingly as she sifted, and rejected, the *eau-de-nil*, the French blue and the moss green.

'The ashes of roses, I think, Flytton,' she said. 'And please don't bother telling me why I shouldn't.'

Flytton pursed her lips but held her peace. Averting another dove-grey disaster had been her only objective, and that, she felt, had been very satisfactorily achieved. The ashes of roses had no trailing train and was eminently suitable, which was why it had been among her selection. The countess would be lost without her; as long as both of them understood that, Flytton was content.

Anna had started reading newspapers to improve her English and her knowledge of the world; not the Barnsley *Chronicle*, which she found – unfairly, given its remit – too narrow and parochial, but the London *Times* or the *Telegraph*, whichever she could get hold of. These were publications of sufficient weight and import, she believed, to properly enhance her programme of self-improvement. She felt wiser and more learned simply by opening them up. She would struggle through the leader columns and the international pages, scouring the difficult words for news from Kiev or any part of the Ukraine. She found a thrilling reference to the presence in London of one Vladimir Ilyich Lenin, and imagined jumping on a train bound for the capital and seeking him out, not because she liked the sound of him but just for the relief of speaking Russian.

'Would you spot 'im?' Eve said. 'London's not like Netherwood, you know – they say it's teemin' wi' folk.'

Anna had seen London. She had never seen Lenin, however, or even heard of him before, but she was confident she would be able to pick him out in a crowd.

'Of course I spot him,' she said, passing the paper over to show Eve his unsmiling face, bald dome and natty beard. 'See?'

Eve looked at Lenin and sniffed. 'Odd-lookin' bloke. 'e'd do well to wear a flat cap,' she said. 'Anyroad, never mind 'im. We've work to do. Fairy pies.'

Anna rolled her eyes. Eve, having heard that the countess was to attend the opening on Monday, had taken the extraordinary decision – in Anna's view – that all the food they prepared for the gathering would be in elegant one- or two-bite sizes. Not pies and puddings and pastries cut into morsels, but whole pies and puddings and pastries no bigger than morsels themselves.

'I'm not 'aving Lady Netherwood wrestling wi' a wedge o' game pie,' she said. 'I doubt she could open 'er mouth wide enough. It's grand for t'likes o' you an' me, but she's used to summat different.' Eve remembered the food she'd seen leaving the kitchen for dinner at Netherwood Hall the night before the party. Slices of chicken breast the size of florins; potatoes peeled away until most of their flesh was in the compost bin and the pale white spheres remaining weren't much bigger than a knur; carrots peeled and cut into identical, tiny matchsticks. 'She's used to fairy food,' Eve said.

So fairy food it was, and though Eve had stuck to her guns, she'd had plenty of occasion to rue the idea once they got started. She roped in Ginger, Alice and Nellie to help, and they worked up at the new kitchen to give themselves some elbow room. The meat for the pies had to be minced, not chopped, and the hot-water pastry raised into thimble-sized cases. The toll it took on their fingers! Nellie, who was known for her remedies, came in with a poultice the day after their first session, a mixture of dried rose petals and rotten apple, which she promised them would ease the ache in the knuckles. It was curiously soothing but the cloying smell wasn't easy to bear. Eve gave up after ten minutes; anyway, she found her aching fingers were more than compensated for by the sight of four trays of raised game pies, none of them bigger than a button mushroom. They also made miniature chicken-and-gravy pies, Anna's pig parcels – they were tricky – and an old recipe of Ginger's called potato pudding-pie, which called for mashed potato, whisked eggs and a splash of brandy – Ginger had some at home, to no one's surprise – baked in puff-pastry cases. Alice, shy and pink-cheeked, brought in a recipe of her grandmother's for a savoury pudding made with stale bread soaked in milk and water then baked with mixed herbs and eggs. It sounded unappetising, but the one they tried tasted just like a good sage stuffing; it came out of the oven a nice even brown, and turned out of the dish as obligingly as a sandcastle from a bucket. They added it to the repertoire, cooled and cut into delicate rounds.

Nellie said they should have something sweet, to counter all the savoury, and Anna said it had to be Eve's Puddings, but they didn't work in miniature without a pudding bowl to bake them in, so they improvised by mincing the apple and stirring it into a sponge mix, then making tiny apple cakes in cases made from baking parchment and snipped around the edges to give them a frill. They waved in the heat of the oven like the fronds of sea anemones.

All the dainties were ready and waiting up at the mill on the morning of the opening, arranged on silver platters borrowed from the Netherwood Hall kitchens. There were no formal invitations – it wasn't a party, after all – but the people Eve wanted there had been asked and the whole Hoyland clan was attending, so there'd be a nice little crowd. The earl was to say a few words, the food would be handed around, those who wanted to have a nosey inside would be welcome to, then everyone would clear off and the real business would begin. That at least was what Eve hoped. Personally, she'd have gone about things with a lot less fanfare. It was Lord Netherwood who was all for the launch, picking the date to suit his diary and sending up crates of Netherwood Hall perry to toast the venture on the day. Eve hadn't liked to point out that Monday was usually wash day in Beaumont Lane. She supposed the world wouldn't end if it all got done on Tuesday, just this once.

Meanwhile Anna, who by now had splashed out on a second-hand Singer to widen the scope of her dressmaking, had come up with their outfits for the occasion after finding inspiration from a fashion plate and its accompanying article in the London *Times*. It was a picture of a Gibson Girl, an American import that had, in her jaunty, liberated, independent outlook and outfit, captured the spirit of the modern young woman. Now, Anna fancied that she and Eve were the embodiment of this wonderful, emancipated creature, so, for the day of the opening of Eve's new enterprise, she had fashioned a whole new Gibson Girl look for them both. Flared skirts, pin-tucked white blouses, floppy black bows at the throat and neat little hats, pinned securely into place at a jaunty angle. The hats had been the only real expense, but worth it, she felt, for the impact they had.

'You must buy a proper looking-glass,' she complained, as they attempted to see their reflection in a tin of liver salts. 'We only see ourselves in parts. It's like jigsaw puzzle.'

'Well from t'pieces I can see, we look a bit full of ourselves,' Eve said. She was worried particularly about the bow. It was meant to look artistic, and was undoubtedly up-to-the-minute, but Eve felt trussed up and more than a little frivolous.

Amos rapped on the back door and opened it simultaneously. He always did this; requested admittance then granted it himself. He was wearing an old suit, probably the one he – or perhaps his father, judging by its antique cut – got married in. The fabric strained at the shoulders and across the back, as if in spite of his good intentions he might break free at any moment. There were signs of strain around his eyes too, which looked bloodshot; he was working nights this week and should have been in bed at this hour, but he wanted to be at the opening. He had resolved, for one day at least, to demonstrate by deed that he'd accepted Eve's capitalist adventure up at Mitchell's Mill. He couldn't stop calling it by its former name though and neither, for that matter, could Eve, even though there was tangible proof of the change in the form of a smart new fascia, black letters on a cream background: EVE'S PUDDINGS & PIES, Proprietor Eve Williams. Amos, in the kitchen now, clocked the two women and performed an exaggerated double-take.

'Bloody Norah,' he said, which hardly helped.

'You see?' Eve said to Anna. 'We look ridiculous.'

Anna glared at Amos, who held up his hands in self-defence.

'No, no, you look . . .' – beautiful, he wanted to say, but didn't – '. . . right smart. Professional, like. It's just not what you usually wear, that's all.'

'You can say that again,' she said, laughing. 'Anyway, you can talk, all dressed up like a dog's dinner.' She thought he looked grand, actually. A suit always did something to improve the appearance of a man, she thought, somehow deflecting the eye from other, less appealing features. He might have left the flat cap at home, though, just this once.

'Dunt want to show you up, like,' said Amos, grinning.

'Got to go, come, come,' Anna said, shooing them like chickens towards the door. The Hoyland contingent – the nobs, as Amos persisted in referring to them – were due up there at ten o'clock, and it was already just leaving half-past nine. Anna opened the stair door and called to the children to come down, which they promptly did, Seth first, followed by Eliza holding Maya, then Ellen looking put out as she always did when she felt she was playing second fiddle to the baby. They were all in their chapel clothes and looked a picture, except for Seth's mutinous expression. The stiff collar always made him cross; it was ruining, for him, the novelty and freedom of a Monday off school. He cheered up, though, when he saw Amos. Amos winked at him, and Seth grinned.

Eve, while everyone's back was turned, had picked up a damp cloth and started wiping away invisible crumbs from spotless work surfaces. It was the only sign that she was anxious about the day ahead. Anna prised the dishcloth from her hands and, taking her by the shoulders, turned her to face the door again.

'Go,' she said. She gave her a little shove. 'Be gone.'

'What about you?' Eve said.

'I follow with Maya in minute,' Anna said.

'No, come now, Anna. I need you up there with me.' Because if you don't leave with us, she thought, it'll be happy families all the way through town for me, Amos and the bairns.

There was a brief, awkward hiatus with Anna inside dressing Maya in her hat and coat, while Eve, Amos and the children stood outside in the yard. It was cold, and there was a noxious smell of human waste because the middens had been emptied just a couple of hours earlier. There was no reason on earth to linger, yet linger they did. Lilly poked her head out of the door of number three and said: 'No Daimler today then?'

266

'She's given t'chauffeur t'day off,' Amos replied.

Eve wondered how it looked to Lilly, standing here with Amos and the children. She wondered, too, how long it took to put a hat on a baby's head.

Amos, understanding, said, 'Seth, lad, shall we mek a start?'

The boy said yes, always eager to put some distance between himself and Anna. Amos looked at Eve.

'We've got some veg business to discuss,' he said, smiling. Then he turned to Eliza: 'Borin' boys' stuff. That all right wi' you, missy?'

Eliza, happy just to have been consulted, nodded, so Amos and Seth took their leave, heads down, walking briskly down the entry into Watson Street. Eve, watching them go, suddenly felt ashamed of herself for hanging back. She should stop caring about the likes of Lilly Pickering, and start caring about the likes of Amos.

'Wait!' she shouted. Holding Ellen on her hip and Eliza by the hand, they jogged after the boys and walked together with them all the way to Mitchell's Mill.

The convoy of Hoylands made its way from Netherwood Hall at a stately pace, attracting a mixed crowd of onlookers as they went, some ardent, some curious and some just plain under-employed. Lord Netherwood led the procession in a brand new Daimler – purchased on impulse after admiring it at the Crystal Palace Motor Show – with a frilly Isabella by his side. Tobias, newly returned from Scotland and cutting a dash in his cream linen motoring coat, drove his own little two-seater, with the permanently affable Dickie waving cheerfully from the passenger seat. The countess was closeted in the landau, though she occasionally popped out her head to enormous cheers. Henrietta, typically and much to her mother's chagrin, was bringing up the rear, driving her own little phaeton. Along they all came, smiling proprietorially at the crowds in a way that made Amos want to break something. There wasn't room for all their various vehicles in the crowded courtyard at the back of the mill, so the motor cars and Henrietta's phaeton had to be moored at the bottom of Mitchell's Snicket, while Lady Netherwood was driven all the way in to preserve her dignity and the fine silk of her shoes.

Amos, forgetting his resolve, allowed a sneer of disdain to spoil his pleasant expression. 'Is she goin' to get out o' that bloody carriage?' he muttered to Eve. 'Or will she stay inside, for fear of infection?'

It was an ill-advised remark, one that he should have kept to himself, and he instantly regretted it because he could see the displeasure on Eve's face. She summoned her children and crossed the cobbled yard, well away from where Amos had positioned himself; this was no occasion, she fumed inwardly, to be rehearsing his rant at the aristocracy. He was a fool if he thought it was, a bigger fool if he thought she'd join in. Under the colonnade she found Ginger, Nellie and Alice, all in their chapel frocks and hats, smiling at her. Ginger said, 'You look a right bobby dazzler,' and Eve blushed because she'd forgotten, temporarily, what she was wearing.

The four women and three children were now in a line under the colonnade, looking out over the courtyard. It looked a picture now; Lady Netherwood had finally been galvanised, as the earl had known she would be, by a visit to the premises during the final stages of renovation, following which she had sent Hislop and a small team of under-gardeners to carry out her plans for the area. The gristmill had indeed been reincarnated as a fountain, the weeds were gone from between the cobbles, and there were stone urns and statuary artfully placed to further enhance the illusion that an Italian count might have once lived in Netherwood. Far from being reluctant to leave the landau, the countess seemed barely able to contain her excitement as she was handed down by her coachman. Her appearance in full, rather than viewed through the carriage window, elicited a sigh of appreciation from the women among the crowd. She was a vision in dusky pink, the embodiment of charm and femininity, a shining example of the rewards of the ceaseless pursuit of perfection combined with a limitless budget. She wore kidskin gloves in the palest cream, and a hat with a wide brim which dipped on one side to give her the appearance of always peeping coquettishly from under it. Eve, to her profound relief, suddenly felt positively under-dressed.

The Hoyland offspring assembled in an informal cluster around their parents and the crowd of friends and sundry locals gathered in front of them. Eve, scanning their faces, saw Samuel Farrimond and Wilfred Oxspring in deep conversation. Lilly Pickering and Maud Platt had walked up together, curiosity having got the better of them. They stood at the back whispering behind their hands, like overgrown schoolgirls. Percy Medlicott had come, and Jonas Buckle stood with him. The Ramsbottom sisters were right at the front and they gave her a wave, jigging up and down a little with the excitement of it all.

The earl cleared his throat, clapped for attention and started to speak, his theme being the inestimable merits of enterprise and industriousness. Tobias, who had behaved himself now for an unbroken stretch of three months, wondered indignantly if the old man meant it for him. In fact, there was no hidden message; it was a straightforward tribute to Eve, who was the one person not actually listening. She gazed about her as he spoke, marvelling at life's unexpected turns. There was Anna, with Maya, standing next to Amos in the crowd. They made a lovely couple, Eve thought idly. Anna was so tiny she made Amos look almost tall. The straw hat had fallen victim to the baby, who had wrenched it off Anna's head and was now waving it in triumph. They were both watching the earl, Amos's expression a study in neutrality, Anna's all concentration as she struggled with his upper-class accent. She'd cracked the Yorkshire dialect, but this was something new. She leaned in a little further, watching the fractional movement of Lord Netherwood's mouth.

'She is an exemple of the indomitable spirit on which we built an empar, end I'm heppy and proud to be her becker in this exciting new enterprise,' said the earl, to Anna's mystification. 'Ey hev every confidence in ha energy, ha telents end ha characta.'

Eve, still gazing rather than listening, suddenly realised everyone was looking at her.

'I give you, Eve Williams!' the earl said. There was enthusiastic applause and Eve joined in until Ginger said, right in her ear, 'Go on, soft lass, 'e means you to join 'im,' and she gave Eve a mighty shove, sending her down the steps and over to Lord Netherwood's side in a sort of ungainly trot.

Lady Netherwood took her first real look at Eve Williams at that moment, and was rather startled to find her younger than she'd realised, and much more beautiful. She had imagined, if she'd thought about her at all, that Mrs Williams would be cut from the same doughty cloth as Mrs Adams; after all, they were both cooks, both widows, so it seemed reasonable to assume – to Clarissa, at any rate – that they would both share the same wide girth and grizzled appearance. But here she stood, a slip of a thing – too, too lovely – wearing a simply divine little get-up that couldn't possibly have been acquired outside Bond Street. Lady Netherwood caught Henrietta's eye and raised an elegant brow. Her daughter returned the look. And there and then, the countess decided to Take An Interest in this charming protégée of Teddy's.

Meanwhile Eve – too, too lovely though she might be – stood mute at the head of the pack of Hoylands, facing the assembled company, completely at a loss as to what she should do or say. The earl beamed at her then nodded supportively, then finally understood that she was in some kind of fear-induced stupor. He leaned in: 'Just a few words from you, m'dear,' he whispered. 'Anything will do, anything at all.'

Eve came to and realised what a fool she looked, so she started to speak.

'I . . .' she said, and stopped. She looked about her, and her eyes alighted on Anna, who smiled so warmly that Eve thought she might cry.

'I . . .' she said again, and the faces in front of her swam out of focus, then back again. And then Anna, propelled by a protective instinct, moved forwards in the crowd. She looked directly at Eve and nodded at her as if to say, 'Go on then, I'm listening,' and somehow this made the difference.

'I'm so grateful to Lord Netherwood,' said Eve, with an unfamiliar shake in her voice, 'for showing such faith in my future.' She paused, and took a deep, fortifying breath. 'And I'm grateful too to Reverend Farrimond over there' – she paused and pointed at the minister, who bowed theatrically – 'for being a friend and writing all those little notices that made people come to my shop.' She was finding her own voice now, the one she recognised, and her anxiety seemed to be leaving her, dissipating into the October sky like the smoke from a garden bonfire.

'I'm grateful to my children, Seth, Eliza and Ellen' – she paused for the crowd to admire them, standing bemused and a little over-awed on the chequered tiles of the colonnade – 'for puttin' up with my ill-'umour and fittin' in with so many changes to their lives. To Amos Sykes' – she found him in the crowd, and spoke directly to him – 'who grieved for Arthur as I did, and who has been such a rock to me and my little family. To all of you' – she swept an arm in an arc that encompassed everyone – 'for coming today to see what's what, and perhaps 'ave a bit o' free food' – she paused for laughter, just like a pro – 'but finally, and most importantly, I thank from my 'eart my dear friend Anna Rabinovich.' Eve hesitated for a beat, feeling an obstruction in her throat that almost overcame her. She breathed, in and out, deep and slow. It was suddenly paramount that she got these words out. 'My dear friend Anna,' she repeated, 'who gave me t'strength and support I needed to endure t'days and weeks after Arthur's death, and far beyond. I couldn't have done it without you, Anna. You are as a sister to me.'

Anna, tears streaming, waved a dismissive hand. The small crowd dabbed at their eyes and looked tragic. Eve thought, this is getting maudlin, so she smiled broadly and upped the tempo: 'Anyroad, this is meant to be day one of Eve's Puddin's & Pies, so let's get down to business.'

There was clapping, cheering and a little whistling. Alice, Ginger and Nellie went inside and took off their hats and coats, and donned clean pinnies, ready to serve the platters of party food. Two footmen from Netherwood Hall had been drafted in to look after the perry, which was being passed around now in crystal flutes. The old mill, scrubbed and restored and full of life, looked magnificent. Eve allowed herself a small gloat at the wonder of it all. No tap dancing, mind, she said to herself. Inside, the earl found her, and pumped her hand up and down as if he was hoping to draw water.

'Well done, well said, jolly well done – thought you'd dried up back there, what!'

Then Lady Netherwood, in a manoeuvre which somehow combined gentility with great rudeness, pushed her husband out of the way to get to Eve. Her cloud of cologne enveloped them both, and she took Eve's hands in her own gloved ones. The kidskin was so beautifully soft that Eve had to fight the impulse to stroke the nap. She'd never beheld the countess at such close range and her legendary beauty, while still in evidence, was a little jaded in the unforgiving light of the October sun, which picked out the tiny, treacherous lines around her eyes. But she was breathtakingly elegant, tiny in every particular, with a figure so beautifully preserved she could, from behind, have been taken for a girl in woman's clothing. She held Eve's eyes in a limpid gaze for a few seconds, then said, 'Do tell – your outfit, dear. Bond Street, no?'

Eve frowned in consternation. The countess seemed to have jumbled her words into meaningless disorder.

'I beg your pardon, your ladyship?' she said.

'Too, too divine,' said the countess. 'Your get-up. Mayfair? Which outfitter?'

The mist cleared a little. 'Oh, thank you, your ladyship. But—'

'Looking at you makes me want to dash home and tear up all my silly chiffon.'

'Oh, don't do that,' said Eve, horrified. 'Your gown is lovely, m'lady.' She plucked at the fabric of her own skirt. 'This is just 'ome-made,' she said. 'Anna made everythin'. Well, aside from t'ats, they were from Butterwick's. There was a discount for two. T'offer's still on.'

It was as if her mouth and voice were functioning without any input from her brain, and she was engulfed by shame. What would the countess care for Butterwick's and their discounted hats? Eve, pink and mortified, cursed herself for a fool, but she needn't have worried; the countess didn't generally listen to what others were saying, and at the moment she was smiling vaguely at her oldest daughter who had bounced up with an outstretched hand.

'Hello again, Eve. I say, clever you!' she said. 'This is just wonderful.' She swept an elegant arm about her, to encompass the mill, the courtyard and everyone there. 'I so admire you. So exciting. I do hope it's a roaring success. I'm sure it will be.'

Eve said, 'Thank you,' though she wished she had something more gracious at her disposal, for it seemed an inadequate response to all that enthusiasm.

'You do look spiffy. Doesn't she, Ma? Terrific outfit. Very much the Modern Independent Woman!'

She gave a proper, firm, ungloved handshake, being built from sturdier stuff than her mother, who seemed liable to waft away on the breeze. Eve smiled.

'Very pleased to 'ave you here, and thank you. Again,' she said. She was starting to feel quite at home with all these Hoylands, though not quite so at home as Anna who seemed to be deep in conversation with Lord Netherwood. Eve hoped she would remember he was an earl and not put him to work.

Ginger waltzed over with a platter of pies. Her curly hair was piled into a riotous topknot and this, with her trademark pillar-box-red lipstick and glamorous pallor, gave her a look of the young Sarah Bernhardt. Lady Netherwood began to feel positively disorientated. Henrietta took a tiny game pie and popped it into her mouth, reaching for another as she chewed.

'Yum,' she said thickly. Ginger offered the platter to the countess, who peered at its load then gasped with delight.

'How utterly charming!' she said. 'Tiny, tiny pies. Enchanting.'

Eve flashed a triumphant smile at Ginger, who flashed it straight back. Lady Netherwood said: 'Do you know, I haven't eaten pastry for years. Such an enemy to the waistline. But what harm can these little darlings do?' She took a pie, perfect and glossily brown, and popped it into her mouth. It seemed rude to watch her eat, but then again it was impossible to do much else. The countess swallowed delicately. She took the merest sip of perry. Then she smiled.

'Clever girl!' she said to Eve. 'What else have you made?'

274

Chapter 35

༄ ~~~~~~~ ༄

The countess tried everything twice and was in ecstasies
quite out of proportion, Eve felt, to the humble fare she
praised. It could only be, she decided, that Lady Netherwood's
palate was so replete with fancy haute cuisine that plain Yorkshire cooking came as a revelation. Plain Yorkshire cooking,
that is, in countess-sized portions.

Tobias had joined his mother. He had a poker game lined
up later and was keen to be off, but since his exile to, and
joyous return from, the Scottish residence, he had managed to
perform his filial duties to the letter while still by and large
pleasing himself. It had been damnably cold at Glendonoch,
and there hadn't been a single girl among the flint-hearted and
puritanical staff who'd been willing to warm him up. A smile
would've been something, but they wouldn't even look him in
the eye to say their name. It had crossed his mind that the
earl might have telegraphed ahead with a warning to the
household to lock up their daughters. Forced into temporary
celibacy, Tobias played golf, fished the loch and furthered his
education in the varieties of single malt, resolving all the while
to play a cleverer game on his return. That is, he would keep
Pater sweet by feigning a new-found, if skin deep, fascination

in the Netherwood estate, leaving himself ample, unsupervised time to pursue his own interests. It was all a matter of balance. So here he was, smiling engagingly at his mother as she spoke, and all the time imagining what Eve Williams would look like naked. She was eyeing him warily, as if she might be able to read his mind. All terribly entertaining, he thought.

'Don't you think,' his mother said, tinkling at him in the oddly flirtatious voice she reserved for her beloved son, 'these darling pies would be just the thing at Fulton House?'

'What an absolutely sensational thought,' said Tobias. He smiled at Eve, a lazy smile that revealed to her just a little of what he was actually thinking. She concentrated furiously on his mother.

'Such a triumph,' she was saying. 'Dainty little working-class canapés.' She trilled with laughter. 'So witty. You'll come, Eve?'

'Do say you will, Eve? *Come*, that is,' said Tobias, delighted with himself and his innuendo. Filthy-minded pig, thought Eve.

'The season can be so dull, every party a replica of the last,' said the countess. 'You, my dear, will be Quite The Thing.' You could hear the capitals in her voice. 'My secret weapon on the society battlefield.' She pealed with laughter again, as if she had bells instead of a larynx.

'Well,' Eve said. She was unsure how to decline, and, anyway, thought perhaps she wasn't in a position to. At least Amos wasn't listening in. Be grateful for small mercies.

'Such fun!' said Lady Netherwood. 'Toby, walk me to the landau. I need half an hour with my diary before dinner. Party planning,' she said to Eve. 'My absolutely favourite pastime. Goodbye, dear. Divine outfit.'

And away she drifted on Tobias's arm. Eve watched her go, wondering quite what she'd been asked to do. Obviously she couldn't go to London. The idea was beyond barmy. Perhaps the pies and pastries could travel alone, by train. First class, of course. She smiled. Her head was throbbing gently from the perry. She had no taste for drink, and no head for it either. People were still milling around, enjoying the occasion, sampling the food, but Eve would happily have left them to it. She longed for the simplicity and the comfort of home.

It turned out that Anna had suggested to the earl that the first floor of the mill, currently empty, would make a wonderful restaurant, selling the sort of hearty home cooking that Eve did best. Lord Netherwood thought it a marvellous idea.

'Oh 'e did, did 'e?' said Eve.

Anna pouted and said, 'Don't be cross. At least miners and their mucky britches wouldn't be in your parlour.'

This was indisputable, but not much of a recommendation as far as Eve could see.

'It's t'work involved, Anna,' she said. 'We can't manage it, on top of t'orders I've already taken on.'

'Hire more staff,' said Anna.

'Simple as that.'

'Just so.'

'Thanks for organising my life for me.'

'You're welcome.' Anna smiled. Sarcasm often eluded her, as if her ear was attuned only to the literal meaning of words, not their nuances.

Eve sighed. It would, she had to admit, make a beautiful dining room upstairs, those arched windows, all that light. But she didn't fancy running up and down the stairs with one-shilling dinners. She'd sleep on it, she thought. See what the morning made of it. Eve yawned, widely. Anna was ready to leave, and had Maya and Ellen with her. Seth and Eliza were long gone, sloping off back to Beaumont Lane to play in the street with their friends. Seth had a back-door key these days, a rite of passage the import of which wasn't lost on him. He barely ever got the chance to use it – if his mother wasn't in, then Anna usually was – but he loved the weight and the feel of it in the pocket of his trousers. It gave him power over Eliza too. She had to stand and wait while he took his time on the doorstep.

'I'll be right behind you,' Eve said. 'Put t'kettle on. I just need five minutes to be sure it's all straight.'

Anna and the little girls left, making slow progress because Maya liked to walk now, though she was still very much a beginner; you needed the patience of Job just to get her down the stairs in the morning. Now, as they went on their way, Anna chided her in Russian, always her language of choice when tired or irritable. Eve, standing outside to watch them go, heard Anna scold. That child, she thought, will grow up with a dread of her mother's native tongue.

'Long day?'

Eve swung round in alarm. Amos appeared from the shadows of the courtyard and stood before her.

'Oh it's you!' Eve said. 'I would've put good money on you 'avin' gone home to bed by now.' She sounded cheerful enough, but her heart was inexplicably pounding in her chest, as if it were a stranger creeping up on her. She wished he'd speak, but he stayed silent, watching her with a benign expression as if she was a pleasant view or a beautiful sunset. It was unnerving.

'Amos?' she said. Then she thought, with a flash of intuition, oh good God, he's going to ask me to marry him.

Amos opened his mouth, then closed it again. Her eyes seemed to be issuing some kind of warning but this business could be put off until his dying day, and then where would he be? Cold in the churchyard for all eternity. He looked down at his hands, away from her face. The words he wanted to say slid about in his mind, dodging his grasp. God knows, he'd rehearsed them often enough at home, in the lonely little house that he'd shared

278

with Julia for so short a time. He loved Eve, and he loved her children, especially the lad, who felt almost like kin. It had taken him a long time, but he'd convinced himself that, if he could but summon the courage and ask, Eve would accept. It would be natural and easy, and he could care for her in the way Arthur would've wanted. Then he could, at last, take her in his arms and feel her body against his, kiss her lovely, familiar mouth, take her long hair between his fingers. He yearned for this, like a parched man yearns for water. And even up to the very moment that he made his presence known in the courtyard, he had been confident. But then he saw her eyes, and all certainty left him, as suddenly and completely as the extinguishing of a candle's flame. A new, miserable future crowded uninvited and unwelcome into his head, but he shook it away, still not prepared to give up hope. He would speak.

'Eve,' he began. 'For a long while now I've—'

She cut in, frantic to protect him. 'Brrrr, it's cold now t'sun's dipped,' she said, too loudly and with an exaggerated, fake shudder. 'Time I got back to t'bairns.'

He looked up now, read the message in her face, and ploughed on regardless, abandoning his mental script in favour of speaking from the heart.

'I love you, Eve,' he said, simply and helplessly. 'Will you marry me?'

It was beautifully done, but he knew the answer, even before he had finished speaking. She stepped towards him, but he moved back.

'Ni' mind,' he said. 'Forget I spoke.'

'Oh, Amos,' she said. This was terrible, cruel. He had the look of a deer brought down by an unseen arrow, bewildered, mortally wounded.

'It's not that I don't love you,' she said, struggling for the right words. 'I do. You feel like part of my family now. But I don't feel for you as a wife towards a husband, do you see?'

279

He held up a hand. 'Enough,' he said.

'I'm so sorry, Amos.'

'Don't say that. Don't pity me.'

'No! It's not pity, it's—'

'I said, enough.' His voice was harder now, his priority self-preservation. He couldn't salvage his happiness from the wreckage of this sorry situation, but he could save his pride.

'I spoke when I perhaps shouldn't 'ave,' he said. 'I misread your feelins. No matter. I'm just as well alone as wed.'

She heard him out, mired in abject misery.

'I'll bid you goodnight,' he said, raising his cap in a formal gesture that made her feel sadder still, as if there was already a distance between them that hadn't existed before. 'Tell Seth I'll see 'im tomorrow.'

'Aye, I will,' she said to his retreating back. She watched him turn out of the courtyard under the arch. She wished she could have run after him, calling his name, telling him she'd been wrong and that yes, of course she would marry him. But she didn't, because it would have been a lie, and Amos deserved better. Nevertheless, when she walked home alone later that evening she felt weary and careworn, and the weight of his disappointment dragged around her like a physical burden.

PART THREE

Chapter 36

The coachman's name was Samuel Stallibrass. He was a Lancastrian by birth, and a friendly soul, but you wouldn't know that from looking at him. Certainly when Eve stepped down from the train at the private railway halt a mile or so north of King's Cross, her heart, already heavy with goodbyes, sank a little further still. He stood waiting on the platform, all top hat and whiskers, arms crossed, legs firmly planted, beefy and forbidding; he looked as if a tornado wouldn't budge him. He didn't shift, either, when Eve's trunk was handed down, followed by five baskets of soft fruit from the Netherwood glasshouses and one full of vegetables from the kitchen garden. As if going to London on the Earl of Netherwood's private locomotive wasn't peculiar enough, Eve had thought, she had new potatoes and spinach leaves as travelling companions. And they were just as comfortable as she had been, nestled in their wicker hamper, cosseted on a bed of straw.

So Eve and the edibles disembarked and three liveried lackeys whom Eve didn't even know had been on the train hopped down, picked up the baskets and jogged off with them, two apiece, towards the waiting brougham. A fourth man heaved the trunk on to a wheeled contraption and followed them.

Only then did the coachman come to life, and as he approached her she spotted a broad smile behind the whiskers, and his handshake was warm and genuine. He reminded her of Sol Windross, without the scowl or the smell.

'Sorry about that,' he said. His accent had the slightest hint of the north. 'Have to hang back or the buggers leave me with the baskets. Samuel Stallibrass, at your service.'

'Eve Williams,' she said, and smiled back at him. His easy manner made her feel more cheerful. Until he spoke, she'd feared she might cry, like a bairn sent off too soon into service.

'Oh, I know who you are,' he said. 'There's been talk of nothing else below stairs.' He set off for the carriage, and she followed, making three steps to his two to keep abreast with him. 'Eve Williams, pie-maker to the earl. That's it, isn't it?'

'Summat like that,' she said anxiously. Among all her worries regarding this adventure, and they were legion, had been the conviction that the kitchen staff would hate her for landing like a jumped-up cuckoo in their nest.

'Oh yes,' said Samuel. 'There's great curiosity in the kitchen as to what . . .' – he paused, searching for the right words – 'culinary magic you're capable of.'

'Oh dear.'

Samuel laughed. 'Fret ye not,' he said. 'I'll keep an eye on you.'

This wasn't particularly reassuring; the idea that someone might need to keep an eye on her compounded, rather than alleviated, her concern. But how to express this to a stranger, however well meaning he might seem to be? A stranger, more-over, who was now fully engaged in issuing directions to the basket-carriers who, having reached the brougham, were making a hash of the business of loading up. An unsteady pile of empty baskets waited by the carriage for the return journey.

'Gormless buggers,' said Samuel. 'Twice, maybe thrice a week they come down, from May to August, and they still haven't worked out how to load the bloomin' baskets. Haven't got the sense they were born with.' He was speaking to Eve, but she made no comment; it was awkward, with the porters right there, taking the verbal abuse. She felt hardly in a position to criticise anyone, standing there mute, knowing nothing about anything.

'Get that out, look,' Samuel said, tugging on Eve's luggage, which currently rested at an angle on top of a hamper. 'Lay this one underneath. Who'd put grapes on the bottom of the pile? Trunk first, then spuds, come on, soft fruit on top. Lift the lids, see what's what.'

Eve stood and watched the palaver as the hampers were reloaded. I'm sitting up top then, she thought; there was barely room for another grape to squeeze in the carriage when they'd finished, let alone her.

'You're by me,' said Samuel, confirming the obvious. He clambered up into the driving seat, then leaned out precariously to help her join him, pulling on her with a powerful arm so her feet left the ground almost before she was ready. 'Better that way,' he said. 'See the sights. We'll take the scenic route.' The porters, carrying the empty baskets from the last delivery, sloped off towards the waiting train with dark looks and muttered asides, and Samuel clicked his tongue for the horses to head off.

'Bloomin' halfwits,' he said.

'Three times a week?' Eve said.

'Some weeks, yes. Depends how many of 'em are in residence. And the countess can't do without her exotics, y'see. Grapes, figs and whatnot. Breakfast and dinner.' He grinned at her, wickedly. 'Keeps her regular,' he said, and winked.

Eve laughed. She supposed Lady Netherwood did have the same bodily functions as the rest of the human race, but it was an unlikely image all the same, and not a welcome one. The carriage behind them swayed a little then settled as Samuel drove the horses out of the cobbled station yard and into the road. Eve swayed a little too; she was higher than she would have liked to be, and there was nothing to hold on to. She sat on her hands, for fear that she might instinctively reach for Samuel's arm and die of mortification.

All around her, this nondescript area of north London got on with its day. It wasn't at all how she'd imagined; before she arrived, all she knew of the city were the colourful facts she'd learned at school. Black death, rats and pickpockets, bodies piled in hand carts, the grim tolling of bells, scaffolds for the beheading of queens, bonfires for the burning of heretics, and the occasional palace or park for light relief. But this looked, just a little, like Sheffield, though the houses they passed were taller and the folk better dressed. The sky, what meagre strip was visible between buildings, was the same dreary shade of chimney-smoke grey as at Netherwood, and the smell of it carried her thoughts homewards; half-past two, Saturday afternoon. Seth and Eliza would be at home, and the house would be empty because Anna would still be at the mill and Ellen and Maya would be in a mutinous mood at Lilly Pickering's, longing for Anna to get home and rescue them. She felt a sudden yearning for Ellen's hot, fierce embrace, her plump little hands clasped behind Eve's neck for a stronger hold, and her face pressed into her mother's cheek. She was losing her independent streak, Eve's little girl. She no longer seemed destined to run the country, wanting her mother all the time now that she couldn't have her. And now look how things stood. She wasn't just busy at work and not home until bedtime. She was many hours and many, many miles away from everything that mattered to her, to make fancy food for a countess who always got her way. A lump formed in Eve's throat. She concentrated hard on what she could see around her. It wouldn't do to arrive with eyes red from weeping.

They turned, quite sharply, into a much wider and noisier

thoroughfare, busy with carriages and pedestrians, all pressing on to their destinations with a collective air of urgency and importance. None of them so much as glanced at a newspaper seller, who stood by his wooden cart, yelling his best headlines in an accent Eve couldn't understand. She stared at him as they passed, meaning no offence, but he leered back at her with an ugly, open mouth, showing brown teeth and a wet tongue. Eve looked away, horrified, and shrank back in her seat. She felt obscurely guilty, as though she'd broken one of London's laws – thou shalt not show curiosity – and slid a glance across to Samuel, wondering if he'd witnessed this encounter. He was oblivious, however, watching the road ahead and whistling 'Rule, Britannia!' through his teeth without a care in the world. In profile, his bushy moustache protruded further than the end of his nose, and twitched in time to the tune. Eve envied him his ease and familiarity with this place; she herself felt like a mouse in a barn full of cats. As her thumping heart settled, she made a fervent little vow to cherish the ordinary when next she returned to it.

The carriage moved slowly now, impeded by the crush and press of other vehicles. Truly, thought Eve, she could have walked faster. She had plenty of time for gazing, though, and the buildings around her had suddenly become much more imposing. One in particular caught her attention; it was long and high, and dominated the outlook with its towers and spires and multitude of windows. Eve, perking up, said, 'Oh! Is that Buckingham Palace?' and provoked in Samuel a roar of amusement loud enough to startle a pair of passers-by arm in arm on the pavement just beside them, the lady squealing at the assault and the gentleman scowling in the direction of the bellow. Unabashed, Samuel let his laughter run its course. Eve knew she must be feeling better, because a rush of irritation made her sit up straighter in her seat. It really wasn't that funny. She'd like to take him to Barnsley, see how clever he was there.

He wiped his eyes. 'Ah, dear me, best laugh I'm likely to have all day,' he said. 'The thought of 'is nibs living cheek-by-jowl with King's Cross station. King certainly would be cross if he had to do that.' He shook with more mirth at his own quip, then finally looked at his passenger and realised she wasn't amused.

'Sorry, sorry, don't mind me,' he said, regaining control and chiding himself for putting her out. 'It's the Midland Grand,' he said. She looked blank. 'Hotel,' he added, by way of clarification. He indicated backwards with his crop, because the great building was now behind them, and in a tour guide's carrying voice said, 'A marvel of British engineering. Revolving doors, ascending chambers, gold-leaf on the walls, three hundred bedrooms – pity the maids, that's three hundred chamber pots as well. Twenty shillings a night they say, if you fancy staying there. Breakfast is extra. Shall I drop you off?'

He roared with laughter again. Couldn't help himself.

Eve gaped, and strained back over her shoulder for another look. She wondered what kind of night's sleep twenty shillings bought a person. A much deeper, warmer, longer kind than she was used to, she supposed.

'I can drive you by Buckingham Palace though,' Samuel was saying, trying to make amends and win a smile. He turned right, and Eve saw trees and the promise of grass. 'Bit of a tour, why not? We can trot through Regent's Park here, down Regent Street and Piccadilly, round Green Park then off down to wave at the king. The flag's flying, so he's receiving visitors. Practically neighbours, we are.'

She nodded, and gazed at the elegant white terraces they were now passing. Any one of those houses would do for a town hall in Netherwood, she thought. She sighed, involuntarily and mournfully, thinking of home again and Samuel glanced across at her. 'Cheer up,' he said. 'Left kiddies behind, have you?'

She nodded again, though she didn't speak, not wanting to risk opening the floodgates. Let's stick to the sights of London, she thought. Much safer territory. Samuel was no mind reader, but he knew a woman on the verge of tears when he saw one. He had just the antidote though; he hadn't yet had a lady passenger new to the capital who wasn't bowled over by the shops on Piccadilly. He picked up the pace, all the quicker to get there. This, he felt, was something of an emergency.

Chapter 37

Lady Netherwood hadn't so much persuaded Eve to work for her in London as assumed she would and proceeded on that basis. Before Eve saw her again, the countess had entered dates in her diary for three parties at Fulton House during the London season, all of which would be catered by Eve. Deaf to any objections, she breezed into the mill with the details – 'Too thrilling, darling – perhaps one or two new nibbles, please, for the later soirées?' – and breezed out again. Dates penned in Clarissa's diary were indelible, as if carved in tablets of stone. And once invitations were sent, when the time was right – too early and one looked desperate, too late and one might be pipped at the post – there really was no turning back. You might more easily cancel Christmas.

The prospect of a long period away from home cast a shadow over Eve from the moment she realised the countess was in earnest, and though the date of departure had been some months distant, she would still wake each morning with a sense of foreboding as it moved inexorably closer. Even Christmas was marred for her. The festive period had been a triumph in every possible way; people had flocked to Netherwood in droves, just to buy her fruitcake and Christmas chutney and the cinnamon shortbread stars threaded with red ribbon to hang on the tree. Such was the demand for her food that Eve had had to hire a couple of liveried delivery boys all of her own, cycling about on sturdy black bicycles with the fare carefully wrapped and packed in their wicker panniers. And all the time, while folk made merry and goodwill was heaped upon her, Eve was trying to imagine herself, come late spring, away from home; and not just away from home, but in London. London! She could form no helpful mental picture of herself in the capital. She was certain she'd be robbed and murdered the minute she stepped off the train.

'Pah!' This was Anna, of course, the world traveller. She had heard Eve out, brow knitted, arms folded across her chest. She'd recently cut herself a fringe, having tired of her severe centre-parting, and with her heart-shaped face and wide blue eyes it gave her the look of a serious child, wise beyond her years.

'Don't you *pah!* me,' Eve had said. 'I'm just sayin', it's a lot to ask. Too much, in fact. I shan't go.'

'You shall, though,' said Anna. 'I stay here, hold . . .' she waved her arms, searching for the words.

'The fort,' said Eve, helpful in spite of herself.

'*Da*. The fort. And you go – for very short time – to beautiful London home of earl, to make food you could cook in your sleep. Easy as pie. Ha! As pie!'

Anna was really getting the hang of colloquialisms. She liked to pepper her speech with them, to demonstrate her command of the language.

Eve sighed. She'd known her friend would be all for it; Anna saw only solutions, never problems. To her, each new day was an opportunity to push forwards in some way, to improve one's lot, to gain more ground. While Eve wanted nothing more than to keep their boat on an even keel, Anna was all for finding uncharted waters. But then, Eve had raised the matter with Ginger too, and she'd said much the same. Told her to jump at it. She'd go like a shot, she said, given half the chance. Eve hadn't bothered asking Alice, because she didn't want Jonas's opinion, but she'd asked Nellie, who had pursed her lips and rubbed her thumb and forefinger together, and bluntly asked what the Hoylands would pay her for the job.

'I, erm, I'm not sure,' Eve had said, slightly thrown by the question. 'Nowt, like as not. They 'alf own me, after all.' This was Amos's sentiment, and she spoke the words ironically. Still, though, she wondered how she stood; the earl's 50 per cent share was in the business, not in her, but no one had mentioned money for her time, certainly not the countess who went through life with the blithe and carefree spirit of an indulged six-year-old. She wanted Eve in London from early May for an unspecified period, though she'd gaily promised her that she'd be home by the twelfth of August for the opening of the grouse season. Grouse season indeed. Did the countess imagine she'd be off up to the Scottish moors when she got home? Lady Netherwood seemed to look at the whole venture as a grand jape, marvellous fun for everyone involved, and it made Eve wonder if she'd ever experienced dread, or fear, or even disappointment. Almost certainly not, she concluded. Mind you, it seemed that neither had Nellie, hard as nails in her starched apron and helmet of grey curls.

'Get thissen to t'estate offices and name thi price,' she had said, as if she was born to the world of cut-throat commerce. 'Never do owt for nowt—'

'—unless tha does it for thissen,' Anna chimed in, triumphantly.

'Aye,' said Nellie. She nodded approvingly at Anna. She might be foreign, but she was nobody's fool.

'Maybe you two should go for me,' Eve said. She was only half joking. It was vexing that it was her name on the company sign yet here she was trying to talk herself out of a potentially lucrative contract. Perhaps she really wasn't cut out for this business lark. She already had more money than she could spend, and it seemed pointless, not to say greedy, to seek more. Then again, Lady Netherwood might value her less if her talents came free of charge. These were the arguments that ran through her mind, contradictory and puzzling.

Once upon a time she would have sought Amos's advice, but he was less approachable than he used to be – still a friend, but always harsh and dismissive where her partnership with the earl was concerned, and a little more sparing with his pleasantries. He would leave Seth at the bottom of the entry these days, bidding the boy farewell and carrying on home instead of calling in to pass the time of day. Eve had tried her hardest, since rebuffing his proposal, to restore their relationship to an even footing, as much like their old easiness as she could manage. But Amos, though gradually feeling the benefit of the healing balm of time, still had moments when he felt bruised and resentful, as if his feelings for Eve had exposed him to the world as a weakling. His response at the time had been to throw himself into issues he felt he could influence, not those he had no power to change. He had convinced himself – brooding at home, brooding at work – that the earl's interest in Eve had thwarted his own destiny; if it wasn't for Lord Netherwood, she would have need of his love. And, rightly or wrongly, this belief fuelled first frustration, then anger and finally full-blown hatred, so that the earl, until lately guilty in Amos's view of nothing worse than aristocratic complacency, became a demonic puppetmaster, whose interests must be thwarted for the good of mankind. His bitterness grew, calcified and stuck fast. The fight against injustice to the working man became personal, and it was not so much an ideal as a mission; Amos would see Netherwood's three collieries unionised, or die in the attempt. It would be his sweet revenge.

So no, thought Eve. She wouldn't go to Amos with questions concerning her business; she was liable to find herself on the wrong end of a diatribe on the evils of capitalism and the glory of an organised workforce. Instead, she gave herself a stern talking to and marched off, for a second time, to the office of Absalom Blandford, who, though it didn't show in any aspect of his behaviour towards her, was almost pleased to see her. Not because it saved him the trouble of posting an already-prepared contract offering twelve shillings a week, plus expenses, for the unspecified duration of her London sojourn, but because there was something rather compelling about her air and appearance. She provoked in him a curious and entirely unfamiliar sensation, and he had to force himself to scowl and fight to remain supercilious. He managed, however.

Where other men found inspiration in a slender ankle, an arch smile or the enticing shadow cast in the crevice of a deep cleavage, Absalom Blandford was captivated by numbers. The beginnings of his unsought interest in Eve had therefore been kindled on the pages of his balance books, in the unnaturally tidy rows of figures that he entered there when Eve's Puddings & Pies had started trading. Nothing thrilled him more than to breathe life into, and extract profit out of, a previously redundant building on the Netherwood estate, so when in this case the numbers quickly began to demonstrate that income was outstripping expenditure, he had to ration his own access to the information, for fear that his mounting excitement might affect his professionalism. He felt it not in his heart – that was a shrivelled thing, not capable of much beyond its most basic function – but in his groin. The effect really could be quite debilitating, and the only saving grace was that he was always alone, seated and behind a desk when he perused his books.

This secret peccadillo didn't strike him as odd or abnormal. What he did find very strange, however, was the gradual transferral of his interest from the accounts relating to Eve's business to the woman herself. No, not transferral, exactly, because the numbers still held him in thrall; it was more that when he laid eyes on Eve these days, though such occasions were few and far between, he experienced the same frisson of excitement. When he looked at her, he saw the numbers too, running down the ledger, credits outnumbering debits. He fervently hoped this was a temporary malaise, having no desire or intention to allow any woman, with all the complications of her blood, sweat and tears, a foothold in his perfect, sterile world. But he had to admit, if only to himself, that Mrs Williams was a remarkable businesswoman, particularly as he knew, of course, exactly where she'd begun and how far she had come. It made him blush now to think that he'd once recommended to Lord Netherwood that Mitchell's Mill be demolished, thinking that at least the bricks could then be re-used to build something rentable. And now look at it: a wellspring of regular profit, veritable hub of the community, proof to the contrary that a silk purse couldn't be made out of a sow's ear.

It was most impressive. She was most impressive. He was most impressed.

The café had opened in February, Shrove Tuesday to be precise, and all day long the smell of freshly made pancakes had filtered through the open windows of the mill, making a pleasant change for everyone from coal dust and chimney smoke, and working on the folk of Netherwood like the Pied Piper's music did on the rats of Hamelin. Free pancakes had been Eve's idea, her way of celebrating the opening of Upstairs, as she referred to the new venture. The large, light room was simply furnished with pine tables and chairs, though Anna had made blue gingham cushions for the seats and matching tablecloths, which added charm to the look of the place. With Eve's new-found confidence when speaking to the earl, she absolutely vetoed anything along the lines of the last opening – no invitations or speeches or anyone in their Sunday best – and instead came up with the plan that anyone who wanted to could come along and enjoy a pancake on the house. Lord Netherwood, very much a pomp and ceremony man, was a little underwhelmed, but, as he said to Eve, it was her business so she should do as she saw fit. This was like him; once he placed his faith in an individual, it was unshakeable.

Nellie Kay on the other hand had plenty to say – not so much about the concept but the timing.

'You want to open a café t'day before Lent?' she said, her face a picture of incredulity.

'Well,' said Eve, 'a slow start won't be a bad thing, will it?' She made it sound as if she'd planned it. 'Anyway, do folk really give up owt for Lent these days?'

'Well, I know I do.'

Nellie looked like a woman who'd never declined food in her life. She wasn't quite five feet tall but she had plenty round the middle, and when Anna had made Nellie's aprons, she'd needed almost as much in width as she did in length.

'She has figure of football,' Anna had said, mystified, holding up the finished article to show Eve, who was helpless with laughter. Now, if anything a little rounder in girth since starting work for Eve – too many samples – Nellie stood before her claiming piety and restraint.

'Very commendable, Nellie,' Eve said, unconvinced, and rightly so. 'I 'ope your principles don't extend to servin' other folk who aren't quite so 'igh-minded. Now, pancakes. Nice and simple, we can all make 'em blindfolded, right?'

Nellie was having to learn to be overruled for the first time in her adult life, but it was the only thing she was struggling with. Eve had chosen well in her three kitchen staff; all of them were capable cooks of the variety in which Yorkshire specialised. No nonsense, nothing fancy, limited repertoire, but perfect results, time and again. They hadn't a recipe book between them, and although Eve was thinking she should perhaps remedy this if only to extend the range of what they offered, they hadn't yet felt the lack of one. Eve had demonstrated her own methods, they had followed them, and Eve was always on hand to check they were right.

In the week before the café opened for business, however, she decided that everything they made – the pork pies, steak puddings, drop scones and Eve's Puddings – should be entered in a ledger for the sake of consistency. The café menu would have to change from time to time, and Eve wanted no mistakes slipping in, no customers going home feeling they could have done better themselves. It meant committing to paper for the first time the exact quantities of ingredients necessary and it was a laborious process, since Eve baked everything by eye and instinct so wasn't certain of the actual amounts herself. She and Anna had spent a day making everything on the menu, weighing flour and lard and fillings as they went, writing down the precise pounds and ounces in a book. The pages were streaked with fat and flour – one glimpse and Absalom would have been cured of his infatuation – but the book became the kitchen bible. Anna's dishes – the chicken soup and the pig parcels – were entered by her as the originator of the recipes, likewise Ginger's potato pudding-pie and Alice's savoury pudding, which they'd enhanced by serving with a thick, caramelised onion gravy. When they'd finished they found they had made a banquet, and they invited Ginger, Nellie and Alice, their husbands and children, and Seth, Eliza, Ellen and Maya, to come that evening to eat it all up. They carried the food upstairs to the newly furnished café, and ate at the tables there.

Anna produced candles and stood them on saucers on the gingham cloths, and it felt like a celebration of everything they'd achieved together. Ginger made a toast to the future, and then Eve, inspired by the candlelight and a sense of life's unpredictable turns, made another toast, to the past.

'To t'memory of Arthur Williams,' she said. 'My good and dear departed 'usband.'

'To Dad,' said Seth emphatically, raising his glass with everyone else. Eve smiled at him, hoping that he, like she, could sometimes now remember Arthur without pain.

They were run off their feet on Pancake Day. There were too many folk with not enough in their bellies in Netherwood, and once word got round that there was free food at Mitchell's Mill, people swarmed in. The café seated forty-eight people, and Eve had to station Jonas Buckle at the door to operate a one-out-one-in policy. Anna joined the four of them in the kitchen flipping pancakes, and the three little waitresses Eve had taken on, Molly Buckle, Sarah Kay and Jennifer Timpson – all school leavers, all in their different ways their mothers' daughters – ran up and down the wide staircase from opening to closing and never seemed to flag. Seth and Eliza came as soon as they could to help wash the pots and Amos appeared too, as Eve had hoped he would, after his day shift had ended. He kept his distance from the women though, standing with Jonas at the entrance on crowd-control duties.

In the kitchen there wasn't time to exchange a word, and by the time the last person left they had made something approaching three hundred pancakes each. At about half-past two they ran out of lemons, but within the half hour a crate of hothouse oranges arrived from Netherwood Hall with the earl's compliments. Fifteen hours at a hot stove, but at the day's end the five women were euphoric. There had been customers that day who they all knew would never be back, not having two pennies to rub together, but none of them cared, not even Nellie. They felt blessed with good fortune themselves and, just for that day, felt like spreading it around.

Chapter 38

Small wonder, then, that Eve felt cut adrift, trotting through the finer streets of London with Samuel Stallibrass and his cheerful running commentary. There wasn't a milliner, a jeweller or a fine hotel that could properly distract her from her current sense of loss. Eve was bodily in London but her spirit was in Mitchell's Snicket with the ladies in the kitchen, and at home in Beaumont Lane with her three children, whose value she felt she hadn't fully appreciated until now. There was so much to worry about she hardly knew where to start. The business was still so new, only six months old, and any number of disasters could befall it. She'd appointed Ginger as deputy in her absence – that went down like a lead weight with Nellie, but never mind – but it felt to her now like a careless act, ill thought through, like handing Ginger a new baby then walking away without a backwards glance.

Then there was home life, which for the children would be chaotic. The little ones would have to spend more time with Lilly because Anna was needed at the mill during the day now that Eve was gone; that in turn meant the myriad domestic tasks around the house all had to wait until the evening. The front-door shop was closed for the duration, though Eve doubted they'd ever reopen – no need for it, when everything was available at the mill. But still, Anna would be spread very thin. She made light of it of course, shrugging off Eve's concerns, refusing to engage with any objections, except to repeat that all would be well if Eve would but trust her.

'Of course I trust you,' Eve had said. 'But you're only human, Anna. When will you wash the linens and beat the rugs, if you've been all day on your feet at the mill?'

Anna, thinking that the linens could perhaps be less than spotless for a few weeks, and the rugs too, simply said, 'That will be my problem, not yours,' and Eve in the end had to accept her word.

And then the children. Oh, the children. Especially Seth, with his up and down moods and his persistent, obstinate, groundless dislike of Anna; she still hadn't cured him of it, or even begun to understand it. She had sat with all three of them the day before she left, and plied them with bread and home-made jam, but it had felt too much like a last supper to help lift anyone's spirits.

'Y'know, lots of things will just be t'same as ever,' she had said. 'Most things, in fact.'

Ellen, not quite following, had smiled at her jammily, but Eliza had gazed at her with sceptical eyes, and Seth wouldn't look at her at all.

'I'll be back as soon as possible. It might seem a long time now, but time flies, y'know. It does. And Amos'll be 'ere, Seth – you'll be busy in t'allotment as usual.'

She had sounded, to her own ears, wheedling and desperate. He stared steadfastly at the table top, but he said grudgingly, 'I know.'

'And Anna's going to be 'ere, just as she is now.'

'It won't be t'same, though, Mam.'

This was Eliza, and there was no denying the truth of what she said.

'Well,' Eve had said. 'It'll be t'same, but different.'

'Can I live wi' Amos?' Seth had looked up now, with eyes brightened by this sudden brainwave. But the shutters came down again when Eve had said no – he was needed at home with his sisters.

'You're t'man of t'house now, Seth,' she had said. 'I'm dependin' on you,' and under other circumstances he might have risen to the compliment, but instead he had glowered at her, as if invoking the absence of Arthur was below the belt.

'Seth, what is it?' Eve had said, gently enough, but he shook his head, said gruffly, 'nowt,' and got up from the table to leave without asking permission. Eve, normally a stickler for manners, let him go. There was much on her mind, and much to be done before she left. She had smiled uncertainly at the two girls, still sitting with her at the table, and Eliza had said: 'Don't worry, Mam,' but her brown eyes had been swimming with tears, and all three of them had had a little weep then, though Ellen wasn't at all sure why.

In the end, when the hour came and she had to leave for the station, she had gone alone. If her children's tragic faces had been watching her from the platform, she had feared she would fling herself off the moving train. Motherhood, she thought, was a cruel mix of pain and pleasure. Two ounces of anxiety for every ounce of joy.

'And here's Fortnum and Mason,' said Samuel, cutting into her doleful reverie.

Oh Lord, more hats.

'London's finest purveyor of fancy comestibles,' he went on.

She sat up and looked left. Not hats. A long shop front, six arched windows, three either side of a central double door, the plasterwork painted a pretty shade of verdigris, the glass so clean it might not have been there. And on display, a lavish selection of luxury groceries: pickles, preserves, tea and coffee, chocolates, truffles, boxes of sugared almonds, bottles of wine, oils and vinegars, wicker hampers spilling fancy goods from their open lids, an embroidered cloth set with glass and silverware as if for a celestial picnic, with champagne and caviar and crystallised fruits.

'Stop!' Eve cried, and Samuel thought her hat must have blown off, but there it was on her head, where it should be. He pulled up alongside the kerb, though, pleased to see her looking interested at last. It seemed to be Fortnum's that had caught her eye. Well, I'll be blessed, he thought; not a diamonds and pearls woman then. More of an anchovies and capers type.

'Can I get down, 'ave a closer look?' she said. She was already clambering out of her seat anyway, ready to drop the distance to the road unassisted. He made her wait; no lady would dismount his carriage without a gentleman's help, not while Samuel Stallibrass had breath in his body. He vaulted down himself, quite nimbly for a big man, then bid her scoot along the leather bench so she wouldn't be risking life and limb in the Piccadilly traffic. He lifted her down and set her on the pavement, but she barely acknowledged him, her gaze intent on the window displays. It was the most magnificent sight she had ever beheld. She wished Anna was here; even she would be impressed.

'What is this?' she said, to the window.

'Fortnum and Mason,' said Samuel, raising his voice a little to be heard across the busy pavement. 'Grocer to the king. Grocer to High Society in general, in fact. Very nice, if the cost of food is of no account to you. Have a look inside.'

'Could I?'

'Certainly you could. Costs nothing to look. I'll wait out here with the horses. Don't be long, mind. They're expecting us at Fulton House.'

She moved to the doors, and they were opened for her by a portly chap decked out in a black morning coat and pinstriped trousers, not unlike the funeral garb of Jeremiah Hague, the undertaker back home. Bit sombre, thought Eve. She thanked him, and he gave the slightest of nods though he kept his chin at a tilt and his eyes elsewhere, as if discomfited by the attention. Inside, she wandered among shelves of mysterious goods, as complete a departure from the stock at the Netherwood Co-operative as it was possible to be. She peered in some alarm at bottles of turtle and terrapin soup – 'thick and clear' said the labels, as if that might recommend it, at seven and six a jar – at tins of boned and stuffed larks – twelve shillings for those, no less – and at what appeared to be jars of snails suspended in brown jelly. *Potage d'Escargots*, said the fancy labels. Just how hungry would she have to be before eating this, she wondered. Only four shillings a jar, mind. She marvelled at what passed for a bargain in this emporium of exotica.

The mingled aromas were many and varied, though the strongest of them was coffee from the counter where beans were being milled and bagged. But like a trained hound which picks out fox from a thousand other outdoor scents, Eve detected the one smell she knew almost better than any other: cooked pastry. It took her mind off turtles and songbirds as she moved through the busy shop to locate the source then, having found it, she stood still for a moment to observe, heedless of the obstruction she caused in the path of other shoppers. They had to veer round her like waves around a break-water and though some of them tutted their displeasure, Eve remained oblivious. None of them followed the line of her gaze, but if they had they would have seen the cold-meats counter; specifically, a pyramid of veal and ham pies, nice enough specimens, glossy and tempting, but which looked to her as if they needed fifteen more minutes in the oven. She liked the triumphant way they were displayed though, stacked on each other's shoulders like an edible circus act, and she made her way over to the counter for a closer look. There were other goods on display: more pies – the duck and venison had a lid of tightly packed cranberries, which Eve duly noted for future reference – and a number of different meat terrines – pork, chicken, game – glistening underneath blankets of aspic.

'Madam?'

She looked up from the counter to see a bright-eyed young man smiling at her encouragingly. Like the doorman, he was formally dressed, but his face was open and his expression perky and helpful. How important it was for the customer to be smiled at, thought Eve. She must pass that on to Nellie.

'It looks smashin',' Eve said, returning the smile. 'But I'm sorry, just lookin'.'

'Don't blame you,' said the young man, sensing an ally and dropping his voice to a confiding whisper. 'I wouldn't buy anything either at these prices.' He winked, rather saucily, and cut off a slender triangle from the veal and ham pie, offering it over the glass top of the counter on the blade of his knife.

'On me,' he said. 'Finest veal an' 'am pie in London.'

Eve took it and popped it into her mouth with as much decorum as she could manage, which wasn't a great deal since the slice was slightly too large to fit, and she felt crumbs and jelly threatening to spill through her lips as she chewed. The shop assistant watched her.

'Well?' he said.

'Mmmm.'

Eve swallowed.

'Beautiful, thank you,' she said, as soon as she was decently able. But as she bid farewell and retraced her steps to the door, she was thinking that, actually, the finest veal and ham pie in London had better not rest on its laurels because, though she wouldn't have mentioned it for the world to that nice young man, it would come a rather poor second in Netherwood. Food for thought, though. Food for thought.

Chapter 39

Fulton House, the London home of the Hoyland family, stood in one corner of a fashionable square, detached from the terraces of grand houses on either side, but built in the same imposing, stucco-fronted style. The house had been bought newly built in 1826 by Thomas Hoyland, the fourth Earl of Netherwood, along with eleven other properties which formed the south side of the square; a stroke of speculative genius, since the annual rents they brought in now added many thousands of pounds a year to the family cause.

The square had been laid out and built on open fields, bought from the scoundrel who owned them for an amount on which he was able to retire. In truth, it had been uninhabited and uninhabitable, and although at the time it was euphemistically known as the Meadows, which conjured an image of wild flowers and lush green grass, the reality was much darker and less inviting: a marshy hinterland between the western edge of the city of London, and the pretty village of Knightsbridge, and much feared locally as a haunt of robbers and ne'er-do-wells.

These days, of course, it was a paradigm of elegant city living; a stylish and desirable address from which to enjoy

London society. A combination of geography and circumstance had helped elevate the area into one of the very best neighbourhoods. King George IV had helped enormously by extending Buckingham House and calling it a palace. Then Queen Victoria took a house nearby for her mother, and before too long, there was no keeping the aristocracy away. It was safe to say that when the Earl and Countess of Netherwood were in residence, they were by no means the most exalted of the titled occupants all around them. Dukes and duchesses were ten to the penny, and even crown princes might be spotted at the right times of year. Certainly it was impossible now to imagine that these towering dwellings, porticoed and royaliced, were ever anything other than permanent features of the London landscape.

There was a pretty, communal garden in the square, hemmed in by plane trees and black iron railings and much frequented by nurses and governesses, who used the excuse that their small charges were in need of fresh air in order to meet, gossip and escape the formal confines of the schoolroom or nursery. But here was one detail in which Teddy and Clarissa triumphed over their grander neighbours: they had no need of the shared lawns, because behind their corner villa, beyond the staff mews and the stables, was a garden of almost two acres – enormous by London standards – which Thomas Hoyland had managed to secure for himself when the houses were built. The plot, at first marshy, difficult and suitable only for toads or wading birds, had been gradually tamed, drained and groomed over the past seventy or so years into the garden it was now: a treasure of a garden, the sort people would pay to visit, if only they were allowed.

Daniel MacLeod, head gardener, rather regretted that they weren't because there were times, as he toiled to maintain perfection for the countess, that he wondered why he bothered. When the family were in Yorkshire, many weeks might pass when he and his two under-gardeners were the only living souls – featherless, that is – to appreciate the splendours within these walls. It would be something wonderful indeed if members of the public were permitted entry; Daniel imagined answering the polite questions of genteel young women – they were always young women, these imagined guests, never old men – and modestly accepting their compliments on his skill and vision.

And it was indeed Daniel's vision, though Lady Netherwood had conveniently forgotten it, that had informed the planting and design of the Fulton House garden. He had come eighteen years before, taking the position of head gardener at the preco-cious age of twenty-one, full of ideas and energy and with six years already under his belt as under-gardener at a fine Stuart house on the Scottish borders. At Fulton House he had pursued his interest, which bordered on the obsessive, in the formal lines and symmetrical planting of the great gardens of the seventeenth century. Not for him the disingenuous informality of the English landscape movement; why strive for years to give the impression that nature has had more of a hand in the garden than the gardener himself?

Like a Cordon Bleu chef producing dishes beyond the reach of the domestic cook, Daniel had made a garden of stunning complexity and accomplishment. There were four levels within the confines of his two-acre plot, accessed on both sides by smooth stone steps, wide and shallow. On one terrace were six rectangular grass plats, precisely bordered by white gravel walkways, on another an intricate lavender and boxwood *parterre*, then came a rose garden with pleached hornbeam arbours, and finally a terrace of immaculately cropped yew cones alternated with clipped and tamed flowering shrubs of an exotic and temperamental nature – hibiscus, pomegranate, anything that could not easily be grown. Down the middle of the whole, dropping into neat waterfalls at each new level, ran a narrow ornamental canal. Its installation had been a great expense and indeed remained so as an electric pump had to continually work to send the water back up to the top to begin its journey again, but the effect was magical, the soft rush of moving water a constant musical accompaniment.

There was no kitchen garden – no room and no need, since everything came down from Netherwood – but Daniel had planted a diverse and jewel-coloured cutting garden for the house, since flowers didn't travel as well as fruit and vegetables. This was contained at the far end within mellow brick walls bearing occasional oval alcoves in which were displayed classical busts of ancient Greek poets and philosophers. These were an inheritance from an earlier Hoyland with a taste for rococo flourishes, and would not have been Daniel's choice. He was not, however, displeased with the effect.

He stood on the York stone terrace at the top of the garden now, surveying his domain, and he smiled at the view before him. Barney, the younger of his two lads, had spent the day on his hands and knees, crawling up the steps and around the paths, winkling out any stray shoots of weeds that had previously been missed. Tedious work, and mindless too, but it made all the difference to the overall effect and Barney was the sort of amiable workhorse who would simply do as he was asked, however menial the task. Fred, older and wiser than Barney, was given the greater responsibility of working his way through the flowering shrubs, carefully pruning so that only buds and blooms remained. Tomorrow the lavender balls would be tidied, the box minutely clipped and the yew cones checked for symmetry. The earl and countess were due to arrive the day after that and, while Daniel never let his standards slip, he was especially scrupulous before an impending visit. But he was happy now with what he saw; he thought, not for the first time, how very splendid it would be to have a real bird's eye view, looking down from high above. From such a vantage point, the garden must surely look like a carefully woven tapestry.

The great clock above the house announced four o'clock in its sonorous chimes. Staff tea would be laid out at the kitchen table; Barney and Fred, dismissed by Daniel half an hour ago, would be down there already, doubtless scoffing more than their fair share. Daniel wasn't much of a cake man – he had a Scotsman's taste for austerity, at least where food was concerned – but he felt a sudden craving for a mug of hot black tea and he turned away from the garden, leaving through the wide archway into the courtyard at the back of the house. As he did so, Samuel Stallibrass made a clattering entrance through the *porte-cochère* and on to the cobbles, hailing him cheerfully with his crop.

'Give us a hand, Dan, as you're there,' he called, as he drew his horses to a standstill. 'Latest fruits from Netherwood on board.'

Daniel, looking at Eve, said, 'So I see,' and gave her his best engaging smile, which on any other woman might have had the desired effect but at this moment was a mistake because Eve, travel-weary and desperately homesick, was in no mood for light flirtation with this man with a strange accent and an unsettling direct gaze. She didn't return his smile, didn't really look at him at all, though she was forced to accept his hand as she climbed out of her seat and down from the carriage.

'Daniel MacLeod, welcome to Fulton House,' he said. He regretted his silly quip and wanted her to look up at him, so that he could show this lovely creature that he was friend, not foe. But it was Samuel who spoke, all paternal protectiveness.

'This is Mrs Williams,' he said, all the emphasis on the Mrs. 'And she's fair done in. So leave her be, and give me a hand with the baskets.'

Daniel grinned at him. 'Ah, Samuel, you old charmer, how can I refuse when you ask so nicely?'

A thin woman with a lugubrious face appeared from a door

at the rear of the house. 'Mrs Williams?' she said. She had a
bunch of keys hanging from her belt, like a gaoler.

Eve nodded at her.

'About time, Samuel Stallibrass. This way then, look sharp.'
This was all delivered unsmilingly, and her tone was brisk,
and some way short of welcoming. Eve looked at Samuel, who
smiled encouragingly.

'Housekeeper,' he said to her, *sotto voce*. 'Mrs Munster.
That's Munster, not monster,' he winked, confidingly. 'She
looks like she's only recently been dug up, and she acts like a
field marshal with toothache, but her bark's worse than her
bite.'

Eve, reminding herself that wailing like a baby was not an
option, braced herself and walked over to the door being held
open for her by this woman with the cold voice and preter-
naturally unfriendly expression. Daniel watched her go.

'Thank you,' Eve said with pointed good manners and grace,
then she disappeared into the house.

A little dog planted itself at Eve's feet where she sat at the
kitchen table. It was some kind of terrier, a cross-breed, with
a short muzzle, brindle coat and soft ears folded over on
themselves. It nudged her skirts with its black nose, and she
shifted her legs away. Dogs in the kitchen, she thought. What
kind of place is this? Daniel, also seated at the table but a
little further along, watched the little dog's valiant efforts to
be noticed, and could relate to its disappointment. Though he
hadn't gone so far as nudging Eve with his nose, he had tried
various other ways to coax a smile from her. He had passed
her the milk jug. He had offered her fruitcake. He had asked
about the journey down. She had responded appropriately –
accepted the milk, declined the cake, answered politely – but

she looked so sad as she did so that Daniel had retreated for fear of provoking tears. In any case, the company around the table was lively, as ever, and he was soon distracted by the banter between the kitchen maids and the footmen, whose conversation was usually mildly scandalous and all the more entertaining for it.

Eve couldn't follow what any of them said. They spoke too quickly in a strange accent about people she didn't know, and the lasses laughed coquettishly at everything the lads said. She drank her tea – it was weak and peculiarly fragrant, as if someone had introduced a few drops of scent into the tea caddy – and glumly took in her surroundings. The kitchen, she thought, wasn't up to much, not compared to the one at Netherwood Hall or her own at the mill, although even in her bleakness she realised that bottomless misery was probably skewing the picture. Still, the work surfaces looked cluttered and floury, and in spite of the high ceiling the room felt airless. Not a pastry-making room, this. Not a single suitable surface. Perhaps she was expected to work in the scullery. She could see directly into it from where she sat; a soft heap of rabbits was piled on the stone floor, ready for a minion to skin and gut. Netherwood rabbits, thought Eve wistfully. Must be. No chance of wild rabbits here in London, where all the fields have been swallowed up. The buildings might be soot-blackened up at home, and the workings of the pits might cast a shadow down the high street, but a short walk in any direction would soon bring you to open land. Eve had never felt fonder of Netherwood than she did now. She sipped her strange brew and surrendered entirely to despondency.

Opposite her the cook, until now in close conversation with Mrs Munster, had decided the time had come to cross-examine the newcomer. Beryl Carmichael, a pleasant enough woman while her sovereignty remained unquestioned, could turn despot at the drop of a hat when she sensed a challenge. She had previous form in this regard; the countess, aware that the best families often employed a French chef to run the kitchen, had made two ill-advised attempts to tamper with the hierarchy. On each occasion, the highly trained messieurs had flounced back to Paris after only a short term, defeated by the redoubtable and, it has to be said, devious Mrs Carmichael, who had made their working lives entirely impossible, resorting even to childish sabotage where necessary. Cold draughts on risen soufflés, salt in the sugar bowl, that kind of thing. She managed all of this without alerting the suspicions of Lady Netherwood, who twice now had thrown herself gratefully – if metaphorically – back into the arms of her faithful cook. To be fair, Mrs Carmichael was not motivated by self-interest alone; she was mounting a rearguard action to protect England from insidious Gallic influence. The paucity of aristocratic old families in France, for which the proud republic only had itself to blame, meant a glut of overqualified French cooks. This was Mrs Carmichael's view, at any rate, and in defending her kitchen, she felt she was doing her bit for King and Country. English cooks for English kitchens was her motto, and she would have had it stitched across the front of everyone's apron if she'd been able. Meanwhile the countess seemed to have been persuaded that Parisian chefs were for occasional use only, and since the earl much preferred a good sirloin of beef or a saddle of mutton over anything fancier, there were no complaints from him either. But now perfidy was in the air again, in the form of this young intruder from Netherwood. It didn't help that Lady Netherwood, innocent of kitchen politics and careless of feelings, had merely sent a blithe message to the Fulton House kitchen telling them to expect Eve on the seventh of May and to purchase any ingredients she might need.

Mrs Carmichael pointedly cleared her throat, and Eve looked up bleakly from her reflections.

'So,' said the cook, loud and clear. 'Mrs, erm, Williams. Why on earth are you here? What is it you're meant to be so good at exactly?'

It was so blatantly unkind, so clearly an attack, that it commanded the attention of the whole table. The scullery maid on Eve's right actually gasped audibly with the drama of it, and for the rest of her life, she never forgot Eve's response.

'I don't know why I'm so tired, Mrs Carmichael, since I've done nothin' all day but sit on my backside,' she said, in measured tones which took all her resolve to maintain. 'Nevertheless, I find I'm too exhausted to bother tryin' to justify myself to you. Tomorrow I may feel differently.'

She was acutely aware, for the first time in her life, of her flat Netherwood vowels, and she was proud of them. She stood, and her chair scraped back on the stone floor, loud in the near-silent kitchen. The terrier at her feet watched her closely, as if a walk in the park might be on the cards.

Eve looked down the table at the assembled faces. 'Perhaps someone would be kind enough to show me to my room,' she said. This, she knew, was a gamble, since Mrs Carmichael's influence on the household staff was clearly much greater than hers. Yet she didn't wish to stalk out of the room alone; she might inadvertently walk into a pantry and lose any advantage she had gained. However, joy of joys, four footmen jumped to their feet in a race to open the door for the heroine of the hour. Eve carefully replaced her chair, nodded solemnly, once at Mrs Carmichael and again at Mrs Munster, then left the room accompanied by the victorious footman. He led her along a corridor, up a narrow flight of stairs and through a green baize door which gently swung itself shut in their wake with a series of soft flumps.

Back in the kitchen, under the table, the dog slumped to the floor broken-hearted and Daniel almost gave in to an

314

impulse to break the astonished silence by leading a round of applause.

Meanwhile, in the privacy of her quarters Eve cried with noisy abandon for a full fifteen minutes. Then, as her tears began to abate, she thought of the lost comfort of Arthur's strong arms holding her to his broad, dependable chest, and she sobbed anew.

Chapter 40

Amos stood on an upturned wooden crate which until recently had held twelve bottles of Samuel Smith's pale ale, but served as well now as a podium as it had for its original purpose. He needed the extra height to be seen at the back since the room was packed with off-duty miners, here in the tap room of the Hare and Hounds. He'd chosen the location so that there was the promise of a pint for any man who attended, and also because Albert Roscoe, the pub's landlord, knew how to mind his own business; nothing he saw or heard in his establishment had ever been used against a living soul. That he was in every other way an irascible old bugger was another matter, and not to the point as far as Amos was concerned.

He'd committed nothing to paper, spreading news of the meeting by word of mouth, approaching the few miners he knew were discontent with their lot. They in their turn spoke to others of a similar opinion, who in turn spoke to others, and so on and so forth in the manner of these things, until it was a widely known but well-kept secret that the inaugural meeting of the New Mill branch of the Yorkshire Miners' Association was to be held on Monday the ninth of May at the Hare and Hounds, at eight o'clock in the evening. That is, before the night shift started work, and before tomorrow's day shift took to their beds. It was coincidentally – and perhaps fortuitously – the same day that the Earl of Netherwood and his family left for their sojourn in London; the earl would hardly have sat so easy in the carriage of his train had he been privy to the information that his blanket ban on union membership, cast in stone – he believed – in 1893, was now being so boldly and coldly disregarded.

Frankly, Amos was wondering why he'd taken so long to get cracking. He never would have believed the numbers that had turned up, if he wasn't witnessing with his own eyes the massed ranks of flat caps and Woodbines. It was a salutary lesson. Never take apparent apathy at face value; the lack of demand for action was not necessarily a signal to do nothing. Now, having got them here, the challenge was to keep them friendly. To speak of representation and negotiation. To save the fire and brimstone for future emergencies that Amos was certain they would face.

'Right, now then, thank you,' he said from atop his crate. The room settled and quietened. All eyes were on him and he had a brief, strange, out-of-body vision of himself at the head of this crowd of men, about to address them. It felt comfortable, apt, natural. As if this was what he was always meant to do.

'I'll keep this brief,' he said. 'There's upwards o' eighteen hundred miners in this town. If tha not a shopkeeper or a landlord' – he waved across at Albert, because it was always worth trying to get a smile out of him, not that he succeeded – 'tha'r probably a miner.'

There was a murmur of agreement at this statement of the obvious.

'And what I'm sayin' to you tonight is, we should all of us, every man Jack, be protected by union membership. There's fifty thousand members of t'Yorkshire Miners' Association.

Fifty thousand men, for t'most part 'ardworkin', God-fearin' men with no desire to bring t'British Empire to its knees' – though we could, if we downed tools, he thought – 'just a strongly 'eld belief in t'rights of miners to decent pay, decent housin' and safety underground.

'Now I'm not sayin' Lord Netherwood is a bad employer. Compared to some, 'e's a saint. But just because 'e's better than most shouldn't mean we're denied a voice. Alone, as individuals, we 'ave no voice. United, as a whole, we can be 'eard. It's time we joined t'YMA, and by so doin', bring Lord Netherwood into t'twentieth century and show 'im that 'e 'as nowt to fear from us.'

A voice piped up from the back of the room.

'Oh aye, Amos Sykes, that's right enough. But we 'ave plenty to fear from Lord Netherwood.'

There was a smattering of laughter and a ripple of interest at this. Sidney Cutts, thought Amos. Mouthy devil. He'd seen him arrive, and knew he'd have something to say.

'What will 'e do?' said Amos, speaking towards Sidney, over the low rumble of noise which duly subsided. 'Sack everybody? Clear us all out and start anew wi' young lads and strangers? T'earl knows as well as we do that 'is workforce is one of 'is greatest assets. Some of us 'ave worked these seams for nigh on thirty years or more. We know them tunnels an' workins better than we know t'way 'ome. Do you really think t'earl places no value on that?'

Actually Amos was far from sure that this was the case, but it was a fine idea at any rate, and it gave the assembled miners something to think about. Most of the men in the room had never considered their existence in terms of value to the earl. They waited for more.

Amos shifted slightly on the beer crate. He would wind things up, he thought, keep it brief. He could talk all night on the subject if he wasn't careful.

'Nob'dy wants strike action. Nob'dy wants a repeat in Netherwood o' what 'appened in Grangely. All I'm callin' for tonight is that we, as a body of men, join t'Yorkshire Miners' Association so that if, some time in t'future, we need to negotiate, we shall have t'wisdom and might of t'union behind us. An' if we join, more'll follow. Long Martley an' Middlecar will take their lead from New Mill an' all. Gents, let's show 'em t'right way.'

This was a masterstroke. The prospect of beating the two other Netherwood collieries to anything was hard for any of them to resist. Amos stepped down from his crate, and moved through the crush of men to a table he had placed near the bar. On it was all the paperwork he needed to sign up new members, supplied to him earlier in the day by the YMA. He was becoming a regular visitor to the imposing headquarters in Barnsley, where he had found the officers were more than happy to help him rally the troops at New Mill, and forcibly steer the Earl of Netherwood into the light.

Next to the tap room at the Hare and Hounds was the snug, and in here, unseen by anyone, sat Harry Tideaway. The Hoyland Arms was closed for business, pending the arrival of a new – as yet non-existent – landlord. Harry and Agnes still lived above, but their days there were numbered. The business had failed when Netherwood closed rank on him, encouraged by Jem Arkwright to sup elsewhere. The earl's land agent was second on Harry's list of most-hated men. Top of it was Amos Sykes, so right now he could barely contain his glee. He had slipped in through a back entrance just before the meeting started, alerted to some irregular activity by the unusual number of men filing in to a rival pub, and what an edifying evening it had proved to be. He stood, and with his head down and his hat pulled low, he skirted the tap room and left the pub. He felt like a man with a keg of dynamite. It was simply a question of when he would light the fuse.

Chapter 41

⚜

Eve woke early the morning after her arrival at Fulton House. This was largely because she had put herself to bed just before six o'clock the previous evening, worn out with wretchedness. But it was also force of habit; she opened her eyes every day in time to get Arthur up for the day shift.

For a short while she lay still, stunned into inactivity by the strangeness of her surroundings. It was a pretty room, and she was alone in it – the first time in her life that she had slept unaccompanied by the sound of another person's breathing. The walls were decorated with heavily patterned paper, pink cabbage roses on a background the colour of buttermilk. The bed was brass, and the linen on it was crisply laundered. A small bedside table bore a green glass jug of water and a tumbler, and, on a shelf below, a black leather-bound edition of the King James Bible. A pale-green satin eiderdown was folded on a chair in the corner of the room, but its extra weight hadn't been needed. The early morning sun streamed into the room, because Eve hadn't bothered to draw the curtains. Nice clean windows, she thought now, with her perfectionist's eye for detail. Not a speck of muck or a rain mark on them. Fancy that – getting a ladder all the way up to the attic. She mentally applauded the effort.

Her spirits were restored by the good night's sleep and, it was true, by the clean window panes. Something about their sparkling clarity was uplifting and promising, and she climbed out of bed and crossed the room with a proper spring in her step. There was a small bathroom for her use just across the way from her bedroom door, with a sink and a flushing lavatory. Impossible luxury, this – no shameful chamber pot beneath the bed, no dash across cobbles to the privy. The footman who had brought her here from the kitchen had said that this floor was always used for visiting staff, and the last occupant of Eve's room was lady's maid to the dowager duchess of somewhere-or-other. He had told her this as if she should be grateful and, actually, she was; if she'd expected anything of her sleeping quarters, it was to have been sharing a chilly garret with a half-starved scullery maid who cried herself to sleep every night. But then, she told herself, she'd also imagined plague-infested rats in the streets and the heads of Catholics impaled on pikes. Instead, she had found Fortnum & Mason outside, and inside the novelty of privacy with a modicum of luxury. Of course, if someone offered her the chance to go home right now, she thought, she'd snatch it and run.

She used her bathroom, jumping with shock when hot water came out of the tap, then dressed quickly from the trunk at the foot of the bed. There'd be time enough to unpack later; she needed to assert herself in the kitchen first. Anna had run up a few more bias-cut skirts and elegant white blouses so that Eve needn't feel like a country bumpkin among the London household staff; the sleeves, which were full, ended in a deep cuff just above the elbow. Pastry-making sleeves, Anna had said. And there were new aprons too, in blue and white ticking with deep waistbands, capacious front pockets and long, wide ties behind, because a generous bow was a thing of beauty, in

Anna's view. No plain old pinnies for her. Eve smiled when she saw them; her friend had perfected the art of reinventing the ordinary.

It was just as well Eve was feeling positive, for there was no good cheer below stairs. The maid instructed by Mrs Carmichael to give Eve a brief tour of the Fulton House kitchens was no more than chief vegetable peeler, yet she clearly deemed the current task beneath her.

'Scullery, pantry, cold store, meat larder, wet larder, vegetable store. Down there's the still room, but that's of no account to you. Main kitchen, back there. Small kitchen, through there. Small kitchen's bigger than the main kitchen, but that's of no account either. That's just the way it is.'

She had a peevish expression, her face pursed and tight around the lips and eyes. Eve was tempted to suggest she loosen her bun to relieve the tension.

'Thank you,' Eve said instead. 'And where will I work?'

'Pardon?'

Eve's question was perfectly clear, but the maid had done this every time she spoke, as if she was using a strange new language.

'Where will I work?' Eve spoke slowly, with exaggerated patience.

The maid feigned bafflement, then said, 'Ah, where will you work!', as if the mist had cleared and a translation had suddenly become possible. It really was very impertinent, Eve thought, particularly since each time the girl repeated her words she made subtle adjustments to the pronunciation, correcting any dropped aitches or flat vowels.

'Yes,' said Eve. 'That's what I said.'

The maid huffed a little and indicated a room off the

not-so-small small kitchen. 'Through there. Pastry room. Is that all clear? Only I have other things to be doing.'

She really was beyond the pale, standing there with that bored, exasperated expression on her pinched little face, offering unsolicited elocution lessons.

'Well, don't let me keep you,' Eve said with studied cheerfulness. 'I can easily see what's what by walking around the rooms myself.' She smiled benignly, correctly judging that of all responses, this was the one most likely to thwart the snippy little madam. Given, that is, that a good slap was out of the question.

Anyway, though she'd been here less than twenty-four hours, Eve was already inured to off-hand behaviour and bad manners. Even the little terrier, clearly a resident of the kitchen, seemed to have switched sides, no longer deeming her worthy of attention. Meanwhile Mrs Munster, the ghoulish housekeeper, didn't seem to have a kind word for anyone; the cook, Mrs Carmichael, was still being exceptionally chilly; the staff in the kitchen, knowing what was good for them, took their lead from Mrs Carmichael; and a brief encounter with the butler, whom Eve had almost literally bumped into while trying to find the kitchens that morning, had been far from pleasant. If she'd realised he was Mrs Munster's other half, she wouldn't have bothered asking him anything at all. But she knew nothing about anything in this monstrously snooty household, and Mr Munster had visibly recoiled, distaste and disdain battling for supremacy in his features, when she made a breezy request for directions. There were so many stairs, doors and corridors between the kitchen and her bedroom, she'd said, that she could've done with leaving a paper trail. His answer, when it came, contained the bare minimum of necessary information and was delivered through an apparently closed mouth, as if he had mastered the trick of speaking through his flared nostrils.

Still, while a friendly smile would have been nice, Eve had

decided she couldn't really care less what anyone thought of her. She wasn't here for long, and she wasn't here to make friends. She had plenty of those at home, and anyway she could always nip out and find Samuel Stallibrass if she wanted amicable conversation. Meanwhile there was work to be done. Not in a begrudgingly yielded corner of the main kitchen, but in the pastry room, no less. It was a source of some relief that she'd kept her poor first impressions of the kitchen to herself, for here she was now, standing on the threshold of a cool, clean room with smooth stone floors and long marble work-tops, beneath which were neatly stored all the paraphernalia of pastry-making. This'll do, she thought.

Working alone, with no one giving her the time of day, she made a batch of sweet shortcrust pastry to acquaint herself with the kitchen, gauge the heat of the oven and – more than anything, if she was honest – keep herself occupied. Her first culinary assignment was to be in three days' time, when the countess had arranged an evening party – a soirée, as Eve kept trying, and forgetting, to call it. In the meantime she was supposed to be settling in, which she would clearly have to try to do alone.

Mrs Carmichael, in Eve's opinion, seemed under-employed. There was a variety of kitchen staff busy at the worktops, but the cook sat in splendour on the large wooden carver at the head of the pine table, entering something into a vast black ledger in an extremely leisurely manner. Eve decided to ignore her until she was approached, and gathered together the ingredients she needed without bothering anyone. Her marathon stint in the Netherwood Hall kitchen all those months ago had given her a fair idea of what would be kept where in a grand house: flour sacks and sugar with the dry goods, lard and butter in the cold store. Alone in the pastry room she busied herself with the task in hand; with her hands in a bowlful of flour and fat, she was at home anywhere.

The batch of sweet pastry had to chill before she could work with it, and she put it on a platter, covered it with a muslin cloth and placed it in the cold store. With half an hour to kill before she could pretend once again to be busy, Eve ventured back through the main kitchen and into the small kitchen which was empty of hostile maids and, indeed, larger than its name implied, though furnished not with stoves and sinks and butcher's blocks, but with fine oak furniture, great dressers and cabinets, laden with china cups and plates and a mesmerising variety of copper vessels and moulds. Nice shine to them, Eve thought, as she peered closely at a row of immaculate little copper saucepans. No verdigris. Back home in Netherwood, there was a woman who'd died from verdigris poisoning. Lottie Naylor, her name was, the vicar's housekeeper before Mavis Moxon. She ate the leftovers of a beef stew that had been kept for three days in a copper dish. Every so often, Lottie's wretched fate passed through Eve's mind, just as it did now. What a shame, she thought, to be known for how you'd died, not how you'd lived.

Next to the dresser was a large linen press, and Eve peeped inside, feeling obscurely guilty. The top section bore piles of blue linen tea towels, white napkins and tablecloths in a range of colours, washed, starched and pressed. Below, in the lower cupboard, were laundered kitchen uniforms, grey dresses and white aprons and, on a shelf of their own, a selection of mob caps. So orderly, and such a gratifying sight, like a pantry full of pickle jars or a cellar full of coal.

'Does it meet with your approval?' Mrs Carmichael's tone was sardonic. Eve jumped to her feet like an inept thief, caught in a bungled criminal act. The cook stood in the open doorway between the two main rooms; her expression was not conciliatory.

'Oh! Yes. Sorry,' Eve said, blushing helplessly. 'I was just, erm.' Truly, she didn't know how to proceed, because she didn't know what she was doing.

Mrs Carmichael raised one eyebrow, an unnerving trick which she'd put to good effect on many an occasion. It conveyed scepticism, disbelief and ridicule, with just one economical adjustment to the features.

Eve tried again. 'I was just explorin',' she said. 'I meant no 'arm.'

'Whether or not you meant any Harm,' said the cook, with a pointedly capital aitch, 'is neither here nor there. The fact is, you're snooping about my kitchen. Spying, for all I know. I would thank you to keep your nose out of what doesn't concern you.'

She turned and stalked away, angrier than she had any cause to be. Eve, shaking a little, stood rooted to the spot. Her second encounter with the cook, and it had been another unmitigated disaster. Now she was suspected of espionage, though quite which dark authority Mrs Carmichael thought she could be working for, Eve was unsure. She considered trotting after her and trying to put things right. Then she considered storming after her and raising merry hell. Instead, she turned and walked in the opposite direction, down a corridor which brought her to a plain wooden door, which she pushed open and found herself able to step outside, on to the cobbles of the courtyard she recognised from yesterday's arrival. With an idea that she might find Samuel, she pulled the door behind her and crossed the yard.

Down in the cutting garden, Daniel MacLeod was thigh high in delphiniums and foxgloves, and apparently impervious to the anxious drone of bees all around him. He had come to

cut blooms for the house, Mrs Munster having informed him
– unnecessarily – that the family would be arriving tomorrow
and flowers were needed for the front and back hallways, the
morning room, dining room and drawing room, and for the
ladies' bedrooms. At this time of year, before the summer's
heat could leach the colour from the petals and the moisture
from the soil, the cutting garden was bountiful, and it was
child's play to fill the willow trugs and have them sent up to
the house to be arranged. At other times of year, everyone's
creativity was challenged; berries, variegated leaves and some
of the prettier seedpods had to do, with celosia, gypsophila,
statice and lavender, carefully dried in his small greenhouse,
interspersed through the foliage. Of course, only when the
family was in residence did these standards have to be maintained. At other times the vases and rose bowls stood empty,
and the flowers bloomed and died with only Daniel's appreciative attention upon them.

He was almost finished in his task, with two baskets loaded
and resting in the shade, when Eve appeared within his view,
though from her unselfconscious manner she clearly thought
she was unobserved. He had the luxury of watching her pass
along the terrace closest to the house, then choose a path down
on to the *parterre*. She was wearing a striped apron, blue – like
the delphiniums – and white, and a white blouse with sleeves
that stopped just above the elbow, showing slender forearms.
Her long hair was off her face, held back in some clever way
known only to women. Remove one or two pins, and down
it would fall. Even from this distance, Daniel could see that
she looked melancholy. He watched her, and wondered at the
response she provoked in him. He was nearly forty years old,
he thought to himself, with no shortage of experience of women
and the world, yet she made him feel like a boy of sixteen,
desire flooding his body in that same unannounced and
afflicting way that it had when he was young. It was with the

greatest effort that he pulled himself together and, bending down to harvest the last of the flowers he needed, began to whistle. He knew she might bolt, but he wanted to give her the choice; he felt like a voyeur, watching her when she believed herself to be alone. At least this way, he reasoned, if she chose to stay in the garden, it would be in the full knowledge that he was here. One, two, three purple foxgloves he snipped at their bases, then three more, from the crop of white ones. Next, unhurriedly, three delphiniums, snip, snip, snip. He forced himself to keep his eyes averted until he had laid all nine stems gently on one of the trugs, then he straightened and looked to see where she was. Wonderful sight. She was walking towards him.

He introduced her to the ancient Greeks: Aristotle, Socrates, Plato; it seemed only polite, since they were there too. To Eve, they all looked alike – bearded and serious in their separate alcoves – but Daniel seemed to know them all and was almost fond of them, said they were his only company on many a day. Their conversation, once it began, came easily. She'd come out looking for the coachman, she said, but as the stable yard was deserted she'd wandered into the garden instead. He said he was glad she had. He asked what her favourite flower was, and she said probably lily of the valley, though she could only rarely find them at home. They talked as they walked through the cutting garden, and he told her the Latin names for the flowers and asked her questions about Netherwood, probing gently for the information which finally emerged: that there was no longer a Mr Williams. He was very sorry, he said, but inside, he rejoiced. He told her he was from Montrose, on Scotland's east coast, and that he hadn't been back there since he took up his post at Fulton House twenty-one years ago.

He'd love to go back, he said. With you, he thought. Then they sat for a short while in the sunshine on a lichen-covered stone seat, facing the house with the garden spread out before them. Eve admired it, said she'd never seen the like, even at Netherwood Hall. Daniel thanked her, but the last thing he wanted to talk about his handiwork, so he took the first opportunity for a conversational turn.

'So. How's it going, down in the engine room?' he said.

'Couldn't be worse.'

She expected sympathy, but he laughed. 'Beryl Carmichael, what a right royal terror. She's very territorial.'

Eve said nothing. She wasn't interested in excuses for the cook's ill humour.

'It's just insecurity. She'll be feeling threatened by you,' he went on.

'Well, there's no need. I'm not after takin' 'er place. I 'ave a life in Yorkshire, and a living to make there.'

Shame, he thought.

'I'll speak to her, if you like,' he said. 'Let her know you're just passing through.'

She listened to the cadence of his voice as much as what he was saying. It struck her that other than his name and birthplace, she knew nothing about him, then it struck her further that it could all be discovered, if she wished it. How odd, she thought, that she should know this to be true, and that she could sit so comfortably by this stranger. She turned to speak, but found him looking right at her and it threw her off her stroke. When she looked away, he wanted to stop her, take her chin in his hand and turn her to face him again because he'd seen a connection, he was sure of it. Now though she was all confusion, and she stood up to leave.

'Ah, don't go,' he said, smiling at her, standing up too. She was flustered, and he wondered what was passing through her mind. If convention and respectability didn't forbid it, he would kiss her and perhaps make matters a little clearer for them both.

'No, I shall,' she said. 'I have pastry to bake. Thank you.'

'For what?'

'Oh, well. Being kind, I suppose. And don't talk to Mrs Carmichael. I shall speak to 'er myself, else she'll always see me as a wet lettuce.'

He laughed again.

'Can't have that,' he said.

She set off through the garden without a goodbye.

'Come and find me again,' he called. 'Any time.'

Then she turned and smiled a thank you, which felt, to him, like a gift.

Eve Williams, he thought to himself. Eve Williams.

At the very bottom of the garden were two majestic cedars of Lebanon and he walked into the shade created by the flat plains of their branches. Growing there, among the parma violets which he had planted for the countess, was a cluster of fragrant lily of the valley, which he had planted for himself. Tenderly, he cut twelve stems of the delicate white blooms and tied them together into a modest bouquet. Then he walked up to the house where he found a housemaid willing to run up to Eve's attic bedroom and leave the flowers there in a small glass vase. He paid her sixpence not to gossip.

Chapter 42

❦

Early on Monday morning, as soon as staff breakfast was over, Field Marshal Munster made a final inspection of Fulton House. She had a gimlet eye in matters pertaining to housework, and her small army of staff understood that nothing slipped her notice. Even Mr Munster, who was the butler and as such vied with his wife for supremacy in the staff hierarchy, quaked at the sound of her step on the parquet floor. She spoke in stern Victorian maxims – 'Idleness hath clothed many with rags' and 'If you hope to obtain favour, endeavour to deserve it' – which she delivered with not even the shadow of a smile. But, in fact, she rarely had need to preach, because it was a matter of honour to the household that whenever the family descended on them, they should feel instantly glad to be there. Most of them had never been to Yorkshire, let alone Netherwood Hall, but nevertheless the place loomed in their imaginations as a pinnacle of fine living. Therefore, they felt, their absolute duty was to maintain a London residence which, while unavoidably smaller than its country cousin, was nevertheless of equal grandeur and sophistication. It wasn't exactly a competition, but they would have been perfectly happy to be judged.

In these last hours before the family arrived, it was as if the building and everyone in it held their collective breath for fear that they might disturb the perfect fold of the drapes, or set loose a petal to drift to the floor. The dining-room table was elaborately set for a late luncheon, with a silver bowl of early roses at its centre. Half an hour before the meal was served, the flowers would be lightly sprayed with water, to give the impression that the morning dew still clung to the petals. Rugs had been beaten and swept, wardrobes dusted and lined. Alice, the still room maid, had prepared muslin sachets stuffed with a heady mix of cloves, cinnamon, dried lavender and cedar shavings, and these were placed in the drawers of every upstairs room. For the gentlemen, crystal decanters were loaded with port and malt whisky, while the ladies, presumed to be less in need of a stiff drink, each had a tiny, precious vial of attar of roses, made to a traditional eastern recipe by the same Alice responsible for the muslin sachets. Elsewhere in the house, inkstands were refilled, stationery replenished and new candles placed in every candlestick. The house was poised in readiness, polished and primed into perfect order.

At half-past eleven, Samuel Stallibrass set off for the station. There was a short debate in the stable yard between himself and Mrs Munster about the necessity or otherwise of two carriages, given that all of the family were arriving in London today. But Samuel, who was one of the very few people who had no fear of the housekeeper, knew best and would concede no ground; if Dickie and Lady Isabella rode with him up top, as he knew they both preferred to do, then there was ample room for everyone else in the carriage. In any case, he said, the earl and young Lord Fulton would very likely be dropped at White's. Why put two more horses and an under-coachman to the trouble, if one carriage would easily suffice? Mrs Munster, whose remit really didn't extend to matters outside the house, was forced to retreat. But she had no real cause for concern; she could see for herself the effort Samuel had put into the cleaning of the carriage brasses and the blacking of the harnesses. If King Edward himself were suddenly to demand the use of Samuel's landau, he would find it fit for purpose.

With Samuel gone and the arrival of the family now imminent, the household assembled front of house, forming two receiving lines down each side of the reception hall, men on one side, women on the other, with Mr and Mrs Munster opposite each other at the head. Daniel MacLeod wasn't present; he was his own man, and had excused himself from this ritual many years before. Mrs Carmichael, who goodness knew had enough to be doing below stairs, was there though, standing next to the housekeeper, while Thomas Hardiment, the under-butler, flanked Mr Munster. Below them, the footmen, the under-footmen, the housemaids, under-housemaids, kitchen maids and scullery maids, grooms and stable lads all stood in obedient lines of decreasing importance, waiting to pay obeisance to their employers. They were as still and silent as waxworks, Mrs Munster having aired two more of her favourite, joyless aphorisms by reminding them that silence was a virtue and the best proof of wisdom was to talk little and listen well. It made for a tense half hour; the merest sniff would earn the culprit a metaphorical black mark that would stain their reputation for ever. Forgive and forget was not in Mrs Munster's repertoire.

Into this eerily soundless tableau came a breathless Eve Williams, who burst through the door from the back stairs in something of a panic. Working alone in her pastry room, preparing the first of her fairy pies for tomorrow's soirée, she was unaware that the kitchen wing had emptied entirely. After all, since no one was speaking to her, how could they possibly direct her upstairs to the reception hall with everyone else? Reasonable enough, at least they all thought so. And Eve, accustomed by now to the absence of conversation, carried on with her batch of miniature veal and ham pies for a good twenty-five minutes after they'd left. It was only when she walked into the main kitchen with a tray ready for the oven that she realised she was alone, except for the little dog who eyed her from his basket as she stood in baffled alarm, looking all around her for evidence of human life.

'Where's everyone gone?' she asked the dog, and felt irrationally betrayed when he didn't reply. Her conclusion, reached in a matter of seconds, was that the house must be on fire and she'd been left to burn alive below stairs by the callous Mrs Carmichael and her mean-minded underlings. Pausing only to pop her cargo into the bottom of the range – well, she might be in mortal danger, but first things first – she flew out of the kitchen, throwing a black look at the turncoat terrier, and up the stairs, hurtling out through the green baize door like a human cannonball.

Her timing could not have been worse. Or, as it turned out, better. For just as she bowled into the reception hall from where she intended to make her escape from the inferno, the large double front doors were pulled open by two footmen and into the house walked the Earl and Countess of Netherwood with Tobias, Dickie, Henrietta and Isabella.

Eve froze. Mrs Munster gave her a swift look of utmost contempt and Mrs Carmichael smirked nastily and with evident relish. Then Lady Netherwood, espying her favourite protégée at the far end of the hall, swooshed past the field marshal, the generals and the ranks of mute and motionless foot soldiers to where Eve stood, alone and beetroot red. To the utter and enduring amazement of the audience, Clarissa clasped Eve in a fond embrace, though rather gingerly in case there was flour on her apron.

'Too, too lovely,' the countess gushed. 'What fun! I hope you like our little London dwelling. Has everyone been charming to you, my dear?'

She turned and beamed at Mrs Munster and Mrs Carmichael, into whose hands she assumed Eve had been placed. They returned two distinctly watered-down smiles, while trying to process the evidence they had before them: that this unlooked-for upstart cook was on hugging terms with the countess. And as if that wasn't enough, the earl now bounded over and gave her an avuncular peck on the cheek, followed by Henrietta, who stood before her in a bias-cut skirt and an intricately embellished blouse and said, 'What do you think? Your friend Anna made me into a Gibson Girl! She took no time at all!' then twirled so that Eve could assess her costume.

Remembering the form, Lord Netherwood turned and addressed his assembled staff.

'Splendid to be here, and to see that everything looks shipshape and Bristol fashion. Thank you all, now don't let us detain you any longer.' He turned to the cook and addressed her directly. 'Mrs Carmichael, Tobias and I eschewed White's today for one of your legendary lunches, so best be getting on with it, what!'

Mrs Carmichael bobbed a curtsy and said, 'Yes, sir, thank you, sir,' and made for the stairs.

Mrs Munster clapped twice, peremptorily, and the assembled household instantly dissolved into their various recesses of the residence. The earl strode purposefully into his study and Isabella raced up the main staircase, Lady Netherwood drifting after her calling that she mustn't be giddy and mustn't be late for luncheon. Henrietta and Dickie made for the rear door so that they might properly greet the London horses. Tobias, leaning languidly against a pillar, the better to display his new linen sack coat and matching trousers, flashed a rake-about-town smile at Eve, who was still rooted to the spot.

'I don't suppose you'd fancy a spin through Hyde Park in the phaeton, Mrs Williams?' he said.

She snorted with laughter. He was priceless.

'Well,' he said. 'It was worth asking the question.' He smiled, unabashed. 'You do look lovely with that flush to the cheeks.'

'Well, that's as may be,' Eve said, putting an end to the nonsense. 'But you're barkin' up t'wrong tree. I'm not one of your foolish dairy maids.' This was no way to speak to the Netherwood heir, she knew that. But he shrugged, smiled pleasantly and nodded his agreement.

'No, indeed,' he said. 'But such a very great shame. Ah well, enjoy the rest of your day. See you anon.'

He sauntered off upstairs, whistling insouciantly, and Eve watched him go. There was no harm in him, she realised that now. She was sure he would never force himself upon an unwilling girl – no need, by all accounts, when so many of them seemed to be on tap. But, she thought, heading back down to the kitchen, he was so entirely lacking in decent, upright principles. Life and love for him were merely sport. Amos Sykes, with his badly fitting suit and his ready scowl, was more of a gentleman than Toby Hoyland would ever be.

Chapter 43

'**W**hy are you wearing your Norfolk jacket, darling?'
Dickie, his mouth full of asparagus and hollandaise, looked across the table at his mother.

'Always ready for the shoot, aren't you, Dickie, old son?' said Tobias. 'Never know when the quarry might appear. He has his gun under the table too.'

'Dickie!' said the countess. 'We simply won't countenance firearms at luncheon.'

Dickie, whose mouth was now empty, said, 'He's joshing with you, Ma. There's no gun.' He picked up another spear of asparagus and pretended to shoot Toby in the head, then dipped it in sauce, and pushed it, whole, into his mouth.

'Even so, dear, your shooting tweeds are hardly the thing.'

'Well, I expect he'll change for dinner,' said Lord Netherwood, in a tone with which he hoped to convey that the subject was too trivial to be given any more attention.

'Don't count on it,' said Tobias. 'I think his tweeds may need to be surgically removed. Do you remember,' he said, beginning to laugh, 'when he turned up at Buffy Mountford's birthday bash in mud-spattered knickerbockers and woollen socks?'

'And the butler thought he was a ghillie and sent him round the back,' said Henrietta.

Dickie, amiable and easy-going, smiled obligingly. 'Actually,' he said, 'it turned out rather well. I had a slap-up dinner in the kitchens and an early night. Buffy Mountford's more your thing than mine, Toby. A dandified ass.'

'Dickie! No asses at the table,' said his mother, provoking a small outburst of hilarity from everyone but herself. It was ever thus; the countess had never entirely shared her family's sense of humour. There was a strong and regrettable seam of vulgarity running through the lot of them, in her view.

The plates, emptied now of their asparagus, were swept gracefully away by the footmen, and clean, hot replacements instantly set down. Munster arrived hard on their heels, bearing a dish of veal cutlets, which he adroitly served: one to each of the ladies, two to the gentlemen. Vegetables – carrots and kale from Netherwood – followed swiftly, the whole operation being designed to preserve as much of the heat in the food and the china as was humanly possible. Like his wife, Mr Munster rarely cracked a smile but his professionalism was never in dispute. Lose not a moment of time between the kitchen and the dining room, he told his footmen, else the cook's labours will have been in vain and the dinner spoiled. Their progress, up the back stairs, through the green baize door and along the corridor to the dining room was therefore always performed in silence and at speed.

'I don't see why I shouldn't be given two chops,' Henrietta said, rather rudely, since Munster was still in attendance at the table when she spoke. 'I'm just as hungry as Dickie and Toby.'

Lord Netherwood sighed. Here we go again.

'Don't be silly, darling,' said the countess. 'Think of your silhouette.'

Lady Netherwood, who barely ate enough to keep a bird

alive, was sure her oldest daughter would run to fat before they found her a husband. She was such a hearty, athletic girl, and though she looked well enough most of the time, one couldn't let one's guard down. Isabella, she was relieved to be able to say, had inherited her own slender frame.

'I'm thinking of my empty stomach, in fact,' said Henrietta. 'I don't want to spend half the afternoon longing for dinner.'

The earl signalled to Munster, who stepped forwards.

'Serve Lady Henrietta with another chop, Munster, there's a good fellow,' he said. These family luncheons were increasingly tiresome, he thought. It was high time these overgrown fledglings began to leave the nest. And now Clarissa was put out at being overruled. He could see from her face that he was in the doghouse. Oh well, he'd been there often enough before, and at least he had Henry for company this time.

'Papa,' piped up Isabella, 'may I be allowed to attend the party tomorrow evening?'

Little minx, thought Henrietta. She well knew that her mother wouldn't permit it, so had directed the question at the earl, who found her almost impossible to refuse. However, he didn't have time to reply before the countess issued a firm no.

'Absurd question, Isabella,' she said. 'You're twelve years old.'

'Shame,' said Toby. 'She could have my place.'

His father eyed him balefully.

'You're jolly lucky to be allowed out of the nursery at all,' said Henrietta. 'I'm quite sure I wasn't at your age. Who's invited tomorrow anyway?'

Her mother perked up; this was the sort of table talk she enjoyed.

'Just a handful,' she said, preparing to count them off on her fingers. 'The Abberleys will be here. The Fortescues. The Fitzherberts. I did ask the Devonshires, but they were previously engaged. The Campbell-Chievelys.'

340

'So far so dreary,' said Tobias rudely. His mother ignored him.

'Oh, and Ambassador Choate and his wife have accepted,' she said.

The earl, who had until this point been with Toby, said, 'Really? The American ambassador?'

'Yes,' said Clarissa, a tad waspishly, since she still wasn't really speaking to her husband. 'And his wife and, I think, a young American woman who's currently staying with them.'

'Well, how very clever of you, dear,' said the earl. 'I shall seek his opinion on Panama. Could be splendid investment opportunities there, boys.' He nodded at Dickie and Tobias. 'The Americans are picking up where the French left off.'

The countess sighed. 'I do not want your obsession with business and industry to dominate the evening,' she said. 'Ambassador Choate will be expecting light relief.'

'Oh tosh,' said Teddy. 'He's a Yank. They abide by a different set of rules to us.'

'What's happening in Panama that's so interesting?' said Henrietta.

'They make hats there, Henry,' said Isabella patiently. 'Don't you know anything?'

And even Lady Netherwood found herself overcoming her pique and laughing.

Veal-and-ham pies, steak puddings, scotch eggs, drop scones, raspberry jam tarts and lemon pancakes. This was Eve's menu for Tuesday evening, and nothing on it would be bigger than bite-sized. While still in Netherwood, she had taken the trouble to write it down and present it to the countess for her approval – the proper way of things, she thought, in grand households. Lady Netherwood had trilled gaily and made a rather fatuous comment about the fun of serving food for the poor to her titled friends, and Eve had taken her leave feeling immensely relieved that Amos hadn't been in the room to hear her.

Since she had first devised the tiny portions for the countess at the opening of the mill, she had fine-tuned the process of making them, getting herself organised with a battery of special equipment which gave her the consistency she sought. She had had the inspired idea to visit the forge at New Mill pit yard, where she'd talked the blacksmith into a bit of freelance work on her behalf. Anna had made a set of drawings to show what they were after: cast iron trays with indentations for pies and puddings, but in miniature. The smith had obliged, producing twelve custom-made baking trays, some of them with rounded hollows for sweet tarts and pies, others with flat-bottomed indentations and traditional sloping sides. He made a set of high-sided cast-iron rings too, just an inch and a half in diameter, and she used these to stop the pancake batter and the drop scones running in the pan. The raised pies she still made entirely by hand, as the slight irregularities gave them charm, but she had a set of twenty-four china thimbles in which she made the daintiest suet puddings known to womankind. They were large for thimbles, but tiny for pudding bowls, so pressing the crust inside them could only be done with her little finger, and even that was a squeeze.

She came back down to the kitchens wondering what sort of reception she might face now that the Hoylands had practically welcomed her as a member of the family. In fact, for a while, there was no reception at all; backs were still turned as she made her way through the main kitchen, facial expressions still set somewhere between neutral and hostile. Mrs Carmichael was nowhere to be seen, although the family's meal was in the final stages of preparation so Eve assumed she would be making an appearance soon enough.

Still, it mattered not a whit to Eve. She had her thoughts

342

for company, and plenty to be getting on with, so she settled herself at her station and began to rub butter into a mix of flour and finely ground sugar to make a sweet paste for the jam tarts. The beaten yolks of two eggs stood at hand, ready to be judiciously added when the time was right. She wanted a very short texture, so that the pastry was no less of an event than the raspberry filling. It was all accomplished lightly and expeditiously, her cool fingers working the alchemy required to turn these few ingredients into something other.

'There wouldn't be half so many failures at the pastry table if greater care was taken over the making of it.'

Eve turned to see Mrs Carmichael in the open doorway. What a peculiar thing to say, she thought. She wondered if the cook had intended a compliment, but was so out of the habit of being pleasant that it came out as an admonishment.

'Well,' Eve said carefully, 't'same could probably be said about most things in life, don't you think?'

Mrs Carmichael nodded thoughtfully. She seemed to struggle for a moment, her mouth working soundlessly as she tried to frame her next sentence. 'I believe,' she said, with some effort, 'that I misjudged this situation.'

'Oh?' said Eve. 'Really? In what way?'

'Well. If perhaps it had been clearer that you were only here for a brief period and for a very particular reason . . .'

She petered out, looking somehow smaller than when Eve had first encountered her. The silence between them grew, and the cook spoke again.

'I bear you no ill-will, Mrs Williams,' she said. No, thought Eve, not now you've seen how things stand upstairs. 'And I hope we can be friendly.'

'Mrs Carmichael,' said Eve. 'I don't think we can be friends, as a matter of fact, but there's no call to be enemies either. I can see I've risen in your eyes today, and I think we both know why. You jumped to conclusions about me that were entirely wrong, and only now, when you see that t'family 'old me in esteem, do you trouble yourself to find out why I'm 'ere.'

Her voice was even and pleasant and caused no stir in the room next door. She had no desire to humiliate, simply to speak the truth, but it was supremely satisfying to be able to do so. Mrs Carmichael looked displeased; the conversation had not gone as she'd intended. She had hoped to bestow her approval on Eve's appointment and had assumed Eve would be glad of it. But there was no arguing with the facts.

'Anyroad,' said Eve, falling into Netherwood colloquialisms in the thrill of the moment, 'if you don't mind, I've work to be gettin' on wi'. Fairy pies,' she added mischievously, purely to baffle.

'Indeed,' said Mrs Carmichael. 'Indeed. And luncheon to be prepared.'

She retreated into the main kitchen.

'Dinner,' said Eve, far too quietly for anyone to hear.

Then she turned back to the preferred company of her perfect pastry.

Later that day, when she'd done all she reasonably could for tomorrow, she took herself off to the courtyard to find Samuel Stallibrass. She'd had an idea and one that Anna, were she here to tell, would approve of enormously. This time Samuel was easily found, sitting on a three-legged stool in the sunshine, smoking a pipe and polishing a stirrup iron.

He looked up as she approached, and beamed. 'Well, well,' he said, talking around the obstruction of his pipe. 'You look happier than when I last saw you.'

'I think that's safe to say,' said Eve.

He leaned in and pretended to study her expression. 'Aye,' he said. 'I think it is too.'

'Shouldn't one of t'stable lads be doing that?' she said, nodding down at the stirrup and rag in his hands.

'They already have,' he said. 'And a poor job they made of it too. How're you getting on with Beryl?'

'Beryl?' Eve had no idea who he meant.

'Mrs Carmichael. Cook.'

'She thought I was after 'er job—'

'So she was nasty to you?'

'Yes. Then she saw Lady Netherwood greetin' me like a long-lost relative—'

'And now she's changed her tune. It's just like Beryl Carmichael, that. Judges a person by how much other people esteem them.'

Eve nodded. 'She sent me some 'elp this afternoon though. Young lass called Molly or Polly or summat. Sound of 'er own voice startles 'er, so I couldn't quite catch what she said.'

Samuel laughed. 'She'll soon learn to speak up. It's the survival of the fittest down in that kitchen, dog eat dog. Give me an outdoor life any day.'

'Never a truer word spoken,' said Daniel, who had appeared through the wide stone arch that led to the garden. A brief flash of pleasure lit Eve's features, which she snuffed out immediately, replacing it with a casual smile, though not before Samuel had spotted it. Aye aye, he thought, could be trouble, though if she's free from obligation in Netherwood she could do worse.

'Eve,' said Daniel.

She looked at him.

'Will you come and sit in the garden for a while?'

This was bold, and she flushed a little. 'I just wanted to ask a favour of Mr Stallibrass,' she said.

'Is that so?' Samuel said, taking out his pipe at last. 'And what is it?'

'I'd like to go back to that shop you showed me. Fortnum . . .'

'And Mason. Would you indeed? Spending your money on canned exotics, are you?'

'No,' she said, wishing she wasn't saying this with an audience. 'I wanted to put a, well, a . . .' – she wondered how Anna would phrase it – 'a business proposition to them.'

Samuel hooted with laughter at this, but Daniel didn't. He said, 'I'll take you. We can walk from here.'

'Can we? Would you?' said Eve.

'Yes we can, and yes I would,' he said. 'Come and sit in the garden for five minutes. Tell me about your proposition.'

So she did, casting an apologetic backwards glance at Samuel, who shrugged as if to say, that's life, and waved her on her way. She'd wanted to see Daniel anyway and had intended to seek him out in the garden after talking to Samuel. She had something for him, wrapped in a linen cloth in the pocket of her apron.

'I wanted to give you this,' she said, taking it out as soon as they were seated. 'To say thank you for t'lily of t'valley. That was such a kindness, sending them to my room. I could smell them as soon as I opened t'door.'

'Plenty more where they came from,' he said. 'You can have them every day, my lady. Well, until they're finished.'

She laughed.

'I'm a gardener, not a worker of miracles,' he said. 'So, what's this?' He took the proffered parcel.

'A pie,' she said, and smiled, because it sounded so prosaic. 'A fairy pie.'

He opened it with careful fingers, and lifted out the perfect little veal-and-ham pie, holding it delicately between thumb and index finger.

'Did you shrink it?' he said.

She laughed again. 'It was never big,' she said. 'I make 'em like that for Lady Netherwood.'

'That's just beautiful,' he said, turning it all angles. 'Look

346

at it. We should leave it under the trees at the bottom of the garden for the little folk.'

'Eat it,' she said.

He grinned at her and put it in his mouth, chewed a few times and swallowed.

'My oh my,' he said. 'Pie heaven.'

Chapter 44

༒━━◆━━༒

The afternoon shift at the Netherwood collieries started at half-past one, and many of the men preferred it to days or nights. There was a leisurely start to the day, a spot of dinner at your own kitchen table and a clocking-off time that, if you moved sharpish, left enough time for a jar at the local. Generally the shift rota was a straightforward alternation between the three: afternoons, days, nights, in an endless cycle. Occasionally, if you were lucky, there'd be a swap with another man who preferred a night shift, or who was laid off with sickness or injury. A two-week run of afternoons almost passed for a holiday, in a life where holidays didn't exist.

Amos, though, was contrary. He would always choose days or nights over afternoons. Days got the shift over with, left you free to grow vegetables, swing a pummel at a knur or waste your money at the dog track; nights were the same. But afternoons hung over you like a threat from the moment you woke, tarnishing your free time with its inexorable approach. You had to watch the clock, on afternoons. You were a slave to the march of time.

This is what Amos thought, anyway. He had spent this Tuesday morning in the allotment, hoeing weeds in the spring sunshine, breaking off every so often to have a look at his fob watch. His cap and jacket were hanging on the handle of a spade, and his snap tin and dudley were balanced on the walls. He had rolled up his shirt sleeves, but it was hot work, and when Percy Medlicott turned up, he paused by the gate and said, 'That's a right muck lather tha workin' up, Amos.'

'Aye, well,' said Amos, keeping his head down.

'That spring cabbage looks grand,' said Percy.

'Aye,' said Amos.

'Them carrots want thinnin' aht.'

Amos said nothing. He didn't mind Percy in general, but on occasion found him as irritating as a persistent horsefly.

'Tha'll be on afternoons, then?' Percy said.

'Aye,' said Amos. 'Well spotted.' He really couldn't be doing with this pointless to-ing and fro-ing like a pair of old women on their back doorsteps. He rammed his hoe into the ground, and turned to collect his cap and jacket. Might as well be off. He passed through the gate, forcing Percy into reverse.

'Your weeds are shootin' up while you stand 'ere chewin' t'fat,' Amos said.

He walked off, thinking how much he valued young Seth's silent companionship in the allotment. Now there was a lad who understood how to garden. They could work side by side for two or three hours, without more than a couple of words being exchanged. Then on the walk home, the boy would talk for England about what they'd done, should be doing or shouldn't consider. He was still after planting a melon bed – Seth had fancy ideas – and wouldn't be dissuaded by Amos's argument that without a glasshouse they had no chance of thriving. And he'd got hold of the top of a pineapple from a kitchen lad down at the hall, having read in his gardening books that they weren't hard to grow. He was bringing the top on at home until it sprung roots, then his heart was set on planting it on a hot bed. He was pestering Amos to fetch some stable dung from the pit ponies' living quarters at New Mill, and Amos – really more of a parsnip man than a pineapple one – found himself catching the boy's enthusiasm and thinking it was worth a crack at it. If he could find time to build a cold frame, they could sit his pineapple top on a hot bed and see what happened. It might take years to fruit, Amos had told Seth. Well, we can wait, he'd said, and Amos had thought – not for the first time – what a fine boy Arthur's son was. Not many young 'uns would have the patience to watch a pineapple grow in Yorkshire.

He was early for his shift at the colliery, so he collected his lamp and his two brass checks and went to sit by Sam Bamford, who had found a sun trap at the back of the stores and was basking in it like a cat.

'Stockin' up on sunlight?' Amos said. 'Grand idea. There's none where we're off to.' He lowered himself to the ground.

Sam kept his eyes closed and his head tilted, but he knew it was Amos.

'Good turn out last neet,' said Sam. 'Now you've got t'ball rollin', we'll be carryin' a union flag through Barnsley before we know it.'

'Aye,' said Amos. 'Fifty-four names. I need more than that to give Lord Netherwood an 'eadache, but it were a grand start.'

'What's thi next step then?'

'A bit more gentle encouragement, a couple more meetin's, a proper agenda o' fair demands. Then we can present t'management wi' a formal letter askin' 'em to acknowledge t'New Mill branch of t'YMA.'

Sam opened his eyes now and looked at his friend. 'Then they'll go runnin' down to Netherwood 'all, and t'earl'll do 'is nut.'

'Aye, more than likely. And we stand firm.' He grinned at Sam, and adopted Reverend Oxspring's sermonising voice. 'Stand firm in the faith; be men of courage; be strong.

Corinthians, Sam, lad. We could sew that on our flag. You any good wi' a needle?'

Sam laughed, then he cocked his head in the direction of the winding gear where the wheels had begun to turn, bringing the day-shift miners up in the cage from the pit bottom. There would be more than one draw, so they sat on a while in the day's warmth, crossing the yard towards the pit bank only when they knew that most of the last shift were up. At the bottom of the steps they joined a small band of colleagues and waited, standing back to let muck-blackened miners pass in the other direction. To a man, they envied them their home-ward journey. It'd be eight hours before they were treading the same path.

As the empty cage went down for the last few men, Amos and Sam walked up the steps. Stan Clough, duty banksman, greeted them.

'Nah then,' he said, nodding. But the wheels were moving again, the cables taut as they took the strain for the upward journey, and there was no conversation among the waiting miners. Silence often fell over them before they descended the mine, as if a few minutes' reflection were needed to prepare for the job ahead. Amos leaned on an empty tub, listening to the music of the mechanism, for want of anything more inter-esting to do. It was as familiar to him as the sound of his own footsteps, this metallic slip and grind of the headstock. And because he knew it so well, he also knew the very second that it altered its tune; Stan Clough and Sam heard it too. There was a discordant squeal of metal on metal, and a quickening of the usual rush and rattle of the chains. Then the cage emerged from the shaft, but not slowly as was usual, preparing to stop at the surface. Instead it moved without intention of stopping, continuing its upward path at great speed and smashing with all its mighty weight into the headgear. The massive steel rope, too thick for a man to enclose in his fist

351

and secured to the cage by a great iron cappel, broke like a strand of cotton on impact with the workings and the two-tier cage and its cargo plunged back into the earth, free-falling for six hundred yards to the unyielding sump at the pit bottom.

All of this took only seconds. Stan said, 'Over-wound. Engine winder must've slipped up. Else workings were faulty and we never realised.'

His face was white with shock, but he spoke placidly as if he was commenting on a bad hand in a game of whist. Which, in a way, he was. You get the cards you're dealt, and you prosper or suffer accordingly. Amos turned and ran down the steps from the pit bank to fetch the manager, pushing past the crush of men who were pressing forwards to find out more. But Don Manvers was already striding towards him across the yard, alerted to the disaster by the ungodly racket he'd heard in his office when the cage slammed into the winding gear.

'How many?' he said to Amos.

'Last draw of t'day shift. Eight, nine.'

'Ah, right. Could be worse.'

'Not for them,' said Amos. 'They'll all be lost.'

They stared at each other for a moment, grim faced. Don dropped his eyes first, and strode on to find the engine winder and the banksman. There'd be officials here within the hour, asking questions, piecing together what had gone wrong, and Don Manvers needed to be a few steps ahead.

Amos, who had been close enough to the advancing cage to see the stricken faces of the men trapped inside, bent double where he stood and vomited.

The Duchess of Abberley peered closely at the plate of tiny offerings being presented to her on a silver platter by an immaculately liveried footman.

'Clarissa,' she said, calling across the terrace in her customary strident manner, 'what on earth?'

Lady Netherwood sashayed towards her. She was in the best possible mood for a number of reasons. First, her gown was superb and up-to-the-minute – a daring, clingy Fortuny silk in lustrous green satin; second, her latest flirtation, Robin Campbell-Chievely, was eyeing her up deliciously often while pretending to attend to his dreary wife; third, the warm weather had held, so they were able to hold the soirée outdoors overlooking Daniel's masterpiece of a garden; and fourth, her divine footmen, specially hired for their height and dashing good looks, were touting platters of highly amusing working-class canapés. The duchess was, at this moment, peering through her lorgnette at an arrangement of tiny steak puddings. Such fun, when everyone had expected the usual fare of shrimp toasts, *foie gras* and mousselines.

'Are these suet puddings?' the duchess said.

'Indeed,' said Lady Netherwood. 'Aren't they the darlingest things?'

Clarissa took one from the proffered plate and popped it whole into her mouth, by way of demonstration. The taste was extraordinary; steak puddings, reduced to their very essence. Eve had pounded shin of beef to a fine pulp with the pestle and mortar, then cooked it long and slow until the meat and its juices had become an unctuous, flavourful filling for the suet-lined thimble basins. Polly Pargiter, the mouselike kitchen girl she'd been loaned, had turned out to be adept with her fingers, and had managed where Eve could not to tie wax-paper lids on each thimble before they steamed in their pan of barely simmering water.

The duchess, sorely tempted and – though she would die rather than confess it – intrigued, followed Clarissa's example and found that the little pudding was easily the most delicious thing she'd eaten since – well, she couldn't remember when.

Some long-ago supper in the nursery, she presumed, because the taste reminded her of childhood. Extraordinary. Carefree days with Nurse, before duty and obligation reared up and bit her. How wonderful that those memories could be unlocked by a steak pudding. Without really meaning to, she picked up a second and ate that too. Then a third. Then she looked up sheepishly.

'I can't seem to stop,' she said. 'They are simply divine.' She had the merest fleck of gravy on the corner of her mouth, which only added to Clarissa's triumph. The countess took a gulp of her gin sling and felt a frisson of internal pleasure as it slid down her throat and made her, momentarily, swimmy-headed. Robin, in deep conversation with Totty Fitzherbert and Dickie, risked a lascivious wink in her direction. Then Teddy, red-faced and large-bellied, boomed across the assembled company.

'Don't be hogging the steak puddings, Clarissa.'

She laughed merrily but thought him awfully boorish. If anyone was hogging anything, it was the Duchess of Abberley, who snuck a fourth pudding before the footman was able to make a dignified dash for the earl. But everyone was in ecstasies over the food; the little veal-and-ham pies had them swooning, too. The countess knew there was more to come, but she was confident that, on the social battlefield, she had already made significant incursions into enemy territory this evening.

Munster appeared, stepping smartly on to the terrace from – apparently – nowhere.

'Ambassador and Mrs Choate,' he announced, 'and Miss Dorothea Sterling.'

There was an audible ripple of interest as the Americans joined the gathering. The earl and countess were suddenly as one again as they converged on the honoured guests, Teddy all manly bonhomie and Clarissa his elegant female equivalent.

Joseph and Caroline Choate were an urbane and sociable pair, more than equal to the present company, and their attractive young companion seemed similarly at home. More at home, perhaps, than was entirely desirable. She stepped forwards when conventional etiquette dictated she should have hung back, and she shook Lord Netherwood's hand heartily. Then, to the badly concealed amusement of all, she did the same to the countess, whose forearm looked about ready to snap under the strain.

'I am so happy to be here,' said Dorothea, wide-eyed with sincerity, wielding the countess's fragile hand in time with her words, up and down like a piston. 'It is so nice of you to have us over. Your garden is just beautiful.'

Mrs Choate, extremely well versed in the niceties of English society, stepped in.

'Dorothea, dear,' she said, taking her firmly by the elbow, forcing her to let go of the hostess. 'Let's go say hello to the young people.'

She steered her in the direction of Tobias, who had brightened up considerably at the sight of this charmingly brash new species. She had such a ready smile, and a sort of innate bounciness that reminded him strongly of his dairy maid back in Netherwood, though he doubted he'd get to know Dorothea quite so well on first meeting as he had Betty Cross. She was striking rather than pretty: small, slim, chin a little weak but eyes large and expressive, which went a long way to compensate for lesser attributes. Her brown hair was extremely modern, cut to shoulder length and not pinned up in the normal way, but held off her face with a rather exotic jewelled satin bandeau. Tobias unfolded himself from the stone balustrade on which he was artfully draped, and prepared to give her his full and undivided attention.

Lady Netherwood signalled discreetly to Henrietta, who promptly joined her in a brief, private huddle.

'What do you make of Miss Sterling?' said the countess.

'Nothing yet,' said Henrietta. 'Haven't had a chance to chat.'

'Oh pish,' said her mother. 'No need to chat to take a first reading. She looks dangerous to me.'

'By which, you mean, she's talking to Toby,' said Henrietta.

'No, that's not what I mean at all. Look at her. She has an extraordinarily bold manner, as if she already knows everyone. Oh, Henry, you don't suppose she's a suffragist?'

That her household might somehow fall under the influence of the appalling Votes For Women brigade was one of the countess's deepest fears, along with premature ageing and running to fat round the middle. Dorothea Sterling's individual style marked her out as deeply suspicious. The countess could quite see her waving a placard and shouting slogans.

'I'm sure not, Mama,' said Henrietta soothingly. 'I really don't think they have them in America.'

Chapter 45

The winding accident was no reason to halt production at New Mill, and Amos and the rest of the afternoon shift were redirected to a wide, single-tiered cage in a ground-level shaft usually used for coal tubs and ponies. Amos had got hold of a list of names of the deceased, and he made sure as many people as possible knew the facts. Lew Sylvester was on it and old Alf Shipley, who had only been down there for a couple of hours to look at a damaged section of the roadway. There were six others. Jed Goddard and his two lads, Henry Schofield, Billy Goldthorpe and young Abe Utley, an apprentice who had only left the screens two weeks previously. The word was that the remains were horrific, the men having been crushed when the force of the fall caused a concertina effect on the cage, collapsing it in on itself as it hit the sump at the bottom of the shaft at a speed of two hundred miles an hour.

It was a black day, and there wasn't much said among the men down the pit as they went about their work. Up on the surface, the bereaved were being plied with sweet tea, though the earl wasn't attending to them in their grief, being away with his family at his London home.

'I reckon nowt of 'im, living the 'igh life while men die in 'is service,' said Sam Bamford.

Amos shrugged. 'Makes no difference who comes, does it? They're dead now. I expect 'e'll be told, anyroad. Telegram or summat.'

In the earl's absence Jem Arkwright had come across from Netherwood Hall, representing the estate, and he was holed up now in a pit office with Don Manvers, putting a story together before the inspector of mines arrived. There'd be an inquest sharpish, thought Amos, and doubtless a great deal of energy would be expended proving the accident hadn't happened through neglected repairs to shoddy equipment. God forbid that the earl's reputation as the great benefactor should be tarnished. Privately, he wondered if this latest tragedy might not galvanise a few more men into joining the union. Death benefits to widows and security for families of the deceased were on the agenda of the YMA. Amos wondered, as he worked, how he might raise the issue without appearing to profit from the disaster.

When he got home that night Anna was waiting, standing like a sentry by his back door in Brook Lane. This was not a usual occurrence. He was almost upon her by the time he noticed her and he stopped in his tracks, astounded. His relationship with Anna had always been friendly, but she had never paid him a visit at home.

'What's up?' he said at once. 'Is it Seth? 'as something 'appened to t'lad?'

'No. Well, yes,' she said. 'In a way.'

He looked at her, mystified and not reassured.

'What I mean,' she said, 'is Seth is safe, but not happy. Can you come see him, talk to him?'

'Now? In all my pit muck?' said Amos. 'What is it that can't wait till morning?' It wouldn't be beyond the boy to need an urgent conversation about melon varieties. There wasn't much Amos wouldn't do for Seth, but right now he needed a wash and a hot meal.

'Please,' said Anna. 'He heard there was accident. He will not believe you are alive.'

The penny dropped. Amos turned at once and began to run down the street towards Beaumont Lane.

'He's not at home,' Anna called after him. He stopped and turned to her.

'He's at allotment,' she said, and shook her head to show that she knew this was madness, but there it was.

Amos set off again, changing his course. Anna followed in less of a hurry. She had had a terrible time with Seth today; frankly, she was happy to hand the problem over to Amos. She was sick of the boy's baleful gaze, which he turned on her so often that she saw it even when she closed her eyes.

Amos, meanwhile, cursed himself as he ran. Among all the thoughts he'd had since the accident, the lad hadn't been among them. It hadn't even crossed his mind that Seth might believe him to be among the dead. He jogged along the quiet streets and out of the town along the Sheffield Road, then swung right on to the lane which led to the plots. By the time he flung open the gate on to his allotment, he could barely breathe, let alone speak. The boy was a sorry sight; he lay face down in the dirt by the potato rows.

'Seth, lad,' Amos said, alarmed, appalled, embarrassed for the boy. 'Frame thissen.'

Seth twisted and sat up, as if he'd been poked with a cattle prod, then he jumped to his feet and hurtled into Amos. He was trying to speak, but couldn't get anything out beyond an incoherent stammer. For a long while they just stood there, Seth's filthy face pressed against Amos's filthy shirt.

'You could've come to t'pit,' Amos said, finally. 'They would've told you there that I weren't among 'em.'

'We did.'

This was Anna, who had just pushed open the wooden gate and arrived by their side. 'Didn't we, Seth? We went to pit, and we spoke to men who told us, no, Amos Sykes was not in cage.'

Amos held Seth out at arm's length, studying his face which had been disfigured by his afternoon of imagined horror.

'Nah then, lad, is that right?'

Seth nodded. Now that Amos was here, in the flesh, he felt weak and stupid for thinking him dead when everyone told him otherwise. He shuddered involuntarily and gave a great, tragic sniff. He simply didn't have the words to express the blind panic that had seized him when he heard the pokers rattling on the fire backs and saw women leaving their homes and their chores to be at New Mill if the worst news came. He had been on his way back to school after eating the bread and cheese that Anna had left for him and Eliza on the kitchen table. Eliza had skipped on ahead and was already in the school yard, but Seth was dawdling along, wishing he could spend the afternoon in the sunshine getting the canes up for the runner beans. Then the clanging had started, passing from one house to the next like jungle drums, and women had emerged into the street, pulling shawls around their shoulders as they half-ran, half-walked towards the colliery. Seth had begun to run himself, all the way to Mitchell's Mill where he knew Anna would be working. She had a fleeting moment of surprised satisfaction that he'd come to her in a crisis, but it hardly lasted a second because he threw himself on her in a fury, pummelling her with his hard little boy's fists, and apparently blaming her, in a barely coherent stream of words, for his father's death and now Amos's.

Ginger had come to Anna's aid, pulling Seth off her and giving him a resounding slap across the face.

360

'Now pack it in, Seth Williams,' she had said. 'Your mother would be ashamed of t'way you're carryin' on.'

There were customers in the shop, all of them gawping at the scene unfolding before them. Anna and Ginger exchanged a look.

'I take him to New Mill,' Anna had said. She was shaking from the shock of Seth's accusations and the uncertainty of Amos's fate.

'Aye, well,' Ginger said. She turned to Seth. 'You behave yersen. And wipe that snotty face.'

She had her own opinion about Eve's lad, and it wasn't favourable. She'd seen the way he was with Anna, and had frequently thought that if he was hers he'd be made to account for his behaviour or suffer the consequences. For Anna, though, a puzzle had been solved this afternoon. She waited until Seth had cleaned his face with the cloth Ginger thrust at him, then she set off with him to the pit, walking in silence. At New Mill three different men told him Amos was safe, but Seth had wanted to see him and this, apparently, wasn't possible. Then he had run away. She had let him be for a few hours – there was so much to do every day that searching for a hysterical, recalcitrant boy had to wait – then, with Eliza at home looking after Ellen and Maya, she walked to the allotment, where she found him. And there he'd stayed, despite all her entreaties to come home, eat, sleep. He hated her, he said, and nothing would ever be right while she was in his home. So finally she had shrugged and left him, and waited for Amos to come home from work and mend it.

They sat together for a long time after Seth had gone to bed. Anna had made a batch of pig parcels for the mill, and she warmed some through for Amos, who'd never imagined you could do anything with a savoy other than chop it small and boil it. They talked about Seth. Anna said she pitied him; all these months he'd carried an irrational grudge, blaming her for being alive when his father was dead. Amos said it was all straightened out now, he was sure of it. He had told the boy, upstairs, that Anna was a good woman and a very dear friend to his mother, and that he, Amos, respected and liked her. It was beyond foolish, he said, to punish her for Arthur's death.

'Your father showed Anna a great kindness before 'e died. He knew what was right, and he would expect t'same o' you. You mun grow up, little man. Stop actin' like a bairn.'

Seth, ashamed, contrite, had listened solemnly then dropped into an exhausted sleep.

'It'll be better now,' Amos said to Anna as they talked about the boy. 'Y'know, easier between t'two of you.'

Anna smiled and shrugged – she could live without Seth's approval – and poured more tea from the big brown pot. They talked a little about the accident and about Lew, who Anna knew vaguely as a customer at the shop. There'd be funerals, probably sooner than later.

'Do you think Eve will come?' Anna said.

'Doubt it. 'Ow would she get 'ere in time? They might not even tell 'er it's 'appened.'

Anna heard the hardness in his voice. 'Are you angry at Eve?' she said.

'No,' Amos said. 'I'm angry with plenty o' folk, but not wi' Eve.'

'Good,' Anna said. She sighed. 'I miss her.'

'Aye,' Amos said. He stared into his cup and swilled the tea around. 'Me an' all.'

Could a *soirée* be too triumphantly successful? The countess believed so. The Duchess of Abberley, enchanted with all she'd eaten that evening, had put her in an extremely awkward position.

'We'd love to borrow your clever cook for a little At Home at Grosvenor Crescent,' she'd said. 'Saturday week?'

The countess, entirely caught out, smiled thinly. Eve was her own discovery. She had no wish to share her. Yet, could one decline a request from a duchess?

'The king will be there, we just heard from the palace. All very hasty, as these things are. You'll come, of course?'

Oh, cruel, cruel. Lady Netherwood nodded her gracious assent. Inside, bitterness and disappointment boiled together, competing for precedence.

'So pleased,' said the duchess. 'We'll keep it small. No more than forty.'

The smile on the countess's face was beginning to hurt. She mustered strength from all the centuries of good breeding at her disposal and said, 'Super. We shall look forward to it,' then she moved away on the pretext of joining her husband, who had spent most of the evening doing exactly what she'd asked him not to, which was talking business with the ambassador. Robin Campbell-Chievely, about to leave with his wife for a dinner engagement – how they could even think of eating, the countess had no idea – gave her a look of longing as she passed. But even this made no impression on her mounting dissatisfaction. To be endlessly overlooked by the king while he graced every other household of note with his presence was bad enough. But to be forced through politeness to allow the Abberleys the distinction of feeding him Eve Williams's heavenly food was simply too awful.

Tobias, all smiles, walked across the terrace towards her, and her spirits lifted a little. Darling boy, she thought.

'Mama,' he said. 'Henry and I are taking Thea dancing.'

'Thea?'

'Dorothea. She prefers it.'

He leaned in and kissed her on the cheek.

'Fabulous party, clever old thing,' he said. 'Might be late, so don't wait up.'

Then he breezed off and she watched him go, thinking he might as well have plunged a dagger in her heart.

Chapter 46

Telegrams are never a welcome interruption, thought Lord Netherwood. In his experience, whatever one was doing when they arrived was always more enjoyable than the news they carried. No happy birthday greetings had ever come his way via a buff-coloured slip from the Post Office; no safe delivery of this or that infant had ever arrived to lift his mood or brighten his day. And this morning was no exception, for as he sat contentedly in his study after breakfast, perusing the share prices and calculating his gains, Munster knocked, entered and presented to him on a silver tray the brutal news that eight of his men were dead following an accident at New Mill.

'Oh, dear God,' he said, after reading it, and he sat back heavily in his chair, just as Henrietta walked in.

'What is it, Daddy?' she said, immediately alarmed. 'Are you unwell?'

He pushed the telegram across the desk and she crossed the room hastily to read it.

'How dreadful. Do we know how it—'

He shook his head, cutting her off.

'I know no more than you,' he said. 'But it's a trip back north for me. Your mother won't approve.'

'Well, that's of no account,' she said. 'You must go. And, Daddy?'

He looked at her.

'Yes?'

'I'd like to accompany you.'

He gave a short bark of astonished laughter.

'Henry. You know, and I know, that that is utterly out of the question. And in any case, what possible use could you be?'

This was uncalled for, she thought, but her father had never responded well to a raised voice, so she kept hers level now.

'I could support you, in the first instance. I could also show, by my presence, that our family is responding appropriately to this tragedy. What would you have me do? Attend a few more pointless parties? Order another dress to add to my vast collection?'

He could see that he had upset her. Since childhood, she had shown the same symptoms when an injustice had been done to her: a high flush to the cheekbones, a slight quaver to her voice, a higher, haughtier angle to the chin.

'Henry, I'm sorry,' he said. 'Of course you would be of use, at least to me, if not at the colliery. But, my dear, you must see that for me to arrive at the scene of the accident with you by my side would be – well, eccentric, at best, entirely unsuitable at worst. But I do applaud you for the impulse.'

She waved away his words.

'I'm not seeking praise, Daddy. I want to come with you because it's the right thing to do.'

'I'm sorry. No.'

'And if this were Toby or Dickie?'

He answered without a moment's pause.

'Yes, they would be welcome to accompany me, though

God knows they're unlikely to offer. But the pit yard after an accident is no place for a woman.'

'Apart from bereaved wives and mothers, of course. There's a place for them.'

'That's entirely different, and you know it is,' said the earl sharply. 'You're a titled young lady with a responsibility to behave in a genteel and dignified manner.'

'Since you mention responsibility, do you begin to wonder if the colliery is as safe as it could be?' This change of direction was deliberately provocative. The earl glared at her.

'Henrietta. You go too far. Please desist.'

She stood.

'Very well. But perhaps you would provide me with as many of the details as you can. The cause of the accident and the names of the deceased, please.'

'Because?'

'Because we have a woman on these premises whose first thoughts will be for her friends in Netherwood. The very least I can do is supply her with the facts.'

He gazed at her for a moment before he spoke. If Tobias had a fraction of her character, the earl could sleep easily in his bed at night.

'Certainly,' he said, a little humbled, and she left the room.

'What's in the basket?' Daniel said, when Eve arrived by his side at just after nine o'clock.

'Pies.'

'A picnic?'

She laughed. 'Sorry, no. Samples. I'm doin' what my friend Anna Rabinovich would want me to do – takin' 'em to Fortnum and Mason. With your 'elp, of course.'

'Right. For your business meeting?'

'It's not exactly a meetin', because I'm not expected. I may well be sent packin'.'

'In which case,' said Daniel, 'we get to eat the fairy pies.'

'Well, you can,' she said. 'I'm sick of t'sight of 'em.'

'And Anna Rab . . .' He paused, stuck for the name.

'—inovich. It's Russian,' said Eve helpfully.

'Right. So why would she want you to go to Fortnum's?'

'Oh, because she's a tyrant of a businesswoman with a thirst for power,' Eve said, and she grinned. 'If I can go 'ome with a licence to supply Fortnum an' Mason with pies from Netherwood, she'll be cock-a-hoop. She thinks I drag my heels, y'see, when it comes to expansion. She's right an' all. I do. Generally speakin'.'

She smiled up at him, and he smiled back warmly. She looked, he thought, utterly charming in a white blouse patterned with tiny pink rosebuds. Who wouldn't buy pies from her?

'Shall we?' he said, indicating with an outstretched arm that they should set off, and they walked together through the *porte-cochère* on to the square. The roads in this residential quarter were quiet, and they strolled along in the warm spring sunshine, chatting comfortably. He wanted to know all about the children, and to a point Eve obliged, then suddenly choked on her words as the urge to weep came upon her at the thought of them. She'd known she would miss them, she said, but she hadn't expected actual physical pain. He was all concern and took her arm, watching her closely to be sure she was quite well. Then he talked, by way of distraction, about Montrose and his boyhood there, and she listened until she felt restored. He didn't release her arm, though, and she didn't remove it.

He took her into Green Park and entertained her with the tale of the philandering Charles II, who reputedly picked

368

flowers for his mistress from what was called, at the time, Upper St James's Park.

'The queen was so furious that she had every blossom and bloom pulled from the ground. She decreed that no flowers should be planted there and ever since it's been Green Park.'

'Is that true?'

'Well, do you see a flowerbed?'

She looked about her. 'Seems a shame,' she said. 'A park with no flowers. Charles II is long gone, after all.'

'Ah, but I'm not sure the present king can be trusted either,' said Daniel. 'Best not to put temptation in his way. I gather, by the way, that you're to cook for him?'

'For who?'

'King Edward.'

'No,' said Eve emphatically, shaking her head and smiling. 'Not me.'

'Well, that's not what I heard,' Daniel said. 'One of the footmen told Munster the butler, who told the earl's valet, who told old Stallibrass that the Duchess of Abberley was so taken with your food that she's stealing you for a regal knees-up in Grosvenor Crescent. King and queen, apparently.'

Eve stopped in her tracks. 'That's not funny,' she said.

'Wasn't meant to be,' said Daniel, though he was grinning.

'But I can't do that!'

'Now, why on earth not?'

'I can't make pork pies for t'king. It's not right, it's all wrong, he'll, he'll . . .'

'Chop off your head?' He was properly laughing at her now, because her face was a picture. 'Better make sure you get the pastry right. He's very irascible, they say.'

She tried not to laugh herself, and failed.

'Seriously though,' she said. 'What am I to do?'

'Think of King and Country, I suppose,' he said. 'And Anna Rabinovich.'

At Fortnum and Mason she insisted he wait outside. If she was going to make a fool of herself, she said, she'd rather do it without him watching.

'Fine,' he said. He leaned against the wall of the shop, arms folded. 'I shan't move from this spot. Unless I'm arrested for loitering.'

She rolled her eyes at him. 'Wish me luck,' she said.

'Good luck,' he said, and waved crossed fingers at her. His smile, to her great surprise, sent a small bolt of joy through her body. It made her feel, on this teeming thoroughfare, that she was the only person he could see. Had anyone ever smiled at her the way he did? She didn't think they could have done, or she would surely never have forgotten.

Into the interior of the shop she went, the great doors swinging open for her as they had done before. But she didn't, as before, stand rooted to the spot in a trance. Instead, she headed straight for the cold-meat counter, as purposeful as any other customer. She scanned the staff for the fresh-faced lad who'd given her a free sample last time. No sign of him. This deflated her mood beyond reason. She'd counted on finding him, she now realised, which was folly when there were clearly many different employees here. She didn't even know his name to ask for him.

'Good morning. May I help you, madam?'

A deep baritone interrupted her frantic thought process. She looked up to see a large man, frock-coated like the rest, hands resting together on the shelf of his ample belly. His fine whiskers were carefully cultivated and gunmetal grey, and they gave him the look of an important statesman. Here we go, Eve thought.

'I wondered if I might see t'manager,' she said.

'Indeed?' he said. 'And for what reason?'

370

Her heart sank a little further. She had a moment's flashback, returning her to Micklethwaite's Household Emporium with Hilary Kilney, the estate offices with Absalom Blandford, the Fulton House kitchen with Mrs Carmichael. She gathered herself in the face of these assembled foes; she had coped with them, she could cope now. And after all, the chap had every right to ask her business.

'I know this is probably irregular,' she said, sounding a good deal more breezy than she felt and lifting her wicker basket up on to his counter. 'But I run a small business making these.'

She lifted out one of her tiny pies and placed it on the glass top. It looked comical there, being too small for its new surroundings, and she had an absurd protective impulse to whip it back into the basket to be with its siblings.

The shop assistant and Eve both looked at the pie, and then at each other. She smiled brightly and he said, 'What is it?'

'It's a veal-and-'am pie,' she said. 'I can do pork too, and game. It's party food, y'see. Rather than slicin' a big one.' She nodded down at the regular-sized specimens under the counter. 'Try it,' she said, and pushed it a little further towards him.

He drew back, as if from wickedness. 'I'm not sure that I should,' he said, but he did look tempted. It was, after all, a delightful little thing, golden brown, with exactly the right degree of irregularity to its crimped edge. At the centre of the lid was a beautiful, minuscule pastry rose. Polly's nimble fingers had come in handy there, too.

'Oh go on,' Eve said. 'I've more in 'ere.' She shook the basket at him, and smiled her encouragement. He smiled back, looking more like a great big mischievous child now than an elder statesman. Overcoming his qualms, he snatched the pie and wolfed it down.

'That,' he said, impolitely, with his mouth full, 'is marvellous. Wait here, young woman.'

And he strode off, through a door concealed in the shelving

of fancy tinned goods behind him. It swung shut very slowly behind him, and just as it settled back into place, it was thrust open again and back he came with another man – there were no women, it seemed, in this establishment – who was shorter, thinner and bespectacled, though not bewhiskered. His general appearance was less impressive than his colleague's, but he was clearly in charge. He held out a thin, dry hand, which Eve shook. He was Mr Paterson, he said, manager in charge of outside catering, and he believed she had something of interest. Eve pulled back the linen cloth covering the rest of the pies and he peered at them through his round lenses, then he clapped his hands rapidly, several times, out of pure joy, and that was before he tasted them. She was whisked behind the scenes, through the same hidden door, to a panelled office where her pies were sampled formally and her answers to a series of questions were scratched in ink by Mr Paterson into a large, leather-bound book, this task carried out with all the import and solemnity of a marriage registration. Name, company name, address. She hesitated at this. Fulton House, Belgravia was home for the time being, she said, which made him sit up a little straighter in his chair until she explained she was employed there, not resident.

'If I make pies for you, they'd be baked in Netherwood,' she said. 'That's in Yorkshire,' she added, because his owlish face was blank. 'And it would have to wait until I'm back.'

'I see,' said Mr Paterson, resting his elbows on the arms of his chair and making a steeple with his bony fingers. 'And let's say we ordered a weekly consignment from, say, the beginning of August. How would you get them to us?'

'Oh, we deliver,' Eve said airily.

'To London?'

'Mmmm.' It was a small sound, but definitely in the affirmative.

'Marvellous,' said Mr Paterson. And they shook on the deal,

Eve's mind in turmoil. What had it come to, that she could smilingly commit to a contract she wasn't even sure she could honour. It was all Anna's fault, Anna and her blessed ambition. If it came to it, Mrs Rabinovich would have to cycle to London with the pies in a pannier.

Chapter 47

They walked back along Piccadilly, a respectable gap between them until a legitimate excuse could be found to be closer. Eve, he remarked, had a spring in her step and she admitted that, yes, she felt brighter and bolder for pulling off a deal with the grocer to the king.

'What'll the countess think of you selling fairy pies on the open market?' he said.

'She doesn't own me,' Eve said, a little tartly. It made her think of Amos, who, in the place he occupied in her head, was saying, 'Ah but she does,' in that implacable way of his. And, in fact, she wasn't at all sure what the countess would think, though she was sure the earl would see the business sense in branching out.

'Anyway,' she went on, to convince herself as much as anything, 'by the time my pies appear in Fortnum's, they'll 'ave served their purpose as far as Lady Netherwood is concerned. They'll be old news by August. She'll 'ave moved on to summat new.'

Daniel laughed. This was an entirely accurate assessment of their employer's character. Her whims and enthusiasms changed with the wind. It was only after years of working for her that he had established a relationship where his own expertise in the garden was acknowledged by the countess as superior to her own, and even now she would sometimes pull rank and insist that something be added to the scheme that offended Daniel's eye. Her tastes, given full rein, ran to blowsy excess.

He changed the subject, all of a sudden.

'Do you have to go back?'

She was in no hurry to leave his side and there was nobody to miss her at Fulton House. This thought made her feel liberated rather than lonely.

'No,' she said. 'What did you 'ave in mind?'

'A spot of refreshment, then, if you don't mind a bit of a walk, there's a place I'd like to show you.'

She smiled her assent, and it required an effort of will not to skip like Eliza along the busy pavement. Forcing herself to walk sedately beside him, she wondered what it was about this man that made her feel like a girl, breathlessly excited and full of hope. He was handsome, certainly. He was tall. He was kind and funny. But it was something far less definable, something, somehow, to do with the way he looked at her; he turned his eyes upon her and she felt like a part of her was melting. She had never before felt this rush of pleasure under a man's gaze; not when Amos blurted out his love for her, not even when, as a seventeen-year-old girl, she had happily accepted Arthur.

Meanwhile there was Daniel, his heart beating a little faster than usual, his breath coming fast and shallow, feeling the strain of the continual effort of not kissing her; and each of them, keeping these thoughts to themselves, presenting a sensible, restrained face to the world and each other.

It was a long walk from Piccadilly to the Chelsea Physic Garden, a small triangle of fertile land bordered on its two longer sides by the Thames on the left and the Royal Hospital Road on the right. As they walked, Daniel, like an enthusiastic academic, sketched a history for Eve, conjuring with his words the seventeenth-century apothecaries who founded the garden for their apprentices. There were plants there, he said, from remote corners of the globe, brought back to London by adventuring botanists in the interests of improving the human condition, advancing our knowledge of medicinal plants. It was, he said, his favourite place in London, aside from his own garden.

'Is it very beautiful?' Eve said hopefully. Her feet were hot and sore in her boots now, and still they hadn't arrived.

'Not in the way you probably mean,' he said. 'It's a bit neglected these days. The Society of Apothecaries fell on hard times. But it's a special place. There's nothing grown there that doesn't have some purpose. It elevates gardening to something akin to science. Left down here.'

He turned into Swan Walk. There was a tall wrought-iron gate set into a high wall built of blond brick, and Daniel lifted the catch, pushed it open and stepped inside, inviting her in after him. It wasn't a public garden, he said, but to date no one had ever challenged him when he visited. Today, it appeared deserted. Eve looked about her. A series of narrow paths separated small rectangular beds stocked with unremarkable-looking plants. The air was heavy with the scent of rosemary. Ahead, a stone statue towered on its plinth, the contours blunt and weathered. There was a scattering of different trees, and, here and there, slatted metal seats, not designed for lingering. It was a pleasant enough place, and quiet, but Eve was slightly at a loss. She'd expected more.

'Come on, have a closer look,' Daniel said. He crouched down by the nearest bed and pointed at the plants growing there. 'Creeping cinquefoil, for griefs of the liver; marshmallow, good against bee stings; dwarf elder, to ease a viper bite.' He looked up. 'Do you encounter vipers in Netherwood?'

'Plenty,' she said. 'I have two for neighbours.' She crouched next to him now. 'Feverfew,' she read. 'My mam used to keep that, dried in a pot. And verbena, look.' She leaned in to read the small sign planted nearby. 'Good for those that are frantic. Ha! I should keep some in my kitchen.'

'Culpeper's notes, these,' Daniel said. 'He catalogued hundreds of herbs, their names and uses, like an inventory of nature's medical chest. But these are all common plants. Over here, look, there are imports.' He stood and moved over to a neighbouring bed. 'These didn't grow here until some botanist on his travels found them and sent them home. *Papaver somniferum*, the opium poppy. Unsurpassed pain relief, but kind of habit forming. *Withania somnifera*, a tonic for fatigue or nervous exhaustion. Native to India.'

He looked at her, and she smiled.

'Am I being boring?' he said.

'You're not,' she said. 'You just make me smile, that's all.'

'Come on, let's stroll,' he said, and they meandered up and down the grid of paths in the quiet seclusion, close enough together for their arms to occasionally brush against each other and each time they touched something physical seemed to pass between them which they stoically ignored, though the effort of staying apart was immense, as if they moved side by side in a powerful force field. Eve felt lightheaded. The afternoon sun was hot for so early in the season, and the air in the physic garden was heavy with the mingled fragrances of flowers, leaves and warmed earth. Wherever they turned, they saw no one else and this added to her acute sense of him, of his presence by her side, the sound of his breathing and his footsteps on the gravel. Finally, like a break in the weather and a sudden downpour after sultry heat, something changed. A small moment of pure understanding passed between them – nothing discernible to an observer, nothing that could be named as the word or the deed that altered everything, simply a glance or a sigh or a fractional movement. Even they couldn't be sure. But suddenly he was holding her and they were kissing like lovers, slowly, intimately and with intent. He lifted her in his arms and moved her so that her back was cradled and supported by the low boughs of a yew tree, and he covered her face in kisses, murmuring her name. She held his face in her hands, directed his mouth back to hers and kissed him with passionate intensity. His hands roved her body and she welcomed them, shifting to allow him wherever he wanted to be. He lifted her skirts, sliding his hands along the length of her thighs, pushing between them, exploring all of her. She gasped and moaned, clutching his shirt in her fists, beside herself with what she was feeling. It was new to her, this liquid, wanton desire. She helped him in his quest, pulling at laces and loosening her undergarments, all the while kissing him and he her. His fingers met warm, damp flesh and she thought she might die with the ecstasy of his touch. He pulled roughly at the buttons of his trousers and she felt the agony of the wait, a desperate longing, then he was free and, with one hand under her buttocks he lifted her higher into the arms of the tree, and entered her with shuddering relief. She clung to him, moved against him, and was lost.

Afterwards they stood welded together for a while, letting the yew take their weight, gathering themselves, allowing the tumult of their breathing to settle and quieten. He looked at her with love in his eyes and said her name tenderly once, twice, three times. She kissed him, more gently now that passion was sated. She knew she should feel ashamed but she couldn't bring herself to. Peaceful was all she could manage. And happy. Then, at the far side of the garden, they heard the iron gate creak to admit someone else, and they hastily arranged themselves into respectability and walked sedately away. The young student they passed as they left nodded politely at them, and they nodded politely back.

They took a deliberately circuitous route back to Fulton House. Neither of them spoke about what had happened; words, with all their limitations, might diminish it. Eve felt some great human truth had suddenly made itself clear, as if part of her – a feeling part, not a bodily one – had never been woken, until now. She knew her old self would have shrunk from such bold abandon, but her new self understood it was as necessary as it was natural. Under a tree, though! She allowed herself a small, private smile at the scandal of it. The base of her spine felt tender, as if bruised or grazed and she rubbed it discreetly, glad it was there. Daniel, for his part, felt nothing but the blessed relief of claiming her; he had not the slightest shred of doubt that she was his.

They were entwined now, his arm around her shoulders, hers around his waist. They meandered along the Chelsea Embankment, anonymous in the throng of people, watching the industrious bustle of the river's population. It seemed to Eve that half the country had congregated here, on and by the Thames; she said as much, and Daniel laughed.

'It's a good deal quieter than it used to be,' he said. 'Canals and railways are sharing the load these days.'

'Well, it's busy enough for me,' she said. 'I don't know 'ow you bear it. The crush. The noise.'

'London's a wonderful city. Headquarters of the British Empire.'

'It's full of strangers. I like to greet folk and be greeted when I walk down t'street.'

'Aye, right enough, I'll grant you that one. You have to be happy with your own company in London.'

'And are you?'

'I am, yes. At least, I was, at any rate.' He stopped walking and, without releasing her, he looked down into her eyes. 'I think, though, that if you leave, I might feel very lonely.'

'I'm sorry,' she said, and she couldn't hold his gaze. 'I can't stay 'ere.'

He leaned down and kissed her softly on her bowed head, because there was nothing to say. Then he began to walk again, slowly as before, keeping her close beside him.

It was another hour and a half before they wended their way into the square, by which time they had pulled apart and were walking with a respectable six inches of daylight between them. From the end of the street they could see all the kerfuffle of a departure at Fulton House. Samuel Stallibrass was atop the landau, and while they couldn't see who was inside as it drew away, there was a large leather portmanteau strapped to the back.

'Someone's leaving, and not just for the afternoon,' said Daniel. 'Strange.'

It seemed no stranger to Eve than anything else that had so far happened since arriving in London, so she felt little curiosity. They turned left into the *porte-cochère*, where a stable lad was busy clearing a pile of fresh manure.

'Very nice, Frank,' Daniel said. 'Another gift for my garden from the horses. Who was that in the carriage?'

The lad ceased his sweeping. 'Lord Netherwood,' he said. 'Called back up north. Eight of his men dead, they say. Accident at his pit.'

All the joyous warmth of the day drained away from Eve with his words, as swiftly and thoroughly as if it had never been there.

'Which pit?' she said, in a strangled voice that Daniel didn't recognise.

Frank, sublimely innocent of the importance of his answer, shrugged nonchalantly. 'Dunno,' he said. 'Is there more than one?'

Eve staggered, just fractionally, and Daniel reached for her. She looked at him desperately, as though he could help her, then she looked away in despair when she remembered that of course he couldn't. He understood entirely.

'I'll get the names for you, Eve. I'll get the name of the pit and the names of the men. Is that what you need?'

Mute and miserable, she nodded. But it was more than that. She was in the wrong place entirely. With every cell and sinew, she wished to be in Netherwood with her family and friends. This was punishment for betraying Arthur's memory. For pretending she was someone else. She left Daniel, without a word or a glance, and entered the house, with no clear aim except to be alone. Watching her go, he felt helpless in the face of the life she had led without him, as if a yawning chasm had opened between them, and she stood out of reach on her side with the people she loved, in the place she knew best. Whose name, on the list of dead men, did she dread to see? Daniel envied him, this nameless miner with a hold on her heart. For the same honour he felt he would exchange places, whatever his fate.

Chapter 48

Daniel's great friend in the Hoyland clan was the countess, but he knew her well enough to realise she would know nothing at all about a crisis in Netherwood beyond the inconvenient fact of her husband's departure. Henrietta, on the other hand, would probably have been briefed by her father and would now be in possession of all the details; for a woman, she made an excellent right-hand man. Therefore it was she whom Daniel sought when he entered the house, hard on the heels of Eve.

He spoke to a footman then waited in the elegant reception hall while his request was conveyed. The flowers he had sent up to the house in a trug, early this morning, rose from a blue china vase in a loose, unstructured arrangement at the centre of a highly polished walnut table. The choice of blooms – cornflowers, poppies, a few sprays of white blossom – had a natural, artless appearance, quite at odds with their formal setting, but all the more striking for that. Not Mrs Munster's work, then, he thought. She took a more architectural approach, preferring tight floral structures with gladioli and irises – flowers with backbone, flowers more like her.

'Mr MacLeod.'

The footman, a handsome blond youth of the type favoured by the countess – matching footmen were all the rage in her set – had appeared soundlessly beside him.

'Lady Henrietta can see you now,' he said, indicating, as he spoke, the earl's study. He led Daniel in, announcing him rather more formally than seemed appropriate, given that he was, after all, merely the gardener. Henrietta, however, welcomed him warmly, standing from where she sat at her father's desk and walking around it to shake Daniel by the hand. She was dressed for riding in a handsome dark-brown habit with a velvet collar, and her hair was tamed and twisted into a thick plait. She rode hardly less in London than she did in the country, though her outings were more sedate in the city, restricted as they were to Rotten Row and other sections of the royal parks.

'Daniel,' she said. 'What can I do for you?'

He hesitated, suddenly aware that his request for the names of the dead Netherwood miners was going to seem peculiar in the extreme. But he was here now, and it would appear odder still if he backed out of the room without speaking, so he plunged right in, and explained that he was speaking on behalf of Eve Williams, who had learned of the colliery accident but not of the details.

'She's desperately concerned,' he said. 'She's been very afflicted by the news and would benefit from knowing the names of the deceased, whatever additional sorrow that might bring. At least, so I believe.' This was tagged rather belatedly to the end of his speech; he could see from her eyes that Lady Henrietta was wondering what Eve Williams was to him. However she was too kind, and too discreet, to ask.

'Ah, good – so she's back?' she said.

Daniel nodded, feeling somehow wrong-footed.

'I did look for her earlier, but the kitchen staff were unable to help. Where is she now?'

'I think she probably went up to her room. She wouldn't head to the kitchen for comfort.' This was excruciating. He felt riddled with guilt for keeping Eve away and for knowing where she was now. But Henrietta seemed unconcerned about the whys and wherefores – the last thing on her mind was an inquisition.

'She must be desperate for news. I shall go directly to her.'

He thanked her, bid her farewell and walked to the door of the study. As he opened it to leave she said, 'And Daniel?'

He turned. 'Yes, m'lady?'

'I shall comfort her, too, if I can. I mean, as well as inform her.'

He was grateful for her understanding and felt a rush of emotion, but betrayed nothing of his feelings when he spoke.

'Thank you, m'lady,' he said evenly, and he took his leave.

Eve sat on the edge of her bed, dry-eyed, white-faced. She would wait there, she had decided, until she heard. She could not continue with her day until she knew if Amos was dead, and if he was, she could not stay in London. The notion that she was perhaps being punished for today was persistent, though in her heart she couldn't feel regret or any sense of sinfulness. She had on her lap the Bible from her nightstand, but it was unopened. Some memory of faith from her past had prompted her to reach for it, but her relationship with the Almighty was complex these days, since he had stood by and watched, as Arthur was smote down. Her fury with God had diminished with the passing of the months – she came to understand it wasn't a personal vendetta – but still she felt she had turned her back on her old, unquestioning beliefs and had therefore forfeited the right to pray, now, for Amos's safety. In any case, she thought, he was either dead or he was alive, and no one's prayers could influence this fact.

There was a brief knock on her closed door, a gentle, tentative tap-tap. She stood and crossed the room to open it, and was astonished beyond words to see Lady Henrietta, who looked almost apologetic to be there on the narrow landing of the servants' quarters.

'I feel I'm trespassing,' she said. 'I haven't been this far up before.' The moment they were out, she wished the words unsaid. Mistress and servant, they seemed to say. Your world and mine.

Eve seemed oblivious. She swallowed, tried to speak, failed. Instead she looked down at a piece of paper that Henrietta held in her hand.

'Do you mind awfully if I come in,' she said. 'I'm so sorry to barge up here, but Daniel – Mr MacLeod, you know, the gardener – said you'd appreciate a few more details about the accident. And I didn't want to send them with a maid, in case, well . . .'

Henrietta's attractive, open face was clouded with anxiety, and Eve felt ungracious, standing there expressionless and silent, but her mouth was too dry to form words. She managed however to open the door wide enough to admit Henrietta into the room.

'Thank you,' she said. 'Now. I shall stay, at least while you read this. It was an accident involving the winding gear at New Mill – oh!'

Eve had stumbled backwards at this unwelcome information, and was clutching the brass bedstead for support. Lady Henrietta thrust the piece of paper at her.

'Quickly, look. These are the names of the men who were killed.'

Eve took the paper and, holding it in shaking hands, she read the eight names. She knew them all, but Amos wasn't there. Amos was alive. She was sorry for the dead, sorrier for the bereaved, but still she was filled with an unfathomable gratitude that manifested itself now in a torrent of tears.

Henrietta stepped forwards and placed an awkward hand on Eve's arm. She would have liked to gather her in an embrace but felt too acutely the distance between them – not on her part, she was all unspent warmth and sympathy, but she was uncertain of Eve, whose evident sorrow seemed to set them apart. For a short while, she let Eve cry, leaving her hand upon her in the hope that this small human contact would be better than none.

Then she said, tentatively, 'What is it, Eve? Have you lost someone very dear?' and Eve, finally able to speak, said, 'No. No. He isn't lost. He isn't named here. Thank you, m'lady.'

She bobbed slightly, deferentially, and Henrietta wished with all her heart that she wouldn't. There was something so utterly compelling about the woman before her, a spirit of independence and integrity that should, if wealth and privilege mattered less, make them equals. We're not so different, you and I, thought Henrietta. Except you are infinitely more admirable.

'I'm so pleased,' was all she said, for she couldn't speak her thoughts. 'I mean – that you're not personally affected. Too severely, that is. Obviously I'm terribly sorry that eight men are dead. Daddy's gone up to Netherwood for a couple of days. The funerals take place tomorrow I think, or perhaps the next day, after the inquest. It's awfully soon, but it's for the best. To be honest, there's been some difficulty . . .'

She tailed off, thinking twice about what she'd been about to say. Eve didn't need to know that the bodies of the dead men were so badly mutilated that they were barely human, identifiable only from the numbers on the brass checks that were missing from the banksman's tally. What remains had been salvaged were to be buried together; they would share a grave and a headstone, just as they had shared their horrific end. Henrietta took Eve's hands in hers.

'Will you be all right?'

'I will,' said Eve. Her face was blotched and wet, but she was beyond caring. She sniffed deeply. 'I'm so grateful to you.'

'Not at all, it was the very least . . . are you sure there's nothing else I can do for you?'

'Well, perhaps . . .'

'Yes? Do ask,' said Henrietta eagerly.

'Just paper, perhaps, and a pen. There are people in Netherwood I need to write to,' Eve said.

'Oh gosh! Of course,' Henrietta said, pleased at how easily she could oblige. 'I'll have some sent up. If you leave them on the silver plate in the hall, they'll be franked and posted for you.'

This was a great kindness, Eve felt. She had never had to post a letter in her life, had no idea how to go about it. She thanked Henrietta profusely.

'Really, Eve, it's nothing. I shall deal with it now,' she said, and she left the room. Eve, alone again, dropped to her knees and had a word with God for the first time since Arthur died, praying for the souls of the deceased and giving thanks for Amos's reprieve.

Chapter 49

It was dark when the train pulled into the family station, and Atkins was waiting for the earl on the platform when he disembarked. The chauffeur's face was sombre, as befitted the purpose of his master's unscheduled return to Netherwood. For his part, and in spite of the grim nature of his visit, Teddy Hoyland couldn't help feeling a lightness of heart at being back so soon. He felt at home here in a way he never could in London. He didn't share Clarissa's need for endless diversion, and, on the whole, London society bored him.

Atkins opened the driver's door of the Daimler, and the earl climbed in. His luggage – very little, since he duplicated most of his essentials in the two homes – was deposited on the rear seat, then Atkins got to work on the crankshaft. It was a little recalcitrant and though the earl loved to drive, he preferred to leave the cranking to Atkins, who seemed to have more of a knack. A chap could soon look a perfect fool, sweating over the blessed handle, and in any case it had a nasty habit of kicking back when the pistons got going. Why risk humiliation or personal injury, when Atkins was so adept at the job? He watched his chauffeur's grimly determined profile as he manfully heaved the engine into life.

No, London might be Clarissa's spiritual home, but Netherwood was his; he could hold his own at any gathering, but he didn't rate the trivial flim-flam of society gatherings. His meeting with the American ambassador last night had been a different matter, of course. For once his wife had invited someone worthwhile; he planned to speak to his broker later about investment in the Panama project. See what he had to say about it. For a man with such wealth, Teddy was cautious about new ventures. Many was the time he pulled back from the brink of a scheme after weeks of deliberation, as if weighing up the pros and cons had, in the end, been his only objective.

On the fifth attempt the pistons fired, the sparking plugs lit the fuel and the motor car's engine settled into a regular, promising rumble. Atkins wiped his hands discreetly down the sides of his coat then, puffing a little from his exertions, clambered up into the passenger seat with evident relief.

Teddy looked across at his chauffeur. The earl planned to visit New Mill before he drove home, and he preferred to go alone; he had never been absent when an accident occurred, and it made him edgy that there were details he didn't yet know about the incident. Henry's rather barbed comment about safety at the colliery had rattled him, too. A quiet word with Don Manvers would set things right. The inquest into the disaster was to be held tomorrow, swiftly followed, if there were no sticky complications, by the burials. If blame was to be laid at anyone's door, Don would know by now. The earl needed as much information as possible if scandal was to be averted. Forewarned was very much forearmed in these cases.

'Actually, Atkins, would you mind walking from here?' he said now.

His chauffeur didn't flinch. 'Of course not, m'lord,' he said, and promptly climbed out of the car.

'Thanks, old chap. I'm off to New Mill, no point you tagging along.'

'Of course not, m'lord,' said Atkins, again. He wondered, privately, if he might hitch a ride with someone else. The walk to Netherwood Hall was a good two miles from here, and there was something intrinsically humiliating about a chauffeur walking home. People would think he'd mislaid the Daimler.

The earl made to depart, then hesitated.

'Atkins, change of plan,' he said.

'Yes, m'lord?'

'You motor back to the homestead. I'll walk back, after visiting New Mill. Been sitting down for the past six hours, could do with a leg-stretch, what!'

He climbed out of the car as he spoke, holding the door open for Atkins to take his place. The chauffeur was perturbed.

'But m'lord—'

'No, no, no objections, mind's made up, subject's closed,' said Teddy. He was already walking away, in the direction of the colliery.

'See you anon,' he called without turning, and he raised one arm in salute.

Atkins, back in the driver's seat, put the vehicle into gear and drove away slowly. He hoped he hadn't shown, in his face or his bearing, any reluctance to travel on foot. The thought that the earl might simply be accommodating him with this new arrangement troubled him all the way back to Netherwood Hall.

The funeral tea was at the mill. It had been Ginger's idea and the earl had approved it, sending word via Absalom Blandford that the cost of the food would be borne by him, and that he would be attending the gathering following the funerals. None of the usual fare was to be provided, just sandwiches and sponge cakes. And there would only be tea to drink, though it would be provided in limitless quantities. If folk wanted something stronger, said Ginger, they could take themselves off to the ale house. She had the girls tie black ribbons on some of the beams, and there were eight wreaths of hothouse lilies sent up from the hall, which Ginger had Alice hang on the doors and the walls. In just the few days she'd been in charge, Ginger's authority had become natural and unquestioned, even by hard-nosed Nellie.

The only person she didn't issue orders to was Anna, who had a status all of her own. Her determined, diminutive figure was a common sight, marching briskly up to the mill to lend a hand, shopping on the high street or at the market for provisions, buying cloth from the drapers. She was still, and would always be, a foreigner in Netherwood and as such was always under suspicion. But the black looks of gainsayers and tittle-tattlers made no impact on her; she was protected by a belief not so much in her superiority as in her own unassailable place in the world. It showed in her expression, and in the way she held herself. Lady Muck, some people called her, yet whatever you thought of her uppity tendencies, you couldn't call her idle; she ran Eve's home like clockwork, cooked for and cared for the children and, in the quiet of the evenings, ran up garments with the same ease that other people buttered a slice of bread or peeled a potato. And when she was needed at the mill, there she would be. Certainly she'd be on duty for the wake, because it was all hands to the pumps. There was nothing quite like a funeral – and free food, said Nellie – to make folk hungry.

The inquest, hurriedly convened in the upstairs function room of the Cross Keys, had been presided over by the district coroner and had swiftly concluded a verdict of accidental death due to a series of 'unfortunate occurrences that, in conjunction with each other, had deadly consequences'. The New Mill winding gear had not been faulty, there was no dereliction of duty on the part of the earl or the pit managers, and there were no recommendations to be made as to the prevention of future such accidents. The blame was placed at the door of Fred Mackie, the engine winder on the day of the accident; the cage had been overwound, and he had failed to react to any of the warning signs. He was laid off work immediately after the incident, and was said to be suffering from an affliction of the nerves. There were no charges brought against him, since a drawn-out court case was considered to be in nobody's best interests.

'No blood on t'earl's 'ands then,' muttered Amos to Sidney Cutts as they both sat listening at the back of the room. 'All that carnage and it's old Fred Mackie we're blamin'.'

'Aye, well, it were old Fred Mackie fell asleep on t'job,' hissed Sidney.

'Or so they say. Did you 'ear 'im defend 'imself?'

Sidney rolled his eyes at Amos, but what he said was true. Fred Mackie, principal witness, was safely out of the way at home. The word was that the earl had been generous, severing Fred's thirty years' employment with a lump sum of six months' pay.

'Half a year's wages to carry t'can,' Amos said, none too quietly now. 'I should ask a lot more'n that, if it were me.'

He found, as he stood in the courtyard at the do after the funeral, that his job as recruiting agent had been done for him, though it was the nailing of Fred Mackie that was the catalyst, rather than the tragedy itself. There was disquiet at the rumour, rapidly setting into a hardened truth, that the old man, whether he knew it or not, had been paid off to take the rap. Nobody could usefully examine the winding gear, since it was smashed beyond recognition. But there were safety devices fitted which were meant to prevent what had happened at New Mill, and none of the pit men could recall when they were last tested for efficacy. It stank of a cover-up, and now here was the earl, moving among the mourners with his customary ease and charm, and there was a general feeling among the miners that his wealth and position had protected him from awkward questions. So without even trying, Amos was being approached time and again by men who felt, finally, that representation and the backing of the YMA might be no bad thing. He couldn't be sure, because the paperwork was at home, but nigh on a hundred and fifty men were now in favour of a New Mill Colliery trade union. When life returned to normal, and the earl was properly back from his stay in London, Amos would approach him with enough hard evidence to support the claim. There'd be branch meetings at New Mill before the autumn. He wondered if Anna might make them a banner. Something fine in red and gold. Something to reflect their pride in what they had achieved.

'Penny for your thoughts.'

Amos laughed. The familiar phrase, in Anna's heavy accent, sounded a little sinister. She bridled.

'What? Have I said it wrong?'

'No, no,' Amos said. 'Spot on.'

'So? What makes you laugh?'

'Oh, just that you said it at all. Not what you expect from a Russian.'

'I am Yorkshire as well as Russian,' she said. 'So. What was you thinking about?'

He smiled again, but didn't correct her grammar. 'I was thinkin' about t'cabbage parcels you fed me on Tuesday,' he said.

She beamed. 'Come any time,' she said. 'Come this evening. I make stroganoff.'

He raised a quizzical brow.

'Come,' she said. 'Then you learn what is stroganoff.' She leaned in, dropping her voice to a stage whisper. 'It's foreign muck,' she said.

He laughed. She was a good woman – he'd often thought it. Not much of her, but what there was was grand.

Chapter 50

The Tideaways were on the move, and the Hoyland Arms locked and shuttered until someone else took it on. It wasn't much of a prospect; Harry's early enthusiasm and entrepreneurship had withered and died; he would be glad to see the back of it. There was a position at the Lady's Bridge Brewery in Sheffield, he had heard, and he was confident that he was the man for the job. Nobody knew more about beer than he did. Granted, he'd never brewed it, only sold it, but what did that figure? A fellow of his experience wouldn't be turned away, of that he was certain. Yes, Sheffield was the place for him. Netherwood was a dead loss and everyone in it could rot in hell.

Their belongings, including the old piano for which he'd had such high hopes, were loaded on to a dray and tied under two great tarpaulin sheets. There was no one there to see them off. This, Harry told Agnes, was because half the town was at the funeral. Agnes, who knew the funeral was already over, nodded. She sat, pale to the point of transparency, on the passenger side of the dray, all wrapped up in wool in spite of the warm sunshine. She was always cold, was Agnes. Thin-blooded, like her dear, departed mother, Harry said. Ada

Tideaway's thin blood had killed her in the end, at least that was Harry's story. Agnes, whose white face often bore the imprint of her father's hand, sometimes wondered if there might not have been another cause.

She was waiting for him now. He had an errand to run before they left, and she was to sit up on the cart and steady the horse until he returned. To be honest, there wouldn't be a lot Agnes could do to stop the old grey nag if he decided to leave town without Harry, but this was an unlikely scenario; he was a placid steed, too elderly to make sudden, impetuous dashes. Agnes sat, gazing at nothing, wondering where she would be sleeping tonight. Speaking for herself, which was something she never managed to do out loud, she quite liked Netherwood and was sorry it hadn't worked out. But she and her father had moved many times, so there was nothing new in these feelings. Privately she thought their itinerant life was bad for her health; a plant that never puts down roots can't be expected to thrive.

She could see her father now, toiling back up Victoria Street. She watched closely, waiting to pick up the crucial clues that would indicate his mood. She shivered, wrapped the shawl tighter around, and swallowed, though she found her mouth was dry. Closer he came with his rolling gait, puffing with the effort required to negotiate the slight incline. He seemed pleased, she thought, with a cautious lift of her heart. She looked on, as he was still a safe distance away. Yes, certainly pleased. There were no tell-tale furrows between his eyes and his mouth was slack, not tight-lipped with anger. He had something in his hand and his progress, though laboured, was purposeful. Agnes, perfectly attuned to the vagaries of her father's moods, allowed herself to relax, and redirected her gaze to her folded hands before he could catch her eye and clout her for it.

He arrived at the cart and with a monumental effort heaved himself into it.

''ere,' he said, slapping a thin bundle of sheets into her lap. 'Make yerself useful and hang on to them.'

She risked a question, since he seemed so pleased with himself.

'What is it, Father?'

He took up the reins and snapped them to stir the horse into action, and he smiled broadly before he spoke, though he didn't look at his daughter.

'Amos Sykes's worst nightmare, that's what it is,' he said. 'Amos Sykes's worst bleedin' nightmare.'

Instead of heading directly out of Netherwood towards Sheffield Road, Harry took a most alarming detour, at least from Agnes's point of view. He turned the cart in a wide arc and set off in the opposite direction, down Stead Lane and out of town past Middlecar. Agnes knew better than to ask where they were headed and she sat, mute, clutching the sheaf of papers her father had entrusted her with. Even when they passed through the gates of Netherwood Hall and headed down the avenue towards the great house, she remained silent, though she wondered at his audacity, bringing their shabby dray with its ungainly load here.

She risked a look about her; it was the first time she had seen the legendary park and grounds. From what she allowed herself to see, it looked to be a marvellous place. How wonderful it would be to work here, she thought. How wonderful to have a place in the household, a uniform to wear, a proper purpose to every day. Agnes, whose external life was barely tolerable, survived by imagining alternatives to her present existence. She cut a surreptitious glance across at her father. His broad face still sported its unsettling smile, as if some grimly amusing memory had come back to entertain him.

He drove the dray around past the front of the house – remarkable, thought Agnes, that they had remained unchallenged – and through the grand arch into the courtyard behind. Here, Harry drew the horse to a standstill and disembarked, silently holding out a hand for the papers. Agnes passed them across. He left her sitting there and strode across the flagstones to a building opposite, disappearing into it without so much as a knock on the wooden door.

Agnes could see him in profile, through the window. He seemed to be agitated now, his hands working as he spoke. He was speaking to – or at – another man, who was seated behind a desk. The man's expression was – what was it? Not startled or alarmed. Disgusted, possibly. Contemptuous. Agnes watched with increasing dismay and her breathing began to come short and shallow. She wondered, even as she knew she never would, if she might run from the cart and into the house, throwing herself upon the mercy of the housekeeper who might hide her, employ her, help her to shake free of him. Inside the building, her father slammed the sheaf of papers down on the desk before him. He jabbed a finger at the man and she could see his face twist with fury. The man, relaxed in his chair with his arms folded, exuded scorn. Now, thought Agnes. If I dropped down now from the cart, I might change my life. I shall begin to count, she said out loud, and if I reach ten I shall go.

But she counted slowly to avoid her own deadline, and had only reached six when he left the office. He stalked back to the dray and climbed up, his face mottled with red rage. He sat, heavily, and she moved a fraction to accommodate him. He turned to her.

'Take that look off yer face or I'll strike it off,' he said. 'Fuckin' stupid waste o' space. You' – he homed in, menacingly close to her face – 'drag me down. You're a burden. And an ugly bitch to boot.'

Droplets of spittle flew from his mouth and hit the back of Agnes's folded hands. He rested the flat of his hand against her cheek in what might have been a tender gesture, then he pushed hard at her face, jerking her head back painfully. He hawked and spat copiously on the flagstones of the courtyard before turning the horse and cart, eager to leave town now that he had accomplished his mission. Well, whatever that jumped-up bastard Jem Arkwright said, he, Harry Tideaway, had just done the earl a great and lasting service. Part of him was sorry he wouldn't have a ringside seat at Amos Sykes's downfall. But most of him was anxious to be long gone by the time Amos discovered who had undone him, and how.

It was late by the time Amos got home. He had gone from the mill to Beaumont Lane, where he'd spent a companionable evening eating with Anna and the children, then lingering a while after they had gone to bed. They found much to talk about; Amos had never been abroad but in his mind he had travelled the globe, and he listened to Anna's stories of her Russian childhood with unstinting fascination. Anna felt indulged by his interest, and she gave him her favourite memories in return for it. He walked home feeling a personal contentment that was unfamiliar, and at odds with the sadness of the day, but then, as he approached his front door, he saw it was already slightly ajar. Close up, he could see the wood was split around the lock where someone had jemmied it open. Cautiously he pushed it wide. His bulldog, Mac, lumbered towards the door, a sheepishness tempering his usual welcome.

'Useless bugger,' Amos said, and the dog shrank against the wall, certain now that he had been found lacking when put to the test. But there was no sound within and no evidence, once Amos entered, of any disturbance. Must be the world's daftest burglar, he thought, breaking into a house on Brook Lane. He wandered through the rooms downstairs; all was as it should be. Upstairs was the same. Mystified, he returned to the kitchen and put the kettle on, thinking as he waited for it to boil that he'd have to see to the lock tomorrow. Tonight he was done in. He gazed gloomily about the kitchen; even without the grim detail of his jemmied lock, this little house had an unloved air about it. There was never a smell of food when he walked in, or the sound of a kettle already building up steam. Then, as he stood with his back to the range facing his small, bare table, he realised what was missing.

Someone had lifted the papers that he'd left on there this morning. A letter from the YMA, detailing benefits of membership. A list of names of men at New Mill Colliery. A letter Amos had drafted to the membership secretary, requesting a meeting as soon as was convenient. It was all gone. Somebody else might have charged about the house searching high and low for the missing documents, in case in an unconscious moment they could've been filed elsewhere, but Amos didn't move, just stood stock still, staring at where they'd been. He knew what was what, just as he knew, now, what was not. Behind him, the kettle began to let out its shrill call. Right, he said to himself, in his methodical way. Somebody else'll tell the earl what I was going to tell 'im anyway. That's no disaster, though it could've been better handled. But some bastard hates me enough to put 'imself to this trouble.

And it was that thought, more than the likely consequences of the theft, which squatted leaden and ugly in his mind.

Chapter 51

London was losing its strangeness as time passed, and the days no longer seemed to stretch out before her with their threats of emptiness and inactivity. She had seized her advantage with Mrs Carmichael and requested a meeting with her and the housekeeper, in which she said she preferred to buy in her own supplies rather than waiting for the rest of the kitchen requirements to be ordered. This way, she said, she could speak to the suppliers herself, check the goods for the quality she was after, and – she added, because she could see the women's faces freezing over – it would get her out from under their feet.

'Really, it'd be less of a nuisance to you,' she said, directing this to Mrs Carmichael. 'And I can order things as I need them, then.'

The cook looked sceptical, but she sensed, correctly, that Eve was telling her, not asking. Mrs Munster said, 'I trust you haven't found the quality of our ingredients lacking?'

'Well,' said Eve. 'Since you mention it, t'flour could be better. Shame you don't have t'Co-op down 'ere.' What she said was only half true, because the flour she'd used was perfectly adequate. But she needed a reason to get out of the house

401

more, and anyway, the looks on her adversaries' faces were priceless.

Mrs Carmichael, stung out of her stunned silence, said, 'Dodson's flour has served us perfectly well for as long as I can remember.'

'Good,' said Eve. 'I wish you well to use it. But I thought I might shop around for somethin' of a finer grade for t'sweet pastries. T'kitchens at Grosvenor Crescent use McSwain's. It seemed excellent.'

She smiled sweetly. There was nothing they could say to her. She'd cooked for the king now and while Eve wasn't generally a person to gloat or pull rank, she found that when she tried it came easily.

'Very well,' said Mrs Munster, who was more at liberty to speak since her pride and reputation were still intact. 'But I shall need all receipts. Bills are settled promptly in this establishment. And I shall need to see the provisions when they come in, to be sure that in weight and measure they agree with the dockets.'

'Of course,' Eve said. She stood to leave. 'Well. T'devil makes work for idle 'ands.' She thought she'd say it before Mrs Munster got the chance. The two senior members of the household watched her go then looked at each other.

'She won't be here for ever, Beryl,' said Mrs Munster.

The cook pursed her lips. 'Finer grade, indeed. You'd think she was somebody.'

The Duchess of Abberley had introduced Eve to King Edward. It had been his idea, of course, and it was because of the Yorkshire puddings. She'd made them in the tiny tart tins, so the batter had cooked and risen to about the size of an upturned chestnut mushroom, minus the stalk. She'd used an extra egg white to make them lighter, and they were almost weightless, rising like small brown clouds in the hottest oven the kitchen could supply. She filled the hollows with a dab of horseradish cream and slivers of rare roast beef which were dipped at the very last minute in rich gravy, just enough to help the morsel go down the royal gullet without compromising the crunch. Eve hadn't known – for how could she? – that beef and Yorkshire pudding was among the king's favourite food, the dish he turned to when his habitual diet of cream-rich, butter-drenched, truffle-heavy twelve-course dinners had begun to pall. But there it was. And while he had laughed heartily at the rest of the lovely, novelty fare, and eaten with his customary gluttony the tiny pork pies and steak puddings served up by the duchess's footmen, the miniature Yorkshires had rendered him temporarily speechless with a kind of dazed joy, as if the one thing his indulged and cosseted life lacked had suddenly been given him, without him requesting it or even knowing it had been missing.

He had wolfed down eight or nine of them in rapid succession – he hadn't acquired his forty-eight-inch waist by exercising moderation in these matters – and then had insisted on congratulating the cook in person. She couldn't be brought upstairs, but there was nothing and no one capable of preventing His Majesty going to her, which he duly did, accompanied by the duchess who had to show him the way. He stalked through the corridors with much the same effect as a beater walking a copse, sending members of the household into a flap like pheasant rising in mindless panic from the safety of their hiding places. There was no time to alert anyone to his purpose; he was in the kitchens before the below-stairs staff could make themselves decent, and to a stunned and dishevelled assembly he boomed out his request to speak to the 'author of the Yorkshire puddings'.

Eve had been standing over a frying pan at the stove, a

bowl of batter in one hand and a teaspoon in the other. The delicate business of forming pancakes no bigger than a shilling was occupying her mind. When Polly – she'd taken her to Grosvenor Crescent because the girl was increasingly indispensable – tapped her on the shoulder and said King Edward was in the kitchen and wanted a word, Eve had laughed.

'Very funny. Now 'old this ring steady for me while I pour t'batter in.'

Polly had stepped back then in respectful alarm, because the king was right there, opulently clad in a plum velvet jacket and embroidered waistcoat. Polly, undeniably nimble with her fingers and helpful to Eve in many ways, was nevertheless completely unequal to the situation, and she fainted, though quietly and undramatically as if the air was gradually being let out of her. Someone pulled her out of the way and Eve, seeing her slide away from the corner of her range of vision, turned from the hot pan to find the monarch an arm's length away from her, smiling. She recognised him from the picture on the children's coronation mugs at home, though he looked more corpulent, and redder in the face. She dropped into a curtsy, still holding the batter and the spoon.

'His Royal Highness King Edward the Seventh,' said the duchess pompously.

'Yorkshire puddings,' said the king, without preamble. 'Absolute triumph. Best thing I've tasted in months. I wonder I've never eaten them before if you're with the Abberleys.'

'I'm with t'Earl and Countess of Netherwood, Your Majesty,' Eve said, with the surface calm that can sometimes be triggered by fathomless shock. 'T'Duchess of Abberley borrowed me.'

He tipped back his head and gave a great bark of laughter.

'Then when they have you back, you must cook for me again,' he said. 'High time I visited Netherwood.'

He nodded at her, then turned and left the kitchen.

'Did that just 'appen?' she said to a white-faced kitchen lad, who was gawping from the sidelines. He shrugged, uncertain how to answer. He'd seen the king in the kitchen, certainly, but the evidence of his own eyes didn't seem enough, somehow, to convince him.

Back upstairs, where he belonged, the king had infuriated his hostess by immediately seeking out Lady Netherwood, who had been trying to catch his eye all evening.

'Clarissa,' he said. 'Time I enjoyed a little Yorkshire hospitality. I'm in Doncaster for the St Leger in September. My man'll be in touch.'

Lady Netherwood, who at last had what she had wanted for so long, smiled graciously, though her mind was whirring with what must be done. At least they had some notice. Even so, if they were to be prepared for a royal visit by the end of August, they should probably return to Netherwood sooner than planned. End of June, at the latest. All of this whizzed through her mind at the heightened speed that thought allows, before she said, 'Thank you, Your Majesty, we shall be honoured.'

'Do be sure to serve beef and Yorkshires,' he said, indicating the now-empty platters of canapés. 'That is, after all, why I'm coming.' He laughed, so Lady Netherwood joined in though she was far from amused that the entire room had now heard that the reason the king was coming to Netherwood was to eat more of Eve Williams's Yorkshire puddings. She said as much to Teddy when they drove away in the landau an hour later, heading for the Royal Opera House.

'Oh, who cares why he's coming?' said the earl. 'Why does he ever go anywhere? Only because it suits him, for one reason or another.'

'Still though,' said Clarissa. 'It was rather shaming for him to make the entire assembly aware of the arrangement. Not to mention that Eve isn't actually our cook. Though I'm sure she'll oblige.'

'Of course she will,' said Teddy. He felt rather sorry for his wife. She looked so crestfallen, sitting there opposite him. She wore a silver fox stole around her pale shoulders, and a new gown in midnight-blue satin which clung to her small breasts and flat belly, reminding him of the girl she'd been. Teddy's tastes these days were for fleshier women, with a proper rump and a bosom you could lose your face in, but Clarissa's elegance struck him now as a quality he was glad of. Proud of, even. He leaned in and patted her thigh and she gave him a startled look, as if he'd trespassed. Then she softened, and rested her own hand on the back of his.

'Fact is,' said Teddy, 'Bertie's coming to stay, and we'll make jolly sure he's never had a better time anywhere, what!'

'We shall have to redecorate.'

'Shall we? Entirely?'

Clarissa nodded. 'Of course. Top to bottom. And who'll come, at the end of August? Everyone's in Scotland.'

'Clarissa, all will be well. Better than well. All will be excellent. Who declines a house party when the monarch is numbered among the guests? Tantamount to treason, I should think.'

'Don't be silly, Teddy,' she said, but she was pleased with him. He really was a dear sometimes, she thought. Dependable. Reassuring. By comparison, Robin Campbell-Chieveley was quite a slight person. He was already on the wane, though he didn't know it yet. Clarissa's passions never lasted long, although even by her standards Robin's star had fallen rather swiftly. But he could be such a sap, making cow eyes over his cocktail glass and forever trying to push her into closets for a fumble. She thought she might simply cut him tonight at the opera, get it over with. She smiled at her husband, and relaxed, just a little. He smiled back.

'You know,' he said, 'they say that when he stayed with the Norfolks at Arundel he took two valets, three of his own footmen, two equerries with valets of their own, a telephonist, two chauffeurs and a little Arab boy to make his coffee.'

She raised her eyebrows. 'Imagine,' she said. 'An Arab boy.'

'Quite. And if he brings the queen, not Mrs Keppel, expect a further eight members of the royal household.'

'His mother was worse,' said Clarissa. 'She hardly ever went anywhere, but when she did she sent her own furniture on ahead.'

They laughed together, united in that moment by the eccentric indulgences of the royal family and the comfortable familiarity of each other's presence.

Eve finally found Daniel in the still room. He had a great bunch of overblown roses, and was pulling off the petals and laying them on wooden trays. He looked at her as she walked in through the door from the garden, and felt the same wash of love and lust that he did every time he saw her. She smiled at him.

'I've been searchin' 'igh and low for you,' she said. She nodded at the petals. 'Is this one of your jobs?'

'No, not really. But it's nice in here.'

She could see why he liked it. It was peaceful, hushed like a library and shady with its shuttered windows that let in only thin slices of light between the slats. The walls were lined with mellow wood shelves and dressers, which bore jars of oils and distilled waters and bowls and sachets of mysterious, fragrant substances that Alice, the still-room maid, concocted, working like an alchemist with the leaves and seeds, spices and petals.

Eve came to him for a kiss, and they stood for a moment in each other's arms. The urgency had gone from their embraces now that they were daily occurrences. They broke away and Daniel turned back to his task while Eve made a slow circuit of the room. Alice had meticulously labelled her ingredients, and they read like the recipes for magic potions, ancient and mysterious. Yellow saunders, orris root, calamus aromaticus. She uncorked a glass bottle the shape of a teardrop and sniffed the contents. Sandalwood, the label said. It was exotic, unfamiliar. She returned to his side, where the smell of roses was one she knew.

'I shall be going soon,' she said, finally saying what she'd come to say.

He stopped what he was doing and turned to her.

'How soon?'

'Middle of next month. Lady Netherwood needs to return to Netherwood. King Edward's going to stay, and there's everything to do up at t'all, apparently. All t'London engagements from July onwards 'ave 'ad to be cancelled. They won't need me 'ere.'

'Eve,' he said, investing her name with a world of meaning.

'I know.'

They looked at each other for a long moment, and it was she who broke the silence.

'I 'ave to go, you know that, don't you?'

'I do.'

'If I was free, I would stay 'ere with you. If I 'ad no obligations.'

'I know.'

'Daniel.'

'I love you, Eve Williams.'

'But—'

'Sssh.' He placed a gentle finger on her mouth. 'I know all your buts,' he said. 'And we shan't let them spoil the time we have left together.' He smiled. 'Four weeks, maybe more. There are any number of things we can do together in that time.

Let's live for the moment, let the future make its own arrangements.'

She leaned in to him, resting her head against his chest.

'You could stay here, y'know. Bring the children down.'

He'd said that before, and she wished he wouldn't, because it demonstrated how little he knew her. Odd, that. She loved him wholeheartedly, and he loved her, but he still thought she could fetch the bairns from everything and everyone they knew. They were Arthur's children, children of Netherwood. They couldn't be transplanted like one of Daniel's perennials. She shook her head now, as she had done before.

'My life's there,' she said.

He wanted to shout at her that her life was wherever she wanted it to be, and that children would live where they were put, and very likely thrive there. But he didn't want to push her away so he said nothing, and instead caressed her face with his rose-smelling fingers.

'Will you come to me tonight?' he said. His rooms were in the servants' mews, behind the house; easy enough, if she was canny, to slip into and out of undetected. She nodded. Tonight and every night, she thought, until she had to take the train north and step out of this adventure, back into her old life.

Chapter 52

The earl didn't pay Amos the compliment of sacking him in person, delegating the job instead to Jem Arkwright, who had cooked his goose in the first place by sending the incriminating papers to London. Jem, to be fair, had been at a loss as to how to proceed; nobody hated Harry Tideaway more than he did, and part of him would have liked to stick the documents straight into the fire and be done with the evidence. But Jem was the earl's man; if Amos Sykes was agitating in the pits, Jem's duty was to keep the boss informed. He still sat on the papers for a few days, though, before finally passing them on and sealing Amos's fate.

The upshot had been instant dismissal and blacklisting, so that no colliery within a ten-mile radius would touch him. Not one of the men on the list of members was sacked, though; Amos had been right on that score. The earl would've liked to send every one of them packing, but by the time he got wind of the situation there were almost two hundred union members working at New Mill, and he wasn't about to dismiss a third of the workforce. He sent them one of his mutual-loyalty-and-respect letters, full of paternal disappointment at their behaviour, but there was a new mood at the pit these days, an awareness among the men that perhaps, after all, their future – or, at least, a say in it – might be in their own hands rather than Lord Netherwood's. His reluctant concession to allow them union membership while in his employ was their first taste of victory. For now, it was enough.

Jem privately felt that the earl was losing a good man in Amos Sykes. He was impressed by his dignity, by the way he'd made the unpleasant task easy; there was no scene, no fuss. When Jem told him his fate, Amos said, 'Aye, as I thought. When d'you want me out of the 'ouse?'

Jem hadn't even thought about that, though Absalom Blandford had, and notice was swiftly served to vacate the premises within the week. Nearly thirty years in the earl's service, thought Jem, and in the end it counted for nothing. Amos took all of this on the chin, though. All he really wanted to know was who'd shopped him. In the days before Jem acted on the information he'd been given, Amos had felt like a hunted man, each day waiting for the axe to fall, or a blackmail demand from the thief to arrive – free vegetables in perpetuity in return for their silence, perhaps, since he had little else to bargain with. He regarded everyone he met as a potential suspect, staring hard at them during any exchange for signs that here was the snake in the grass who'd stolen his paperwork. It said a lot about Amos's usual demeanour that no one noticed a difference in him. He'd fixed the broken lock himself, unwilling to involve Absalom Blandford in the mystery before he had to, and there had been no further signs of disturbance since. And each day, when he presented himself at the pit-yard time office, fully expecting to be met by a furious Don Manvers, or a lynch mob from the earl's estate, he was merely nodded at as usual and handed his helmet, lamp and checks. It was unsettling in the extreme. So when he finally received a summons to the estate offices from Jem, it came almost as a relief. And when Jem told him it was Harry Tideaway's doing, he actually laughed.

'That's not the reaction I expected,' Jem had said.

'Tideaway's an arse'ole,' said Amos. 'Rather it were 'im than some'dy I work with.'

So, he was without a job and almost without a home, though not yet without hope. He'd managed to save a bit, being a single man with no dependants, and something would turn up, he was sure of it. Anna had already offered a berth in Beaumont Lane, though to be honest, he wasn't that desperate. The last thing he wanted was Eve coming back to find him living under her roof. No, he'd find a job above ground – working in daylight, what a novelty – and he'd rent a room that wasn't tied to the estate. Today he'd been up to the brickworks just after first light, asking to be considered if anything came up. There was nothing at the moment, but they took his name. Then he'd spent a couple of peaceful hours in the allotment before strolling back to Brook Lane for a bite to eat.

There were two letters on his door mat when he got there, and one of them was addressed in Eve's tidy, meticulous hand, so, for the time being, the other one was eclipsed. He sat down at the kitchen table, his heart beating a little faster at the thought of her taking the time to write to him. It was on thick paper with the Countess of Netherwood and Fulton House, Belgravia embossed in black across the top of the sheet, which he could've done without, but he supposed she had no other option. He didn't know what he was hoping for – he'd ceased trying to comprehend his feelings for Eve – but in the event the letter was a little sterile and disappointingly short; she hoped he was well, had been so relieved he was safe, was sorry for the bereaved and had written to them too, was missing everyone but would be home by the summer's end.

There was no news about herself, no way of knowing from her letter whether she was happy in London or sad, no

412

indication whether her life was too full for the written word to do it justice, or so empty that there was nothing to say. Missing everyone didn't mean she was crying herself to sleep at night, he thought. Not that he'd want her to. He wished her well, really he did, even though he loathed the way she'd jumped up and left when Lady Netherwood snapped her fingers. Anna, of course, took issue with his position on this matter, and she was a feisty, articulate adversary. She kept Amos on his mettle; he felt he was sharpening up his debating skills every time he talked to her. Anna refused to see Eve as a servant of the earl and countess. Eve was in the driving seat, Anna reckoned; she had the skills they needed, and was being paid handsomely for them.

'She doesn't need their money, but they need her,' Anna had said. 'I would say that puts Eve in charge, yes?'

'Codswallop,' said Amos, who used these colourful colloquialisms in the hope that Anna would echo them later in the conversation, because it never failed to amuse him when she did. 'Complete codswallop. Eve didn't want to go, but she 'ad to.'

She had given a short, derisory bark. 'Ha! So this is basis of your great, ideal world? We all do only what we want to do?'

There she went again, turning his argument upside down and using it as a weapon to beat him with. It was Anna's speciality. When he pictured her, it was making just such a point, her small chin jutting forwards and an expression of Slavic contempt clouding her pretty face. She should run for parliament, he'd said. They should give her the vote and she might, she'd replied.

Amos put Eve's letter to one side and picked up the other. It was postmarked Barnsley, though he didn't recognise the handwriting. Perhaps this was the blackmail note, he thought. Bit late now.

It wasn't, though. It was a letter from the secretariat of the Yorkshire Miners' Association, inviting Amos to apply for the post of regional recruitment officer for Barnsley and district.

'Well, I'll be blowed,' he said out loud.

Tobias was in love with Dorothea Sterling. No matter that he'd met her for the first time just three weeks earlier, had seen her only four times since, and had spent none of those times alone with her. He was in love, he was quite convinced of it – had known, in fact, the first evening he met her that she was the one for him; she was bold and independent, and she sparkled with vivacity and wit. Henry, in that maddening way of hers, had been quick to point out the recessive chin, but even she conceded that, while no conventional beauty, Thea had something special about her, something that turned heads when she entered a room. She was so spirited! Tobias felt pepped up by her presence, as if she transmitted invisible waves of enthusiasm and *joie de vivre*. She was something new, really she was. She was a masterful horsewoman, but she didn't ride sidesaddle like every other girl in the capital; they'd ridden out, she, Tobias, Henry and Dickie, in Hyde Park and Thea had worn a new style of redingote that allowed her to sit astride the horse without showing more than a modest flash of ankle. It was an incredibly stirring sight, seeing her straddle the horse's back in that way. People stared and Tobias, eyes on stalks, had almost come a cropper watching her instead of the path ahead. Everything about her – her clothes, her manners, her voice – was different from what he knew, and therein lay the appeal. He was so unutterably bored by the girls his parents favoured. Thea shunned chiffon in favour of exotic shot silks in hot colours; she shook hands like a man and opened doors for herself; she could play poker and baccarat

414

as well as bridge, and when Tobias lit a cigarette in the club that he and Henry took her to, she took it from his mouth and enjoyed a couple of long drags before handing it back, stained with red lipstick. She wasn't fast though. He'd come not even close to getting his hands on her. Something told him that this thoroughly modern young woman, who danced to Scott Joplin and taught Toby the cakewalk, drank bourbon on the rocks or whisky sour, studied Greek and Latin and mathematics and was in England to attend a summer school on Elizabethan literature, would nevertheless require a marriage proposal before she loosened her stays.

'Mama won't like it,' said Henrietta, when he confided his intentions.

'Why?' said Toby. 'She wants me married, doesn't she?'

'Not really,' said his sister. 'Not if she's honest. And certainly not to an American.'

'She's from an excellent family.'

'Trade,' said Henrietta. 'Iron manufacturers in Connecticut. Her ancestors made a fortune supplying the American Revolution with arms, so they're not even covert monarchists.'

'Well, we're trade too if it comes to that. Mama can hardly throw that up as an objection. How the dickens do you know these things, Henry?'

'She told me. I'm not so distracted by her as you are. We've had some interesting conversations.'

'Don't you think she's divine?'

'No, not especially. But I like her.'

And Tobias had had to be content with what he considered an exceedingly shabby and lukewarm response to the object of his infatuation. Henry had been spot on, though, about their mother's reaction. He'd waited until breakfast the following morning and then had dropped it into the conversation in a careless manner, as if proposing marriage was of no greater import than requesting the salt for a boiled egg.

Lady Netherwood was quite composed, under the circumstances.

'No, darling. Don't be absurd,' she said, when Tobias made his opening gambit. She smoothed her napkin over her lap and poured a second cup of tea with a hand that was completely steady, so sure was she that the matter was closed.

'Clarissa,' said Teddy, somehow reproving and conciliatory at the same time. 'I rather like Thea Sterling. She has a good head on her shoulders.'

Tobias gave his father an appreciative smile, but his mother replaced her cup in its saucer in a decidedly combative manner.

'No one marries an American unless they have to,' she said. 'If we were destitute, I might consider it. As it is, you'd be a laughing stock. The Sterlings scream trade from every pore.'

Henrietta smiled knowingly across the table at Tobias, but he was glaring at his mother.

'As do we,' he said. 'Do you think society forgets that our money has everything to do with industry? Do you think we've somehow managed to cover our tracks? Let me tell you, Mama, everyone knows where we've come from, as plainly as if we had coal dust on the soles of our shoes.'

Everyone stared. In the history of family gatherings, no one could remember Tobias ever speaking with such harsh authority. And to his devoted mother, too. She blanched elegantly, and made a little show of collecting herself under the assault. Then she nodded at Munster, who was steadfastly pretending to have heard nothing. He stepped forward, blank faced, to assist her out of her chair and out of the room. At the door, she turned.

'If you propose marriage to Dorothea Sterling,' she said carefully, 'I shall kill myself.'

'Clarissa, dear,' said Teddy, but it was a feeble protest, a half-cocked attempt at bringing her back, and it failed.

'Well!' said Henrietta.

'I say,' said Dickie.

416

Isabella snivelled, but she was ignored, even by her father. He looked at Tobias.

'That's torn it,' he said.

Now that going home was a tangible prospect, Eve would have hastened her departure if she could. This seemed perverse, given her feelings for Daniel, but she looked at it differently; pain postponed cast a pall over everything. If she had to separate from him, let it be swift – that was her reasoning. The thought of being without him caused a sensation of pure panic, and yet she had lived without him well enough before, and perhaps she could again. In any case, she longed to see her children. She missed Anna, too, and the women at the mill. She had thought she would be absent for the summer months, when they planned to put tables outside in the courtyard if the weather was warm. Anna remembered a street café in Bremen where she and Leo had sat together on their long journey from Kiev to England, and she'd described it to Eve; there were canvas parasols over the tables for shade, and people weren't chivvied away, but lingered over coffee and cigarettes. Why not bring some continental flair to Netherwood, she'd said, and Eve had said that anything was worth a try. And now she would be there to oversee it; the tables and chairs were being made at the foundry, and she and Anna would paint them white, or yellow, or perhaps pale blue. There would be a new summer menu, with lighter fare – open flans and fishcakes and egg mayonnaise on homegrown lettuce with fresh bread and butter. She filled her mind with these pleasant meanderings, and they protected her from dread.

And then Lady Netherwood summoned her to the morning room one day and said she could pack at once. The whole family would be travelling back to Netherwood at the end of the week, an emergency, she said, though she didn't elaborate except to reassure Eve that it had nothing to do with the collieries. Samuel Stallibrass would take her back to the station whenever she was ready.

'You don't mean today, m'lady?' Eve said, her heart suddenly pounding in her breast.

'No reason why not. Tomorrow, if you prefer. Is there a problem?'

'I, well, I thought you'd planned a party on Saturday, m'lady? Certainly the food has been ordered. I did it myself yesterday.'

'Cancelled,' Lady Netherwood said crisply. 'Haste is of the essence. Tobias is in danger and I'm removing him to the country.'

'Oh! Is he ill, m'lady?' Eve had seen him just this morning, looking right as rain and whistling as he sauntered through the courtyard to collect the phaeton. To Eve's great relief, he seemed to have stopped eyeing her up. In fact, she'd felt all but invisible as he passed her without so much as a sideways glance.

'A malady of the mind, not the body,' the countess said enigmatically. Then she dismissed Eve with no more ado. And now she was seeking Daniel in the garden with a desperate urgency that exposed her previous attempts at calm acceptance as flimsy pretence. She found him on the *parterre* and, ignoring the lasciviously grinning presence of both Barney and Fred, she threw herself into his arms and let the tears flow, feeling relief, at least, that she was properly acknowledging her grief at having to say goodbye.

Chapter 53

Eve disembarked at Hoyland Halt at half-past two on Saturday afternoon, and Absalom Blandford was on the platform. How very awkward, she thought. What a stroke of bad luck. But it turned out he was waiting for her, because he sidled over and attempted a smile.

'Welcome back to Netherwood, Mrs Williams,' he said. 'I brought the carriage, and thought we might take the opportunity to talk en route, as it were.'

She looked at him blankly.

'Is this your trunk?' It clearly was, since it was the only item on the platform and she was the only passenger.

Still she stared. Undeterred, Absalom barked orders at the porter to load her luggage on the waiting carriage, then he offered her his arm.

'What are you doin'?' she said.

'Accompanying you to the carriage, Mrs Williams.'

'Why?'

He hesitated, feeling a shred of unease. Several weeks had passed since his Damascene conversion to the merits of romantic attachment, and during that time he had thought of Eve – and her accounts book – every day. But, he conceded to himself now, in his excitement he had neglected to give Mrs Williams even the slightest indication that he had chosen her. He chided himself inwardly, though he had no doubt that the situation was retrievable. And there was no time like the present.

'Mrs Williams,' he said.

'Yes?'

'In the months since we first met I have come to very much admire your, your, your, let's say, your assets, and I find that the thought of you causes me some considerable agitation.'

'Oh,' she said. 'Sorry about that.' She had no idea where he was going with this.

He grimaced and dropped down on one knee. She stepped away, as if from a lunatic.

'Please, no need to apologise,' he said, suffering all the loss of dignity to which knee-height subjected him. 'Mrs Williams, I intend to do you the honour of making you my wife.' That sounded wrong, even to him, but he let it be.

'Pardon?'

He stood now, dusting the gravel off his knee and thinking what a silly business proposing marriage was. Had to be done, however.

'Wedlock, Mrs Williams. Holy wedlock. I have a pleasant house and secure prospects. If you wish, the children can come with you, unless other arrangements can be made . . .'

Eve finally cottoned on, though her amazement knew no bounds. The man was out of his mind.

'Thank you, but no thank you,' she said, and she laughed incredulously. ''ave my trunk sent home. I'm walkin'.'

She turned from him and left the station without so much as a backward glance. He watched, open-mouthed. Had she just spurned him? He believed she had. For the first time in his adult life he felt the unpleasant after-effects of humiliation. And in the merest fraction of a moment, his admiration of

Eve Williams twisted itself into hatred; he marvelled at how seamlessly the change was made.

The porter, having done as he was bid, returned to the platform with the empty trolley.

'Have that trunk removed from my carriage,' Absalom said.

'Sir? And do what with it, sir?'

'Whatever you like,' he said. 'It's of no account to me.'

Eve walked through town sparing not a moment's thought for the surreal encounter with the earl's bailiff. She was occupied instead by the strange sensation of being at once displaced and at home. The familiar sights of Netherwood lifted her heart, but the complete absence of Daniel dragged it down. She carried a small carpet bag – a gift from Henrietta; it could be used to hold personal effects, but also it opened out flat into a travelling rug, intended to keep off draughts in railway carriages, though she hadn't felt the need today, and doubted she'd be making many more journeys by rail in the near future. It was a pretty thing though, fashioned out of a fine Persian rug.

'For your trouble,' Henrietta had said. 'For coming to London with little notice, and for going home with even less.'

It was kind of her, thought Eve. Women in Henrietta's position rarely gave a thought to how others might be inconvenienced by their actions. Certainly it wasn't a quality Henrietta had learned at the countess's knee.

In the bag was a book, a parting gift from Daniel. She'd said farewell to him last night, knowing that it would be impossible this morning, and they hadn't made love, but instead lay in each other's arms and talked, about everything and anything but her leaving. She had finally crept from his room at four o'clock this morning in order to prepare for departure at six, and he'd handed her a small parcel. She should open it on the train, he said, and keep it close to her at home. He loved her, he said. He always would.

She had waited for the train to leave London, then had unwrapped the present. It was a small book, bound in olive-green cloth and decorated with an illustration of a daffodil. *A Dream of a Garden*, it was called. A collection of poems by Ellen Clare Pearson. She opened it, and inside was a pressed lily of the valley, perfectly formed and still fragrant. He'd written: 'Dream of our garden, my darling Eve. You are the life I should have led. Ever yours, Daniel.'

She had cried again then, and was crying now, at the thought of him.

'Eve, lass?'

She started. Clem Waterdine, of all people, stood before her on the lane. His old face was creased in consternation.

'What's up wi' thee?' he said.

She smiled, wiped her eyes. 'Nowt, Clem, nowt. Summat in my eye.'

A likely tale, he thought, but he lifted his cap and moved on. No welcome home, no pleased to see you. Yorkshire men didn't stand on ceremony, especially old ones like Clem. Any fondness they felt was implied, not spoken. Eve smiled again as she watched him go; the fact that he'd stopped and said anything at all was Clem's way of saying he was glad to see her back where she belonged.

She walked on, feeling brighter, and instead of heading for Beaumont Lane she turned towards the mill where she reckoned she'd find everyone she wanted to see. There was a new shop on Mill Street, bow-fronted with a fancy gold fascia declaring the existence of Franklin G. Pickles, Pharmacist. The window displayed three vast glass bottles of jewel-coloured liquid: one red, one yellow and one purple. They looked full of the promise of magical properties, which was presumably their point, thought Eve. She walked on, wondering what else she'd missed and feeling a little indignant that anything had dared to change in her absence. Mitchell's Snicket looked the same, though. She felt a leap of the spirits at the sight of her business, the elegant, substantial building facing her at the end of the lane, and she broke into a run as she approached the arched entrance. In the courtyard she found Ellen, pottering about on the edges of the millstone fountain. The child saw her at once, and, abandoning her game, jumped up, ran across the cobbles and, damp from the water, hot from the sun, barrelled into her mother. Eve scooped her up. She smelled of toasted teacakes, and she pressed her little face against Eve's until it hurt.

Thea, unbeknownst to Lady Netherwood, had left London for Stratford-upon-Avon, where she was to spend two weeks studying Shakespeare before returning to the capital. So when Tobias agreed, quite meekly, to join the family migration back north, his mother thought victory was hers. She was completely wrong, of course. In fact, with the earl's blessing, Thea had been invited to Netherwood in mid-September with Joseph and Caroline Choate; they would stay for a few days before travelling together to Glendonoch for the shooting. Tobias had high hopes that a first-hand viewing of the ancestral home and the Scottish seat might prove irresistible to Thea, if she wasn't already won over by the attentions of an earl-in-waiting. Teddy, for once in agreement with his oldest son, was biding his time before speaking to his wife. It broke all manner of ancient rules and rituals to invite guests without the prior knowledge of the hostess, but Lord Netherwood felt that, just this once, needs must. Clarissa could be won over, he was sure of it. For what it was worth, the earl felt that Thea Sterling could be the making of his son. If he was entirely honest, he thought she probably deserved better.

Anna was thrilled about Fortnum and Mason; it sounded to her like just the sort of establishment they should be supplying. The pies would travel once a week by train, to be met in London by a Fortnum's delivery vehicle. Splendid arrangement, and one which brought honour on the business. King Edward's interest impressed her less, however. She'd heard about his antics and didn't approve.

'Scandal follows him around,' she said. 'It isn't kingly.'

Eve laughed. It was hard to believe in any of it, now she was home. She had kept Daniel to herself, for just that reason. She didn't want to discuss him with Anna as if he was history, as if it was over. Better, she thought, to keep him to herself. She took another sip of tea, and sighed.

'This is t'first decent brew I've 'ad in six weeks,' Eve said. 'Proper, dark-brown tea. T'stuff they drink in London's disgusting.'

'Why?'

Eve shrugged. 'Tastes like perfume. And it's wishy-washy.'

'Wishy-washy,' said Anna, filing it away for later use. 'Perhaps it was Earl Grey. Or Lapsang Souchong?'

'You what?'

'My father sold it in our shop in Kiev. There are many different types of tea.'

'Really?' said Eve. 'I thought tea was just tea.' She looked at her friend admiringly. She was a mine of information.

They were back home in Beaumont Lane, in their favourite spot on the back doorstep. Already, the novelty of her homecoming had faded and the children had drifted away to play. Lilly and Maud had nodded hello, staunchly and deliberately underwhelmed by her reappearance. The house, Eve thought, needed a proper clean, but she would have cut out her tongue sooner than mention it. The children looked well though. Really well. Rosy and cared for. Seth was a little taller and had started filling out around the shoulders. He was first reserve for the knur-and-spell team, he said. Amos wouldn't be able to play some Saturdays and Mr Medlicott had asked Seth to take his place.

'Why won't Amos be able to play some Saturdays?' Eve said.

'Rallies and whatnot,' said Seth, and Anna clapped her hand over her mouth.

'Oh my,' she said. 'You don't know about Amos!'

'Know what?'

Anna and Seth exchanged a glance, but Eve could see from their expressions that there was no black secret. Seth spoke up. Amos was sacked for recruiting miners to the union, he said, then walked right into a job at the YMA. He wore a suit to work now, and had a pen in his top pocket.

'He gets t'train to Barnsley every day. He lives in lodgin's on Sheffield Road. It's a better job, safer like,' said Seth. 'But 'e can't get to t'allotment so much. It's more mine really, now.'

'It was always yours, love,' Eve said. He smiled at her. He looked younger, for all that he had grown. He looked, in fact, happy.

'When did all this happen?' she said.

'Just,' said Anna. 'When was it, Seth?'

'Wednesday,' he said. 'He started Wednesday.'

'That's right,' said Anna. 'And he came here to tell us and stayed for dinner.'

'Tea,' said Seth, and they shared a smile.

They're friends, thought Eve. Anna and Seth are friends.

A week passed effortlessly by, then another, then another. Life fell into its old rhythm. Ginger handed back the reins to Eve, graciously hiding her disappointment that she was back so soon. Anna stepped back from duties at the mill and returned to domesticity, though she had a nice little sideline as a seamstress these days, and was threatening Eve with a new summer uniform for herself and the mill girls; skirts were getting higher, she said, and less full, and they'd all be less mithered in the heat if their shins were free of fabric.

'Mithered?' Eve said.

'Yes. Hot and bothered,' Anna said.

'I know what it means! It's just, you never said it before.'

'Oh, codswallop,' said Anna, just for effect.

She kept the book of poems in a cupboard by her bed. They were lovely, but what she read most was his inscription. She had thought she would write to him, but there was too much to say. And in any case, he didn't write to her. She thought, it's all for the best. She had the lily of the valley framed, though, and hung it on her bedroom wall.

In the estate office, in a new daily ritual, Absalom Blandford studied the ledger relating to Eve's Puddings & Pies with a saboteur's eye. One of these days he would discover a discrepancy or a deception, even if he had to invent one himself. It would have to be clever and convincing; something small, perhaps, but worrying enough to trouble the earl with, and from that seed of suspicion, who knew what might grow? He could wait years, if he had to, for the ruin of Eve Williams. The longer it took, the more satisfying it would be. He whistled as his finger traversed the pages. He had never felt more content.

One Sunday in August, Anna had taken the children to the common with Amos, who had bought a kite in Barnsley and wanted an audience for the maiden flight. He'd come back to Beaumont Lane after chapel, and shared their Sunday roast, then all of them had gone, loud and excitable, moving like a maelstrom out of the house, down the entry and into the street. For Eve, the treat was being alone in her house. The business took so much of her time now. Eve's Puddings & Pies was doing a roaring trade, and people travelled to Netherwood from other towns, just to shop and eat there. It still astonished her that she could be their destination, when once upon a time selling to her neighbours had seemed ambitious. With the wages from her spell in London and the weekly income from the business, there was too much money, really, to keep safely in the house, even after wages were paid and ingredients bought. Samuel Farrimond suggested a bank account, and she promised to think about it. Anna suggested a bigger house. There was a fine stone villa for rent on the edge of town, detached, with views across the common. Five bedrooms, an indoor lavatory and a kitchen as big as this backyard, she said. Eve could practically buy it outright with what she had stuffed in the housekeeping tin. She promised to think about that too. For now, she just needed to return to normal.

She dealt with the dishes, washed them, dried them, put them away. Nothing was ever left to drain when she was in charge. She carried water from the rain butt to the set pot, and poured it in. Wash day tomorrow. Then she wrapped what was left of the roast beef, and put it away. If it was up to her, there'd be hash tomorrow but Anna probably had other plans, involving paprika. Then, finally finished, she stood for a while, looking at nothing through the kitchen window. In these moments of absolute stillness, few enough though they were, she was vulnerable to melancholy. It lurked in the silences, waiting for its moment, and it stole up on her now. She wondered if, after all, she should have gone with the others to the common, let the fresh air blow away her sorrows. It wasn't too late, though. Before she could think again and submit to the miseries, she took her red jacket from the peg at the foot of the stairs and shrugged herself into it. She stepped out of the house and pulled the door shut behind her, then headed off up Watson Street so brisk and purposeful that when Daniel MacLeod rounded the corner from Allott's Way, she landed right in his arms, as squarely and perfectly timed as if it had been their intention all along.

She took him to Bluebell Wood, not to the common; all those awkward introductions and significant glances between Amos and Anna could wait until later. The bluebells were done, but you could see where they'd been, the ground an unbroken bed of tender green leaves, spent and flattened as they worked at sending their strength and goodness back underground for their show next May. He'd be here to see them, he said. They sat, side by side, on the long, low bench formed by a fallen beech tree, and contemplated a life together.

There was a post at Netherwood Hall, he said. Old Hislop was being pensioned off, and the countess had mentioned it to Daniel, half-heartedly, because she thought he was entirely wedded to his garden at Fulton House, but found she was mistaken.

'You're to be 'ead gardener?' Eve said.

'I am,' he said.

''ave you seen t'size of that garden?'

He nodded. 'A lot of work,' he said. 'But thirty-four under-gardeners. *Thirty-four*.'

428

'And you'll need every one of 'em. Who'll tend your garden? I mean, at Fulton 'ouse?'

'Fred. He's already older than I was when I started there.'

'Daniel.'

She sounded serious; he looked at her and found she was.

'You must be absolutely sure,' she said.

'I am, I—'

'No, listen. It's marvellous that you're 'ere. A miracle. But everything'll be different for you now. So different.' She laughed, not because the differences were funny, but because they were legion. 'You like London, you told me so. Netherwood's small and mucky and everyone talks like me, or worse. And that enormous garden, working on t'estate – you won't be your own man.'

'No. I'll be your man.'

He turned his smile on her, which, it seemed, was all he needed to do, because all her doubts and fears proved as insubstantial as gossamer in the wind. He pushed himself down from the bough so that he could face her, then he folded her into his arms and held her close enough to feel the beat of her heart against his chest. For a while he stood silently and breathed her in. Then he spoke, and she could feel his voice in her hair.

'Life is full of uncertainty, Eve, twists and turns we don't expect, a future we can't predict. So, in the end, the only really important thing is who we love, and who loves us back in return.'

'Well,' she said. 'I love you.'

'And I love you.'

They left it at that, because there was no hurry any more, no urgent sense of time contracting. Their days spread out before them, unthreatened by train journeys and other people's plans. There were, however, folk to meet. He lifted her off the bough and set her down, and they walked together out of the woods to find the rest of her family, up on the common.

Did *Netherwood* whet

your appetite for an

authentic taste of

Yorkshire?

Then try your hand

at the following

recipes from

Eve's kitchen.

Recipes From Eve's Kitchen

Raised Pork Pie

Ingredients
(For the filling)
A pound and a half of lean, boneless pork from the leg
Half a pound of fat, boneless pork from the belly
A dash of anchovy essence
3 tablespoons of stock
Salt and pepper to taste

(For the hot water crust pastry)
12oz plain flour
A quarter teaspoon of salt
4oz lard
A quarter pint of water

(For the jelly)
A quarter pint of good, reduced meat stock, made with bones,
gristle, onion, carrots and herbs.

Method

Dice lean and fat pork and mix together. Add anchovy essence and stock. Leave to stand while making the pastry.

Sift the flour and salt into a large mixing bowl. Heat the lard in the water until melted. Add the flour to the hot liquid and stir vigorously until well blended. When the dough is cool enough to handle, place on a floured work surface and knead energetically until smooth. Allow to rest for one hour at room temperature.

Roll out the dough. Lightly grease and line a seven-inch raised pie tin. Cut a circle of pastry the depth and circumference of the sides of the tin, then mould and shape the dough into place. Bring the crust a half-inch above the top of the tin.

Put in the filling, then cut out a circular portion of dough for the lid. Cut a small hole in its centre, then place it on top of the pie and seal the edges and trim. With the left over pastry, fashion a rose, large enough to sit over the hole. Decorative pastry leaves may be added at this stage too. Brush with an egg wash.

Bake in a moderate oven for about three hours, though it may be more, or less, depending on your oven. Lower the heat after two hours if the pastry seems to be catching. When ready, remove the pie from the oven.

Carefully remove the rose from the centre and pour in the reduced stock. Leave the pie somewhere cold for several hours for the jelly to set.

Serve in wedges with homemade chutneys.

Steak and Kidney Pudding

Ingredients
(For the suet crust pastry)
Half a pound of plain flour
A good pinch of salt
4oz suet
Cold water to bind

(For the pie filling)
One and a half pounds of chuck steak
Half a pound of ox kidney
One onion, sliced
Seasoned flour
Worcestershire sauce
Good beef stock

Method
For the suet crust, sift the flour into a mixing bowl then sprinkle the suet in, mixing lightly with your hands to distribute evenly. Gradually sprinkle in cold water and mix with a round-bladed knife until you have a smooth, elastic dough that leaves the sides of the bowl clean. Rest the dough for five minutes, then roll out for use.

Line a greased two-pint pudding basin with the dough.

Chop the steak and kidney into small pieces, toss in the seasoned flour, scatter the onion slices into the meat mixture and add to the pastry-lined basin. Pour in the stock to about three-quarters of the way up the meat filling. Add a dash of Worcestershire Sauce.

Roll out a pastry lid, dampen its edges, and press and seal well on top of the pudding.

Cover with a muslin lid, or greaseproof paper, pleated in the centre to allow the pudding to rise. Tie securely into place with string around the neck of the basin.

Steam over boiling water for five hours, adding more water to the pan beneath the steamer as necessary. Turn out onto a platter and serve with seasonal vegetables.

Yorkshire Pudding

Ingredients
8oz plain flour
3 eggs
Half a pint of milk
Pinch of salt
Beef dripping, for cooking

Method one
Sift the flour with the salt. Make a well in the centre and add the eggs. (An extra egg white may be added at this stage for a higher, lighter pudding.) Gradually whisk in the milk – you may not need to use it all – until you have a thick, smooth batter that easily coats the back of a spoon. Leave to rest.

Heat the dripping in a roasting tin until smoking hot. Add the rested batter and bake for about three-quarters of an hour, or until golden brown and crisp. You may need to reduce the heat when the pudding has risen.

Cut into portions and serve with gravy.

NB For small puddings, use moulds as for fairy cakes or buns, and reduce the cooking time to half an hour.

Method two
If you're roasting a beef joint, you may bake the pudding in the tin used to cook the meat, first straining away the juices for use in your gravy, but leaving the fat in the tin.

Pour the batter into the tin and cook until nicely browned. The meat should be returned to the oven to finish on a rack above the pudding, adding its juices to the batter. This method is delicious, but does give a flatter, crisper pudding.

Anna's pig parcels (golubtzi)

Ingredients
1–2 large Savoy cabbages
Pork sausage meat
Chopped mixed herbs
Chopped tomatoes
One onion, chopped
Good chicken stock

Method
Take off the largest leaves from the cabbages, and in a large saucepan of boiling water, blanch them until soft. Remove and pat dry.

Mix the herbs with the sausage meat, and place a spoonful in the centre of each leaf. Fold the leaves, wrapping the pork inside, and fasten with a wooden toothpick, or with twine.

Gently fry the onion in oil in a wide, shallow pan until soft and sweet. Add the chopped tomato and fry for a minute or two. Season with salt and pepper.

Pack the cabbage parcels into the pan, as snugly as possible. Pour over the stock to just cover.

Bring to the boil, then simmer gently for half an hour. If the parcels rise above the broth, turn them over from time to time. Butter beans, soaked overnight and cooked, may be added to the sauce before serving.

Drop Scones

Ingredients
4oz plain flour
1 teaspoon of baking powder
Pinch of salt
Pinch of sugar
1 egg
A quarter pint of milk
2 tablespoons of melted butter

Method
Sift flour, salt and baking powder into a large bowl. Stir in the sugar and – if you wish – a few raisins or sultanas. Add the egg and the milk, and beat well until you have a smooth batter. Add to this the melted butter.

Grease a griddle and put it on the heat. Test by dropping a small spoonful of batter onto the griddle and if the heat is right, small bubbles will form within a short while on the surface of the batter.

Drop large spoonfuls of batter onto the griddle, flipping them over after two minutes to cook on the other side for the same length of time. Lay the cooked scones on a clean cloth over a wire cooling tray.

Serve with butter and homemade jam.

Eve's Pudding

Ingredients
A pound and a half of best Bramley apples
4oz sugar
lemon juice
4oz butter, softened
4oz caster sugar
2 eggs, beaten
4oz plain flour
1 teaspoon baking powder

Method
Peel and core the apples, then slice them thinly. Put them in a pie dish with a splash of cold water, the sugar and some lemon juice. Bake in a moderate oven until the apple slices begin to soften and break down.

Cream together the butter and the sugar until soft and pale. Gradually add the beaten eggs to the mixture, little by little, then sift the flour and baking powder and fold it in.

Spoon the sponge batter over the top of the baked apple mixture, and put in the oven for about fifty minutes, or until the top has risen and is pale golden. Sprinkle with sugar to finish.

Bibliography

Adams, Samuel and Sarah, *The Complete Servant* (Southover Press, 1989).

Arthur, Max, *Lost Voices of the Edwardians* (Harper Press, 2006).

Bailey, Catherine, *Black Diamonds: The Rise and Fall of an English Dynasty* (Penguin Books, 2008).

Davies, Jennifer, *The Victorian Kitchen Garden* (BBC Books, 1987).

Davies, Jennifer, *The Victorian Kitchen* (BBC Books, 1989).

Dawes, Frank Victor, *Not in Front of the Servants* (Century, 1989).

Elliott, Brian, *A Century of Barnsley* (Sutton Publishing, 2000).

Elliott, Brian, *Yorkshire Miners* (This History Press, 2004).

Elliott, Brian, *South Yorkshire Mining Disasters*, volumes I and II (Wharncliffe Books, 2009).

Howes, Geoffrey, *Around Hoyland* (Sutton Publishing, 1989).

Mulvagh, Jane, *Madresfield: The Real Brideshead* (Black Swan, 2009).

Patten, Marguerite, *Classic British Dishes* (Bloomsbury Publishing Ltd, 1994).

Threlkeld, John, *Pits* (Wharncliffe Publishing Ltd, 1994).

White, Florence, *Good Things in England* (Persephone Books, 1999).

Reading Group Discussion Points

Netherwood draws heavily on class distinctions in early twentieth-century Britain – did you find the attitudes discussed surprising or shocking?

How would you compare and contrast Eve and Henrietta?

What is the central theme of the book and how did it resonate with you?

There is much food imagery in this novel. Can you explain why imagery is so important in the story and how effective it is?

How are relationships between the classes portrayed in the book?

Who is your favourite/least favourite character and how true did each of them feel?

What do you think will happen in the next book in the series?

There are a number of significant – and very different – male characters in this book. In what ways did each of them help or hinder Eve?

There are various different businesses described in this novel – how does working life differ from today?

What do you think Anna's presence in Netherwood says about the political situation in the wider world?

The turn of the twentieth-century was a time of great political change in Britain too – how does *Netherwood* reflect the catalysts for that?

Do you think Eve, Henrietta and Anna are typical of their era and class?

Q&A with Jane Sanderson

Have you always wanted to be a writer?
Yes, and I've always written to one extent or another, though for many years it was as a journalist and not as a writer of fiction. When I was eleven, though, I wrote an extremely emotional and heartfelt piece about the lives of pit ponies at my dad's old colliery – perhaps that was the beginning of *Netherwood* . . .

How did you research *Netherwood*?
Well I've just mentioned my dad, Bob Sanderson: he was very much my chief mining consultant and he has the most amazing recall of authentic detail. His own working life started the day after his fourteenth birthday at the local colliery, and although it was the 1940s, not 1903, lots of his memories were still tremendously valuable to me. The food – all those pies and puddings – was what my grandma, Nellie Sanderson, used to cook for me. Other than that it was books, books and more books – my desk and windowledge are piled high. I had a lovely view towards Hay Bluff when I began, and now I can barely see it!

What is your writing day like?
Ah, I wish I could say I wake with the larks and write until lunchtime every day. In fact, my writing days are never the same. Life in the country with three children, two holiday cottages and a small menagerie has a habit of filling up time, so basically I write whenever I can: some days are very productive, some are hopeless. I just have to go with the flow and make the most of my writing time when I find it. I should probably be more disciplined, but there we go. I find I can't write if my head is full of other things that need doing.

What does it feel like to see your debut novel published?
Absolutely, completely, overwhelmingly wonderful.

What advice would you give to aspiring novelists?
I hardly feel qualified to say! But the best piece of advice I ever heard was, just make a start. Get something down, because you can always go back and improve on it, but you can't edit a blank page. And don't worry if you don't know the ending, or even the middle. Start writing and you'll find you're going somewhere. Finally, I would say don't stop reading other books when you're writing one yourself – we all find our own voices by learning from others more experienced at the craft.

Where do your characters come from and how do they evolve?
My characters are a real mix of people I knew when I was growing up and people who exist only in my imagination. Eve Williams and Nellie Kay, for example, were both inspired by my grandma, although she was only a starting point – there's certainly nothing biographical about *Netherwood*! There's a huge cast of characters so at times it felt like a bit of a juggle to keep them all going, but the protagonists were very clear in my mind and that made the writing easier; they developed and grew very naturally and sometimes it felt as if it was in spite of me and not because of me. That sounds very odd, but honestly – they took on a life of their own. I always found that if I didn't know what to write next, I could write about Anna and she would show me the way. Everyone should know an Anna Rabinovich.

Did the writing of *Netherwood* throw up any surprises for you?
Not surprises exactly, but I learned a lot about the mining community I grew up in and its relationship at the turn of the twentieth-century with the local aristocratic family. The Earl and Countess of Netherwood are fictional, but were typical of the landed ruling class of the time. I also learned that the famous Yorkshire characteristic of dropping 'the' in favour of 't" is called a dental fricative – I've been doing it all my life and never knew what it was called!

Do you have a favourite character in *Netherwood*?
I grew to love all of the main characters. I was so sad to have to kill off Arthur! Eve, Anna and Henrietta are all women I would like to be friends with. Amos is wonderful – a composite of all the dry, dour but kind men who populate towns like Netherwood. And I have to confess I have a soft spot for Tobias: well, who wouldn't?

Will there be a sequel?
Most definitely, and it will pick up precisely where *Netherwood* leaves off.

What do you think of TV period dramas? Who would you cast in the TV adaptation of *Netherwood*?
I'm a great fan of period dramas; they're wonderfully escapist and gorgeous to look at – perfect Sunday-evening viewing. I love those big, overpopulated stories such as *South Riding* or *Cranford*, where the main storylines intertwine with the small dramas of daily life. As for *Netherwood*, well . . . as long as they can pull off an authentic Yorkshire accent, I shall be happy!

You portray two strong women in Eve and Henrietta. How are they similar, despite the differences in their circumstance?
Eve and Henrietta are spirited, strong and capable – typical Yorkshire women in fact. They don't suffer fools gladly, although from time to time they both have to. I feel a little sorry for Henrietta though; in spite of – or perhaps because of – her great wealth and privilege, she is less free than Eve to fulfil her potential. Henrietta admires Eve greatly and is also, I think, a little envious of her independence.

What do you enjoy reading?
A mix of classic and contemporary novels. I just finished *Wives and Daughters* by Elizabeth Gaskell, but before that I read and really loved *The Northern Clemency* by Philip Hensher. I like books that span a few years and encompass the lives of a lot of people. Every five years or so I revisit Jane Austen and read my way through the complete works as a special treat.

If you enjoyed

Netherwood, turn

the page for the first

chapter of the next book in

the series, published by

Sphere in September 2012

Chapter 1

High on the northern side of the mining town of Nether-wood was a wind-blown swathe of common land – not vast, certainly not a wilderness, but wide and varied enough for a person who walked there to feel unfettered and alone. It wasn't much to look at: coarse grass more yellow than green, pockets of unchecked scrub, spiteful, unruly gangs of hawthorn, the occasional jagged, craggy outcrop hinting at a wild and different geology before man roamed the earth, let alone farmed or mined it. According to a bill of commoners' rights, the people of the town could put their livestock out to graze here, but in this community of miners it wasn't much of an advantage. The grass was kept down by a small herd of retired pit ponies, stocky little Welsh breeds that had survived the rigours of their long, underground life and been given the freedom of the common in return. Once in a blue moon someone managed to acquire a pig but the common was unfenced, and while the ponies always managed to understand the boundaries, pigs seemed cursed by curiosity and wanderlust: a rudimentary pen built by Percy Medlicott a few years before had failed to contain his Tamworth sow. The pen, against everyone's predictions, was still standing but the sow had met an early end on Turnpike

Lane in a collision with a coach-and-four. Percy had had to share the spoils with the driver, who had been unseated from the box by the accident; the man had travelled home to York the following day with a fractured collarbone, a half-leg pork joint and a packet of loin chops, by way of compensation.

So Netherwood Common, not being of any great practical benefit to anyone, was simply enjoyed by the townsfolk for what it was: a natural open space – rare enough, in this grey industrial landscape – where children could play out of earshot of their mothers and a working man could smoke a Woodbine in peace. The common in its present form had evolved over the past hundred years and it owed its existence to the three collieries that dominated the town, because as coal production replaced agriculture as Netherwood's *raison d'être,* the fertile land became infinitely less valuable than the stuff beneath. The area's farmland origins could still be seen in the hedgerows and ancient field boundaries that criss-crossed the common, but it was over a century now since the soil there had been tilled or crops planted.

Like everything else in the neighbourhood the common fell within the vast acreage of the Netherwood estate, and from its highest point, and facing south, an observer could map the principal features of the earl's Yorkshire dominion. New Mill, Long Martley and Middlecar collieries, positioned respectively north, east and south of the town, dominated the outlook, their muck stacks, headstocks and winding gear stark and graphic against the sky. The residential terraces, long rows of coal-blackened, doughty stone houses, stood like stocky bulwarks, built to withstand the worst of the four winds. Victoria Street, Market Street and Mill Lane claimed precedence on the south side of town and formed its modest commercial centre, where small shops, stalls and barrows plied their trade and vied for custom with the Co-operative Society, whose premises, like its profits, seemed to grow annually. One town hall. One town hall clock tower. Three public houses. Three churches – one high, two low. And then beyond Mill Lane and Middlecar Colliery, but still visible from the common, the road gradually narrowed and dipped, following the contours of a shallow valley and leading to the gate – one of four – to the ancestral home of the Earl and Countess of Netherwood.

The great house itself, Netherwood Hall, was tucked away, out of sight, a remarkable feat, given its size, and a fortuitous one. Not only was great privacy accorded the aristocratic family within, but also they were spared the unlovely sight of the scarred landscape of the Yorkshire coalfields.

But beauty is in the eye of the beholder. Eve Williams and Anna Rabinovich, standing on this clear August day on the highest point of the common, saw nothing to offend the eye as they regarded the familiar vista before them.

'See?' Anna said, arms spread before her in a proprietorial way, as if she was personally responsible for the view. 'World at your feet.' Her accent, her hybrid dialect of Russian and Yorkshire, made most of her statements sound comical. She had no end of colloquialisms to hand, but somehow never remembered to use the definite article.

Eve laughed. 'Always knew it was only a matter of time,' she said.

'But imagine, Eve. All this, ours.'

'Aye, ours and three thousand other folks'. It's a common, y'know, not a back garden.'

Anna shrugged. Mere detail, and detail was the enemy of an adventurous spirit. She had brought her friend up here, dragging her unwillingly away from all the things she should be doing, to look at a house. It was the only property on the common, a large, detached villa, deeper than it was wide, double-fronted with generous bay windows and its name and date carved in stone over the door: Ravenscliffe, 1852. Like everything else, it belonged to the earl, though it had been designed and built by the same architect who was responsible for most of the dwellings in Netherwood. Abraham Carr had sought and been granted permission from the present earl's father to erect a house for his own use and at his own expense, and had named it nostalgically for the Yorkshire village of his birth. Then, just five years after taking up residence, he had passed away: born in one Ravenscliffe, died in another. The house was bought by the Netherwood estate, absorbed into all its other possessions and instantly put to work. Various tenants had taken it in the forty years since Mr Carr's demise, merchants, mostly, or people from the professional classes whose wages stretched further than those of the miners. Now, though, it was empty. Unfurnished. Unloved. And Anna wanted to live there.

Something about the house spoke to her, and you should listen to a house, she believed. She wasn't in any other way a fanciful person, never looked for meanings or omens in everyday happenings, never tried to interpret her dreams or fathom the patterns of the stars, but a house was another matter. There were good ones and bad ones and the two could look identical, but while one would bring happiness, the other would bring only misery. As a child in Kiev, in another life and time, she had lived in an imposing mansion with towers at each end and six wide steps up to the front door. It was her father's statement to the world that he was a successful man, but for all its fineness Anna knew, even as an infant, that it was riddled with misery, from its foundations to its roof tiles. She never understood why: some houses were afflicted, that was all. When her parents disowned her for marrying a Jew, when they spat on the floor at her feet and told her never to return, she had thought, it's the house speaking: you two have been here too long.

This house on the common, though, this Ravenscliffe, held the promise of happiness. Its hearths were empty and cold,

451

but there was warmth here nevertheless. Anna had stood before it, looked it in the eye, and recognised this at once. So her mission in persuading Eve that the rent – though four times what they currently paid – was of negligible concern compared with the ease and comfort it would bring, came directly from the heart. She felt compelled to win this battle, overcome her friend's reservations, press her point. In any case, from a purely practical point of view, they were bursting at the seams in Beaumont Lane. And when Eve and Daniel were wed, he would be there too, because Eve and the children couldn't live in that doll's house they'd put him in at the hall. And then babies might come. No. There was simply no other course of action.

They walked back down towards the house, and Anna could tell that Eve's mind had drifted elsewhere.

'Bedrooms for us all,' she said, to pull her back to the matter in hand. 'Space for your children and my little Maya. Fresh air.'

'Mmm, as fresh as it gets round 'ere, anyroad.'

'And kitchen big enough to dance polka. And bathroom, Eve. No tin tubs and outdoor privy.'

'Yes, Anna. I know. It's just . . .'

'I know. Beaumont Street was Arthur's home,' she said, with the slightest hint of weariness, as if she'd heard it once too often.

'Don't say it like that, as if it's not rational of me to think of it.' Eve, provoked, stopped abruptly so that when Anna turned to face her she had to trot back up the slope a little way.

'That's not what I meant,' Anna said, though it was, in part. 'What I meant was, I understand how you feel, how leaving Arthur's home would feel.'

'It's not just me,' said Eve, setting off again. 'I mean, I'm not only worried on my account.'

Anna sighed. 'Seth?'

'Aye. 'e's already 'ad too much to take on.'

No more than Eliza and Ellen, thought Anna, but she held her tongue. Eve's oldest child made heavy weather of life, in her view, and was as rude and withdrawn with Daniel as he had been with Anna herself, when she first moved in to Beaumont Lane eighteen months ago, after Arthur was killed. It was a long road ahead for Daniel, if her own experience was anything to go by. All of this ran through Anna's mind as the two women walked in silence down the slope, then rounded the bend towards Ravenscliffe. Her heart lifted at the sight of it.

'Eve,' she said, quite urgently, so that they both halted again. Her friend turned to her questioningly.

'When you and Daniel marry,' said Anna, 'wouldn't it be better for everyone if you made new home, and left one you had shared with Arthur?'

Eve sighed, looked at the ground. This conversation, kindly meant, was nevertheless unsettling. 'Probably,' she said. 'Yes.'

'Arthur lives on in your children, you know, not in bricks and mortar.'

'Aye. I know that.' And she did. But still, she thought, it was a link with him. She didn't want her love for Daniel to eclipse her memories of Arthur: that would be wrong, disrespectful, less than he deserved. While she lived in her little terrace in Beaumont Lane, she could still picture him, at the table wolfing his dinner, or in the tub sluicing off the coal dust. Where would he be in Ravenscliffe?

They went in, though; like a cat burglar Anna had cased the joint and found a sash window that had been left unfastened. She opened it now and ushered Eve through it, holding up her skirts and giving her a gentle push into a large square entrance hall. There was never any resisting Anna when she was on a mission. They stood for a moment in the profound stillness of the empty house.

'You'll get us arrested,' Eve whispered. She was half-impressed, half-scandalised at her friend's resourcefulness.

'No need to whisper,' Anna said boldly. 'Come,' and she set off through the ground floor with a certainty of purpose that suggested she'd been here before. There was nothing to be done but follow her, so Eve dispatched her disapproval and allowed herself to be led from one large, impressive room to another. Abraham Carr had done a fine job. There was a fair amount of dust, and the spiders had claimed all the corners, but there was no getting away from the fact that this was a glorious house, flooded with natural light, substantially built and sure of itself, adorned with Victorian flourishes – lavishly tiled floors, plaster cornicing, marble fire surrounds, a sweeping mahogany staircase – and positioned to make the most of the views of Netherwood Common, from the front and from the back. How odd it would be, thought Eve, as she gazed through one of two windows in the large kitchen, to look out every day on grass and trees. Anna joined her and Eve said, 'Makes a change from looking at Lilly and Maud's bloomers on t'washing line, doesn't it?'

'At least when their bloomers are up you can't see privies.'

They laughed, then Anna wandered across to the other window and Eve turned to study the black range. It was rather fine, a Leamington Kitchener, twice the size of her range in Beaumont Lane and with no visible faults that a pot of black lead and a rag wouldn't solve. It was set back into a recess, which was bordered on its two long sides by carved columns and across its top by a handsome mantel in the same classical style, giving the range the air of a prize exhibit. Eve placed her hands on the top of the stove. She wondered how long it had stood cold.

Anna said, 'You could watch Seth play knur and spell from here, see?'

Eve turned back to the window and joined her friend, who

454

pointed up the hill outside towards the wide clearing of trampled grass where men gathered most Saturday afternoons with their pummels and knurs. Miners' golf, some people called it, though it was tougher than golf to master, and as much about strength as strategy. Seth had watched his father play ever since he was old enough to be taken along to matches, and now he used his dad's pummel, which was too big for him, really, but try telling him that. If the competition wasn't too fierce or if they were a man short, Seth was asked to join in; along with the allotment, it was the one thing that could make him smile.

Eve moved to Anna's side, saw the same long wide slope, and the same clearing. But she didn't see Seth there. She saw Arthur. Jacket discarded on the floor, shirt sleeves rolled above the elbows, facing the spell and its finely balanced knur, his eyes never leaving the ball as the spring launched it up and he swiped it long and true with the pummel his own father had made for him. That's where Arthur would be at Ravenscliffe, she thought. Not in the house, but up there, on the hill.

She turned and walked out of the kitchen so abruptly that Anna was sure she had taken against the idea of the move, once and for all, and as they clambered back out of the window Eve was silent. But then as she pulled open the front gate, which hung lopsided, its top hinge having splintered away from the post, she said, 'That'll need fixing for a start.'

Beside her but unseen, Anna smiled.

If you loved Netherwood,
don't let the story end here.

Go behind the scenes at
www.jane-sanderson.com

~

Read the latest news and reviews.
Download exclusive reading group notes.
Test your period drama knowledge with a fiendish quiz
or roll up your sleeves and download one of Eve's
wonderful recipes.

~